What people are saying about

"A sassy, humorous, and gripping novel that had me wrestling with raw emotion. If you consider yourself smart and cautious, you need to read this book!"
– Jackie Andrews

"Touching and sincere, this is an important story for all of us looking for love in the twenty-first century."
– John Ogden

"A real life wake-up call on modern love – odds are it's happened, or is happening now, to someone you know...Definitely read this book if your online special someone says, "I love you, send money."
– Cheryl Thompson-Purcell

"Great read, interesting story, funny with a good message for all planning to date online."
– SJ Johnston

"I love the references to music, food and art…and the end – it's uplifting! Online dating? Now…count me in, I'm ready!"
– Beth S

"I can't tell you how many times I had to stop reading, put the book down, and just say, wow."
– WRW

"A perfect companion for those signing up on a dating site for the first time. Be prepared: read the book then go forth and find your special someone…in that order!"
– Erin Whyte

"This book made me laugh out loud, even while reaching for tissues. I love you, send money is entertaining on many levels, and really packs a punch."
– T Lara

I LOVE YOU,
SEND MONEY

By Jordan M. Alexander

I love you, send money Published by Pangaea Press Limited New Zealand

A catalogue record for this book is available from
the National Library of New Zealand.

Alexander, Jordan, author. I love you, send money/Jordan Alexander

ISBN 978-0-473-36479-3 (paperback)
ISBN 978-0-473-36480-9 (ePUB)
ISBN 978-0-473-36484-7 (audio)

Pangaea Press Limited
P O Box 19027 Courtenay Place
Wellington, New Zealand 6149
pangaeapress@gmail.com

Cover Design by Rhiannon Bassett (www.rhiannonbassett.com)
Typesetting by Jon Huang (jonhuangdesign.com) and Rhiannon Bassett
Proofing/Editing by India Lopez (www.colesandlopez.com)
Author Photograph by Sage Alexander-Wood
Printed in New Zealand by yourbooks.co.nz
Printed in USA by bookbaby.com

DISCLAIMER
This novel originated from an actual online dating experience. The characters, incidents, time frame and dialogue are based on reality. I have tried to recreate events, locales and conversations from my memories of them. In order to maintain their anonymity, in some instances I have changed the names and identifying details to protect the privacy of individuals; in other instances, I supplement these with fictitious characters and incidents that are merely products of the author's imagination. Any errors are the author's responsibility.

All's fair in love and war.[1]

Contents

Preface

We all have lasting impressions of that perfect evening of indulgence. Your host greets you at the door like a spring breeze. Is that outfit new? You've not seen it before; it's most complementary to her skin tone. You notice it's pressed, not tumble-dried. That little extra effort extends to her make-up: it's more than usual, but balanced with the 'hello, I'm a harlot' red lippy. Even her tousled hair is pinned up with a casual elegance. Her impeccable appearance is punctuated by her relaxed demeanour, likely aided by a glass of wine while she was cooking.

Her partner steps out of his *GQ* ad to accompany her. Where did she find him again? Half expecting a knock at the door from the paparazzi, you attempt to clear the fire-hazard congregation at the entrance, following Mr Buff's bottom up the stairs. Legs in motion, your brain alerts you: *Don't drool. It's impolite. And creepy.*

You stop in your tracks, your olfactory sense captured. The lingering molecules thrust into the air by the entrée tease you with a foreshadowing of the menu ahead. Spritz-like bursts of heaven from the vase of fresh and ripe white lilies join in the tennis match. Each demands attention. Your senses continue to widen as your host glides you into the lounge. Is this the dining room or the set of a *Better Homes and Gardens* shoot? You note a strict adherence to the long-standing restraining order Emily Post imposed between crockery and stemware.

The inner sanctum welcomes you. It's UGG-boots cosy (sans UGG). The well-worn leather couches beckon you to sit next to the crackling fire (now an environment-friendly gas insert). You appreciate the soft lighting, which makes everyone look ten years younger. You don't appreciate your deteriorating vision; you cannot discern whether the Drawbridge hanging nearby, *Pacific Horizons*, is real or a copy. Either way, you like that New Zealand is a small country with very large talent.

As you recognise Peterson's quartet, the volume of it seems to increase. Your feet start to tap; you're feeling a little playful. Perhaps it's that provocative piano. Duke Ellington's nickname for Peterson, 'the Maharaja of the keyboard', is fitting; you impress your host by commenting on it. Peterson is the ideal choice. Perky, sexy, smooth. Sipping on the aperitif, you poise your palate: your salivary senses stand at the ready. You willingly succumb to the palpable excitement overtaking you. Feeding frenzy foreplay complete, you are fully prepared to indulge, anticipating a meal to put Gordon Ramsay to shame.

A similar experience awaits you on the following pages. Your epicurean reading experience is about to begin. Partake, if you will, in this love story with a twist. Each chapter offers you a culinary delight, a beverage to match, art to 'capture the moment' and some mood music. And to finish? Perhaps you might enjoy a new lasting impression.

Bon appétit. Let the experience begin!

Chapter One

Introducing Alexis Jordain – Impulsive Gemini

Eat		NZ Bluff oysters
Drink		French champagne – Dom Perignon (go big or go home)
Look		*The Armada Portrait* (circa 1588), attributed to George Gower
Listen		'Thinking Out Loud', Ed Sheeran

♥ ♥ ♥ ♥ ♥

For seven years, the eyes of Queen Elizabeth I in *The Armada Portrait* have kept a watch on me.

Visiting the Long Gallery at Woburn Abbey, where the painting hangs, you wonder at Elizabeth's strength. The art piece commemorates her successful defeat of the Spanish Armada sent to depose her. Liz's pale white hand deftly settles in command atop the globe: today, the Spanish Armada … tomorrow, the world! It brings to life Simon Schama's comment that 'Great art has dreadful manners … the greatest paintings grab you in a headlock, rough up your composure and then proceed in short order to re-arrange your reality…'[2]

The rendition of the Queen, way back when, captured such power and composure in her insipid face, yet underneath all that hot air concealed by puffy sleeves and gold brocade, the façade could not contain a discomfort that appeared to permeate her slenderness – her private place being free of the pomp and circumstance. One can only imagine how gentle that interior would have been, the lonely inside life that leadership bestows. She is also beautiful, personifying strength *and* femininity – a heady combination that, long prior and since, continues to petrify suitors. That a woman can be intelligent, powerful AND have real-worldly charms (and needs) makes the world of love and lust most interesting.

It is refreshing to meet a woman who embodies this paradox, punching stereotype in the guts and releasing notions that strength, beauty and love are mutually exclusive. They are not. The ability to hold a position of power and appear 'together' may just be the work of the clever utilitarian corset, a strange hold that over time weakens its grip.

Let us move inside the painting, the portrait, and explore the paradoxical world concealed within.

Aperitif is from the Latin verb *aperire*, which means 'to open'. The word most often refers to an alcoholic drink consumed prior to a meal. The aperitif serves to whet the appetite and prepare the taste buds for future courses.

We 'open' with some deep, unconditional and eternal love lyrics for ambience, while noting that Sheeran could have been a little more optimistic and pushed out the chorus a decade or two. C'mon, Ed, everyone knows seventy is the new sixty, sixty is the new fifty et cetera. Plus, the trend in population demographics show that this older-person bulge is expanding (in more ways than one), meaning it's likely teens and tweens are using the credit cards of these baby boomers to download your wonderful song!

Reach for that elegant, delicately engraved, extremely heavy silver serving tray (use two hands). The one bequeathed by late Aunt Edna. Yes! Unshackle the notion of its purpose being 'display only'. Throw caution to the wind as you pop the cork on that bottle of bubbles which cost more than your monthly retirement-plan contribution. No matter what age, this is the special occasion you've been waiting for.

A quick spit and polish later, select and carefully arrange a dozen plump, fresh, crimson, bursting-with-juicy-sweet-flavour organic strawberries. See if you can arrange some quartered slices of lemon in Jenga style, and add Maldon sea salt and fancy ground peppercorns. Last but not least, the feature act. You really cannot call yourself a foodie or connoisseur if you've never had Bluff oysters from New Zealand. Seriously, you have not lived if these succulent suckers haven't saliva-river-rafted down your throat. Luxuriate in anticipation of these fresh, delicate, decadent and delicious creatures.

How many can Edna handle, you might ask? Good question.

How about fifty?

Casanova would start the day with fifty oysters, then proceed to enjoy five or six orgasms a night. 'Venetian Viagra', according to biographer Ian Kelly.[3] It brings new meaning to *breakfast of champions*, doesn't it? Not sure Edna's up for it, but Kelly shares Casanova's oyster game, how he'd pass the delicacy back and forth, mouth to mouth, eating them off breasts and other body parts. The first body shot, perhaps?

So is it fact or folklore? The oysters, I mean. Are they an aphrodisiac? Could they help with longer lovemaking? Casanova's experience does embody a reasonable sample size of n=more than a hundred women (and a few men).

Consider some scientific facts.

The average male ejaculates between 0.1 and ten millilitres of semen. *Please note, amounts and velocity can vary widely.* Increases depend on duration between activity and amount of foreplay. With each explosion, a male loses more than just his load. Based on an average serving size of around three-quarters of a teaspoon (yeah, right), males deplete their bodies of various nutrients: vitamins B6, B12 and E; plus calcium, magnesium, selenium and zinc. Most losses are trace amounts, but zinc (key for testosterone action), selenium and copper really give it up for the cause. So as the semen searches for its next lunar landing wet spot, the male testosterone, serotonin, acetylcholine and dopamine lower and prolactin rises. Result? Sleepy, tired and throw in a bit of moody for good measure.

Enter our unsuspecting appetiser.

In 2005, those wild and crazy folk at the American Chemical Society conference in San Diego verified the science linking bivalve molluscs and increased levels of sex hormones. Imagine the number of pointy-heads and thick-black-rimmed specs at *that* event! They confirmed oysters as *the food* with the highest zinc concentration (over thirty-three milligrams per serve) and as *exceptionally good* for sourcing vitamin B12 and trace minerals. So, centuries later, science vindicates Casanova's diet of shellfish and his associated sexual prowess (though the scientists mentioned nil about the body shots).

Good to know.

It's the little, seemingly insignificant details like ejaculation and semen content that really add to our understanding of partners and the opposite sex. Expanding our relationship toolkit must improve our chances of relationship success. After all, you don't need to *like* everything you read in, say, *Men Are from Mars, Women Are from Venus*, but like most things these days, knowledge *is* power. In the search for love, the more you know, the greater the chance of victory.

So, women out there, and those sensitive gay males, please don't take it personally when your man rolls over after sex wanting to go to sleep. Truth is he's legitimately tired. And gentlemen? Just eat the oysters. Lots.

♥ ♥ ♥ ♥ ♥

Reaching for a bottle of 'Sophia' from her well-stocked cellar, Alexis brushed off the dust. Like a genie, each rub brought forth a recalled scene from the Hawke's Bay experience when the case was purchased.

Her sales manager boyfriend at the time could drive home any car on the lot. He chose a brand new Cayenne as their 'ride' for the winding hills of the region that weekend. Of course, they aptly christened the vehicle at the last bend in the road before crossing Napier's city limits. The car would be fully loaded with many fine specimens by the time they returned to Wellington.

Mr Porsche knew Alexis had needed a change of scene. She had been working full-time by day, renovating a rental on weekends and evenings and, in the remaining hours, setting up a new business. He tried to *man-help* where he could, but wasn't particularly handy, and did not come equipped with the Energizer Bunny batteries she did. He'd often head to bed, and she would join him in the wee hours of the morn. Waking when she came to bed, he would always help her *wind down* before softly kissing and cuddling her to sleep. His bunny was getting more exhausted by the day, and her upcoming birthday was the perfect excuse to 'take her away from all this'.

Alexis remembered the tray of cheeses and canapés he brought outside, along with an armful of *NZ House & Garden* magazines. He insisted she read at least one cover to cover, as he leaned forward and took her laptop away with a mischievous smile and sloppy kiss. Her chivalrous knight wrapped her in a big blanket so she could enjoy the last of the setting sun among the vines. A queen on her throne, gazing at her kingdom, replete with olives and grapes, she enjoyed her stunning panorama. The fresh, cool air was invigorating, as she stayed cosy and warm in her regalia. By evening, it was time for entertainment in their simple and rustic but well-appointed castle. The heat from the roaring open fire led the royalty to disrobe. In their birthday suits, it was a *joyeux anniversaire* after all. The pair enjoyed the jesters perform in *Pulp Fiction* and ate breakfast at dinner, because they could and because he knew it was her favourite meal of the day.

She took the bottled treasure upstairs and gently removed its cork.

Alexis appreciated how the bottle was still old school. Screw tops were easier, of course, and led to less corkage, but there was something special about having to work at getting into the wine. That's how Lexi thought about love – to get to the good stuff, you needed to put in some effort. Her career demonstrated how good things take work, and she was prepared to put in the time to get what she wanted, even if that meant some ridicule from her friends on occasion.

At her fortieth birthday, her good friend Edie had toasted: 'Let's raise a glass to Lexi, the inspiration for the screenplay *I Don't Know How She Does It*. You make us laugh and are the kind of person we would love to hate, except that you're so damn charming. Cute as you are, though, let's hope this year brings you some luck in the love department.'

It surprised many of her friends that with all her energy and joie de vivre, Alexis had little success in relationships. Edie Purcell, known for her 'shoot from the hip' style, often ventured into the Alexis-love-life minefield. She called Lexi's history *deplorable*. 'How can you get divorced a second time after only five weeks? C'mon, Lex!' A lot of people couldn't cope with Edie's honesty, but Alexis appreciated her no-bullshit approach, even if it did ouch on occasion.

Edie wasn't the only one to judge the reign of Queen Alexis as lacking any Armada. Oliver, her BFF, also knew that gaining and keeping territory were not among Lexi's strengths.

It was during that infamous weekend away that Lexi bumped into Oliver at the stunning Craggy Range tasting room. Oliver had taken his new squeeze, Paul, for a dirty weekend to the Bay. As Alexis reread the words on the label about the 'true expression of the great Gimblett Gravels vineyard and the hand selected Merlot and Cab Franc grapes', the scene replayed.

'"Sophia" bottles will cellar well for five to ten years,' the cashier advised the friend group mulling around the till. It was then that Oli glanced at Lexi's boyfriend.

'That's unfortunate for you,' he simpered. 'It's unlikely you'll be around to enjoy it.'

It was 2008. Mr Porsche never made it to 2010, let alone today, when 'Sophia' was finally uncorked. Maybe it was time to overhaul her 'old school' ideas about love and relationships.

Swirling 'Sophia' in her glass, Alexis was delighted with the deep burgundy colour, great legs and full nose. She closed her eyes and took a sip. Ahh, heaven in a glass – divine. The crimson bus tour burst with flavour in her mouth. First stop, front of her tongue, then sides, and as she breathed in to enjoy the long finish, the rich chocolate and cherry lingered like aftershocks post coitus. She opened her eyes, wanting to share her tasting experience. 'Sophia' was too special to drink alone. She should be shared. 'We both should,' Alexis thought.

Not since she and Mr Porsche parted company had she enjoyed the lingering finish of male company. The desire to share more than her lovely wine crept up on her like a panther in the wild. She didn't see it coming, but she felt its presence as she let the alcohol carry her to a different plane. A better place, where being single didn't matter. The time-bound place, for a few sips later, the bus took a sharp turn south.

A few more led to total distraction. Her wandering mind left her heart exposed – fully unguarded prey.

The next time she closed her eyes, she submerged herself in the whole concept of love. She considered several colleagues, those matched up, either married or in serious, grown-up relationships, most with seemingly unlikely candidates. Lexi would say to herself, 'I don't know what she sees in him.' You know, *that* guy, your mate's boyfriend who might be obnoxious when drinking, or perhaps totally uncoordinated on the sports field, or maybe unemployed with no job prospects. Does she see only what she *wants* to see, missing his flaws? Or perhaps she *sees* nothing, because, as they say, 'love is blind'. Or is it? What does that even mean?

Pouring another glass, Alexis decided to take a closer look at the 'blindness' part of love (pardon the pun). On Google, Paul Acquasanta provided her with a starting point: 'A blind person, in reality, is the only person who can truly see. They know first hand what true love is, without the use of eyes, but with the heart. And that is the truest form of love, and they harness it.'[4]

The third glass got her creative juices flowing, and she made the connection to modern times with Katy Perry's lyric 'one man's trash is another man's treasure'. Between Paul and Katy, Alexis interpreted 'knowing' with the heart as trumping anything one might 'see' with their vision (even though hers was starting to blur). Proud of herself, she concluded, 'So, the dude who might appear to be awkward or obnoxious to me is "known" to my mate because she "truly loves him". She sees with her heart what is not apparent visually to me, or others.'

There was something safe and alluring in the 'blindness' concept. It sort of transcends the media's expectations of perfection, giving those of us who see ourselves as 'less than tens' by magazine/media standards a chance to find 'true love'. It raises hope that someone will see perfection despite our 'features and benefits' (because no one really has flaws ☺). The thought that someone might love us, warts and all, is alluring. It satisfies our deepest human desire to be loved unconditionally. Remember all the 'awws' when Mark Darcy tells Bridget Jones 'I love you just the way you are'?

Alluring indeed.

As she drifted to sleep on the couch (aka passed out), she faded into the romantic notion that someone would fall in love with her, deeply in love, relying only on their heart for guidance, sight unseen. Someone to consider her *their* treasure, *just the way she is.*

Now that would be something, wouldn't it?

The next day was crisp but sunny on the waterfront, invigorating Alexis as she made her way to St John's to meet Oli for lunch. Remnants from last night's trip down memory lane poked her sore head with thoughts about love, possibility and how to take a change of heart.

Oliver was no stranger to a change of heart.

Probably the last to acknowledge he was gay, it took him decades to come out. He wasn't overtly camp or feminine and didn't have any special gay tells. It was just something people around him knew. Lexi had a suspicion during their 'behaving-badly twenties' in Parliament – always cosying up to the other side. Then later, in their (somewhat) responsible early child-rearing thirties, he was never truly happy as a husband. Father – absolutely. Married? Not so much.

His proclamation left a wake of lost friendships and estranged family. It was little comfort Lexi stuck by him as he struggled with his new identity. Lack of acceptance from his beloved children, and, of course, the vitriolic blame and hate cast upon him by his then wife for ruining her life, trumped the airspace of his coming out. But that was *so* yesterday. The water was much calmer now, in their fab forties, both older but wiser, and the battle scars were worth it, fully morphing into authentic skin.

Oliver had already ordered a platter of oysters and a bottle of Pinot gris. No 'by the glass' for him. Lexi got comfortable. She knew some parts of his younger days persisted. They'd likely be there for the afternoon.

A voracious reader, Oliver had a full library of every self-help book to suit any occasion. Naturally, each was at easy access on his iPad. He carried that thing with him like Linus and his blanket. Oliver's iPad was his reference book, the preacher's bible, if you will, always at the ready with a photo or quote to support his case, or to check a reference. Of course he had 'just the book' when Lexi raised her topic of love.

'Oh my God, Oli, the last thing I need is another self-help book,' Lexi protested. She had to add shelving to expand her library to accommodate the number of fix-yourself-at-home books she had accumulated over the years.

'You're just scared, love. You just need to jump in and take a fucking chance. You've been single far too long, and you were made to love – you ooze passion, sweet.'

Shoving the platter of oysters in her face, Oliver insisted, 'You get in the right head space. I've something to read to you.' Convinced his perfectionist friend could find a happy love life if she just overcame her fear of failure, Oli read Lexi an excerpt from David Richo's *Daring to Trust* book: '… our need for safety and security is part of living in a relationship … but only the survival part. The second … part of our need is for mutual love and personal fulfillment, manifested in the form of the five A's (attention, acceptance, appreciation, affection, and allowing). When these were associated with the letdown in our original experience of life with others, we will have trouble trusting later. That "trouble" has to be called by name: fear. Our fear in intimate relationships is not of closeness but of the disappointment we imagine will surely follow commitment, since once burned, twice shy. This superstition can be refuted as we accept the fact that though some people hoodwink us, others do not. In any case, we can survive being let down by others – and we can grow in the process.'[5]

'I'm not scared!' protested Lexi. 'I'm just too busy! Who has time to find the love of their lives anymore, with full-time work and kids and … well, Oli, we all cannot be as lucky as you and Marley.'

Lexi knew luck had little to do with it. Marley was Oli's live-in Thai import boy toy. Wait, she thought, that is unkind. He was much younger than Oli, that was true, fourteen years (what's the male equivalent of cougar?), but the pair was deeply in love. Nearly at the bottom of the bottle, Lexi was about to hear the story of how Oliver met his match. Again.

Oliver and Lexi shared a common background. Both had been raised in alcoholic families, and both had experienced their fair share of disappointment – and felt they disappointed others as well. Breeding self-confidence was in short supply at their respective homes. The pair connected deeply just based on shared experiences of emotional parental negligence. Both swore they would make the lives of their own children different to what they had endured. They worked so hard at trying to provide a stable home life that they often worked too hard and didn't play enough. In trying to end the narcissism and neglect in this generation, they often relied on the same crutch of their forefathers. Intentions are wonderful creations, sometimes even fruitful, but always great sentiments just the same.

'You're not too busy. You are just not focused. C'mon, Lex, you and I both know if you are really fucking serious about your happiness and finding true love, you need to make an effort! Oh, do not be a bore. You know I went through months of dating men who were interested in just sex before I went online.' Oliver winked then giggled his signature forced deep laugh, which reminded Alexis of Grover on *Sesame Street.*

He continued, 'After all that sex – and, as you know, doll, there was a LOT – I found I wanted something more than just a physical relationship. You know me, traditional to the core.'

'Yes, Oliver, you ooze tradition.' Alexis played along.

'Well, going online helped me weed out a lot of fuck-buddy prospects. It was actually more efficient dating time. I only pursued those interested in something real. When I met Marley, it didn't take us long before we knew we wanted the same things in life. We met up when I sent for him to visit New Zealand, and, right away, we knew we were made for each other. Neither of us has looked back!'

Oliver had *fully* explored his newfound sexuality in the early change-of-heart/coming-out months. Lexi worried about how promiscuous her dear friend was being before she came to appreciate the subculture of gay males in Wellington. Whereas she had preferences for *select* wines, shoes and clothes, many of the male gay community seemed interested in choosing *every and all* candy on the shelf. And even before picking a favourite, they might choose again and again – sometimes the same flavour – just to be certain they hadn't missed out on anything that anyone had to offer. Oliver tried to play hide-the-parcel with various lovers, but always got his heart trampled on by players far better versed in the game than he.

Oliver wasn't like the masses. He actually wanted a full-time, committed relationship. He found that in Marley, and Lexi was overjoyed for him. Of course, it was not an easy road. For Oliver, his former gay liaisons would pressure him to partake in other *sweet treats* even after he started seeing Marley. There were a few indiscretions when

Marley would return to Thailand before the two settled into a fully monogamous relationship. Now coming up three years, they were the poster couple for gay men wanting serious, amazing monogamy. As a couple, they were the envy of all Lexi's single friends looking for love.

She had often dismissed it, but Lexi had to admit to more than an occasional fascination with and attraction to the internet dating thing.

'I know, and you're deliriously happy. And I'm happy that you're happy. Really I am. So you've told me the story a million times, Oli, but maybe now just focus on the internet part of the dating. Like what websites to go on, and how you present yourself, and how you decide who to go out with.'

Alexis was surprised by her what-you've-always-wanted-to-know-about-internet-dating-but-were-afraid-to-ask questions. Clearly this was something her subconscious had prepared earlier!

'I've heard horror stories about people lying about their age and weight and careers and all sorts. I don't want to waste my time on a bunch of pork pies,' she said as she signalled to the waitress they were ready to order.

She could sense her conscious mind shifting. She needed substantial food to keep down the butterflies starting to take flight in her stomach. Her heart was put on notice. Internet dating appeared imminent.

The change of heart was not lost on Oliver, who recognised this as the first time the 'relationship disaster' ever *seriously* asked questions about internet dating. Delighted at the possibility that his gorgeous, warm and loving friend might at long last find her Marley, Oliver trod carefully so as not to scare the delicate, tentative, anxious and weary lass.

'Fuck off – no way! You're going to do it, aren't you?' The wine had lubricated not only Lexi's logjam of reservations about going online but also Oliver's propensity to use the F-word.

'That's fucking great. Yay. You won't regret it. I can totally help you write a profile. We can vet the thousands of guys who will jump at the chance to date you.'

'Hang on, Oliver.' Lexi wore down her heels trying to stop the freight train, but it was too late. That damn iPad was out again. Match.com, Be2, FindSomeone – he pulled up several sites and started his sell job, indicating pros and cons of each. Whether Lexi was on board or not, she was now Oliver's pupil on internet dating. She would later wish she had paid closer attention to the fine print and Oliver's advice.

Lexi and Oliver left St John's several hours and a bottle of bubbles later. During the time there, they covered a good intro to online dating. They discussed the dozens of friends who had tried it; Lexi recalled several Auckland girlfriends who would simply go online or use their cell for dial-in sex, now aided by Tinder. Lexi was sure that she was not into that but, not wanting to be judgmental, admitted that for some, the service had utility. The whole online thing *did* seem a great way to meet someone without any preconceived notions about looks, money or status. A 'naked' bare-all, while keeping your clothes on, tyre-kicking expedition.

It wasn't clear who was more excited about Lexi's decision to give online dating a go. Certainly Oliver was overjoyed he had a new project, and, while apprehensive, Alexis too was excited about taking control of a part of her life that had been neglected. She agreed she would go into it completely open-minded. Positive about the possibilities. She looked forward to that intoxicating feeling of being 'in love'. She now, however, needed to detoxify in time to get home to make dinner for her gorgeous girls.

♥ ♥ ♥ ♥ ♥

Returning home, Lexi asked the cabby to let her out in the pullout just down from the house. She got out of the taxi and plonked herself down on the park bench, taking a moment before going inside. A lot was discussed that afternoon, and, before entering the Narnia of children's math problems, homework and perfect pasta, she needed a time to collect her thoughts. Was she serious? Was she really going to try online dating?

The thought of sharing what she had created in the bay filled her with joy and delight. Edie would say that Lexi was the captain of her ship-like home, working as she did overlooking the bay near the prow and bridge, which made her feel like Kate Winslet on the *Titanic*. She was independent, sure, but her heart was meant to love. Her toils and hard work meant to be shared. She wanted her Leonardo DiCaprio – or even Jack Dawson, pre-hypothermia.

She recalled when she put in an offer to buy the 1914 beach bach that originally guarded the bay. She had no recollection of the house she had viewed some hours before. No idea of number of bedrooms, appliances, the flooring. What captured Lexi's heart was the most idyllic view she'd ever seen. She would later build her architecturally designed glass house and, of course, never throw stones. She would raise her children there. The ones who would complain of being 'beach-sick' if ever away for too long.

It was there that she said goodbye to the girls' father after divorce number one. There that husband number two walked out weeks after marriage, tarnishing forever her faith, goodwill and trust in the opposite sex after he sued her for half her paradise. No wonder Alexis kept her heart and family behind a locked glass cabinet like a Fabergé heirloom – to be seen and not touched.

Maybe it *was* time to venture back to the dating scene. She considered the possibility.

Together with her new first mate (they could take turns playing captain; she wouldn't mind), she could rock on the porch swing. They would be entertained by the view that had captivated her for nearly two decades – watching the planes, ferries, sailboats, kayakers, surfers, swimmers and fishing boats. They would enjoy coffee on the kayaks in the morning, take a blanket for an impromptu dinner on the beach or sit under the stars in the hot tub, where moonlit nights made the bay come alive.

Yes. She was ready to share again. She was ready to reach out and try to love. She was open to the possibility of finding Mr Right. And she was open to the notion she would find him online.

Going inside, entering the kitchen, Alexis saw Paige was on the computer googling. It definitely was *not* homework, she found when she came in closer to investigate.

'Miley Cyrus is a topic on the school curriculum again, eh?' she asked Paige.

Awaiting a reply, Alexis noticed a pop-up box in the lower left corner. It was advertising Be2.com – a dating site.

She laughed to herself. 'Seriously, is this a sign or what?'

Putting the water on to boil, Lexi asked the girls if they thought it was time she got a new boyfriend. Surprisingly, they agreed, though what love advice does one expect from a ten- and a twelve-year-old? They discussed online dating and how it worked. They were less interested in the outcome and more in coming up with the online name for Mum. With Skye their yellow Labrador and Paris the cat representative of their former naming skills, Alexis appreciated perhaps she hadn't fully thought this through.

In the end, the trio agreed on 'Funny Girl'. It was not too 'kids' pet name-ish' and actually was part of Alexis's personality that she deemed an asset. 'Humour in adversity' was her catch-cry growing up in the hood. It would work just fine for her premiere entry to the online dating world.

It was the nineteenth of September. Nearly twenty-five years since her dad died. *That went fast,* she contemplated. The quickening evaporation of time over the decades meant little focus on the past, on missing her parent. *C'mon, Tata, you'll need to offer me some help from the other side if this is going to work.* It was about time he came to the party with some support.

As Alexis climbed the stairs to the bedroom, she was inspired by Sir Edmund conquering Everest. Being positive about taking control of her love life, she knew she'd need to make an effort. Oliver was right – fear was holding her back. She was sure Hillary would not scoff at rising to the challenge. By the landing, she had decided to complete her profile and get the ball rolling. There was no time like the present.

There were a lot of dating sites out there, but Lexi knew Be2 was hers. They had offices throughout the globe, and Alexis liked the idea of casting a wide net to catch her man-oyster. The process was all fairly straightforward: enter your 'online' name, pay some money and go shopping for your 'special someone' (however you define them). Funny Girl signed up for premium membership for six months. *Surely that's long enough to find the man of my dreams,* she thought as her MasterCard cha-chinged $270 NZD somewhere in Hünenberg, Switzerland.

She put on her crampons and grabbed the pickaxe, ready to diligently conquer the uncharted Funny Girl territory. No one mentioned it would require a packed lunch and camel ride to complete her profile. Nor did she appreciate that being online and dating was a full-time job.

Profile for Funny Girl

I look forward to getting to know you. Why not write to me?

Facts

Smoking: Non-smoker.
Drinking habits: I regularly drink alcohol (when going out or at parties).
Children: Children who live with me.
Pets: Cat.
Eye colour: Blue.
Hair colour: Blonde.
Ethnic group: European/White/Caucasian.
Religion: Christian (Roman Catholic).
Zodiac Sign: Gemini.

About Me

How Funny Girl's friends would describe her:
Interesting, funny, passionate, bubbly, warm-hearted.

What makes Funny Girl laugh:
Laughter is the best medicine (and proven to reduce stress too, so whoopee!). I like to find humour in everything. Life isn't meant to be taken too seriously. I like to have playful banter with my partner – nothing like a cheeky smile to brighten the day!

What Funny Girl does on a bad day to make herself feel better:
Let's hope it doesn't last a day! Refocusing on the many wonderful things in life can easily turn around a bad mood/ emotion. Being quiet/contemplative can help. At the end of the day, feeling good is the most important thing we can do to be happy.

Funny Girl's dream home:
Home is where the heart is. I can make anywhere home. Given a choice? My dream home is on the water – the coast near a beach, or on a lake. I love the mountains and a country setting with wide-open space like the Otago landscape or Kootenays in British Columbia (a true dual Gemini).

What Funny Girl would like to do one day but hasn't gotten around to yet:
Trans-Siberian Railway trip across the continent from Novosibirsk, then ending in St Petersburg. I'd love to get my helicopter pilot's licence. That one is probably on a longer timeline :) – would love to take it to visit remote locations!

Other things Funny Girl would like to share with you:
Be yourself and I will too. No point in pretending. Anything that lasts is based on a solid foundation and honesty. Let's respect each other's time and energy. I'm open-minded for this process. Let's have fun and enjoy getting to know each other. :)

Lifestyle

Music that Funny Girl likes:
Indie, pop/rock, R&B/soul, jazz, dance/DJ/techno, country/folk, classical music.

Food that Funny Girl likes:
Italian, Mexican, Asian, French, Indian, Greek.

Holidays that Funny Girl enjoys:
Beach/water sports, visiting famous landmarks, exploring exotic/adventurous places, just staying home, visiting family, outdoor sporting activities like cycling, hiking or skiing, relaxing or wellness.

Leisure activities that Funny Girl is interested in:
Sports, music, reading, theatre/opera/cinema, outdoor activities like hiking and walking, museums/exhibitions, cooking, travelling, cars/motorcycles.

Sports that Funny Girl enjoys:
Badminton, basketball, bowling, billiards, boxing, soccer, golf, hockey, cycling, writing, rolling, swimming, sailing, skiing, squash, dancing, diving, tennis, volleyball, hiking, yoga. Plus I love to watch almost any live sport!

Views

Relationship & Preferences:
Value of faithfulness/monogamy: Very important.
Need for attachment in a relationship: Relatively low.
Children's upbringing: Relatively liberal.
Dealing with unpleasant tasks: Wait until last minute.
New experiences: Open attitude.

Goals & Expectations:
Luxurious lifestyle: Quite important.
Career: Very important.
Creativity: Very important.

Dedication to others: Very important.
Intellectual needs: Very important.
Outward appearance: Quite important.

Lifestyle and habits:
Healthy eating: Often.
Fond of animals: Very.
Reliability: Quite important.
Punctuality: Relatively important.
Shopping habits: Not price-conscious.
Contact with family: Regularly.
Vegetarian: No.
Going out to parties etc: 2 to 3 times a month.
Sleeping habits: Early bird.
Tidiness: Tidy.
Preferred lifestyle: In the city.

The last summit – upload a photo. The chosen pic, at the Calgary Stampede, portrayed a little of Lexi's face and a lot of Lexi's cowboy hat. Opting for the *love is blind* approach, she and hat would remain locked until the potential candidates from Be2's 'unique and psychology-based *Personality Partner Search*' proved worthy.

Exhausted but satisfied, Alexis planted her achievement flag atop her newly acquired land. Excited and tentative, she climbed into her Cali King bed, tossing off the monogrammed *L'Amore* pillows, glancing at her scented candle collection. Every night she would slide into 'her side' of the sheets. Edie told her she could save fifty per cent in laundry costs if she just changed sides rather than sheets each week. *Just wait,* she thought. *Before long I'll have someone exploring my uncharted territory.* She would enjoy an Armada-like victory, then, as queen with her new king, successfully reign over their love kingdom, each climbing into their respective side of the now fully utilised bed, ruling together: two hands, not one, on the coveted globe.

She smiled as she turned out the light.

'Lord, please grant me patience … and hurry up!'

Chapter Two

Be2 Gentle: It's My First Time ...

♥ ♥ ♥ ♥ ♥

Partaking in online dating requires one to travel through a romance portal to the 'new world', moving from the traditional to a modern-day matchmaking service.

Bridging yesteryear, we are reminded how winemaker Millton marked the new millennium with a 'celebration of tradition in these hurried and faceless times'. 'Muskats @ Dawn' provides a 'gentle sparkle [that] delights the senses with tropical fruit and the first blossoms of spring'. It gently guides the taste buds with the same care as Rousseau's

The Avenue in the Park Saint-Cloud guides the onlooker through the plethora of trees.

All objects d'art are eager to please to the end. For the imbiber? The motivation is to enjoy fully to the finish. For the souls on the Avenue? Reaching the really, really tiny architectural masterpiece collection point on the horizon. And online dating? It has to be *the meet* in the PlentyofFish.com sea, where the freestyle swimmers impress that special species to take their next plunge together.

Choices abound, in art, in drink, in food. Just look at the abundant, evolving options since the humble Eggs Bene with poached eggs, English muffin, ham and hollandaise sauce. First the meat options were extended to bacon, then salmon, and for vegetarians, replaced by some spinach or asparagus; now the staple muffin has morphed to potato cakes or scones! Our love affair with all things Spanish now adds chorizo, guac and chipotle to the menu. Ah, at least the traditional hollandaise remains.

All treasured delights in life evolve, traversing the age-old traditions and creating new ones.

Alexis could be forgiven for needing some assistance in this new *find a mate* online world. Feeling like Alice, she had no rulebook as she jumped down the rabbit hole on her new adventure. The path was less clear than Rousseau's art. Luckily, the heady glee of finding and falling in love continues to entice both sexes and endures the test of time.

Top down on her Peugeot, Alexis wound around the bays to work. Wellington was having a perfect late-winter day – crisp, sunny – these were her favourite. This was the biggest high she'd had in months. The new star of the 'Walking on Sunshine' song from uni days, she was taking charge of her love life. Wind in her hair, she felt great heading downtown to where she loved her work and loved her colleagues – even the Australians. Feeling as she did, she could only think of her new adventure as full of promise and possibility. Boasting to her bestie to share the love seemed the right thing to do. The phone dialed on the hands-free.

'I did it,' she bellowed to Edie through the wind. 'I'm internet dating! Well, at least I started on-the-line yesterday.' Her retro tech views mimicked Vince Vaughn's in *The Internship*.

Never willing to miss a beat, 'You mean *online* dating?' Edie corrected.

'Yes,' said Alexis, exasperated. 'You know what I mean. I'm excited. Cut me some slack, Edie!' You had to deal back hard to Edie, or she'd keep coming at you. Edie was too clever for her own good. One of the few people who could do the hardest crosswords without help. But nothing was going to get Alexis down this morning. Well, almost nothing.

'What'd you go and do that for?' Alexis knew the tone. Edie did not approve, and now she'd hear why. 'The *line* is full of crazies and people pretending they're younger and skinnier and smarter than they actually are.' The elation Lexi felt about making her first move was quickly deflating with Edie's pinprick. 'You're a clever woman, Lex. C'mon, surely we can find you a real man. Not someone who needs to hide behind the screen.'

Lexi was not sufficiently grounded in her decision to stave off Edie's attack. She had agonised on and off since her last male encounter about online or any other kind of dating. That was over six months ago. She was tired of doing nothing, and it was far too long since she'd last had sex.

'Are we still on for book club tonight?' Ostrich Alexis went to duck and cover. She preferred to delay or avoid the ensuing discussion. 'I'll bring over my potential suitors list and we can review it together. It will be fun. This way my clever friends will help me make some good choices.'

'Yup, book club is on. And sure, bring the list of suspects. We'll weed them out for you.' Edie wasn't on board with online dating, but best that she and Oliver duke it out over dinner. Alexis didn't want to spoil her mood on such a glorious morning.

'Perfect. See you tonight. Have a great day!' The pair signed off and Lexi resumed her glass-half-full view of *on-the-line* dating. She was determined the blue *online* pill was the right choice for a Wonderland of options. All things happen for a reason, and her finally signing up last night would pay dividends. She was investing in her future, and she would find the love of her life. She just knew it. It was time.

♥ ♥ ♥ ♥ ♥

What would *you* do for love?

Nothing in this material world quite compares to the feeling of connection with another human being. Whether it's the closeness of holding another's hand or the art of sex, people are inherently built for *other* people, to love and to be loved. It would be difficult to argue that humans should forgo the innate desire for intimacy. Look at our Lego-shaped bits, for goodness' sake, that naturally click together. No further evidence required. But add that *your person* 'is into you' or thinks you're awesome or pretty or amazing, or all of the above. Such is the desire for attachment that we go to many lengths to experience it. Love *is* the drug, and it's easy to get addicted. Loving and being loved just make life all the more incredible.

So what would Alexis do for love? She truly believed in her heart, really deep down at the core, that *one day*, 'Mr Right' would walk into her life. Time was ticking, and she had been with a lot of *Mr Right Nows*. She convinced herself she just wasn't evolved enough to appreciate the acquired tastes of former lovers. Older and wiser, and much more motivated, she was ready, willing and able to taste the real thing. And no, that doesn't mean a Coke.

Alexis wondered about the dearth of *heterosexual males seeking females* in New Zealand's capital. The 'dating pool' just seemed smaller. It wasn't even big enough to fit on her tattoo. The artist's rendition of the Mercator projection carved into her flesh had no green ink left for New Zealand. With home located at the southernmost place on the planet, she regretted her short-sightedness and inability to say 'you are here' using her ankle. A mistake Edie and Oliver were quick to point out whenever they saw her exposed inner malleolus.

The artist, like many in North America, would mistakenly place a proximate tag near Australia, or just miss the presence of the jewel of Oceania altogether. When dating the American, his father criticised the distance as hindering a proper courtship. He eloquently advised his son that 'New Zealand was a long way to go for pussy'. Yankees have an uncanny knack for a turn of phrase. And yet they remain perplexed if given a hard time when travelling.

Since Alexis moved from Canada in the mid-nineties, her Canuck counterparts had also been quick to judge. New Zealand was a mysterious and largely anonymous locale. It was pre-*Lord of the Rings* fame, when Peter Jackson was still a plump, jolly and less familiar hobbit, long before Godzone's tremendous landscapes graced the big screen and popularised Aotearoa. Even now, with Jackson a household name, finding New Zealand on a map is still a *Where's Wally?* exercise. Even the Aussie cousins remain challenged when pinning NZ's tail on the cartographic donkey – or perhaps sheep is more apropos.

Kiwis and sheep jokes are a favourite pastime for locals and foreigners alike, especially Aussies. Holidaying here without bringing home at least a few new sheep jokes as souvenirs is unlikely. Travellers soon gain new appreciation for the versatility of the furry creatures.

The stereotypical sheep references for Down Under are popularised in countless (usually tasteless) jokes. For the PG crowd, we focus on the more tame variety: *What do you call a sheep covered in chocolate? A Candy Baa.* Or *How do sheep in Mexico say Merry Christmas? Fleece Navidad!* and *What do you call a dancing sheep? A baa-lerina.* For the adults-only set, we relocate to the gutter, where jokes are less refined and downright crude.

Canadian and Yank border-mates enjoy a similar rivalry to the trans-Tasman pair. Aussies love to call Kiwi counterparts 'sheep-shaggers' and 'ram-rooters'. Shagging (of Austin Powers fame) and rooting (not the famous 1973 Canadian brand of clothing) renders further explanation futile, right? These kissing cuzzies play on their respective accents and the preponderance of sheep (*Ovis aries*). A farmer may be asked if he should be *shearing* the sheep, to which he might reply, 'I'm not shearing this sheep with anyone!' The 'ewe-phemisms' apply to songs, jokes and politics. In 2000, Grant Gillon, a then MP, sparked controversy debating on genetic engineering: 'I want to ask the minister whether, no pun intended, it's appropriate in this case for a woman's body parts to be inserted into a sheep when that has normally been the domain of Tory males?'[6]

Witty repartee extends to myths about *sheep to people* ratios. To set the record straight, it's actually only about six sheep per peep. The country is home to around 4.5 million people and just under thirty million sheep based on 2015 stats (the lowest number since World War

II). The ratio is still high relative to other countries, but has changed dramatically since 1773, when Captain Cook Ubered them from Europe. In 1982, New Zealand was home to over seventy million, or more like twenty-two sheep each! Things went from baaaad to worse for the furry flock from the mid-1980s, when wool prices tanked, droughts hit and competition from those cows and other land-intensive industries like forestry led to a decline. Post Brexit? Who knows, but for Alexis, the steady decline in sheep numbers seemed directly proportional to the degeneration of the pool of single, interesting and available Kiwi male population (that's humans, not sheep). Being a Pollyanna looking for love sure takes you to some crazy-ass corners of life.

♥ ♥ ♥ ♥ ♥

Alexis slipped her Chenin blanc next to the chilling Sav, Pinot and bubbles and helped herself to the open sparkling in the fridge. Edie's was always self-serve. She'd ask if you needed a drink then direct you to the kitchen. She would also be gravely offended if you didn't treat her casa as your own.

'We could still discuss the book if you want to.' She heard Edie's sarcasm all the way from her reupholstered retro chair in her throwback parlour. 'Sharon likely never read it anyway.'

The fifties was the site for today's book banger bash. Not a theme night; Edie just lived in a different era. Her haircut was fifties, her car was so old it *looked* fifties and she'd always be wearing one of her beloved bowling shirts. You know the style, like Charlie Sheen on *Two and a Half Men* or Wally on *Leave It to Beaver*, depending on your preferred decade of reference. Today, her hula girls were accompanied by someone else's hospital pants and accessorised with a plastic lei and gumboots (she'd been gardening before her guests arrived). Edie *never* wore lippy.

Sharon had cancelled at the last minute, so it was just Alexis, Oliver and Edie. Sharon had recently had a baby, which meant she was often tied up doing newborn-mum things or leaving early with her built-in milk truck to give the little guy a feed. She was sad to miss a night out with her bookies – it was one of her only social events without the newborn. Her life seemed destined to be a Groundhog Day of endless nappy and wardrobe changes, mountains of laundry, infinite categories of crying, excretions and newfound states of exhaustion. She agreed with the others that raising children was an incredible experience and that you *really* didn't know what it was like until you had your own!

Alexis took a seat in her favourite chair, next to the nibbles, and placed her glass by the napkins. *Some call it cocktail hour; to me it's a support group.* It summed up their group perfectly. Not that anyone would believe they were a book club. Any *real* book club (i.e., where they actually read and discuss books) would categorise this loose collection as a middle-aged drinking club. Hardcore bookies would be mortified at the lack of attention to, well, *books* for one thing, and would have issued a variety of infringement notices. The group of four, at different times, would each have breached some aspect of established book club tradition, not to mention generally displaying some morally questionable behaviour.

Like when Oliver didn't have time to read the book (quelle surprise). On the drive over, he watched a YouTube video of the author talking about the book. During entrées, the girls were most impressed by how he somehow managed to offer significant insights they had missed. Halfway through the main course, however, he got too sauced to keep up the façade and spilled his guts, laughing all the way through. Or there was the time Edie lit up at Lexi's smoke-free abode, educating her 'supposed to be sleeping' girls about intimate details of sex and the challenges of being an intelligent woman amongst a plebeian society dominated by men. Alexis had some serious explaining to do the next morning. Or when Lexi read half the book and still participated in the discussion about the ending, although she had no idea what happened. Then of course there was the taste of the classics selection of Jane Eyre, where the group decided to go see the movie instead of discussing the book (they'll never know if anyone even bothered to read Austen's classic).

After meeting for three years, they liked the guise of discussing a book but were resigned to the purpose being more a drinks-and-dinner club where you talked shite about anything and everything. Over time, the dinners got more extravagant, and now, the group had got to the point where you'd need to take the afternoon off work to do justice to the food prep. At each session they would cover topics from world peace to the art of husbandry. The book content was optional.

'Or we could read my online profiles and find me a date.' Lexi offered an alternative. 'I brought the raw data,' she said, holding up a list of profiles she'd printed before leaving home.

'Yes, yes, yes.' Oli topped up the drinks. 'Brilliant idea. I didn't read the fucking book anyway.'

The coven enjoyed an amazing meal, as always. Edie outdid herself with the dessert. In antique blue glass goblets, she served a gorgeous Black Doris plum crumble with crème fraîche and homemade vanilla ice cream. No one was getting up in a hurry.

'Time to get down to business.' Alexis took advantage of her captive audience and grabbed her briefcase. Oliver got more wine.

Lexi explained the intricacies of the task at hand. She had printed out the top six matches on the Be2 personality-based partner search. In each, the potential suitor scored over ninety. The group agreed to each take two men, consider their profiles and rank them according to how they'd 'fit' with Lexi. Then the group swapped profiles and repeated the process to moderate the results. Simple. Top score would proceed to the next round.

'Let's get in the mood for luurve.' Oliver poured fresh glasses all around. 'There is much work to be done, and we need to stay hydrated.' He Grover-giggled.

In the end, all roads led to 'Jcarl' as the man of the match, the architectural masterpiece at the end of Rousseau's pathway. All three agreed he was the best candidate 'on paper', and even the Be2 computer gave him the highest rank on the personality-match index – a whopping score of 110.

'So Jcarl is *the* favourite.' Alexis positioned the paperwork to make her decree. Oliver gave a drum roll (along with a hiccup or two) and read the facts aloud:

Find out how well you are suited:

Compatibility Report with Jcarl – Your Be2 Index with Jcarl: 110
Your personality is compared here to that of Jcarl for each relevant personality aspect. You will find areas of great compatibility and factors that could generate tensions in a relationship. Every relationship is a mixture of both of these, and slight divergences in your personalities can have a positive effect.

Rationality versus emotionality
(Jcarl more emotional)
You both like to let your heart lead you when making a big decision. In areas of shared opinions, this is a great advantage. You will understand each other and feel understood. In areas of dissent, however, it will be hard to judge the other's perspective rationally.

Traditional versus innovative
(perfect match)
You are both open to new experiences and love variety. A certain sense of curiosity drives you. Research has shown correlations in this area to be important for the success of a relationship.

Distance versus attachment
(both close to attachment side)
Both partners are impulsive and tend to react strongly. Pleasant situations can lead to mutual euphoria. Negative, strained situations, on the other hand, can lead to considerable tension.

Observation versus feeling
(Funny Girl more toward observation)
You are both fascinated by the same type of information. Content should be clear and appeal to the senses. Purely intellectual, abstract deliberations and intuitive conclusions interest you less or not at all.

Structure versus integration
(Jcarl slightly more toward integration)
You both love situations that offer you a number of alternatives. For both of you, openness and flexibility are important. You prefer multiple options to clear guidelines. You show a high correlation in this regard.

'Proceed?' Alexis asked.

The group collectively proceeded to dissect the profile of Jcarl, starting, as expected, in the deep and meaningful place – his online photo.

Even Edie liked this game. Her suppressed childhood dream was to be one of Charlie's Angels, so she was thrilled with the challenge that lay ahead.

'Judging from his casual button-down work shirt, he seems business-like, but since his cuffs are turned up, he's probably a bit more down to earth, not a snobby pickle-up-the-butt. That's important. You don't want a fuddy-duddy, crotchety old suit now, do you?' Edie, private dick, was on the case.

Jcarl's stated age was fifty. He looked much younger, and Lexi was quietly happy with a more mature but youthful man. She did not want a learner driver and, naturally, craved someone with business sense. Tick.

'But what about that silly stache, Lexi? I know you're not a fan of facial hair,' Edie pointed out.

Always there to help a friend in need, Edie once purchased Lexi's boyfriend an electronic ear and nose hair clipper and elegantly presented it in the plastic shop bag it came in. Lexi was not there to see the look on Gary's face when he opened it. She did hear about it instantly. Luckily, it was taken in the spirit it was intended, an unexpected and yet practical gift from a well-meaning friend. Win-win.

'It doesn't look too big and bulky.' Lexi smiled. 'I could probably manage to find his lips under there somewhere. Or over time, maybe convince him to *take it off*.'

'Oh yeah, baby, you'll get him to take it off ... all off,' Oliver said in his sexiest voice, giggling to climax. 'You've got all the *tall, dark and handsome* criteria covered, girlfriend.'

Lexi was nearly five foot nine, and with Jcarl at 182 centimetres, which the gang calculated to six feet, his height was perfect *and* allowed her to wear up to three-inch heels without looking Amazonian. Excellent. Tick.

'He seems to have a gentle and kind face, and a nice smile. I also like that he's a railway engineer. I've always loved trains, and as a transport policy person, I think we'd have some good work-related discussions,' said Lexi, trying to get back to business and sounding all grown-up-like. It was impossible to let her rational brain sit out this dance.

'Choo choo,' Oliver cooed with a wink, bringing seriousness back into perspective.

Alexis got up for a jug of water, paying respects to the four dead wine-bottle soldiers in the kitchen. There was no way she was getting anything more productive out of this group.

'Okay, I'm going to reply to Jcarl, then I'm calling a cab. I've got to release the babysitter, and we all have work in the morning.' Lexi was a *responsible adult* seeking a serious relationship. She needed to stay focused.

'Just one more drink. C'mon, Lex.' Oliver was having too much fun living vicariously. He loved the excitement and romance of the honeymoon phase of a relationship.

'No, I really need to go, but thanks so much for your feedback. I feel more comfortable knowing we are all in agreement *on the same profile* at least.'

As Oliver poured Lexi a water, and another Pinot for the pair staying on, Lexi wrote her first of what would be many emails to Jcarl.

Be2 Email:
To: Jcarl
From: Funny Girl
Sent: Wednesday, 19th September, 10.30 p.m.
Subject: Hello

Hi there, this is the first time I've been on a dating site, so bear with me. Why did you choose Be2 as a site? I wasn't sure which to register with, but I suppose you need to start somewhere ... I'm in Wellington. What made you choose Nelson as a place to live? What's your favourite part of your job? What's your master's in? Cheers,

Funny Girl

'Will that work? Short, simple, just to get the ball rolling?' Lexi asked her rapidly deteriorating advisors.

Several replies came back.

'Sure.'

'Why not?'

'Fucking boring.'

But she needed to start somewhere, and let's face it, Jcarl was a total stranger. She was hardly going to ask, *How wedded are you to your facial hair?*

As she left Edie's, Alexis smiled, grateful for her bookie friends. They'd still be at it for a few hours. The joys of motherhood. She thought of Sharon, and was grateful being a mum called her away before things got too messy. She would be thankful in the morning. Her mates would surely wake with sore heads to nurse at work the next day. Besides, Alexis would need extra time and to have her wits about her. She would need to reply to the first incoming email from Jcarl.

♥ ♥ ♥ ♥ ♥

Lexi woke up with anticipation of a six-year-old on Christmas morning, wide-eyed and grinning, failing miserably to contain the excitement of what pressies might be in store.

She created a tangle wrestling off her Egyptian cotton sheets, nearly capsising during the process. There would be absolutely no regard for bed-making this morning.

With trepidation, she turned on the computer. A queasy, anxious feeling took over, starting in the pit of her stomach, as her body synchronised with the waking of her technology. Meanwhile, the irrational thoughts just kept coming: *What if he didn't reply? He may not even be on-the-line. Was my message appropriate? Interesting? Enticing enough? Why did I agree to go online dating?*

Finally, the Be2 welcome screen appeared. She logged in. It was there. He had replied. Her first emotion was that of relief. Until that moment, she wasn't sure that anything would actually happen. Now she was having her first online dating interaction. How exciting.

At Christmas and birthdays, she was usually one of those painstakingly patient present-openers, carefully opening ribbons and cards, un-taping corners of sticky tape. Now she became a rip-off-the-paper-haphazardly, desperate-to-see-what's-inside type. Click. Taking a deep breath, she read:

Be2 Email:
To: Funny Girl
From: Jcarl
Sent: Thursday, 20th September, 6.30 a.m.
Subject: Re: Hello

My name is James Norman. I live in Alpine, New Jersey, at the moment, but due to the nature of my job, I travel a lot, so right now I am in Norway. I was just in Nelson a few days ago on a business trip.

I'm a railway consultant. I can sell to companies to construct/ repair railways in most parts of Asian and European countries. It is a pretty hectic job, but I love it, although I am looking at retiring at the end of the year.

I've heard so many good things about women in New Zealand, which gives me a special interest in you. In fact, my assistant is married to an Australian, who was born in New Zealand. They are so happy together. He actually signed up to this website on my behalf.

I've been married, but now widowed. I've a son who means a lot to me and I always want him to be happy. Things have been unbearable for him since he lost his mom eight years ago, but he is gradually getting his bearings.

I am looking for a woman to love and who will love me and spend time with me. We can laugh together, share jokes, hold hands, go on walks together, talk about and do everything together and live forever in love and happiness.

I know I live far away at the moment, but I visit Australia and New Zealand very often because of my business, and I believe this can work if we want it to. All it takes is time and commitment.

I always tell people that when you eventually find the person that you can spend the rest of your life with and you can love, then age, distance, height and weight become just a number.

I'll prefer to write to you directly, as I'm not comfortable talking about myself here.

Hopefully I'll read from you again.

Regards, James

She exhaled. She had been holding her breath the whole time.

'Yay!' She was overjoyed. He didn't sound like a lying, cheating scoundrel. He sounded lovely, and articulate, and interesting, and …

'Mum, is breakfast ready?' she heard Bella asking from the kitchen.

Children. Yes, thought Alexis. *Must feed children. Must get dressed. Must reply to Jaaaaames.* Schoolgirl giddiness kicked in.

What a sophisticated name, she was reflecting when her phone buzzed. It was the alarm reminding her to fix the leak at the rental down the road. She would need to pause her James daydream and tend to immediate events.

'Okay, go fast,' she told herself. But she really wanted to say something in response to James's email. 'I have time to send a note – just a quick reply before I leave.' She managed to squeeze out more than a quickie.

Be2 Email:
To: Jcarl
From: Funny Girl
Sent: Thursday, 20th September, 8.30 a.m.
Subject: Re: Hello

Hello James, thank you for taking the time to write a full reply to my email.

Spring has sprung in Wellington and it is a bright and sunny morning. Your work sounds very interesting. One of my must-dos on the bucket list is the Trans-Siberian. I'm very much looking forward to that one day. I'm off to fix a leak in a property down the road this morning, and will later have a day in meetings for my consulting business. I started out in transport, so I am familiar with the railway circuit, only just ☺ I was actually born in Canada and moved to NZ for transport work in the mid-1990s.

If you'd like to write me on my work email, please do so. It is: Alexis@gondwanaconsulting.co.nz. I really must fly now as it is a busy day, but will write more to your personal email when you send one.

Warm regards, Alexis

Alexis raced through the day. She checked in on her bookies (both nursing hangovers), put in eight consulting hours bouncing between locations, installed the new traffic guard on the leaking balcony and somehow managed to collect the kids from netball practice before anyone called child welfare. She didn't have tons of time to contemplate Jaaaaames that day, but she did notice some restrained excitement that he sounded a reasonable sort, and apparently not a serial stalker (at least not yet). She needed and wanted some fun in her love life and hoped James might be the one.

Should I have written a fuller response to James? she wondered. What *was* the messaging protocol when you met someone online? Alexis was unsure of the correct balance, wanting to show interest but not wanting to appear too keen (and, hello, desperate).

She didn't have to wait long for an answer. A reply from James appeared the next day.

From: James Norman
To: Alexis Jordain
Sent: Friday, 21st September, 1.46 p.m.
Subject: Hello Alexis

Hello Alexis,

Thank you for your message. I am very delighted to have received it.

We seem to have a lot of things in common. You know exactly what you want and that's very admirable. I don't desire a woman who's confused. I like your drive, intelligence and determination for achievement. It is very attractive.

I'd like to be friends with you first. Friendship breeds love. The reason why a lot of relationships have failed today is because they were never friends with their partners. I'll look forward to talking every day, sharing our experiences (bad and good), telling our funny stories, hearing about your work and your family and kids, laughing together and becoming great friends. Great friends always turn out to be the best lovers.

I always tell people that a relationship is like a piece of cake, where friendship is the cake itself, and love is just the icing.

Like I said, I want someone to love and be happy with. I am not looking for someone to mess around with. I want someone I can show love to and be happy with, for the rest of my life. All these years, I've not been with any woman. After the death of my wife

8 years ago, just like you, I've dedicated my life to my work, and suppressed my needs and my ability to be a great lover. I'll give anything it takes to be that man again. Time will tell.

So tell me a little more about you. Tell me more about what you do. Do you enjoy your job? How long have you been on the site and are you talking to other people? Do you believe in love and all its attributes? Do you want to get married again? Do you believe in God?

I will like to know your views on these issues.

I can be that man that you want. I am not perfect, but I am a good man, and you're definitely the kind of person I am interested in knowing.

I hope to read from you soon. I've attached a picture of me, Mike and his friends, taken 3 weeks ago.

Anything else you want to know about me? Please ask. I'll be more than happy to answer. If you give me your number, I will like to call you and hear your voice. If you are also on MSN, we can chat often, as I have it installed on my mobile.

Regards, James

James's eyes were intense. They seemed to jump off the page and actively delve deeply into Alexis's soul. Yes, intense, while still being kind and sincere. Combined with his sweet, almost crooked, shy smile and dimples, she found him to be a most welcoming, 'come hither' type of guy. Michael, his son, resembled the father, but was a much slimmer 'mini me' version. He was just dorky enough to scream 'I'm going through puberty', and she could imagine him tripping over those long, slender giraffe legs.

Alexis saw an almost vulnerable look in Mike's eyes that she figured was a result of growing up without a mother. She also considered that standing next to his six foot tall father, of course he'd seem diminutive. She wasn't sure what to think of the pair of *Sports Illustrated* swimsuit models in the photo. Alexis was saved from the pangs of jealousy climbing from her well of insecurities when the phone rang. It was Oliver to the rescue on the phone.

'Lex, great fucking news! You are compatible! In your head, heart and, most importantly, the bedroom.' An advocate of astrology, Oliver had taken it upon himself to conduct a full analysis of the James-Virgo, Lexi-Gemini combination. Oli was desperate to share his new hard evidence.

'Good morning, Oli. What have you done?' Alexis loved that Oliver was overly protective. She also thought it sweet that the romantic in him lived vicariously in any opportunity for love.

'Well, according to the stars, you are both quite intelligent, rational and practical and see the world just as it is.' He sounded like he was reading from a pre-prepared note. He was. The assessment was fresh off the 0900 phone line Oliver called earlier. He had started the conversation with the unlikely phrase *I have this friend...* Oli continued.

'Both of you love to talk – well, that's a fucking surprise,' he ribbed Lexi, 'and you both will find your conversations pretty interesting – thank God. However, the banter of the Virgo is much more purposeful than the Gemini, who is more experimental, doing odd things just for the sake of experiencing it. The Virgo is more cautious and careful.'

'Okay, well, that sounds promising.' Alexis was innocently sliding into the black hole that captures astrology *non*-believers every morning while waiting to collect their caffeine hit at their favourite haunt. Step one – trying to look nonchalant, you have a GoPro moment to scan the environs, checking no one sees you as you lock on the relevant star sign.

'I know we will have a lot to talk about, as I already find his work and business interesting!' she added. Step two – rationalisation of advice with real-world events and people.

'Yes, but wait, there's more,' Oliver, as-seen-on-TV commentator, announced. 'While you both are realistic about and not prone to emotional outbursts, neither of you are able to express your feelings easily. This may lead to some misunderstandings that may relate to compatibility problems.'

'I can express my feelings!' Alexis said defensively.

'Honey, you express your feelings about as well as I did when I was living IN the fucking closet. You know you could use work in this area. C'mon, doll.'

'Whatever.' She recognised her outburst was tipping away the justice scales of innocence by the second. 'What else does it say?' She tried not to get wound up.

'On the positive side, Lexi, Virgo brings some sort of stability to your Gemini nature – we all know you could use some stability.' Alexis wished they were online so Oli could see her RBF (resting bitch face). 'And it says you can teach him passion! So, quid pro quo, dear friend. You'll need to brush off his tendency to be critical, you BOTH need to be honest with each other, and he'll need to learn to respect your freedom and appreciate your tactlessness.'

'It doesn't say I'm tactless.' Alexis wanted to hear more about how she and James were compatible, not how they clashed and what they'd need to change. Her freedom, for one, was a non-negotiable. Would James be a control freak? She wondered.

'Well, overall, I guess there is the possibility for a good relationship. We'll just need to think about a few of the pitfalls of the tactless, unstable Gemini!' Alexis stopped herself, realising she was swimming in suppositions. Step three – seek positive signposts for the future.

'That's the best part, Lex – if you do all I've said, the cards say this love match can definitely work! Isn't that great news? You're on the right track, sweetie – not only are you compatible but it can definitely work. Great, right? This is your first connection on the net – and what if he's "the one"?!' Oliver was so excited at the prospect of double dates and dinner parties and going dancing with James. And Lexi, of course.

'Thank you for sharing, Oli. I know you always have my back,' Alexis conceded, 'and it IS exciting. I must learn to express my feelings – well, I'm nervous but excited. Very.'

'I know, right? It's made my day sweet! So I thought it would make yours too. Better dash. We're off to brunch. Love you.'

'Love you too, Oli. And thanks again.'

Alexis found herself mulling over words from Oli the Oracle several times that day. She also contemplated her reply to James. She wouldn't have any alone time until late that night, but she appreciated the smile on her face and the feeling of happiness and warmth that accompanied her throughout her daily activities. Recalling the need for them both 'to be honest with each other', Alexis tried to 'express her feelings' when she wrote that night.

From: Alexis Jordain
To: James Norman
Sent: Saturday, 22nd September, 12.54 a.m.
Subject: Re: Hello Alexis

Dear James,

It was lovely to receive your photos. Mike sure looks like you and he seems to love his dad with his cheeky grin. I notice in the photo, it looks like you are still wearing your wedding ring. Might I ask why (if it's not too difficult/personal a question)?

I agree with you that friends make the best lovers and that friendship is needed for a relationship to work. It is very easy to jump into bed with a stranger and wonder why a few weeks/ months down the track, the people find they have nothing in common – so what was the gain/benefit? I love your cake analogy about relationships ☺ – I often use analogies and metaphors to explain things, most often mixing them together, which is quite humorous, and it allows me to laugh at myself. We must not take ourselves too seriously, I feel.

I would like to communicate with you, although a daily email may prove difficult as most days are pretty full on with work and children and life admin. I have been 'online dating' for all of three days now. My two girls and I were doing some homework three nights ago and a web ad came up for Be2. My 12- (nearly 13) year-old, Paige, and I started filling out a profile for fun (she helped me pick a name), and then we had some explaining to do when my 10-year-old daughter, Bella, asked what we were doing! We all got in on the fun, and so, at day 4, I'm pretty happy with having met you – you seem like a reasonable and normal person ☺ (although friends have told me some horror stories about online fellas).

There seems to be a lot of action out there for a newcomer, and it is reasonably easy so far to sort through some of the noise on the site (Be2). I am not registered on any other sites as yet (just starting out) and have only given you my personal email address. To be perfectly honest, I'm not sure how I am going to manage different conversations with different people. It could turn out to be a full-time job! Ha ha. I guess I thought I would like to give it a try – everyone is doing it these days, and I really do not want to waste time with people who are not aligned to my beliefs and with what I want in the future. How many women are you juggling 'friendships' with at the moment? Have you been online for long? Experiences so far (good/bad)?? Any advice? ☺

I have two girls, as I mentioned earlier, whom I adore. They live with me mostly and see their dad every other weekend (they are with him this weekend, so, after a lovely morning walk with a dear friend and breakfast, I have free time to write ☺). William (the girls' father) and I got separated about 8 years ago and are now divorced. We have a fantastic relationship and I still love him as the father of my children. He has a new partner, Anne, and a son from a previous marriage, who I also love. His name is Allan and he's 21 and recently moved to NZ too. William is Canadian but lives here now. I took the girls back to meet his parents in Victoria BC for the first time in June this year as well as seeing lots of relatives in Toronto and my sister in Vancouver. My mum lives out here in Wellington also. One of the reasons William and I split up was over a difference in beliefs. You may say that I should have known beforehand about core beliefs like God, views on family (it comes first for me) and future dreams. I am a very spiritual person (not a bible-thumper by any means). I was baptised Roman Catholic, my mum is Greek Orthodox and we grew up more around the Greek Orthodox traditions. The kids go to the Catholic school, but I never did. We do not go to church regularly, but have strong faith. I am on the school board, and was chairperson for several years. My definitions/ interpretations on God are much broader than the average bear, so I may save this topic for another day.

I am a crazy romantic and believe in love and marriage and forever (despite my track record of a few failed relationships and divorce). As I've gotten older, I have realised how much work it takes to be in a relationship, something I don't think I appreciated in early years. I'm probably learning more every day about what I need and want and how compromise is important on the little things. I'm pretty strong-willed on the core stuff: love, integrity, honesty, passion for life and living, family. It would be lovely to one day get married again, knowing what I now know, but I will not be rushing into anything.

I love my work, and will discuss it more later. I love being self-employed as it gives me flexibility and freedom, both of which are important to me.

Let's get to know each other a bit more before we get onto the phone. I use Skype, but not MSN (a bit of a techno write-off, really – learner driver on my iPhone still ☺).

It must have been challenging raising Mike after your wife passed away. How long were you married? How have you managed raising Mike with your work being away often? How old is he now and what are your favourite things to do together? Do you have other family near you? Where is 'home' for you?

Warm regards
Alexis

PS – You mentioned you will retire this year – What has made you decide this? Partial or full-time retirement? You seem to love your work – will you seriously be able to let it go?

♥ ♥ ♥ ♥ ♥

Alexis considered how death left such a void in her heart. She had lost all her grandparents, but the first significant loss was her father. Even though he was an alcoholic, not having her dad was devastating.

He was mostly a happy drunk, always making jokes and entertaining everyone around him. He was the 'Everybody Loves Raymond' of the Croatian community. Unfortunately, he toasted one too many times and died of a pickled liver. Sclerosis at a mere fifty-six years young. In the end, the once-sturdy Rat Pack lookalike and his handsome force majeure became a superior farce. Jaundiced, slender, feeble and weak, he died in a hospital bed just after Alexis turned eighteen.

The plot of land to bury him was purchased with proceeds from the sale of her Trans Am. The three thousand dollars she got was just enough to buy it. They sell them in pairs. We'll take two. How romantic. But it made sense. Alexis did not like the idea of him alone there forever.

Life following Tata's death was difficult. He died without a will and there were no cash reserves. They lived day to day with proceeds of whatever business she could drum up at the family auto body garage and car lot. Lexi deferred law school that year to stay and support them. She would do anything for her family.

Empathising with James was easy. Alexis could understand the challenge and personal difficulty he had endured – losing his wife, raising his son alone, his young boy left motherless. This man could use a bit of love and support in his life, she thought. Alexis knew she had lots of love to give – both to him as a partner and, of course, to his motherless child.

From: James Norman
To: Alexis Jordain
Sent: Saturday, 22nd September, 12.21 p.m.
Subject: Re: Hello Alexis

Hello Alexis,

Thank you for such a lovely email, I had to read 2 or 3 times just so I could keep smiling. I like how detailed you are. It is very impressive that you write so well. It is a major attraction already.

Thank you also for all the nice compliments. It was very nice of you. How are you today? I've an early flight to London in the morning, so I will stay up all night and work on my computer and sleep on the plane. I've not got used to taking my wedding ring off yet. My late wife and I were married for 7 yrs. and it took me a lot to get over her death. It has been really hard to raise Mike on my own. I couldn't forgive myself for her death, as I kept thinking there must have been something I should have been able to do, even though she died from breast cancer.

It was so hard. It felt like everything had come to an end. She was my friend, my only friend. It was one of the saddest moments of my life. I hate to talk about it. I gave up on love. Almost gave up on life itself, but I stayed strong because of Mike. Mike is 16 now. We travel the world together. He loves to sight-see. We go fishing and sailing and watch most of the basketball games together. He calls me his best friend. I talk to him as I would talk to my girlfriend. LOL.

Home for me is Alpine. After Angela died, I bought a house here and moved. It is very beautiful, quiet and relaxing here. Mike loves it. I am also in Europe a lot. Most of the contracts are from

Asia and most parts of Europe. I had to buy a small house in London to be able to mobilize effectively.

I am going to take time to answer the questions that I asked you. Like I already told you, I'm a railway consultant. I run a company that conducts and supervises the construction and repairs of rails around most parts of Europe and Asia. I can say that I've been very successful in my job because I've the God factor. He's the only reason for my success. I've worked for about 15 years as a railway consultant and I've been very successful. It's the only reason why I am retiring so early. I didn't see the need to continue working. Many of my contracts have been through him, and I'm so grateful.

My job requires that I travel very often. I've been to about 32 countries in the course of my job and somehow, I enjoy it.

I've been on Be2 for a few days now. My assistant convinced me to sign up after so many years of being alone and lonely. I am not in talks with anyone else at the moment. I've a busy schedule and I can't be distracted. Plus I am already enjoying reading your emails. I look forward to them already.

I believe in love and all its attributes and it's such a beautiful feeling when the one you love loves you back. Like I always say, I would like an honest, loving and caring woman who will always be there for me. Who would let me love her and care for her too. A woman who can be my best friend and I can tell everything to. Laugh, talk and walk together. If you can be that woman, then yes, I want to get married.

I read books and I love to watch movies, as there is a new thing to learn from every movie.

I think each word we write brings us closer and closer to each other. Soon we'll become best friends. I cannot wait. I am so excited.

I attached some pictures of me. I hope you like them.

If you can download MSN on your phone, it will help us a lot in communicating, as we both have busy schedules.

Looking forward to talking to you again.
Regards, James

♥ ♥ ♥ ♥ ♥

Forbes ranked Alpine, New Jersey, as the most expensive ZIP code in the United States. Twenty-odd kilometres north of Manhattan, the less than two thousand residents share a median house price of four-and-a-quarter million. No trailer parks or white trash in this neighborhood. Alexis was well on the way to ensure her third-time-lucky husband would satisfy Edie's plea that the next intended she would marry for money. Alexis did love North America's Eastern Seaboard. She would seriously consider moving to this fifteenth-ranked 'Best Place to Live', not for the money but for love and family.

From: Alexis Jordain
To: James Norman
Sent: Saturday, 22nd September, 6.28 a.m.
Subject: Re: Hello Alexis

Hi James

Do you need toothpicks to keep your eyes open, or have you already boarded and are away with the bedtime fairies dreaming of your next port of call?

I thought I would try to catch you before you head away. I know what it is like travelling around somewhat (not 32 countries, mind you). It has its moments, but working abroad is very different from holidaying abroad (I think I prefer the latter)! Do you enjoy London? Was your trip to Norway successful? Part of the reason I contacted you on Be2 was that I felt a railway engineer must be happy in their work. I imagine a man's most preferred occupation would be playing with trains for a living. Many men are still boys at heart, I find – are you? I'm sure trains are a winner with Mike also.

It sounds like you've had it pretty rough the past while. As a total stranger, I will not proffer advice or claim to know how you feel. I appreciate it is difficult to talk about. Thank you for sharing some of your private thoughts. As I read your email, I remembered a poem in the service booklet that I received at the funeral of a dear colleague of mine. Bruce died earlier this year from cancer. We had worked together for about 15 years on and off. He was a lovely man and only 55 years old. Anyhow, I thought the writing was so beautiful and gave a message that I would quite like to share when that moment arose for me. I am sharing it with you now, as it seems the right thing to do. I do not know if Angela might feel the same way, and I hope you are not offended by my gesture. It comes with a hug.

Okay, back to London. It reminds me of a trip a few years back. I was meeting a potential investor for a mobile phone company. He was having me to dinner at his home to discuss the business. I got onto the subway and was several stops away from the hotel when I realised I had no idea where I was going. I brought the bottle of wine, but forgot the address. By the time I jumped off the subway, got reoriented (I am very spatially challenged for a geographer) and got back to the hotel, I was dreadfully late, so jumped in a taxi only to be stuck in traffic and truly more than fashionably late. Luckily, the evening was recovered and ended successfully. I also enjoy the markets when I am there, and sipping on cocktails at my favourite bookstore, Waterstones, after giving the Visa a good workout. I always leave with way too many books for any sane person to be carrying on a plane ☺. You mentioned you like to read. What sorts of books? Do you Kindle? It took me ages to get over the need to hold my book – my home is like a library-in-waiting. I now read both real books and e-books (which are great for the beach and travel).

Basketball games, gosh I miss them. It isn't as popular Down Under as it is in North America, though the Tall Blacks did very well last year. Which team do you back? If you could pick a game to take me to, who would be playing? Do you play any sports? What do you do to stay fit (other than chasing after your teenager ☺)?

It is a glorious sunny day here in Wellington. I have to prepare for an open home. I bought a property for my mother to live in, but as she gets older, she needs a bit more attention and care. She will stay with us for the first while when the property sells, and then head to Vancouver to stay with my little sister for 4–5 months over spring/summer. Do you have any family? Siblings? Does Mike have any cousins to kick around with?

What do you do for fun? When are you back in the USA?

I'm off to select a movie for an evening by the fire with a lovely Pinot noir. Do you enjoy wine?

Happy travels, Alexis

Alexis sent him an excerpt from the writing of Henry Scott Holland (1847–1918, Canon of St Paul's Cathedral) that was used in her late colleague's recent funeral service:

Death is nothing at all.
I have only slipped away to the next room.
I am I and you are you.
Whatever we were to each other,
That, we still are.
Call me by my old familiar name.
Speak to me in the easy way
which you always used.
Put no difference into your tone.
Wear no forced air of solemnity or sorrow.
Laugh as we always laughed
at the little jokes we enjoyed together.
Play, smile, think of me. Pray for me.
Let my name be ever the household word
that it always was.
Let it be spoken without effect.
Without the trace of a shadow on it.
Life means all that it ever meant.
It is the same that it ever was.
There is absolute unbroken continuity.
Why should I be out of mind
because I am out of sight?
I am but waiting for you.
For an interval.
Somewhere. Very near.
Just around the corner.
All is well.

Alexis missed Bruce. They had worked together on projects that often stretched the way of thinking in a very traditional property sector.

He always spoke about travelling, and *one day*.

He was fit and funny and very particular. He was the social club treasurer at work, for example, and took the job *very* seriously. Alexis recalled the first time she asked for credit at Friday afternoon drinks. Bruce immediately obliged, and then proceeded to pull out his little black book, carefully recording the new debt. Bruce had a dry sense of humour, and though serious at times, was also incredibly funny and easy to kid around with.

His life ended so suddenly and at such a young age. Alexis was sure his idea of *one day* differed from the curt reality.

Her recollections of Bruce reminded her how short life really is. She didn't want to waste time with mere pleasantries and small talk. She wanted to be open and honest with James. It was important to live each day as if it were the last. One day it would be.

Why waste a single moment?

From: James Norman
To: Alexis Jordain
Sent: Monday, 24th September, 1.52 p.m.
Subject: Re: Hello Alexis

Hello Alexis,

Thank you for such a lovely email. I don't know what I am going to do if I ever stop getting your letters. I felt a lot closer to you as I read it and I couldn't stop myself from smiling. I've done nothing but think about you since I got back to London. I just keep smiling to myself at random times. LOL. Oh, by the way, my trip was great. I had a glass of red wine on the plane and slept like a baby. I didn't even know when we landed.

I love it here in London. It has a relaxed atmosphere and the people here are very polite and accommodating. Norway has a bit of a language-barrier problem, as not everyone speaks English, but I've rescheduled a meeting for next week so I will be going back there soon.

I actually do love what I do. I love things that require special skills and expertise to handle. It makes me feel unique and special. Ha ha. Your story about your experience in London was hilarious. You needed to have seen me laughing aloud like I was at a stand-up comedy.

It will be really nice to see you and spend time with you. I've been thinking about you too much lately. I'm a bit confused on my feelings and how I've grown to like you in such a few days. I have no idea what is happening to me. I'm a strong man, but I sincerely believe in love at first sight. I'm so happy when I see your mail in my inbox. I am so excited and I lose control of whatever I am doing at that moment. I am usually stronger than this. Reading about you, who you are, what you like and don't like, just has a way of bringing me closer. I will check with my assistant and communicate to you what time is convenient for me to come over and spend time with you so you can reconcile it with your schedule.

Well, I'll tell you more about me. Let's start with the kind of food I like. I love chicken, cheese and fries, but I am addicted to Chinese food. Maybe it is because I feel comfortable eating that, rather than just jumping on anything every country I visit has to offer me. I also really like Italian cuisine.

I love to cook. I always like to feel like I am some kind of international chef, but Mike always says to me: 'Dad, please don't ever quit your day job trying to be a chef. We would be poor.' Ha ha. He is so cute when he talks like that. I love him.

I love to read. I read a lot of inspirational books. I have read a lot of books by Robert Ludlum. My favourite right now is *The Matarese Circle*. I also love books by Anne Rice and Stephenie Meyer.

I like coffee. I am one of the 'coffee starts my day' kind of men. LOL. I think I got addicted a long time ago. I like to do a lot of exercise. I like to be fit and strong because my work requires a lot of energy sometimes. So I'm involved in a lot of physical activities. I also like to watch the news. It helps to keep abreast of what's going on around the world and brace myself for upcoming travels and events.

I can count how many basketball games I've missed. I am a die-hard fan of the New Jersey Nets. Supported them since I was a little kid, before my mom and dad separated. I had to move with her to South Africa for a number of years. She was Australian. I am not sure I mentioned this.

I'll take you to see a game between the Lakers and Jersey Nets. It will be amazing.

Favourite color? I have a lot of white shirts, so if I say any other color as my favourite, I feel like I am cheating on white. LOL. But I love blue and purple too.

I love movies a lot. There's always something new to learn from a movie. I've a library of movies back home in Alpine. I feel like I could start a video club. LOL.

What irritates me is rude people. I just don't feel there is enough time in your life to be rude. 'Please' and 'thank you' or 'excuse me' would not hurt to be used when it's necessary. You should always respect one another, no matter what the culture is. Even if you dislike, never say you hate. Also, I despise people who think solely about themselves. Always be willing to help if you can.

I also dislike bad smell. I can't stand anything that smells bad. I cannot stand bad breath and bad body odors.

I love music. It's food for the soul. I like rock sometimes, but I prefer R 'n' B. Some of the words inspire to me to look at life from a different perspective. For instance, I was listening to this song: 'Unbelievable', by Craig David (http://www.youtube.com/watch?v=TI_Tz2JLESY) and I couldn't stop thinking of you. I know it is a bit too early to feel this way, but I hope you like it.

I hope to talk to you again pretty soon.

Did you get around to downloading MSN? Still don't have your number. I don't even know what you sound like, yet I feel this way already. My number here is +4474666585, just in case you get around to texting me.

Have a great week.
Regards,
James Norman

From: Alexis Jordain
To: James Norman
Sent: Monday, 24th September, 12.34 a.m.
Subject: Re: Hello Alexis

James, it's official, I can be committed.

I am dreadfully tired and had taken myself off to bed, saying I would return your letter in the morning. Well, not long after my pillow and head got reacquainted, I found my legs pulling my body out of bed and getting the laptop. It is now on my lap in bed (I suppose that is what they were designed for – laps, that is, I'm not sure about a fixture in a bedroom ☺). Righty-ho, my reply … lest I can get some shut-eye!

I was delighted to hear you like vampire novels – the first thing we can disagree on (I was getting worried – it was all too coincidental until then). I love Ludlum, but haven't read him in ages, but I must be the only one on the planet who has never seen any of the *Twilight* movies or the other vampire series (I don't even remember what it's called). Perhaps it's all just a conspiracy and I am the only one left standing who is not on the 'dark side'.

One glass of red wine and you passed out – woke up in a different country – sounds like the makings of a good novel. I'm glad you were able to sleep on the plane and are settling back into London. I giggled at the thought of being a distraction for you. I take absolutely no responsibility for any spontaneous actions, decisions or otherwise. You are a grown man, and it is perfectly normal to send a complete stranger some intimate music halfway across the globe. (It was a great song, by the way, and I love receiving music.) I am sure this new distraction is frustrating you as much as you being on my mind is challenging me also. It is quite a funny scenario really. Less than a week ago, I spontaneously join a random dating site that I have never heard of, having never done so previously. Then, against any advice friends have ever given me, provide you with my personal email. Perhaps I could have committed myself earlier than this evening.

The thought of you coming to visit is exciting and petrifying at the same time. Let's hope our schedules are sufficiently busy to at least delay the possibility of this happening in the too near future. Today I received confirmation of a new contract to advise on the merger of several government agencies. I really wanted to get involved in the transition project, despite having some other work on at different departments. A client is returning from PNG later this week and I believe there may be some additional coaching work with him while he is over there, so all in all, I am heading into a pretty full-on time workwise to Christmas. In NZ and Oz things slow down between Christmas and mid/late January – most businesses have the 'gone fishing' sign out and remain closed. The better weather here is in late January/Feb–

March, when summer seems to settle, but I just remembered, you have your own Kiwi information booth back in NJ.

Food – hmmm. Chicken, cheese and fries – that's a classic American fare ☺. I enjoy these also. I'm crazy for my cheeses, but I suspect my love of blue cheese, gorgonzola etc. may not be shared by a man who is very clear on his desire for all things 'non-stinky' – I laughed at your bad breath and body odour comment. I feel the same, but cannot imagine stating it so baldly – do keep that honesty, it is refreshing. I enjoy all Asian foods, love seafood and do try the local fare in new countries (but I don't travel as often as you – perhaps tried and tested may work as part of your routine). I love Italian, especially if authentic, preferably in Tuscany ☺. I got lost travelling through there one summer and was literally in a farmer's field when some black Mercedes came out of nowhere and asked us to 'follow him' in broken English. Having seen too many *Sopranos* episodes, I thought we were goners for sure. I was most surprised when he led us to a restaurant in the middle of nowhere, where I had the best gorgonzola gnocchi of my life. You certainly cannot judge a book by its cover …

Speaking of which – you surprisingly have not asked for a photo. I am intrigued as to why not? I loved your photos, and while you have a love affair with white, my favourite colour is blue, and I must say, I liked the twinkle in your eyes in one of the photos you sent where you were wearing a blue shirt!

I love coffee. I start my day with it also, though I am now on decaf, having gotten used to 8 double espressos a day for years. I realised it wasn't great for the body when I went to a health retreat in Australia two years ago. I haven't gone back to caffeine since (if I have it now, I shake like an addict, its comical). I have a lovely Italian espresso machine and put the unloaded brew in and voila – liquid gold. Yum.

So your mum is an Aussie? You hadn't mentioned that. Is she living there now, or still in South Africa? Is your dad still around? If so, where? It sounds like you've spent a great part of your life moving around. What made you settle in NJ? I am excited at the prospect of the basketball game. Let me know where and when and I will check my schedule ☺.

I have downloaded MSN to my cell, but for the life of me have no idea what to do next. I tried entering Hotmail addresses and other emails, but you may need to walk me through the intricate details. Pathetic I know. Technology and photocopiers, they have it out for me … My cell is +6421115599, for your future reference.

I share your love of movies. The girls and I have movie nights as often as possible, and my DVD collection is growing (along with a lovely selection of the old videos – the girls don't quite know how these work – 'what's rewind?' they ask – it is cute). I agree each movie carries a message if you are paying attention. I enjoy all kinds of movies – rom coms, action and foreign films too, particularly French, but I need to be in the mood for subtitles. I love being entertained and relaxing with a good movie (I saw *The Ides of March* on Saturday night with Clooney and Ryan Gosling, and loved it).

I share your disdain for rude people – no excuse for it really. Good manners are important. I have a very eclectic music interest – everything from rock and R & B to classical, country, indie and pop. Having two young girls keeps the new music flowing, and several friends are also always sharing new sounds with me. I shall send some music soon. Right now the only music I wish to hear are the lapping waves carrying me off to sleep.

Enjoy the rest of your day, don't work too hard (or get too distracted ☺) and I shall speak to you again soon. I look forward to hearing from you.

Warm regards,
Alexis

It was nice, she thought, interacting with James, getting to know him, no façades, just simple conversation about simple things, connecting and getting to know each other. Slowly. The courtship was the best part. Maybe that's why they call it the honeymoon period. She admired what she was seeing in James: his work ethic, his adoration of his son, his views of love. From his replies, he liked what he saw too. Alexis loved that she remained sight unseen. It made it more alluring. They were in their own black-and-white film, like the ones she enjoyed as a child. The whole movie was about the romance, dancing and swooning. The first kiss (never with saliva exchange) saved until the climax. Falling for him would be easy. He was recovering from her heart the hardest piece of the Alexis relationship puzzle: her desire for unconditional love in a normal relationship.

Casting herself as Audrey Hepburn, she tried to translate *Roman Holiday* to modern times. The world had changed so dramatically. Transitions from courtship to kisses truncated to sexual encounters on the first night in the twenty-first century. No transitory glimpse of what made the other tick, nor a desire to know. Soon Alexis would transition from the security of the computer screen to actually *speaking* to James in real life – in real time. She was mildly apprehensive. Were they moving too quickly?

The cellphone was unfamiliar terrain. She hoped she would cope and that the encounter would not end up some reality TV show, like an emotional episode of *Naked and Afraid*. LOL.

From: James Norman
To: Alexis Jordain
Sent: Tuesday, 25th September, 2.51 p.m.
Subject: Hello Alexis

Hello Alexis,

I am sorry for the delayed response. The last couple of days for me have been very overwhelming, but I never stopped thinking about you.

You write exceptionally well and keep me glued to my computer screen. I can't even dare get a cup of water. LOL. I don't want to miss a word of what you have written. You have no idea what your words do to me. I am smiling from cheek to cheek and I can't help myself.

I am not easily bamboozled with nice words and beauty. I am not a teenager. I can't afford to go in and out of relationships, if not for anything else, for my son. I have thought about this. It is a priority to me now. I don't expect a completely smooth sail, as we would probably have our differences, but this is what I want to do.

I want to be with you, Alexis. You are definitely worth the risk. I see the honest, pretty (I expect that you would send me pictures in your next email), smart and enthusiastic woman in you and all I want to do is love you.

I completely understand if this is a huge step for you, but if we put our hearts to it, it will work. This feeling is unusual, especially for someone I've never met. I can't explain it. I also want to meet you as soon as possible. I spoke to my assistant today about plans to see you. I'll confirm the exact dates to you in a few days.

Don't get it wrong – aside from the fact that I've let my emotions control me, I've also thought about this. I've thought about the possibility of living in another country forever, or you moving here. I've thought about a new life with you and Mike. And I see this happening. I see it clearly and I'll do all it takes to make it work.

I've the gift of discernment. It is not very common, but I can tell when something would work or not. It has never failed me. Just give me your hands and let me take you to a happy place.

Let me warn you about my accent. I do not sound American. A lot of people say I sound English, some say Welsh, and even South African. LOL. In 2006, my company started a three-year project in Freetown and I kind of picked up on some of the accent there from mimicking the locals. It stuck, LOL. How unlucky can I be, right? It's hard for me to keep up on my accent because of my regular traveling, but you will decide for yourself when I call you.

I already sent you a text. Please let me know if you got it.

I am very excited with the thought of us being together. I cannot think of anything else. I am completely overwhelmed. It is the first time I am doing something like this. In fact, it was Charles (my assistant) that put me up for this and I was very reluctant. At one point, he got very frustrated and registered the site himself on my behalf. I can't let him in on how happy I am now. I don't want to give him that satisfaction. LOL.

You are such an adorable woman. I understand that you can never completely know someone. You only know as far as they want you to, but I can see beyond those words that you write to me. I can see a woman who knows how to love, but has been deprived of the act itself.

I don't know everything and I am not a perfect man, but I am ready to give my all into this, to make us happy forever. I'll pay attention to every detail. It's such a difficult commitment to make, I know, but I am ready. I understand that you might not be mentally ready. I can take it as slow as you want. I just want us to be happy together. I hope we talk soon. Please call me when you wake up. I am dying to hear your voice.

If you have downloaded the MSN, you need to have a Hotmail or Windows Live ID. If you don't currently have one, you can sign up for one at www.hotmail.com. My ID is jameskarlten688@live.com. Invite me and it's all done.

So many many things I want to write about and talk about, but we will take this step by step. Rome wasn't built in a day.

I attached one of my favourite songs by Javier Colon. I hope you like it: 'Stitch By Stitch' (https://www.youtube.com/watch?v=JylVuny5Kwl)

I also attached a picture of me and my best friend Richardson in Canada. In May, I was there with Mike for 4 days.

Regards, James

When the unfamiliar number appeared, she knew right away it was James. Nervous to answer, her hesitation felt like forever. In tangible time it took mere seconds for her curiosity to win out. She pushed green to take the call. She was hoping for auditory confirmation of a voice match to charming paper-based personality.

'Hello, Alexis speaking,' she commanded like an army sergeant, overcompensating a desire to sound professional. She was straining to contain her hyper-anxiety and to remain calm whilst the stomach acid welled up in her belly like she'd just eaten a bowl of Carolina Reapers. Reapers are a cross between the red habanero and a ghost pepper (the former Guinness record holder) and currently rated the world's hottest chilli pepper. They were bred in South Carolina by Ed 'Smokin'' Currie at the PuckerButt Pepper Company (true story). Alexis was having a pucker-butt moment of her own.

'Alexis, darling, it's James. So nice to finally speak with you.'

Eh?

She made out 'darling' and 'James' between the phone lines cutting in and out. Even incomprehensible as he was, her butt cheeks unclenched as he mumbled those first greetings. As he continued, she received more of his emotional Pepto-Bismol tonic, settling her stomach lining, leaving a pleasant, warm feeling instead.

Each of his earlier photos came to life when she first heard his voice. He *was* real, she thought. He is not a writer on the other side of the world – he has a voice – a strong voice and lovely belly laugh. She smiled at the thought of his laughter on the other end of the phone. She laughed a lot too. She couldn't understand him much of the time, but tried to home in on the frequency of his different accent – like dialling into that part of the brain to receive Radio Moscow – beep beep.

Twenty minutes later, the novelty of trying to have a conversation with James waned, replaced with exasperation. Lexi could find no appropriate dials for Radio James. His background noise filling the airwaves, she knew her day's to-do list was long, and patience short. She concluded it was perhaps best to *accidentally* hang up on her newfound love interest. It was sufficient that she heard his voice to prove he was real and not a figment of her imagination. She could ruminate on how she might communicate in person with her romantic interest over the coming days. Meanwhile, she had a busy day ahead. She smiled thinking about meeting James face to face and how the universally accepted language of love would most certainly not require a translator.

Looking around for CCTV, she pushed call end.

The rest of the day and into the next, Alexis wrestled with competing emotions of *protect the heart* and *take a chance on love.* She knew she was thinking too much when she reached for her yellow notepad. Crawling into bed, she captured her musings on paper.

From: Alexis Jordain
To: James Norman
Sent: Thursday, 27th September, 8.38 p.m.
Subject: Musings from last night …

Good morning James,

I fell into bed early last night, very exhausted. The kids had a school concert Wednesday night and I have been working late/ up early this week to fit in a few extra contracts. Sending you my thoughts from last night in the attachments (old school writing on paper, hope you can read it). I trust you are well. I look forward to speaking to you soon, though just not sure when ☺ – things can get pretty full on, but it is nice to have an escape in our conversations. Do write soon when you have a chance.

I miss hearing from you. Tell me of your travels/adventures.

Sending smiles your way,
Alexis

Attachment:
As my eyelids predict the imminent end of another fully packed day, I cannot even get up to reach for technology to facilitate communication. Perhaps I should think again about caffeine …

We last spoke, almost spoke, but two days ago. It feels like ages. Part of me is excited and curious. And dreamy. And jumping ahead to the last page of the novel. Smiling at the old couple holding hands at the waterfront lake house. Part of me recognises that with stilted conversation, and gaps in days, and the tyranny of distance, this may not be smooth sailing. It feeds my *Runaway Bride* tendencies. (You really must see the movie – I have some similarities here, unfortunately.)

I find it easy to write and connect with you. Perhaps I am more a writer than a conversationalist, though as I write this, it doesn't quite ring true. I can communicate very well indeed, although, to be fair, speaking of my emotions may actually be quite a challenge.

If I am honest with myself (as I must be, lest I not be honest with anyone else either …), I am willing to try to love, but at the same time I am afraid. I'm scared of being hurt. I'm scared of not being able to let down my guard (Tower of London Beefeaters have nothing on my suit of armour).

Part of me is willing to jump off the cliff, believing full well the parachute will open and gloriously land me at the end of the rainbow. Part of me realises the folly in jumping without checking the ropes and ties, and certification of all operators, pilots, air traffic control, etc.

Which to go with?

Your song selection, 'Stitch By Stitch', probably is the best middle ground. My interesting-accented man across the miles who I have only just met. Yet, like strangers on a train, I feel it is so easy to communicate with the safety of distance and anonymity. There is something comforting about revealing myself to someone who is miles away, not even occupying the same day as I am. Am I a coward? Just cautious?

The romantic in me smiles from afar. The thought of a chance interplay on a similar day, miles away. Total strangers drawn together by fate. No other explanation suffices. Neither reason nor logic fits. I smile; in some ways it can be so easy. If we let it. In other ways barriers – insurmountable – can surface, if that suits to keep the armour intact.

I already mentioned I am spatially challenged. I fear that even with the map I would get lost. What of this, then, where I have to admit: no compass, not an internal guidance system (I was not equipped with one it seems), or perhaps it is just buried and needs digging out like some national treasure. Ah, my kingdom for a map! Alas, I cannot interpret it …

Where to begin?

I do not want to bore you with my ramblings, my confusion and my apparent inadequacies on matters of the heart. I just feel due diligence is in order, particularly for an overseas buyer. I have champagne tastes while cooking on a camp stove. I'm not even sure I've got matches ☺.

Don't get me wrong. I am fiercely independent and can and do withstand all adversity and manage life's curveballs quite well – lots of practice. It's the simple stuff – the things I crave most of all – where I am a learner driver. I'm not sure if any of this makes sense. I'm very tired, and may have gone way beyond any semblance of sensibility. Do indulge my rant.

I wanted to communicate, from a million miles away, and these were the bits and bob that came out today.

Signed,
Searching for gaps X

From: James Norman
To: Alexis Jordain
Sent: Friday, 28th September, 10.17 a.m.
Subject: Re: Musings from last night ...

Hello my darling,

I am sure you are asleep by now. Your letter just stirred a lot of emotions in me, and I don't know how your words have so much control of me.

As you well know, I am in Spain at the moment. I've had such a hectic week, but thoughts of you in my head just made it better and kept me smiling. I got recommended as a favourite for tomorrow's bid of the contract, so that kind of brightened my day a little.

Coming back home to such a lovely email made it even better. Thank you so much for being so sweet.

Every word that you say to me brings me closer and closer to you. I cannot believe what you've done to me in the past days. It is so amazing.

If I had the chance to go back on the past few days, I will still choose you. You are all kinds of amazing. I lose my concentration nowadays thinking about you. Thinking about all the beautiful places we can visit together. The thought about introducing you as my wife to people overwhelmed me, and made me smile.

You're not a coward, darling. And sometimes being cautious is a good thing. There's no rush. I just want to be happy with you. Eventually.

Your letter made me feel close, like I was lying down just beside you and I could smell you and kiss you. Sometimes, we don't need to make a lot of sense. We don't need to explain our feelings and the things we do. People may not be able to relate, but we know what our heart says, and that's all that matters.

I want you to know that I'm not perfect. I'm a man who might have some flaws. And my life has been a bit of a roller coaster. You could never imagine what pain I went through losing my late wife. I know all about the lonely heart. But you have woken mine up, and now I have something to look forward to, and my heart just always smiles now.

I look forward to our time together, and that is what I want to focus on. I can't wait to love you.

I also look forward to spoiling you with my love, and you spoiling me too. I thank God for sending you my way, and giving me the chance to love someone for real again. My heart is just bursting and my smile glows once again. Thank you, my dearest Alexis, for being who you are.

You are a part of me now and I don't want to ever lose you. I don't say all these words just to make you smile or be happy. I actually mean them. I believe in a lot of things, especially in the law of karma that says 'what goes around comes back around'. It keeps me in check, especially with my utterances, so I don't promise what I cannot deliver.

Knowing this, I promise you today never to hurt you and to be there when you need me, always. My feelings for you would never be compromised. It has gone way past a physical attraction. I will do anything to make you happy and I'll stay with you forever. This is a promise. You've hit me in a place that no one has been able to, and I can't express how I feel. It's such a strange feeling, especially when I have never met you, yet it seems like we have been together for so many years.

I just want you to be safe around me and know everything about me. I stay in 36 Clayponds Gardens W54ER, in a small apartment here in London. While it's small, it is beautiful. In America, I live on 39 Tamarack Road, 07620, Alpine, New Jersey. It's a duplex with a beautiful garden and a pool.

I will also like to know where you live. I trust you, like you trust me. I know we were meant for each other. Please don't ever lose faith in us, okay?
Did you get around to fixing MSN? Please let me know …
Have a great night. Hope to talk to you soon.
Regards, James

From: Alexis Jordain
To: James Norman
Sent: Saturday, 29th September, 6.58 p.m.
Subject: Re: Musings from last night …

Hello James

Thank you for writing yesterday, I know you are very busy with work, and I do appreciate hearing your words as well.

I did not know you were in Spain. And I'm not certain if you are still there, in Norway or back in London. At least I am relatively certain you are somewhere in Europe/UK ☺. I know you will do well with the contract and despite work being frantic, remember you love it, and it is still only one part of your life. I've also said a little prayer for you. Do let me know how the tender goes.

I'm ready to jump into the shower to get ready for a charity gala tonight. I wish you were accompanying me. It is for intellectually handicapped people (IHC). There is a big auction and a lovely dinner and entertainment and we always have a great deal of fun. It's a great opportunity to dress up. Do you like functions? Going to the theatre? The ballet? I know so little of your tastes (besides chicken and cheese and chips ☺). I really must go. I'm cutting it fine as it is.

I've got MSN working, I believe (followed your instructions, thank you), so do let me know if you can see the connection. We will speak at some point, I hope. I've been also thinking that maybe meeting on neutral ground may work – perhaps somewhere in the Pacific Islands, Fiji or Hawaii or not sure where, you may have a suggestion. It could be an interesting first date …

I look forward to the next installment – travel well, warm regards,
Alexis

The doorbell announced her escort for the evening had arrived.

Switching her attention, Alexis was partway through greeting her date and leaving instructions for the babysitter when the phone rang. It was James. She was already running late and didn't want to be rude to any of her growing number of attentive audiences.

The rushed nature in Lexi's voice didn't stop James asking a dozen questions about who was accompanying her, where she was going and when she'd be back. On one level, *sweet that he cares*, but Alexis really didn't have time to appease a jealous inquisition. She apologised as she needed to go. She would deal with any fallout later. Now it was show time.

♥ ♥ ♥ ♥ ♥

Charity auction galas were always so much fun.

Alexis totally enjoyed schmoozing with colleagues and friends and acting like Ivana Trump, with her credit card and fancy ball gown. The food was always good, and, with wine flowing freely, the bids would skyrocket. That was the point, though, to donate to a good cause, feel good lending a hand and have a bit of fun while doing it.

She didn't think about James much at the event, other than when she bid and won a weekend away in the country. Her 'date' winked at her purchase, understandably believing they might enjoy it together. It also explained why Alexis spent much of the evening repositioning his roving hands, and her corresponding *Matrix* moves when avoiding the saliva-swap tongue-down-the-throat-filled goodbye at the evening's end.

Alexis would need to be clearer in her communication to reaffirm his 'friend-only' status.

♥ ♥ ♥ ♥ ♥

It took three doorbell stanzas before Alexis processed she had a visitor. Her desire for a sleep in thwarted, she climbed out of bed and down the stairs and did the airport-security frisk to ensure her clothes covered her private parts before opening the front door.

'I've brought croissants from Pandoro,' Edie announced, pushing past sleepy Lexi and heading toward the Goliath coffee machine. Lexi had to give in to the moment.

'Fantastic.' She tried to sound awake and appreciative.

Edie knew strong coffee and fresh croissants were just the ticket to start Lexi's perfect weekend. If she didn't push her way into Saturday morning, Alexis would just work all of Saturday and Sunday away. Edie needed to know where things were at in the growing love life.

'So, what's the goss?' she inquired.

They ate, drank and eased into the morning, swinging on the porch chair and watching all the fitness hounds run and walk along the waterfront, showering the pair with guilt around inactivity and poor diet. They caught up with details of the events of last night and the calls from James, and Edie updated Lexi on work at the airlines, the status of her bathroom renovation and her interim assessment of Lexi moving to Alpine.

'What the …' Lexi pushed back the swing, nearly toppling the Poole pottery. 'Well, yes, I've google-mapped his house, and although it *appears* to be spectacular, and in a flash location, you still haven't ever met him, and you need to be cautious. He could be a gold-digger, Lex. Some crazy scammer preying on a good-hearted woman like you. How do you know he even lives in Alpine, or London, or anywhere, really?'

They sat in silence for a bit. Edie knew Alexis was processing. Alexis knew Edie knew that she had received her serve and was processing. Such is the value of a close friendship. Sitting in silence, blinded by the rising sun and perhaps the truth. It was easier to close her eyes than squint from the sun.

Alexis was initially hurt, not because of what Edie said about James but more that her friend seemed to have a lack of faith in her judgment about love. Surely she was learning what to do and not do in relationships. She questioned her ability to discern fact from fiction in the romance game. She knew her perspective on love called attention to exaggerated, not-drawn-to-scale romance, like the trees in Rousseau's painting.

She took Edie's words to heart as they rocked to and fro gently. What did she know about this total stranger? Nothing. Not anything real or tangible. She was tired and vulnerable, and she knew Edie cared. She brought French baked goods.

Mission complete, Edie received Lexi's assurance she would proceed with caution. Edie could almost hear Charlie from the distant LA teleconference box on Bosley's desk. *Great job, Angel.*

♥ ♥ ♥ ♥ ♥

The next time James rang, Lexi's body armour was in DEFCON 1 protection mode. She let it go to voicemail.

It was very difficult to keep guarded, as, when she played back his message, he had rung to share good news about winning the tender in Spain. Alexis was so proud of his accomplishment. She picked up her pom-poms, with a high kick, yelling, 'Go, James!' Then set them alight, truly torn.

Part of her wanted to dive in, boots and all, sharing in James's success, but she agreed with Edie to keep her feet on terra firma. Alexis needed to figure out if she was standing on bedrock or quicksand. Why didn't she pay better attention in geology class?

From: James Norman
To: Alexis Jordain
Sent: Tuesday, 2nd October, 1.59 p.m.
Subject: Re: Musings from last night ...

Hello Darling,

It was so good to talk to you today, even though it was short and the call ended abruptly. It made me really happy. Talking to you always makes me smile. I cannot help myself. It is 12:57, and I just got in my hotel. Charles (my assistant) and I had a long night out to celebrate. We had so much to talk about. I told him about you and how I feel about you already. It's hard for him to understand how I feel like this so quickly, and, to be honest, I wasn't quite convincing.

I keep thinking about you. I hate the communication breach between us. I am sorry I keep calling at odd hours. I've only just figured out the time difference between us. Sorry, I just want to call sometimes and wishfully think you might be awake. You seem a bit distant after my last email. I didn't even get a proper reply. I didn't get your address. I hope I am not putting any kind of pressure on you. Please let me know if I am.

I was hoping that by now we would talk every day. At least do a little chit-chat on MSN so we can know much more about each other before we actually meet up. But I understand that we are both busy right now.

It is a whole new beginning for us and we need to start right, in friendship. Communication is one of the keys to a healthy relationship. No grudges, no secrets. If something bothers you, tell me and be sure that I'll do the same. Mike is going to love you. He loves immaculate and smart people. They thrill him. I am so happy about this. I am smiling cheek to cheek as I write you this email.

Do you want me to still come? Please let me know so I can start to make plans. I really want to see you, Alexis. I think about you all the time, wondering what you're like in real life. What do you smell like? I want to hear you laugh, feel your hugs and to feel if they are sincere. To kiss your lips, and see if they are as soft as they look.

I leave Madrid on Wednesday morning. Tomorrow I've got to sign documents and I also have a short meeting with the Minister of Works and Housing here in Madrid.

Hope to talk to you again tomorrow.
Regards, James

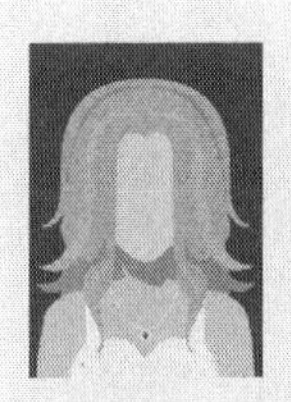

From: Alexis Jordain
To: James Norman
Sent: Tuesday, 2nd October, 12.48 a.m.
Subject: Re: Musings from last night ...

Hello James,

I tried taking you into the bath with me today, but since my laptop is my work computer, I thought it might not be a good risk-management strategy with non-backed-up files and a great deal of water. Out of the tub now and ready to hit the pillow, but jotting a few notes down to reply to your lovely email, which I got after coming home tonight. I do love hearing from you.

First of all, I'm so excited for you winning the contract in Spain. I was chuffed that you thought to ring me to let me know – how I wish I got the call! Well done. I'd love to hear all about it, truly.

Second, you are gorgeous with your concern about my being distant ... you do realise I am just about as far away from you physically as is possible ☺. We are both busy right now and need to be patient, and I agree with you, completely honest with each other. I have been honest so far and intend to continue that way. I can totally understand Charles's reaction of thinking you are crazy. You can blame him for putting you on the site, I suppose. I have contacted and corresponded with one person from the site (you) and am disregarding all other emails I have been sent since registering. This probably is not how it is meant to work for online dating, but then again, I wasn't really serious about getting into it. It was a total fluke that we connected – I'm calling it divine intervention – and will leave it at that, until such time as we choose to part company or live happily ever after.

My note the other day was brief as I was being collected to go to the charity ball in 45 minutes and hadn't started to get ready. I very much wanted to connect with you despite my running late. Sorry if I came across as distant; it wasn't the case. In fact, I thought about you attending with me (that's why I asked if you liked dress-ups and events and going to the theatre etc). I also sent you an MSN message from the auction. I suspect you have not been on, as I've sent two messages to your address. I've never used it for conversations, so when you finally get on there (after the hurry to get me on there ☺) I will see if I can work things from my end and speak to you properly. Despite the distance, please know you are never far from my thoughts. I often think of where you are and what you are doing. My #1 distraction! 'Now and Always', by David Gray (http://www.youtube.com/watch?v=JaZLm5-geSY&feature=related).

James, I was not elusive about my address, rather just being cautious. I needed to think about sending you these details. So, I'm going with the 'trust the guy' option – another learner-driver activity for me, so be gentle please. I live at 1252 Bay Road, in beautiful Wellington – the land of the long white cloud, Aotearoa, or New Zealand. I love living by the sea, I am a water baby – I could live on the water, I am happiest on the water/waterfront. I am an ardent supporter of the All Blacks and love watching NZ sport, except for cricket – I'm thinking cricket is a waste of a good lawn. Supporters say there is much strategy to it, and perhaps there is, but my patience is not sufficient to learn the rules/strategy. I would love for you to come and visit at some point, but also agree it would be great to know a bit more about each other first. How awkward would it be travelling so far away to find that we may not click, or you cannot cope with my hugging style (I assure you my hugs are the best BTW – in fact, you'll have never had a better one). The reason I suggested meeting somewhere neutral was to give us both a chance to get to know each other gently, over a bit of time, even though it's a contrived circumstance at some chosen location. I thought going somewhere we might explore together could be fun, and still give us some space to retreat to if things got too intense (remember *Runaway Bride* here again, just keeping a safe personal distance) – 'How My Heart Behaves', by Feist (http://www.youtube.com/watch?v=sNYIvIRJJU4&feature=related).

Speaking of which, I was perplexed that a man who can sell the Spaniards could not convince Charles! We aren't sending out wedding invites just yet. Tell Charles not to panic ☺. A personal assistant relationship is very close, I know. They know us very well, as they see us at the highs and the lows and how we react. He is a loyal friend to watch out for you.

I have to say, I love hearing your voice on the phone, but to be truthful, I do not always understand what you are saying. It may be the accent or the phone line. I feel like an old granny saying pardon and sorry and please repeat ☺. When you speak slowly, I have no problem understanding you. Wouldn't that be fun, not being able to understand each other in person (I shall start learning to mime and to sign).

Oh my, it is nearly midnight. I better go to sleep. I'm up early to walk with a friend. I sent you a photo on MSN of a walk last week on a perfect, calm morning. We get just the opposite in stormy weather; I love the contrast. Many moods (like me). Okay, I will try to ring you in the morning, but I have a breakfast meeting before my work. I'm starting extra early and ending late to fit in other client work. It's a particularly crazy time, but remember, 'I Will Wait', by Mumford & Sons (http://www.youtube.com/watch?v=rGKfrgqWcv0).

Warm regards
Alexis

Lexi knew she was holding back in her email. She had played her cards close to her chest in the love game.

Part of her was willing to jump in, but in true Gemini fashion, she had doubt, some cast there by her well-meaning friend. Muddled by these competing emotions, she acknowledged how she had always been the responsible one, taking care of others first, not wanting to waste time on the self-indulgence of a boyfriend or serious relationship. She was a mother and a businesswoman; she needed to act appropriately.

Alexis felt the mini-tsunami growing in her soul, pushing through her risk-management strategy, eloquently captured by Anaïs Nin:

And then the day came,
when the risk to remain tight in a bud
was more painful than the risk it took to blossom.

Alexis loved her poetry. It was like dessert to her – decadent and satisfying. The fullness of a flower is far more beautiful than the bud's body armour. Take an orchid. Unfolded, felt-like tongue, pride of a Māori warrior, bold, powerful, unique. Surrounded by admiring petals, each opened with a new challenge from life, it grew to be this beautiful.

She desperately wanted to *blossom* as Nin suggested. She wanted to fall for James – to take the risk. She had to believe in herself – in her own ability to grow into a strong and beautiful flower.

'Just make sure this James creates a love partnership, not partner-shit.' Edie's reminder from breakfast on the swing caught Alexis in an undertow. She would need to prove Edie wrong and put her own mind to rest, but how?

Nin provided inspiration for Alexis, who was now feeling like the goddess Veritas.

'Flowers! Of course,' she said out loud, smirking like the Grinch before he stole Christmas from the Whos.

She would reveal the truth of the romance with flowers. The merits of her new romance would be strengthened once she revealed James was genuine.

The guise of congratulations on winning the contract in Spain gave her the perfect alibi to send a bouquet of 'poised to blossom' buds. Once she could prove his residence in London, even Edie would need to cut Alexis some slack that maybe, just maybe, James might be the genuine article.

Going online, at www.eflorist.co.uk, Alexis learned from Goldilocks: it should not be too large, to avoid being a try-hard, nor too small, lest he thought her *too* cheap and cheerful. She carefully selected the 'just right' sixty-pound medium-size 'Autumn Sunshine' bouquet. A perfect selection for the object of her desire. Delivery address (she hoped) was 36 Clayponds Gardens, London.

She typed in the details and a message:

Congratulations on Spain, James!
I woke up this morning to the most blissful message from you.
You take my breath away.
Enjoy London, A x

She left special instructions with the flower company: 'This is a new and very special man. I hope you wow him ☺ thank you!' As she loaded her credit card details and hit send, she hoped some lovelorn florist would take up her challenge to totally impress.

Tucked into bed, Alexis realised just how much she remained on the fence. Would he really be in London, where he said he would, to receive her bouquet?

She was no longer walking on sunshine – more like eggshells post breakfast Bene. Alexis needed this reassurance as much as Edie. James receiving the bouquet had become the object of her affection, the focal point in the horizon of Rousseau's path. At least part of her thought Edie might be right. 'If it seemed too good to be true,' Edie would say, 'it probably was.'

But there was suddenly more at stake than just being right.

Alexis was falling in love.

Chapter Three

Love at First … Write

♥ ♥ ♥ ♥ ♥

In the museum district in London, one might choose cafés from modern to country classic, each featuring replica statues, *objets d'art* and prints of classic paintings. One setting beckons you to sit, with its bright bouquet of yellow flowers perched delicately on a white lace tablecloth contrasting the wrought iron base. You enter to enjoy the multitude of feel-good home comfort selections as the on-site bakery scents the air at daybreak.

One of the perks of the Commonwealth is the juxtaposed cuisine, sometimes simple, adding a bit of the best from the colonies to complement the food chain. Maple and pecan scones infuse a New World charm to one of Mother England's favourites. Using all of nature's offerings, like indigenous for generations before, those adventurous settlers would satisfy their nutrient needs, using any and everything at their disposal, like taking wild blueberries to create wine, the Great White North grog. New ideas grew from necessity in the harsh climes of the north – that same mother of invention that inspired Klimt's most famous work.

The homely cottage welcome mixes rustic and romance with *The Kiss*, hanging just in your view. It features a combination of simple forms, bright patterns and a courageous collision with religion, introducing the gold leaf. It captivates. Even now, glancing at your table setting, the replica's mosaic of colour echoes in each variety of glassware on direct loan from grandma's pantry or local antique shop.

The picture is a cut-down rectangle, like the countless reproductions found on postcards and souvenirs. It is not like the original, nearly six-foot, perfect square. Obviously. Less obvious is the state of mind of the artist just before creating this Austrian national treasure in 1907 (now worth hundreds of millions). Klimt's career was in crisis. He had *seemingly* botched up life at home with the nudity in his works *Philosophy*, *Medicine* and *Jurisprudence*. Criticised for 'pornography' and 'perverted excess', he had no North American adventure parachute in which to escape. He wrote, 'Either I am too old, or too nervous, or too stupid – there must be something wrong.'[7]

The call of adventure, the call of the wild and the call to romance. It was all far too intoxicating, sitting there enjoying the Klimt, the scone, the tea. By the time Chet Baker started on that trumpet of his, even Edie, the greatest cynic, could not help but fall in love. Right there on the spot.

The *call* took the form of an email acknowledgment from the florist: 'We are pleased to inform you that your order WA232994 to 36 Clayponds Gardens was successfully delivered on 04 October.'

As soon as he received the bouquet, James rang. He left the following message: 'In all my years, no one has ever sent me flowers,

Alexis. You totally blow me away.' He sounded totally smitten. His voice was soft and emotional. 'In such a short space of time, sight unseen, I cannot imagine my life without you. You are an amazing woman. Thank you. Thank you so much. Thank you for just being you. Call me.'

It would appear from his message that upon receipt of the beautiful bouquet, James decided to unfurl from his own bud.

'Whew, what a relief.' Alexis clearly received the call. She was ready for the adventure ahead, boarded the ship bound for the great unknown. She was reassured that the earth was not flat. At least she wouldn't fall off the end when answering.

From: James Norman
To: Alexis Jordain
Sent: Friday, 5th October, 1.43 p.m.
Subject: Can't stop thinking about you

Hello Alexis,

Its 2:02 am and I am here sitting in the corner of my room, thinking about you. I can't get you out of my head. Believe me when I say I've tried. I just thought I'd send you a short email to express a small piece of my mind.

I don't know how to say this without sounding like a fool, but I am completely in love with you. I don't mean to freak you out. I know Love is not a word that you throw around just because you want to sound sweet and romantic. I actually do love you, Alexis. I don't even know how and when it happened. I cannot trace its origin, but at the same time, I can't think of anything else. I keep hearing your voice playing in my head like a skipping record, and I cannot get a grip, no matter how I try.

You mean everything to me now. You make my life so beautiful. These past days have been fantastic for me. Love just makes you glow in a special way. People around you can see it. They know that there is something new in your life. I am happy that I met you, Alexis. It has been the highlight of my year.

I am devoted to making this work. I will do all it takes. It is easy to say, but I am a devoted man. I am in a position that I just want to love you till I die. I have the most awesome conversations with you, smiling from cheek to cheek like a mentally ill patient. You need to see me reading one of your emails. I am completely overwhelmed by how I feel, and I don't want to stop feeling this way. I can't wait until I hug you and kiss you and look you in the eyes to say how much you really mean to me.

I know how you feel about this and how you want to take baby steps, but please trust me. I know how delicate your heart is and how skeptical your mind is. But like you said, sometimes, we just need to let go. Just give me your hand. I ask you again, let's just be happy together. The last thing I want to do is hurt you. I would treat you like a man should treat his woman and I promise we would be happy together.

I don't know how I feel like this so quickly. I always thought I could control my emotions. Sometimes I am so scared that I love you too much already, and that I need to slow down. It is almost like I've known you my whole life. I am so comfortable with you. I can't wait until Mike meets you and loves you too.

I am leaving for America in a few days to see Mike. I'll keep you informed with all my plans and travels – 'To the Moon and Back', by Savage Garden (https://www.youtube.com/watch?v=zD8KvL1aFNQ)

Have a good day, and please send my regards to the kids.
James.

From: Alexis Jordain
To: James Norman
Sent: Friday, 5th October, 4.48 a.m.
Subject: Re: Can't stop thinking about you

Hello James, it's 4.30 am and I've been up since 3 am, thinking of you. First the moonlight kept me company, then I waved to the fishermen heading out to sea. I had prepared a wonderful note sharing my thoughts, but before I sent it, my computer crashed. I will write again when I wake up properly, but even putting pen to paper (so to speak) helped me clarify my thoughts. The gist of it included:

If I think about how you make me feel, the way my mind races with possibilities and the warmth of emotion I have felt over the past days, I would not know what else to call it but love. That it is such a short duration is irrelevant. The heart knows what the heart wants. Mine wants yours.

I have waged war on my rational saboteurs. In the past they have been insidious and prevented any friend or foe entering the parapet. I shall take the offer of your hand to hold as I do my best to remove the armour and all its trappings to win the war. I wish to reclaim my heart and its freedom to love unconditionally, with your help. I may falter and I feel you will help steady me. I want this. Very much.

If sleepless nights and distraction through the day move us closer to understanding ourselves and each other, what a small price to pay. I am elated, and while I initially responded with 'why nots', I have moved swiftly into wonder and gratitude. What a special feeling to share with you. We are so very fortunate indeed.

I'm back to bed. I shall dream of you. I hope you are having a brilliant day.
A x

'Stick With Me Baby', by Robert Plant & Alison Krauss (http://www.youtube.com/watch?v=4yyofgq2I30).

Best to keep mum on the mention of the three little words, Alexis concluded. She knew her friends would go mental if they knew that James, aka complete stranger, said 'I love you'. Oliver might be okay, but she knew Edie would blow a gasket and criticise her for falling in love too easily. She could share later, when the timing was better.

From: James Norman
To: Alexis Jordain
Date: Saturday, 6th October, 12.10 a.m.
Subject: I love you

My darling, the one that I love and I adore. The one that I constantly think about. The one that would make me smile no matter what. The one that taught me a new level of love I had never experienced before. My heart longs for you. My body is dying to touch your body. My lips, my lips are waiting to be introduced to your lips. When I think about it, I cannot control the smirk on my face.

I read your emails again. Such lovely words, Alexis. I can almost hear you speak straight from your heart, and I know that you mean everything you say. We are going to be so happy together, baby. Live together in love and happiness. People will always talk about how much we love each other. You make it so easy to love you. I have completely and totally given myself, and all I have and own, to you. I cannot love anything or anyone else. There is no more space in my heart. Talking with you brings so much joy to my heart, and a smile to my lips. I can never get enough.

I keep falling deeper and deeper. There's surely no going back on this one. I have realized that love is all that you need to make it work. Working on love fixes everything, so all we really need is love. Thank you for loving me the way that you do. Thank you for all the nice things you said about me. I don't even realize when I am doing these things. You bring out the best in me. Chats about your life, your kids and friends and family just made me realize how you are a very special woman and I am a lucky man. I am so glad that I met you. That song was beautiful, by the way. I loved it …

You constantly think of me even when I am asleep and care about me without an iota of doubt. You are so sweet and loving.

I promise to tell you if I have had a bad day and if I need some help. I'll let you help me. You are now my best friend, Alexis. When you fall in love with your best friend, nothing can go wrong. There are no surprises. I am so glad that you came into my life. It's been such a short time, but seems like forever. I can't wait for us to go on walks and I can kiss you midway and tell you how much I love you, face to face, eye to eye.

I had a short rest, then I woke up at about 1 am. Now I am having a cup of coffee as I am writing you this email. I am also trying to keep up with the news. I like to be up to date. I like to know everything that's going on around me. I also like to know a little about everything to help me for conversation purposes in business. After this, I will take a shower and try to go back to sleep.

Alexis, I know all of this is happening so fast and you can't catch your breath. But I love you, baby, and I really want to make this right. You make my life so beautiful.

I would send this off now and I will talk to you later. I love you. Regards, James.

The introduction of MSN as a communication channel for the happy couple added a new dimension to real-time dating. It was also easier to understand James in written English rather than trying to decipher his hard-to-pin-down vernacular. Saturday's MSN started the first of many such communiqués.

MSN – 6th October

Alexis Jordain 10:41:49 a.m.
How was your day, darling?

James Karlten 10:41:16 a.m.
It was all right. I had a lot of meetings today. I met with some Chinese people from Hong Kong. I am looking at selling the company to them as soon as I retire. So it was a bit hectic. How was your night?

Alexis Jordain 10:41:49 a.m.
Are you ready to let go of the business?

James Karlten 10:42:16 a.m.
Well yeah, I don't see any reason why I should still be in it.

Alexis Jordain 10:42:20 a.m.
Edie and I had fun. We drank too much wine and watched Bridesmaids and laughed for ages …

James Karlten 10:42:43 a.m.
Oh, I can imagine, I can't wait to replace her.

Alexis Jordain 10:43:35 a.m.
LOL. Just thinking about what you said about your unique skills and applying them. Might you still consult back, or are you looking for a clean break?

Alexis Jordain 10:43:51 a.m.
Hey, it is easier to type on the computer, this is actually very easy :)

James Karlten 10:44:33 a.m.
Well, I am not sure, I just want to spend time with my family. I've had a decent 22 years of hard work. It's time to get some rest.

James Karlten 10:44:41 a.m.
Tell me about it, baby ...

Alexis Jordain 10:44:58 a.m.
Sounds perfect. I think it's very sensible, and better now than when you are 60! I'll need to find things to keep you entertained I suppose.

James Karlten 10:46:00 a.m.
Yeah, besides I'd have the most beautiful and charming woman with me. What more can a man ask for?

Alexis Jordain 10:46:08 a.m.
Indeed.

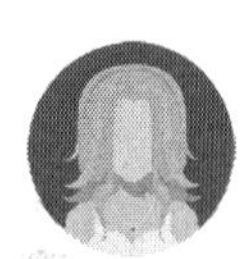

James Karlten 10:46:11 a.m.
All I want is you ...

Alexis Jordain 10:46:49 a.m.
It's pretty wonderful to hear that.

Alexis Jordain 10:47:26 a.m.
Have you been to Melbourne Cup?

James Karlten 10:47:35 a.m.
You know that I mean all that I say to you, right? It's not just an attempt to sound sweet or anything.

James Karlten 10:47:47 a.m.
No I haven't.

Alexis Jordain 10:48:12 a.m.
Were you trying to sound sweet? Would you like to have a first date there? Melbourne?

James Karlten 10:48:58 a.m.
That would be nice. I thought we were thinking Hawaii.

Alexis Jordain 10:49:17 a.m.
That would be fine too. Just always thinking … too much probably. This morning was interesting … I just couldn't get you out of my thoughts.

James Karlten 10:50:14 a.m.
Well, I like that you are involved in this almost as I am. It helps me to feel sane. When you think about me, what do you think about?

Alexis Jordain 10:50:31 a.m.
Oh please do not use me as a sanity barometer! Lots of things. Companionship, romance, adventure, intimacy.

James Karlten 10:51:11 a.m.
Hmm ...

Alexis Jordain 10:51:45 a.m.
Sharing experiences, simple family stuff, attending functions together ... I think about having a strong connection with you that allows me to feel like we can do anything, anywhere – and still find home in each other's arms.

James Karlten 10:53:17 a.m.
It's amazing how we share the same thoughts.

Alexis Jordain 10:53:28 a.m.
It's limitless really. I too have worked hard for a long time. I want to enjoy life.

James Karlten 10:53:44 a.m.
Something bothered me – when we eventually get together, where do you want to live? Do you still want to stay in NZ or do you want to move to Jersey with me?

Alexis Jordain 10:54:11 a.m.
Residence ... tricky conversation. I suppose we should see if we actually like each other :) then ... There was a time I said I never wanted to leave NZ.

James Karlten 10:55:40 a.m.
Like? I am in LOVE with you, Alexis. I don't mince words.

Alexis Jordain 10:55:40 a.m.
Where do you want to live? Mike loves NJ, you mentioned earlier. My eldest daughter starts college next year (that's high school in North American terms). I want her to have a smooth transition – are you sure you want to get involved in the pre-teen years?

James Karlten 10:57:26 a.m.
Of course, Alexis. She will be the daughter that I never had.

Alexis Jordain 10:57:51 a.m.
Are you interested in NZ? We have trains here too :) and running water.

James Karlten 10:58:04 a.m.
I am expecting a lot of challenges and I am ready for it. I want to be with you. Nothing, absolutely nothing will discourage me.

Alexis Jordain 10:58:17 a.m.
Ok. If you could live anywhere, where would you choose?

James Karlten 10:59:12 a.m.
I love it in Brisbane. I went there for work one time and I liked it. I was going to buy an apartment there 2 years ago but it turned out that someone else beat me to it.

Alexis Jordain 10:59:39 a.m.
Brissy is nice. Good climate. Reasonable work opportunities, it's growing also. Where does your mum live – still there?

James Karlten 11:00:35 a.m.
She has passed on now. May her soul rest in peace.

Alexis Jordain 11:01:15 a.m.
Sorry to hear that. Did she know Mike?

James Karlten 11:01:31 a.m.
Yeah, she adored him …

Alexis Jordain 11:01:48 a.m.
Wonderful. It's important to have connection with our heritage.

James Karlten 11:02:26 a.m.
I totally agree.

Alexis Jordain 11:02:49 a.m.
Gosh, the thought of location on top of diving into this emotional experience is overwhelming.

James Karlten 11:03:15 a.m.
I can take it slow if you want. I am sorry. I just like to plan things ahead.

Alexis Jordain 11:03:19 a.m.
I'm trying to sort out arrangements now with my mum, given the house will be sold shortly. It will be a chance for all of us, with her coming to stay here. I understand the planning aspect. I too have planned in the past. As I get older I'm trying to go with the flow more.

James Karlten 11:03:46 a.m.
Okay, she's moving in with you?

Alexis Jordain 11:04:35 a.m.
In the interim, yes. She will go up to Vancouver to stay with my sister in a few months for at least half the year.

James Karlten 11:05:12 a.m.
Okay.

Alexis Jordain 11:05:32 a.m.
I would like to be closer to my sister too, and have thought about whether coming back to Canada would be good for the kids. I have a lot of relatives in Toronto. Lots of links back to Croatia as well.
It feels like there are a lot of change dimensions going on right now. I'm not certain where they'll all land.

James Karlten 11:06:36 a.m.
Oh great, what about work? You know you didn't really go into detail about what you do exactly.

Alexis Jordain 11:08:18 a.m
I have a successful consulting business, mostly me and I contract out a few bits and pieces. I do strategy, planning and management consulting for government, private sector and NGOs. Some coaching with CEOs and a few judiciary, etc. I love my work, but do too much. It's transportable, thankfully, as long as my brain and experience stay intact.

James Karlten 11:08:46 a.m.
Oh that's great. I can tell that you enjoy it from the way you sound.

Alexis Jordain 11:10:29 a.m.
I've done a lot in NZ. I've played in Aussie a bit and in Singapore. I started working in British Columbia and worked on the east coast in Halifax ages ago (the east coast is my favourite part of Canada, apart from the Yukon and QCI).

James Karlten 11:10:35 a.m.
That's a lot of experience. I used to have that passion for my job as well, but it started fading out.

Alexis Jordain 11:11:00 a.m.
I'd love to talk to you more about everything. I'd love to be able to hear your story and listen to your heart and understand where you've been, and then consider where you are going … where we are going …

James Karlten 11:12:00 a.m.
I am here. Do with me whatever, darling. I want us both to be extremely ecstatically euphoric (in a calm and peaceful way).

Alexis Jordain 11:13:18 a.m.
☺ I need to dash, I'm sorry. I could stay online with you, though I really would prefer the real thing. You must be getting ready to rest after a very long and tiring day. Let me tuck you in with a kiss and tonight, just relax, imagining I am there next to you, stroking your forehead as you drift off to sleep.

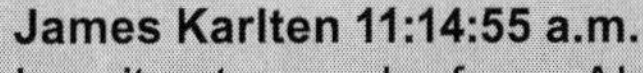

James Karlten 11:14:55 a.m.
I can't get enough of you, Alexis. I hope we can do this again soon. I will just sit here and write you an email before I hit the sheets. I love you. I would love that … I wish you could just appear on my bed right now.

Alexis Jordain 11:16:10 a.m.
I've not mastered time travel just yet. Give me a few days … Sleep well love, I'll speak to you in the morning, x

James Karlten 11:16:42 a.m.
I trust you to do anything Alexis. LOL. All right darling.

The time Alexis and James spent together was steadily on the increase. He was becoming a permanent feature throughout the day and occupied time in between in her daydreams.

From: Alexis Jordain
To: James Norman
Sent: Saturday, 6th October, 10:43 p.m.
Subject: Re: I love you

Dearest James,

Surely Japanese water torture is next to follow the sleep deprivation. We must really get into a groove of proper rest. We'll never make it to Hawaii at this rate! BTW, when are you off back to America to see Mike?

Thank you for your lovely note. You are very sweet and I love that you can communicate how you are feeling. I am so happy that you are happy, AND I am happy that I am happy also. I also sound ridiculous at times. I guess that's why they say crazy in love … 'Crazy in Love', by Beyoncé and Jay Z (http://www.youtube.com/watch?v=k-0S1F99N7U).

There is so much I want to ask you about, and tell you about. You never mentioned whether you had an interest in theatre or the arts/culture. Do you dance? Sing? I realised I had forgotten to mention the day spa I opened here last year. I would love to tell you more about my consulting work too. I have great clients and do some really rewarding assignments.

The girls are now over with their dad for a few days so I will catch up on some overdue work and house maintenance starting tomorrow. There are never enough hours in the day it seems. The next few weeks are a bit hectic workwise also, with a bit of internal travel required. I have looked at my forward commitments and could perhaps do first weekend in November to meet you (Hawaii??), just for a few nights – arriving late on Friday 2 November, back to NZ on late Monday 5 Nov (the dateline is a bugger) – so 3 nites max, or I could stay longer first weekend in December, perhaps up to a week. Gosh we are a long distance away …

I'm turning in now, desperate for a good night's sleep. I may try you in the morning on MSN. I'm starting to nod off already … I hope you have a fantastic day – Saturday when you wake – perhaps you may rest a bit? I hope you were able to get back to sleep last night.

PS – I like your name. It sounds very noble.

PPS – I'm not sure if you should be putting English as your first 'spoken' language (sorry, I guess I just had a little bit more cheeky left in me b4 bed ☺).

♥ ♥ ♥ ♥ ♥

Lexi thought it would be nice to post James a card in Alpine so he had a letter to open when he was back in the States:

> Saturday, 6 October
> Darling James,
>
> I am attempting to keep one step ahead of you in your travels. This is no small feat.
>
> I am following you with a heat map as you light up the globe en route to East Coast USA.
>
> It has been wonderful connecting with you from faraway shores, and now that you are home with family, I am smiling the most.
>
> Enjoy your time together. I am sending lots of love your way.
>
> A x

She also enclosed a heart-shaped card she purchased from Typo – one of the kids' favourite stationery stores. On the front, the cardboard heart carried a simple message: *You & Me*. On the back, there was room to add a personal note. The card then disassembled into puzzle pieces. James would need to put the puzzle back together again to decipher the note from Alexis. She thought it might be fun for him to test his engineering skills. She imagined his loving hands putting the heart together again and his smile when it was completed. She just knew he would love it – both receiving and assembling it.

Before sealing the envelope, she added a small card for Mike, so he would feel included. She had already started a bond with this young man, James's son, who his father simply adored. *He is such a wonderful father,* thought Alexis as she wrote to Mike:

Saturday, 6 October
Dear Mike,

I wanted to take this opportunity to say hello while sending a card to your dad. He has spoken so fondly of you. I look forward to meeting you one day.

If you're confused at all by the strange circumstances, please join the club. We have two founding members and I suspect several more joiners to come ☺. I am certain all of this will make more sense as time passes and life unfolds. Try to be patient with your dad. I think he has learner wheels on his love bicycle (we both do).

Anyhow, I look forward to hearing about what you are studying, and how school is going for you. My eldest daughter, Paige, starts high school next year. The terms here run by calendar year. It takes some getting used to after living in Canada. I also have a younger daughter, Bella.

Have you been Down Under? To New Zealand or Australia? We are in spring now and the days are longer and warmer. It's the best time of year to visit. Enjoy your weekend at home with your dad. He's missed you a great deal.

Warm regards, Alexis

Unfortunately, like Humpty Dumpty, the puzzle would not be put back together again. Mike would never feel the warmth intended by her note. Her thoughtful package would never arrive.

Mother Nature had another scene in mind, as she started brewing Hurricane Sandy.

Even though meteorologists re-classed Sandy as a cyclone before her centre reached land, the technical distinction did not lessen the devastation. The impending storm would cause much damage, altering the lives of all in its path. Sandy and her hurricane-force winds would still leave a state of emergency for all concerned.

From: Alexis Jordain
To: James Norman
Sent: Sunday, 7th October, 12.06 a.m.
Subject: Another level …

Dear James

Just when you thought it couldn't get any more pathetic … I now have your photo sitting on my desk. Say nothing … It is actually a collage – please do not laugh – I'm killing myself laughing watching myself be so silly. So, I've got the 'corporate' one in the blue shirt (told you blue was my favourite colour), the 'come hither' shot of you in the yellow shirt that was on Be2 (what were you thinking!) and the 'James at home' in a black t-shirt (probably Iron Maiden) with your friend Richardson in Canada and Mike. Three moods of the man. I love it. It's also ridiculous at another level … You are quite cute though ☺ I love the intensity of your eyes – you have a genuine ability to connect with those baby blues. Wow, I can't wait to see them in real life. Oh, you said you sent me a shot with Mike and his mates a few weeks ago, but didn't. The one with Mike in it has him at about 13 maybe? You and him outside a house somewhere, no mates. I'd love to see a recent pic if you have one please.

Today's been a working evening, and a busy day for a Sunday. I'm ready to hit the hay and start another humdinger of a week. I've put one contract to bed and advanced two others, so I'm making progress. Brunch with Grandma (my mum) went well. I think we have a plan. I'm unable to pack her due to work commitments, so we'll get someone in to do all that and just put most things in storage, hopefully sell some things at the auction. She's accumulated so many things over the years. I sorted through some old books today – funny how you can remember some things so clearly 40 years ago and cannot remember something from yesterday.

Okay, back to getting to know you more …

- Do you speak any other languages than 'near' English ☺?

- What made you agree to let Charles put a profile on the site this time (I suspect your friends would have been prodding you to get back in the game before now)?
- What is your favourite alcoholic beverage?
- If you were to make me dinner ☺ what would your international chef standard (sans Mike's review) cook for me?
- When are you most comfortable – at work, at home or ?
- Do you have any fears?
- Have you ever broken any bones?
- What kind of a laugher are you?
- How tall are you?
- What's your favourite fruit? Veggie?
- Do you ride a bike? Paddle a canoe/kayak?
- Can you swim?
- Do you scuba dive?
- What is your favourite thing to do when you are alone (keep it clean, it's a family show ☺?)

I'm a pretty independent woman. I love spending time with people, and I am also a firm believer in alone time. I like to recharge my batteries with some quiet time, solitude. Don't get me wrong, I love doing things as a couple and spending time together, but I also need my space. I'm pretty energetic, and being quiet helps me balance my yin and yang energy. It's kind of a paradox, really, the desire to be taken care of, pampered and loved to the extreme, but with the freedom to pursue individual interests, different friends, time apart. I think we're doing extremely well on the time apart – we've nailed it. I think we can move on from that ☺.

I've never dated a man with a moustache before. Have you always had one? I wonder if it tickles to kiss you. I wonder what it would be like ... So, you grilled me on my hugging ability ... what about yours? What kind of a hugger are you? During a hug, would you (a) be able to drive a long combination *road train* or *Rocky Mountain triple* between us? (b) squish a kiwifruit if I had one in my pocket (c) lift me up (provided you are very strong, I mean really – start bench-pressing now ☺) (d) not let me go ... Okay, getting steamy in the bay, best move on.

Time for bed. I haven't spoken to you today, and despite being busy, I've missed you. No doubt you are entertaining the Chinese with your tremendous breadth of knowledge and experience of their cuisine. I cannot wait to hear your answers to the questions above. I need to manage expectations that you are perfect ... Just thought of another one – neat freak or messy man or ?

I'll take your smile (with a moustache) to bed with me. Hope you have a super day, and I will leave you with a song I'm listening to now ... for my railway man, thinking about retiring so he can hang out with his new love, A x

'Death Of A Train', by Daniel Lanois (http://www.youtube.com/watch?v=5HMjzHtlAZk).

♥ ♥ ♥ ♥ ♥

Alexis was rapidly becoming an MSN junkie. She sent James a few short messages every time she passed by her computer that day.

MSN – 7th October

Alexis Jordain 9:05:23 a.m.
Good morning from the land of the long white cloud, darling. I wish you could see the sunrise and waves crashing against the shore, and the cheeky grin on my face when writing to you. I am off to breakfast with my mum to go over moving logistics. It's an emotional time. Please send some strength my way. I miss you. I hope your day was wonderful, and that we connect soon. Sending kisses from afar, A x

Alexis Jordain 3:06:11 p.m.
Hi there, just lost the weekend of 2–5 November – forgot about helping at church for First Communion group! Down to 9–12 Nov or a week in early December ...

Alexis Jordain 11:07:51 p.m.
PS, I don't think my text messages get through to your phone. Please let me know if you got my text today.

PPS, Don't worry about connecting if you are busy. I'm happy doing all the talking (promise). At least this way you cannot disagree with anything I have to say … sleeping now, Funny Girl over and out x

Am I falling in love too easily? Hopping into bed, she wondered if she was acting like a stalker. It was hard for her to pull back once in full throttle. By morning, any weird and nutty behaviour of hers was vindicated.

From: James Norman
To: Alexis Jordain
Date: Sunday, 7th October, 11.19 a.m.
Subject: Re: I love you

Hello Alexis,

Thank you for all your lovely messages. I don't know what I will do if I ever stop getting them. You've taught me a different way to love, like we are the only ones in the universe, and I just want you to know that I am contented. I don't know why anyone would want to lose you. It has been a very busy weekend for me (unusual). Like I told you, some experts from China are negotiating on buying my company as soon as I retire, so there has been some rigorous reviewing of our portfolio and it takes a lot of time, especially when we got to the point where the financial aspects had to be audited. But looking at the upside, we had a good Chinese meal after the meeting yesterday LOL. It went well and I am meeting with them tomorrow again. I am also trying to finalize the paperwork for the Madrid contract so we get the mobilization funds and begin our work as soon as possible.

I think that our story of love is one of the most beautiful considering the almost immediate passion and all we have talked about and shared since we started corresponding. I don't want any other person. You will be my last love, because you already are my everything.

There are no more reservations, and no fears to express. All my heart wants is you. I always thought it was impossible to feel like this about anyone until I found you. Our love and feelings cause me great excitement and joy. I will cherish them forever. I love you intensely now and I will be pleased to do my most important task: to love you permanently and completely and build a strong and true union.

You have hit me where no other woman can ever reach, and I just want to say thank you. I've no iota of doubt that we are meant to be together.

A million words I can speak of you and the lyrics would be the same ... I love you now. I always will. Sometimes it's hard to believe that I've you all to myself. It's like a dream come true. It is such a beautiful feeling when you love someone and they feel the same way about you. You can't even imagine how good it is. I completely adore you, baby. You are so tender and so affectionate. I like how you are very interested in the things that concern me. I know true love when I see it and I can only say one thing: I am the luckiest man in the world.

You've completely taken possession of my mind and heart. Charles says that I've not been able to complete one sentence lately without saying, 'I wonder what Alexis thinks about this,' LOL. I am just a man in love with the best woman in the world. These are the happiest moments of my life and I cherish it all. I would do anything to feel this way forever. I wake up every morning with a love song on my lips and I am just smiling, knowing that someone is thinking about me and cares about me. I don't know how this happened so fast. I can't answer a lot of questions about how I started to love you. I don't know how I got here and I don't even care, but one thing I do know is I love it here and I don't want to ever go back. Loving you, baby, is what I want to do.

Well, I am going to send this off now and go to bed. I love you, baby, a lot more than my words could say.

James

Wow, Alexis thought. This man is seriously committed. It was wonderful and also a bit scary. *Is he acting like the stalker?* She was also starting to fear that *she* may not live up to his expectations of her. And what if she wasn't physically attracted to him after meeting?

Oh dear, how can my heart be so full of love and yet my mind send such mixed signals about a future together? She decided a Vienna Convention was needed. She granted herself a day of diplomatic immunity to give her head and heart an opportunity to agree a position.

From: James Norman
To: Alexis Jordain
Date: Monday, 8th October, 7.31 a.m.
Subject: Re: I love you

I just can't stop thinking about you, so I wrote you this:
My precious love,
So far and yet so near.
Your name sits there in vivid blue
And I know that you are there.
At first I wondered if it wise
To use my time in search
Of something no computer feels
Without a human touch.
But as I grow to know you
Through lines upon the screen
I saw a depth of beauty
So clear though never seen.
And as we talked of love and trust

And kindled our desire
I felt myself become entranced
And caught within your fire.
For though I have not met you
Your earthly form not seen
I feel your soul within the words
Upon that magic screen.
Oh, love how you stir me
Your passion strong and bright
Brings to my full but lonely life
A wondrous glow of light.
The obstacles of the world between us
Cannot stop us from meeting
And so be ensured that my love for you
Is beyond eternity.
I love you with all my heart Alexis.
Regards, James

From: James Norman
To: Alexis Jordain
Date: Monday, 8th October, 8.03 a.m.
Subject: Re: I love you

Hello darling,

I am going through your emails again and joy overflows in my heart. I am leaving for the US on Tuesday night to see Mike. I would be there for a few days and return to Madrid as regards the contract. I am looking at the 8th of November to meet up with you. Please let me know if this is okay with you so I can tell Charles to begin with all the necessary bookings. Talking about this makes me really happy. I am looking forward to this with all my heart. Thank you for all your compliments, LOL. You are so cheeky sometimes, it makes me love you all the more. I almost have omitted the picture of me and Mike, I have attached it to this email.

Do you speak any other languages than 'near' English ☺?:
LOL, I speak a bit of French as well but I am not perfect yet.

What made you agree to let Charles put a profile on the site this time (I suspect your friends would have been prodding you to get back in the game before now)?:
I don't have a lot of friends, but Charles and I are really close. I am not sure why, but he just thought that it was time for me to get a woman and he was very persistent.

What is your favourite alcoholic beverage?:
I like ciders, and I drink a lot of white wine as well.

If you were to make me dinner ☺ what would your international chef standard (sans Mike's review) cook for me?:
Hmm, tough one. I want to surprise you on this one, so watch this space, baby.

When are you most comfortable – at work, at home or ?:
I spend more time at work, but I am more relaxed at home.

Do you have any fears?
Not really. I am a very optimistic person, and I believe in positivity, so I really don't dwell on fears.

Have you ever broken any bones?
No.

What kind of a laugher are you?
LOL, Mike says he loves the way I laugh, but sometimes I think I am rather loud.

How tall are you?
6'1".

What's your favourite fruit? Veggie?
I love pineapples.

Do you ride a bike? Paddle a canoe/kayak?
No, I hate bikes, LOL. But once Mike and I went on an adventure and I had to paddle a canoe with him. It was fun.

Can you swim?
I am an Olympic champion LOL.

Do you scuba dive?
NO.

What is your favourite thing to do when you are alone (keep it clean, it's a family show ☺)?

I like to watch the news. I have some shows I randomly watch, but I am never able to keep up, so it doesn't make any sense to try.

I am looking forward to your answers on these questions you have asked me. I have not always had a mustache. I started growing one after my late wife passed away. I admire all your attributes and I can't ever get enough of you. I wish I was good with words the way you are so I could express how I feel. I will write you another email in the morning.

I've attached some other pictures of me where Mike made me do a cowboy. I hope you like it.

Have a great day. I love you.
Regards, James

Alexis was certainly getting a barrage of positive reinforcement from James. Later that night, he reached out on MSN.

James Karlten 10:22:11 p.m.
Hello darling, I love you more than words can describe. I know you are having hectic days. I wish you could come home to me and let me kiss you all over your body and massage your feet and tell you how much I love you. You make me so happy and I can't live without you. I hope you know that I mean all that I say to you.

Alexis Jordain 10:22:46 p.m.
According to MSN, James Karlten is writing – how is this possible, when he's already sent such lovely words across the miles ... I was just about ready to head to bed and your light popped up. I was watching the video you sent. I'm really liking the thought of that – kisses all over, massage, hmm – I could get used to that. Charles will have my head for distracting you so much!

James Karlten 10:25:10 p.m.
You don't distract me. You are priority at this time.

Alexis Jordain 10:25:18 p.m.
I loved the photos btw. And your poem, wow, fantastic. Is that priority for this morning?

James Karlten 10:26:00 p.m.
For life. Thank you, Alexis. I was expecting pictures of you too …

Alexis Jordain 10:26:55 p.m.
How does one respond to such words? I put some up on MSN with the girls – did you see them?

James Karlten 10:28:00 p.m.
I didn't get them.

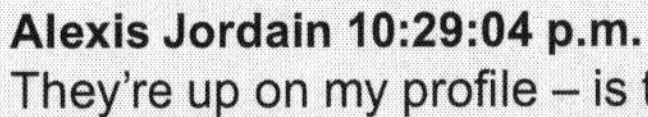

Alexis Jordain 10:29:04 p.m.
They're up on my profile – is there a security process to release them? Do you need any more evidence of my technologically challenged-ness!!!

James Karlten 10:29:53 p.m.
I left Be2 since I fell in love with you. I don't even know my password or username. LOL, just send them via email. You are beautiful, Alexis, just like your heart …

Alexis Jordain 10:32:02 p.m.
I'll try to send some pics by email. I was going through some papers on the weekend and came across my Be2 sign-in (on 19 Sept). You were a steal at $270.

James Karlten 10:33:25 p.m.
LOL, I am not that expensive. You should cancel your profile, Alexis.

Alexis Jordain 10:33:38 p.m.
How are the discussions going with the Chinese? Were they impressed with your knowledge of their cuisine? I'm sure that is part of due diligence.

James Karlten 10:34:27 p.m.
LOL, they are not concerned with food, but it's going on well. I am sure we would be able to close the deal when I get back from the US.

Alexis Jordain 10:34:45 p.m.
I intend to, just haven't got around to it as yet. I always delete the emails that come in. Did you approach them to exit or did they woo you (no pun intended)?

James Karlten 10:35:23 p.m.
They would keep taking money off your account.

Alexis Jordain 10:36:59 p.m.
Okay, fair enough. I thought it was a one-off for 6 months. I wasn't paying a great deal of attention, really. It started out as a bit of a giggle with my girls after homework. I never imagined. I was drawn to the ad at the right moment, glanced across the kitchen, and, weeks later, here we are! I was meant to connect with you, obviously, and only you. I am not interested in anyone else.

James Karlten 10:39:03 p.m.
That's a pretty nice thing to say. You know how to make me smile …

Alexis Jordain 10:39:28 p.m.
I simply speak the truth.

James Karlten 10:39:56 p.m.
I wish we could meet next week. I am dying to meet you.

Alexis Jordain 10:40:16 p.m.
Me too.

James Karlten 10:41:06 p.m.
I am leaving for the US tomorrow night.

Alexis Jordain 10:41:43 p.m.
I haven't had a chance to reply to your notes from today, but if you can manage the weekend in November 9th I think? – I think flights from NZ arrive late on Friday night. It's a dreadfully long flight. How long will you spend in NJ? Maybe we can celebrate a signed deal by then.

James Karlten 10:44:21 p.m.
I am not sure. I will let you know when I arrive and send you my numbers as well. So you want me to come to NZ, right? No longer Hawaii?

Alexis Jordain 10:44:54 p.m.
Are you okay? Not working too hard. Hmmm? No Hawaii sounds fine. Wouldn't that be great? I'm in Honolulu and you arrive in Wellington! I kind of worry about you sometimes. I know you are more than competent, but I don't know, just want to be there for you.

James Karlten 10:46:35 p.m.
I just want to be with you, Alexis. I don't care wherever.

James Karlten 10:47:27 p.m.
It's okay, Alexis. This time difference. Sometimes, I want to share a joke with you or I want to tell you about something that is bothering me, but I know you'd be asleep.

Alexis Jordain 10:47:53 p.m.
I would prefer meeting you on neutral ground. Just us. No familiar trappings, no responsibilities. Maybe I need to install a special red phone that only you ring, just when you need me. Like on Batman … I think it was Batman.

Alexis Jordain 10:51:12 p.m
Well, I know it's not ideal right now, but seeing as we are both pretty flat out, it (being on different continents/islands) is probably the only thing that's keeping us sane. Could you imagine trying to close the deal with the Chinese if I was around the corner asking you to come and play?

Alexis Jordain 10:54:24 p.m.
I understand you are busy. I really do not have any expectations. I would love to have you on tap, but it's not really possible right now. I am being remarkably patient for a 'now' girl. I guess I think about how long it has taken for you and me to finally connect – we were both ready at nearly the exact same time – we have to go with that divine intervention and be pretty happy with it … Sweetheart, I've some papers still to read before bed, and I've a very early start. I'm going to have to say bonne nuit and sign out. Just know I'm thinking about you always. You always make me smile and I feel amazing knowing you are there. I really feel loved. It's wonderful.

James Karlten 10:57:45 p.m.
I totally understand that, Alexis, but when I say you're my priority, I mean it. Okay, Alexis, I love you. I love you so much.

Alexis Jordain 10:58:48 p.m.
I will write more tomorrow. If we don't connect before you leave, safe travels. I need to figure out why my cell cannot send you texts. I love you also. Very much. Huge hug (and rain check on the all-over-body kisses please).

James Karlten 11:04:42 p.m.
Thank you baby, I love you too.

From: Alexis Jordain
To: James Norman
Sent: Tuesday, 9th October, 5.27 a.m.
Subject: Some photos …

Good morning James,

Here are a few random pics:

- Mum and I at the US/Canada hockey game in Queenstown (of course Canada won ☺)
- My friend and I just before the charity dinner two weeks ago
- The girls at the Botanic Gardens on our day together last Friday – very windy but lovely spring tulips
- The view from my desk (our double rainbows – we each get one)
- Out at dinner with friends earlier this year
- The girls and I at The Cow restaurant in Queenstown last year for Winterfest

I hope these don't crash your system! More soon … I love you,
A x

From: Alexis Jordain
To: James Norman
Sent: Tuesday, 9th October, 6.28 a.m.
Subject: Re: Another level …

Good morning sweetheart,

Just a quick reply to my Spanish inquisition from the other day…

Do you speak any other languages than 'near' English ☺?:
I speak some Ukrainian, Croatian and Russian, and can get by in France (a master of none). I read/write very basic Cyrillic alphabet. I learned Russian at uni so I could correspond to my Ukrainian grandparents as they didn't teach Ukrainian at Queen's uni in Kingston.

What made you agree to let Charles put a profile on the site this time (I suspect your friends would have been prodding you to get back in the game before now)?:
Something called me over in the kitchen to go to the computer where Paige was doing homework. I trust my instinct and it told me I needed to click the online dating button. I never registered for a dating website in my life before. I was just called to it.

What is your favourite alcoholic beverage?:
I love my wines – all kinds, many moods. More reds in winter and whites in summer. I'm a bit of a wine snob. I know what I like and believe life is too short to drink bad-quality wine. At sports events/watching the game or barbecuing, I drink beer. Cocktails are just for fun. I love to sit and people-watch in another country with a cocktail in my hand (not sure why).

If you were to make me dinner ☺ what would your international chef standard (sans Mike's review) cook for me?:
I would like to know more about your palate first, and select a meal that I think would be a stretch, but you would enjoy. Of course the setting, lighting and music would be perfect.

When are you most comfortable – at work, at home or ?:
I mostly work from my home office (have sent you the view). At home I am always casual and I love the flexibility of coming and

going as I please. I'm enjoying working on-site for this contract, the interactions with people, being part of a 'team'. I also like facilitating (leading groups). I'm definitely most comfortable at home, or travelling.

Do you have any fears?
Like you, I really don't dwell on fears. I too am very optimistic and positive. I watch my language to be careful with what the universe hears to manifest for me. I have been thinking/ imagining my ideal mate would find me. This thought makes me smile. He has (or I found him) – we can argue about this playfully for years (the universe is also laughing I think).

Have you ever broken any bones?
No.

What kind of a laugher are you?
I would love to hear you laugh. I can be quite restrained depending on the situation. When totally comfortable, I laugh. Actually, come to think of it, I could laugh a lot more. I'm way too serious. You'll need to start collecting funny stories. I love to laugh. Bridesmaids the other night, I laughed my pants off!

How tall are you?
I'm around five foot eight and a half (often wear high heels – lucky for you, so I can reach your lips).

What's your favourite fruit? Veggie?
I love papayas, melons, kiwifruit, mandarins, apples, pineapples, cherries, berries – I love berries – they're my favourite – blueberries, strawberries and raspberries. Veggies – I love all kinds, love salads, and broccoli and tomatoes, bok choy, carrots, oh – love asparagus. I love food generally, good food especially. I disliked in Canada how everyone is always eating pre-packed and processed foods. We don't do that as much down here. Food is sacrosanct really. I love good simple eating. Especially sharing food with family and friends. I love cooking for others.

Do you ride a bike? Paddle a canoe/kayak?
When I find time I cycle and paddle the sit-upon (a lazy kayak) out the front yard ☺. I spent a few years in BC writing their provincial cycling policy and promoting cycling. It was lovely to go back this year and see how far things have come.

Can you swim?
I will chase you around the pool. I will enjoy catching you.

Do you scuba dive?
Yes, but only in warm water. I'm a wuss in cold water.
What is your favourite thing to do when you are alone (keep it clean, it's a family show ☺)?

Go slow. I enjoy reading the paper (hardly ever get to do it – it usually gets picked up and put into the recycle bin, or if I read it, it's a quick flick-through). Coffee and paper with some warm croissants and homemade cinnamon and maple butter, preferably in bed, early in the morning – that's perfect. During the day, just puttering around, the main thing being go slow. Cooking relaxes me also. I love to pour a glass of wine and spend time slicing and dicing. The girls and I like to bake/cook together.

Okay, off to start another day. I'm really missing you right now. I know you said it didn't matter about where we meet up, but what would **you** prefer? I only have a few days in November. I could do more in December. I was just thinking halfway might be easier for us both, given the lack of time right now. If you want to wait until December … (but actually I'm keen for November – I want to see if your hugging is as good as you say ☺). Let me know how you feel about this, please. I'm not wedded to any place in particular – just wanted somewhere neutral – and for you to be there ☺.

I know you said yesterday that I was a priority. I'm trying to wrap my head around this notion – it is a very, very foreign concept to me. I've never felt like I was anyone's priority, so be patient with me. I really need to digest that. It is easy for me to be all-consumed by you – giving for me is very easy. Loving you for me is very easy. Receiving, ah, let's just say my love bicycle has training wheels (learner driver, like lucky you). I do feel your love and your words and your eyes. You are there in my heart. It comforts me knowing you're there. More depth will come in time, I know it. I feel it. I'm so lucky to be on this journey with you. Exploring the complexities of the heart and soul with someone I inherently trust is magnificent. I know loving you will continue to be magical. I cannot wait to hold you in real time. Let us plan a rendezvous soon. It will give me something to look forward to (did I say I miss you already? ☺).

Okay, I really must dash, 7 am meeting in town this morning and still need to shower! I love you. I love you darling. Go well, A x

After several hours on the job, Lexi's workday was interrupted by James calling her and then trying her on MSN.

Alexis Jordain 9:46:52 a.m.
I love hearing your voice.

James Karlten 10:00:27 a.m.
Why did you cut off?

Alexis Jordain 10:04:06 a.m.
Every time I'm on cell to you it cuts out.

James Karlten 10:04:53 a.m.
I called back like 2 times and I even texted you.

Alexis Jordain 10:05:10 a.m.
I was gibbering on before realising u were gone.

Alexis Jordain 10:05:30 a.m.
My texts don't get to you.

James Karlten 10:06:03 a.m.
That's very sad … I miss you.

Alexis Jordain 10:06:18 a.m.
I miss u too, terribly! It's so hard to concentrate.

James Karlten 10:07:08 a.m.
I feel like I don't talk to you enough. I don't want to do without you.

Alexis Jordain 10:08:18 a.m.
We don't talk enough. It will never be enough.

Part of her wanted to indulge in talking to James, but her professionalism and work drive forced a quick exit. She could attend to her love life back home. Right now, she needed to focus on earning a living, especially given her future plan to hit the tropics.

From: Alexis Jordain
To: James Norman
Sent: Tuesday, 9th October, 9.18 p.m.
Subject: Re: A quick good morning note ...

Hello, darling, I love your cowboy outfit, really. I decided at Stampede in Calgary this year that I am definitely a little bit country. Do you ride horses – or just dress up ☺? The picture I put on Be2 was from Stampede this year when I visited my friend from law school. She lives there with her husband and she's a cowgirl through and through. We had such fun.

I am so excited about meeting you, James, and for us to spend some time together. There are a million things I want to know about you, and I just want to touch you to make sure you are not just someone I have dreamt up (though in many ways you are the man of my dreams). I have printed some of your lovely poetic notes so I can read them through the day like a lovesick schoolgirl. I giggle sometimes walking down the street, like I have some secret to happiness tucked in my pocket. I feel as light as a butterfly these past few days, imagining what it will be like to finally be in your arms and laughing because I have no idea what you are saying (while still finding your accent very charming and sexy). Ah, so many things I want to show you and introduce you to. I cannot wait!

Well, by now you will be close(r) or at home. I hope it feels good to be back there. I very much hope one day to be sitting with you in the kitchen or in the lovely garden you spoke of and discussing the highlights of your trip. You have touched me very deeply, James. It is a new and incredibly light and wonderful feeling. Yay!

Speak soon love, A x

Text to James – 9 October, at 10.18 pm:

Heading to bed, darling, v tired. I hope you have a wonderful day and safe travels back to America. I tried texting again and calling on the landline. I sense your frustration over the distance and understand. I miss you, James. I wanted a tuck-in before bed, but it's just me and the man of the house, I guess, Paris our cat. A poor second choice. I love you. ☺

From: James Norman
To: Alexis Jordain
Sent: Wednesday, 10th October, 12.36 p.m.
Subject: Re: A quick good morning note ...

Dear Alexis,

It's almost midnight and my flight has been delayed. I am in the lounge so I thought I'd write you a short email just to say a few things. I miss you so much. I feel like I am repeating myself too often. I wish there were other words to describe how I really feel about you, but words fail me at the moment. I think about so many things, Alexis, our lives together, our adventures, sex, everything. I just can't get my mind to do something without it drifting off for a bit to you.

What is there not to love? Why me, Alexis? I am sure a million and one men hit on you every day and night. Why did you choose me? Why do you love me? I just can't get enough of you. I can't make any plans without saying to myself: 'I wonder what Alexis will think about this.' I am so scared that I've gone too deep into this and I cannot go back. I've never loved like this before, and what makes it amazing is that I've never met you.

Love is a beautiful thing, but when it hurts, it hurts really badly. My heart surely cannot take another hurt. It is too fragile. But it's also too late to be careful now. I am in with both legs and I am completely helpless. I love you, Alexis. I can't wait to tell Mike everything about you.

I am going on now. I'll call you as soon as I get to Jersey.
Love, James

Alexis didn't expect to hear James express any feelings of insecurity. Was his intuitive nature picking up the vibes from Edie? Perhaps he was just tired and questioning Alexis's commitment due to jet lag. Using words like 'I'm so scared … and cannot go back'. He did not strike Alexis as the wallflower type. He had presented himself as strong, and his traditional views came out in his masculine voice during their phone engagements.

She appreciated that James, like her, would be in a delicate emotional state, exploring the New World love territory for the first time in a long time. Both had faced loss. Both were vulnerable. Both had the opportunity to create a Klimt masterpiece out of necessity. He needed her as much as she needed him. Alexis could reassure him so he did not feel so exposed to this unknown adventure.

She wanted him to know he had nothing – absolutely nothing – to worry about. She went into the place where she protected all her really deep emotions – the 'feeling zone' replete with the colours and intimacy of *The Kiss*. She would write him a poem to make him feel loved and cherished, safe and secure, sharing a moment like the subjects in the painting. She would write what she would want to hear if feeling insecure.

They may have fallen in love quickly, they were not school-aged, but both seemed to share a similar commitment to the other. It felt like they were exploring together and should support each other when needed.

It was easy for Alexis to connect with her feelings for James. She had no reservation in their coming together. Both wanted to bloom. She knew inside that she cared deeply for him and would do anything for him.

Anything.

Chapter Four

The Jersey Boys

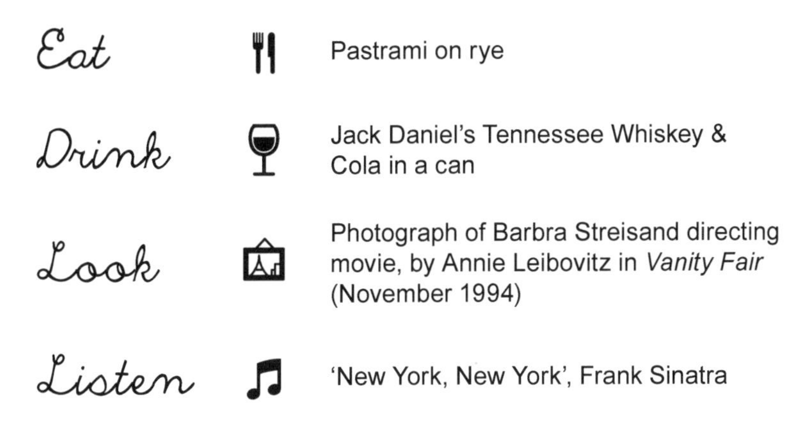

♥ ♥ ♥ ♥ ♥

If America is the land of opportunity, you're likely to find the door it is knocking on is somewhere in New York City. Perhaps Annie Leibovitz's grandfather thought this before emigrating from Romania. The photographer requires no trademark. Her unique lens on people has journeyed a long way since the family trips around America in the station wagon. Her sister points out Annie's first frame was the car windshield, looking down the highway.[8] She captures the strength and sensitivity of Barbra Streisand, another NYC brand name, in her portrait featured in *Vanity Fair* (November 1994).[9] The visual dichotomy extends to her life journey.

'S.W.F., divorced, runs her own business, gym-fit, loves beach walks in baggy sweaters, spiritual exploration, children, C-SPAN, and *The Economist*, seeking handsome Democrat not put off by crowds and paparazzi,' reports Michael Shnayerson, comparing hugely successful Barbra, who still gets nervous before dating, to a 'high-school senior going out to the prom'. With such a wide contrast of strength and softness, it is unsurprising males have little understanding of what to do with the opposite sex. Barbara's theory of why men fear women is posited in the article.

'You have to go back to caveman times. The man doesn't know he has any part in making that baby. All he sees is: the woman opens her legs, and out comes human life. Well – she must be a god! The man had to be in awe. He had to be frightened: if she can give life, she can take it away. I think it started there.'

As the years pass, Barbra talks about becoming more accepting of things as they are, releasing some of the suffering associated with resistance to what is. Go grow, Barbra! She's come to appreciate she is 'good' and her 'imperfections are OK'. Yes, the amazing Barbra is most impressive in her humanness – her desire to live, love and learn – captured in one amazing photo, by one amazing NYC artist.

There's no place like home, thought Lexi as she tapped her ruby-red slippers together and started dreamily thinking of what she'd pen in a poem for James. Home is where the heart is, and she found James a place in hers. He would be winging his way back home now to all the familiar places, and of course to Mike. She considered NYC, how immigrants (then and now) really make the place, and considered her own experiences there.

You could find all the world's cuisine in NYC, with the global people-drift sharing homeland fare in their new digs. New York is so influenced by Jewish heritage. She recalled Katz's Deli, 'the most New York restaurant in New York', where she enjoyed a sandwich with mountains of peppery sliced meat surrounded by hearty rye – a deli feast as classically New York as yellow cabs or Yankee pinstripes. The lively possibility that oozes on Broadway and buzzes on Wall Street. NYC has so much to offer.

Alexis often considered how different Canada's east coast was to the cousins in the south. She wondered if the Maritime provinces had matched up with the Americans, instead of connecting west for confederation, would they be more financially stable?

James, at least, had found his fortune, his home, his land of opportunity, in the Alpine borough of New York.

Alexis smiled recalling the jokes she and Edie made about Lexi moving to NYC and dining with the snooty neighbours. In her mind, by the time she put pen to paper, Alexis had swum in James's pool, had a run-in with Consuela, his house cleaner and talked to Mike about 'girls', including those scantily clad hussies from the early photo. She liked the notion of being a mom to Michael, even as the 'also ran' to his 'real' mother. She also liked the notion of a deep and meaningful relationship with James. He meant so much to her.

From: Alexis Jordain
To: James Norman
Sent: Wednesday, 10th October, 7.44 p.m.
Subject: Why you ...

Good morning, my darling,

You will be back in America by now. I have thought about you as you crossed the Atlantic and am excited about you being home and seeing Mike. I have written a response to your last email in the attachments. I would be so excited to hear your voice again. I love listening even though at times I have no idea of what you say ☺

Have a perfect day,
With love, Alexis x

Wednesday, 10 October, 10.30 p.m.
To my darling James,
Why you ...
Because you see me, even though I am not there.
Because you feel me and know that I care

Because you love me
Really, madly, deeply love me. The way you love me leaves me oxygen deprived
seriously –
I have to remind myself to deep breathe;
I feel so giddy sometimes. We connect in our minds, in our hearts
and in our souls.
These connections are not common to make at one level …
But three?
Such good fortune begs for gratitude, elation, joy, true joy, and happiness. Why you?
I love loving you because you get it.
You feel it.
You believe it.
You know it.
I know these things because I read your words
and feel your soul
I think of you and our hearts connect
I hear your voice
and I haven't got a clue what you said ☺
I listened to your voice message a zillion times
My telecom provider contacted me
to see if there was an issue
I ran over the max time on my plan.
I listened to your voice
because despite not hearing the words,
I could feel you.
You are articulate with your feelings
please do not doubt your ability to communicate so eloquently how you feel.
I read your words to me over and over again
Each time they make me smile
Each time I want to be near you more. Why you?
I have such respect for your hard-working nature
kindred spirits in this regard
But too, I feel we both want more than work.
I feel we share a passion for living and want to do just that
Live!
When you said you had a full life, but a lonely one,
That resonated with me.
I'm always surrounded by people and laugh and entertain on cue,
but with you –
with you it's different.
It seems that what started as two strangers,

created an instant bond
Common circumstances?
Perhaps. Right place, right time?
Right state of mind?
Maybe – the rational brain seeks the sensible solution.
But there's the rub.
This isn't rational – you and I are both rational to an extent,
yet find ourselves swimming in magic,
bathing in such a wondrous light
Neither wants to stop.
We are on this journey together
discovering as we go.
Why you?
When I look at your photos
I see such sensitivity and softness behind a strong façade
Not minimising your strength (for that too is a desirable trait,
very much so – even the Chinese want some ☺)
The softness has been neglected.
I appreciate the softness needs attention and I so want to give it.
I want to wrap you up sometimes, just softly caress you as I said before,
stroke your forehead as you lie my chest,
peacefully drifting to sleep in the knowledge
all is well because we are together.
All is safe. And conversely,
I more than anything
want to lie on yours and to feel the same.
Why you? I can imagine us on camels and carpets and mountains and dales.
Smiling and holding hands
Knowing. It's the deep down knowing without words (says the verbose one)
that we share.
That we are on opposite sides of the planet does not worry me.
Together we could change that in a heartbeat.
We both are strong and could make anything happen, so this I do not fear
or worry over, we will make it work.
We will have adventures together, irrespective of physical address
Home is found in each other's heart.
You feel like home to me, James.
I have been a vagabond in my life.
I see home in you. A place where my heart can flourish and be safe.
And grow. And learn. And deepen in intensity and passion.

Together.
Why you? There are many men, James, yes, many.
What did they see in me?
One dimension, perhaps two?
What they can possess, or conquer, or tote on an arm.
I feel you were different.
You fell in love with me before falling in lust,
or calculating what you might possess.
I believe your interest in me is true.
I feel you have seen me naked with no form, nor substance
and loved the unseen
The spirit and soul – the essence
of who I am.
I have willingly shared and exposed myself in your gentle hand
And what you saw you loved.
Our beginning is unlike any other and cannot, nor will, be repeated.
On us they broke the mold.
Our starting point, so unique, is our solid foundation.
Of a million and one; I have found the one.
And that's why.
My one is you James.
Always remember. I love you.
That's why.
Ax

From: James Norman
To: Alexis Jordain
Date: Thursday, 11th October, 12.08 p.m.
Subject: Re: Why you …

Hello Alexis,

I just tried to call you. Mike was looking forward to saying hello to you, but as usual, you didn't pick up. I had a long flight back here. I miss you. I could only think about you. I can't get enough of you.

I miss when I am not talking to you, Alexis. I feel so empty and lonely. I just don't know what to do with myself when I'm not talking to you. I think about you every second of every day, baby. I often find myself daydreaming about you, like I am in some kind of trance. I can't get a grip.

I think of you constantly. I can't get you off my mind. I am smiling to myself, like this is the first time I was in love. I can't get you out of my mind. I can't believe that I feel this way already, Alexis, like I will do anything for you. I didn't think I would ever love anyone again in my entire life. My heart was completely shattered. I didn't think I could ever bring the bits and pieces together. Then I met you. You made it easy to love you. The first day I said to you that I loved you, I wasn't even sure what it was, but I couldn't stop thinking of you.

I went through hard times, darling. I was completely useless. I could hardly do anything by myself. Every time I took a walk and I saw a married couple, happy with their kids, I could not help but shed tears knowing that I couldn't do anything to save her. Have you ever watched someone that you love die and you couldn't do anything, even when you had the resources? My financial success became useless. My life became useless. I couldn't even eat. I didn't know what I was living for. I had to be strong for Mike, but I wasn't strong enough. It took me almost a year to go back to work.

When I love, I go very hard. I love with everything. I don't just say words. Words are easy to say. Love never dies. It heals all bitterness or hatred. It heals everything. I don't want to ever lose you. I am far from perfect. I have my flaws, but one thing is sure, that I love you and I want this to work. I'll do everything to make it work. I can't wait to be with you and kiss you every morning and say good morning and make you a cup of coffee. I can't wait to have face-to-face conversations with you and have good laughs and kiss you whenever I want.

As I always say, good things fall apart for better things to come together. I never want to see you hurt. I never want to see you cry, or be sad. I'll do everything I can to make you happy.

Baby, we would get old together and our love would multiply. I am so excited when I talk to you, I feel like I am 17. Please ask for anything. Ask about anything. Don't hesitate to ask. That's why I am here. I love you.

Mike would not stop asking questions about you. He wants to know everything. He wants to come with me to Hawaii to meet you, but my NO was very firm. LOL. I printed out your letter so I can read it every morning and night. You give me a fever with your words. You make it so easy to love you. I couldn't stop myself from smiling as I read it. I just fell in love with you all over again.

I forgot to comment about the picture you sent to me. You look gorgeous, Alexis. I just want to do bad things with you. I can't wait to meet in person.

I love you, Alexis. Now and forever. Please give my regards to the kids. I can't wait till we all become one happy family.

I'll text you with my landline number here in Jersey so you can reach me anytime.

Love, James

After her bare-all poem, Alexis did not expect this response.

She had to reread his email several times. The first time, only the weird aspects stood out in yellow highlights to her:

- Mike, his son, coming to Hawaii;
- that James wanted to do bad things with her; PLUS
- the 'like usual, you never answer' …

WTF???

She knew she was a very sensitive person and prone to taking things out of context, but she struggled to get her head around James's obvious criticisms – not answering her phone when he called – like, she worked, and what, in a meeting was she meant to excuse herself and speak (or try to speak) to her unknown, what? Was he her boyfriend? It was all so odd.

Alexis enjoyed intimacy, but, sight unseen, she worried about what James might be like in the sex department. That and there was no way in hell that she'd entertain the notion of a seventeen-year-old chaperone on their first rendezvous in Hawaii. What the hell was he thinking even mentioning that?!?

And 'bad'? she thought. *Hmm, how does he define bad?* What if he was some guy who's into S&M? To do bad things with her? Spanking?

Tying her up? Is this good Christian man into anal? OMG! Was she walking into the next sequel to *Fifty Shades of Grey*?

Her tirade about James the Terrible ended when he called.

Somehow he was able to reach down the phone line and tug at her heartstrings sufficiently to cats-cradle a slipknot to mend her injured feelings. All it took was reminding her about how lucky they were to finally find each other and how much she should believe in the power of their love and in fate, and not be tainted by her past hurts.

She needed to believe in the possibility of an amazing loving relationship. Thus, reconnecting with James the Adorable, Alexis dropped her simmering notions of his wicked and enigmatic ways and replaced these with the sweetest of dreams.

After a good night's sleep, she woke and found herself back on the Love Train.

From: Alexis Jordain
To: James Norman
Sent: Friday, 12th October, 6.40 a.m.
Subject: Flights

Good morning sweetheart,

It was wonderful to speak with you last night. I felt like I was in high school. I'm still grinning.

I've looked into flight timing for the weekend we are looking at in Hawaii. Air New Zealand flights to Honolulu depart Wellington on Saturday morning, arrive Honolulu at 8:35 pm Friday night, 9th November. There isn't anything prior to that for the weekend (though I haven't checked other airlines). I'm thinking that might work from my perspective, and I would head back Monday night, 12th November, departing 9:35 pm. That gets me back in time for a working day on Wednesday. This gives us three days/ nights together.

It may be useful for Charles to know roughly when I might be arriving when booking your flights, so we can maximise our time together. Once he's finalised your bookings, if you/he lets me know, I'll make arrangements this end. Let me know which hotel too, please. Despite your good looks and charm, I would feel more comfortable having my own room ☺

Please say hello to Mike. I hope you boys have a fab day together. I'm off to another fun day of meetings and interviews! Don't be put off calling me today (even though I never answer), as I love hearing your messages!

I love you, A x
PS – very excited about seeing you.

From: James Norman
To: Alexis Jordain
Date: Friday, 12th October, 11.03 p.m.
Subject: Re: Why you …

Hello Alexis,

The last couple of days have been very blissful. Mike wouldn't let me touch my computer. He says, 'NO work, Dad, just the both of us for the next few days.' I've tried to phone you a couple of times, but you do not pick up. I miss you so much. I can't function properly without talking to you.

I can't begin to tell you that no words can express the love I have for you. I can't tell you enough the joy you have brought into my life. You have brought hope, love, laughter and pride into my life. I am so lucky. All I want to do is kiss tenderly with loving affection and to show you the love I have for you.

I can't stop thinking of how happy I am with you. I couldn't have asked for anyone else. I am completely overwhelmed and I cannot get a grip. I love you so much, and I would never let you go, even if you stopped loving me. Know that I will be there for you. I will be a good husband and loving father. I know how easy this is to say, and I've also taken into consideration the implications of my words and the enormous sacrifices I may have to make to make this work, and I've 3 words to say to you, baby: I AM READY.

I love you. No one can take that away from me. I am not even sure how it happened to me. You got me addicted, but no rehab can heal me. Whatever you do, wherever you go, be sure that someone, somewhere, cares and loves you more than you can ever imagine.

Regards, James

From: Alexis Jordain
To: James Norman
Sent: Saturday, 13th October, 5.40 p.m.
Subject: Touching base …

Hello darling,

I know you boys will be catching up and getting into all kinds of trouble back in Jersey. I hope you are having way too much fun! I'll just write and fill you in on goings-on here, so when you get a chance, you can catch up.

It is the end of two weeks of school holidays here for the girls. They're back at it on Monday. Last night, I hired the local skating rink and took a dozen girls rollerblading (a few pics attached from phone). It was so much fun, but I've really walloped my leg going up a ramp, or down a ramp – I can't remember – I have a bruise the size of Sri Lanka on my leg. I hope it's gone by Hawaii, or passers-by will think we are kinky or you beat me! The kids had a blast, and Paige and Bella each had a friend sleep over afterward. Needless to say, sleeping was the last thing on the agenda. We did some baking this morning and played Wii before I took them home. Now time to get caught up on some work and domestic chores ☺.

Next week I'm down to Christchurch to work. They've asked me to come and talk to them about a proposal from the Ministry to close/reconfigure/new-build schools post-earthquake. I will speak to them about needing to collaborate across their existing schools (they do not do this now because funding is based on school roll – larger roll, more money, so it breeds the I-want-all-the-kids mentality). Pitting one against the other will not benefit anyone, I feel. I believe post-earthquake we need to be prudent with investment, and, given declining demand in some areas and poor performance in others, we need a robust whole-of-area strategy if we are to respond effectively.

I cannot just take their money doing one-offs (my integrity will not allow it), and I feel that a more sustainable solution CAN be achieved and is required for all concerned. So I'll work on prepping to convince them of a different plan of attack. I've also got to write a few papers, finish a work plan for another client and get on top of invoicing (I need to borrow Charles, please).

Enough of work, though. It is terrific to have the kids back after a few days with Dad. I'm sure you are enjoying time together again with Mike. What are you getting up to? I imagine you will watch some flicks together. Do share your stories. I'm interested in hearing about what boys get up to (I really haven't much experience with boy stuff – just girl stuff) ☺.

Speaking of girl stuff, I am still thinking about you all the time. Still feeling silly and still wishing I could speak to you more than we do. It was fabulous speaking to you Thursday nite (Wednesday for you). I've tried you on MSN and I don't have a Jersey number (so sorry, no texts yet ☺). Just know that I am very, very, very excited about seeing you (meeting you for the first time – in person – wow!). I do hope we can make this weekend in November work into your schedule. I have imagined what it might be like kissing you for the first time. What your touch might be like. How it will feel to hold your hand … and to wrap my arms around you. Yum, doing a lot of thinking about us in Hawaii.

Enjoy your time with Mike, darling, and do try to get some R & R. I miss you very much.

Sending lots of love to the boys in Jersey,
Alexis x

From: James Norman
To: Alexis Jordain
Date: Sunday, 14th October, 6.04 a.m.
Subject: Re: Flights

I have a million and one words to say to you but I don't even know where to begin: I am so excited about meeting with you. Every morning when I wake up, I cannot stop looking at all your pictures. I love you more each day, and I can no longer contain my feelings. I cannot express my joy enough. I leave here on Tuesday morning to Sri Lanka. Charles has all my bookings sorted out. They are as follows:

I am leaving Jersey on Tuesday morning back to London, where Charles and I will fly to Sri Lanka on Thursday night. I will be there for about 14 days and return to London.

On the 9th of November, I leave London (LHR) to Honolulu (HNL). Airline: Delta (DL 9). Departing: 14:05. Arriving: 19:00.

Charles hasn't finalized the hotel bookings yet, but he should have it sorted by Monday morning.

I know words are not enough to say how I truly feel, but it represents a bit of what I feel in my heart, so I wrote you another poem.

How can I write a poem about my love for you?

Words can't begin to convey the way my heart goes into overdrive when I think of you.

What phrases can replace the light that glows within when I imagine us together?

I could write you a love song, but no music can express the depth of what I feel for you.

No song can stir me the way the sound of your voice does. You're the notes rising above life's din, crossing rivers and climbing over mountains to reach my heart.

In My Dreams ... When you awake to a golden dawn, know that I love you, and that I envy the very sun that shines above you. And as you go about the day, remember that

I'm thinking of you, and that my heart is with you in all you do.

And when you close your eyes tonight, know that I'm holding you tight in my dreams beneath the starlight.

I love you, James

MSN – 15 October

James Karlten 5:05:06 a.m.
Baby, are you there?

James Karlten 5:07:12 a.m.
Mike goes everywhere with me, he's insisting on going to Hawaii, but my response is still very firm. Anytime I try to phone you so he can talk to you, you don't pick up. He's getting a bit frustrated, but I understand that you are very busy.

James Karlten 5:08:03 a.m.
The last couple of days have been very relaxing for me. Mike had saved up a lot of stories/incidents to tell me. Trust me when I say they are a lot. He won't stop chatting ... LOL, I love him.

James Karlten 5:08:57 a.m.
I miss you so much, like a part of me is missing, I can't live without you. It's not possible anymore – our hearts were meant for each other. You are just so adorable, and I say thank you for loving me too. I am writing you an email now. I hope to speak to you soon.

Alexis Jordain 6:04:23 a.m.
Good morning, are you there?

James Karlten 6:04:57 a.m.
I am here, gorgeous.

Alexis Jordain 6:05:04 a.m.
Yay! At last.

James Karlten 6:05:09 a.m.
How are you? I just wrote you a couple of emails. Did you see them?

Alexis Jordain 6:05:27 a.m.
I'm still just waking up, so bear with my sleepiness. It's 6am. Haven't logged into email yet.

James Karlten 6:05:53 a.m.
Oh, I am sorry. I miss you baby.

Alexis Jordain 6:06:02 a.m.
Just made a cup of tea and jumped on computer. I miss you. It's freezing here, raining and cold. I need to get bundled up with you in a big duvet.

James Karlten 6:08:24 a.m.
This internet has some stability problems.

Alexis Jordain 6:08:37 a.m.
Lucky it's just the internet, not love-struck grown-ups acting like teenagers.

James Karlten 6:09:14 a.m.
LOL, did you sleep well?

Alexis Jordain 6:09:23 a.m.
Yes, thank you.

James Karlten 6:09:29 a.m.
Haven't spoken to you in like 5 yrs now.

Alexis Jordain 6:09:38 a.m.
Just 5? Feels like 10 – are you having fun?

James Karlten 6:10:10 a.m.
LOL, well, not really. There's never enough fun without you ...

Alexis Jordain 6:10:20 a.m.
:) I'm up early on a Sunday to try to get a jump on some work. I'd have much rather slept in, but speaking with you is now worth it! What have you boys been up to?

James Karlten 6:13:59 a.m.
A LOT. We have been to all the decent restaurants in Jersey, saw one of the games, watched about 3 movies now. Sigh.

Alexis Jordain 6:14:15 a.m.
Remember you need some R & R too. Please do explain to Mike about the time difference and my work and things, and that I would pick up the phone if I were able. I am not avoiding you lovely boys, promise.

James Karlten 6:16:19 a.m.
It's fine, I am sure he understands.

Alexis Jordain 6:16:23 a.m.
I love this time of day. No one is around and the sea is totally mine. The weather is keeping the dog-walkers away too. I wish you could see it! I've been thinking about you non-stop (as usual).

James Karlten 6:17:21 a.m.
I know, I can't wait. I am beginning to think that 4 days is too short of a time to spend together, Alexis.

Alexis Jordain 6:17:35 a.m.
I thought about you at skating, and would have loved to see all 6'1 of you stumbling around.

Alexis Jordain 6:18:20 a.m.
I know. I did think about delaying until December when I can have more time, but I so want to meet you. Plus, with your work, I'm not sure about your availability. What to do?

James Karlten 6:21:15 a.m.
No, December is too far away, it's out of the question. And I am retiring at the end of the year, so I have plenty of time to throw around.

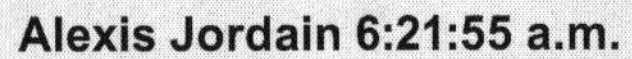

Alexis Jordain 6:21:55 a.m.
I love how you can be so forceful. I think it's so cute.

James Karlten 6:22:11 a.m.
After this project in Sri Lanka, there is another one in Madrid and that's it …

Alexis Jordain 6:22:15 a.m.
Okay, well there you go, time will not be an issue for you shortly.

James Karlten 6:22:46 a.m.
I will do anything for you, Alexis, never forget that.

Alexis Jordain 6:23:50 a.m.
I want to see you, and I'm smack dab in the middle of this gig that has a big changeover date of 19 Nov. Lots to do prior, so 4 days is even pushing it. I think it's worth it, though.

James Karlten 6:23:52 a.m.
And I am not just saying that, I mean it …

Alexis Jordain 6:24:16 a.m.
That is very sweet, and I feel that you are not just saying that. You make me smile, James – a great deal. That is a very good thing. Gosh I miss you.

James Karlten 6:25:25 a.m.
I miss you too, very much.

Alexis Jordain 6:25:59 a.m.
If you were here, I would have milked my skating injury, claiming the need for massage and pampering … I could have really played it up ;) I have added the cowboy dad photo to my shrine of James photos.

James Karlten 6:27:13 a.m.
LOL, I love it when you say shrine.

Alexis Jordain 6:28:03 a.m.
What do you boys usually do for Christmas?

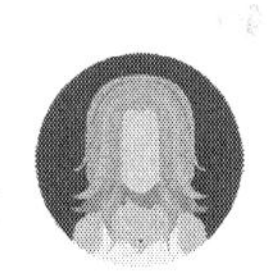

James Karlten 6:29:01 a.m.
Well, it's just a time to bond, just stay home basically. Did you get the old picture I sent?

Alexis Jordain 6:29:27 a.m.
I've not jumped on email. I'll take a look now.

James Karlten 6:30:00 a.m.
Oh, okay. So you are excited about Hawaii?

Alexis Jordain 6:30:19 a.m.
OMG! Don't you guys look sweet. No wonder he looks like a girl in it. He has a pink sweatshirt on with a Disney princess!

James Karlten 6:30:50 a.m.
LOL, don't tell him I sent you that picture, he will kill me … He hates it.

Alexis Jordain 6:31:14 a.m.
Okay, are you sure it's him!!! Those lovely curly locks.

James Karlten 6:31:59 a.m.
LOL, I've only one child, who else can it be?

Alexis Jordain 6:32:34 a.m.
And what about dad – you're looking very cool and sexy. At least he looks very happy. Where were you two in the picture? And all that hair, James!

James Karlten 6:40:40 a.m.
LOL, I know. That was my first house. It was in Pennsylvania.

Alexis Jordain 6:41:13 a.m.
My granddad left Croatia to make his fortune in the mines in Pennsylvania. He went back to Croatia and bought a village and built a grain mill and employed many. When communism hit, they lost everything. My dad ended up coming to Canada, and one of his brothers was killed there.

James Karlten 6:41:25 a.m.
Oh wow. Great your granddad remembered his base. Sorry about your uncle.

Alexis Jordain 6:42:21 a.m.
So seriously, two more projects and you're done work? Sri Lanka and Spain then. Two more and you're out.

James Karlten 6:42:58 a.m.
Yes, darling, two more projects. I was going to cancel on Sri Lanka, but I already got paid half of it … and it is a lot. Yes, baby. I don't have any need to work anymore …

Alexis Jordain 6:44:42 a.m.
It will be interesting to see you pre and post business. Well, I'll only see you really post, but won't you get bored? I'm sure you will have other interests to keep you occupied. I could perhaps help you with that …

James Karlten 6:45:54 a.m.
Well, I won't … I am working on a major project for disabled kids, an orphanage for kids age 0–16. It will keep me busy.

Alexis Jordain 6:46:17 a.m.
Where? (and very cool)

James Karlten 6:47:05 a.m.
Well, I was going to do it here. We just put in an application for a license, but we haven't gotten a response yet.

Alexis Jordain 6:47:23 a.m.
You need a good consultant!

James Karlten 6:47:46 a.m.
We've looked into acquiring some properties here as well, but the logistics and other things have to be taken care of.

Alexis Jordain 6:47:54 a.m.
I'm not sure you could afford me, though …

James Karlten 6:48:13 a.m.
I do, I do need a consultant. I leave everything to Charles. Sometimes I reckon it's too much work. LOL, you name your price and divide it with a good lasting kiss and sweet loving sex … What does it come up to?

Alexis Jordain 6:49:30 a.m.
Gosh you drive a hard bargain. I see I'll need to polish my negotiating skills.

James Karlten 6:49:46 a.m.
LOL, you need to.

Alexis Jordain 6:50:15 a.m.
Perhaps you should give me a sample so I know how to value it. A robust valuation strategy is key in such matters.

James Karlten 6:51:41 a.m.
LOL, you would have a full dose of this sample in Hawaii, darling. I can assure you.

Alexis Jordain 6:52:01 a.m.
Well then, I will need to postpone our further negotiations until then.

James Karlten 6:52:26 a.m.
That's okay.

Alexis Jordain 6:53:08 a.m.
You may wish to reconsider your position as well. Following the sample. We shall see if you are as good a negotiator as you think you are.

James Karlten 6:53:51 a.m.
LOL, I am a man of few words, my dear … I'll let my actions speak.

Alexis Jordain 6:54:28 a.m.
I'd better book my tickets then. I really cannot wait to meet you in person.

James Karlten 6:54:47 a.m.
You hadn't?

Alexis Jordain 6:55:10 a.m.
I was waiting to see that you could actually physically get there from Sri Lanka.

James Karlten 6:55:11 a.m.
I am ready to meet you, Alexis. I've absolutely no doubt about this. Do you?

James Karlten 6:55:20 a.m.
Oh, of course I can …

Alexis Jordain 6:55:36 a.m.
Doubt about what?

James Karlten 6:56:04 a.m.
About this, us, our future, our lives together …

Alexis Jordain 6:58:00 a.m.
I don't have doubts, James. I have so many dreams and hopes about us. I have grown over the years to become a more cautious woman. Please do not take my pace as doubt. It is not. Slow and gentle please.

James Karlten 6:59:23 a.m.
Oh no I do not, I understand your caution. I accept it, it's only natural, but I've thrown caution to the winds. I want to love you till I have no love left in my heart to express …

Alexis Jordain 7:00:35 a.m.
… and I feel the same inside for you. I want to throw caution to the wind.

James Karlten 7:01:50 a.m.
Take your time, Alexis. No pressure. I want you to love me at your own pace.

Alexis Jordain 7:03:31 a.m.
Please know that the depth of my love is there. It's life admin and responsibilities that up the stakes and slow the pace. If it were only you and I, I'd be in Jersey by now.

James Karlten 7:04:27 a.m.
That last part made me smile like a retard …

Alexis Jordain 7:05:30 a.m.
You must show me this smile of yours. And you must stop calling it retard. I do a lot of work with special needs kids here – I'm sure you can think of an alternate – articulate as you are. What an interesting looking couple we will make sitting by the pool …

James Karlten 7:05:47 a.m.
LOOOOL.

James Karlten 7:08:03 a.m.
You are so adorable … I wonder how I can ever live life without you …

Alexis Jordain 7:08:11 a.m.
Stop wondering. Just keep imagining life together.

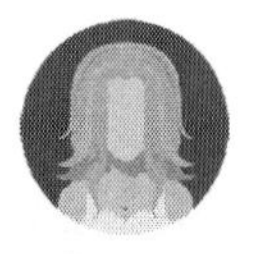

James Karlten 7:08:44 a.m.
I already do and it's amazing.

Alexis Jordain 7:08:46 a.m.
We do not need to dwell anywhere other than bliss. I know. It is pretty fantastic.

James Karlten 7:08:58 a.m.
I will let you in on the hotel by tomorrow … sorry, Monday.

Alexis Jordain 7:09:15 a.m.
Okay. I'm going to book my flights now. Verrrrry exciting. I can't wait.

James Karlten 7:09:49 a.m.
Me too, Alexis. You make my life so beautiful …

Alexis Jordain 7:09:55 a.m.
I'm off to make coffee now.

Alexis Jordain 7:10:02 a.m.
I want to make you coffee too.

Alexis Jordain 7:10:06 a.m.
How do you take it?

James Karlten 7:10:21 a.m.
Ok, I like my coffee black.

Alexis Jordain 7:10:31 a.m.
Short or long?

James Karlten 7:10:36 a.m.
Short.

Alexis Jordain 7:10:48 a.m.
Why mess around with all that water, hmm?

James Karlten 7:11:17 a.m.
LOL, well …

Alexis Jordain 7:11:38 a.m.
Okay love, I need to get some work done before my gorgeous girls wake up.

James Karlten 7:11:43 a.m.
Well, I will leave you now and I will give you a ring later so Mike can say hello. I love you.

Alexis Jordain 7:11:53 a.m.
I love you very much – have a fantastic rest of your day.

James Karlten 7:12:32 a.m.
I love you too, Alexis, a lot more than words can illustrate … you too love – kisses on every part of ur gorgeous body …

Alexis Jordain 7:13:23 a.m.
Yum. Now how am I supposed to concentrate? You are a such a distraction, James. I'm signing out x

James Karlten 7:13:34 a.m.
LOL, love you.

Alexis Jordain 7:13:55 a.m.
☺

From: Alexis Jordain
To: James Norman
Sent: Monday, 15 October, 9.41 a.m
Subject: Re: Flights

And I will track your beacon as it traverses the globe until yours connects with mine in the tropical paradise of the Pacific. I have just booked my flights, arriving Air New Zealand Z0010 at 8:25 PM on Friday night November 9, departing 9:35 PM on Monday 12 November. So it is done – we are officially going – non-refundable ticket!! Yippee. I loved reading your emails this morning. I love how you make me feel, James. I cannot wait to see you. I will write more soon, loving you,
A x

♥ ♥ ♥ ♥ ♥

Alexis had her ticket to ride. Her 'vagabond shoes' would be packed and ready to 'make a brand new start of it' on the ninth of November. Her story would join countless others of the immigrants journeying to the land of opportunity. Maybe one day even Annie Leibovitz would create a lasting impression of their family portrait.

She thought about waking up next to the love of her life.

Aloha Hawaii. Aloha James. Aloha love.

'Start spreading the news!'

Chapter Five

Foreign Affairs & The October Crisis

Eat	🍴	Borsch
Drink	🍷	Samohonka – Croatian firewater – vodka by any other name
Look	🖼	*The Bolshevik* (1920), depicting the 1917 Russian Revolution, by Boris Kustodiev
Listen	♫	'Romance', op. 97 (featured in The Gadfly), Dmitri Shostakovich

♥ ♥ ♥ ♥ ♥

Contrast: 'the state of being strikingly different from something else in juxtaposition or close association'. Russians do contrast really well.

Take Shostakovich's 'Romance', op. 97, which transits dream to reality, creating a longing for beauty amidst a majestic expanse in a country of extremely difficult terrain. Classical aficionado or no, hearing the solo violin, it is impossible not to feel your spine tingling, experience repetitive shortness of breath and find your natural Stevie Wonder head-sway. Within the beguiling melody, you find typical 'what was that' moments of contrast with a powerful bitch slap like you're being punished for not paying attention.

Russian art offers more contrast. Who else can take the October Revolution and make it look like a scene from *Willy Wonka and the Chocolate Factory* (queue 'The Candyman' song)? Boris Kustodiev's *The Bolshevik* (1920) stays loyal to depicting colour and cheer, regardless of topic. Even with the Revolution, his painting captures a sense of playfulness, with his larger-than-life Lenin (taller than the Stay Puft Marshmallow Man from *Ghostbusters*) carrying the verrrrrrry long, all-encompassing flag of the Revolution high over the people and tall buildings, effectively leading the way forward for all to see and follow. But together, of course. (Well, just as soon as they all grow twenty odd feet, or he takes Alice's blue pill and slides down an onion dome roof).

The well-travelled Kustodiev held great love for his 'blessed Russian land', depicting the scenery and portraits with an air of joy and colour, despite his humble beginnings as a tenant in a wealthy merchant's home. These early impressions of wealth would continue to influence his work in oils and watercolours throughout his career. His great love for his country permeates his work. His art is simply beautiful, using colour to beguile, even with nationalistic sentiment and politics aside. And of course, the joy and the brightness in his efforts are even more incredible knowing that in 1916, suffering from tuberculosis, he became a paraplegic. The stereotype of the inherent strength of Russian character is typified in Kustodiev, remaining joyful and productive despite his physical paralysis.

It is not surprising, then, that Russians would teach their children, 'What doesn't kill you makes you stronger,' now, is it? They've lived with hardship, harsh climate, a tumultuous path. Yes, if you survive, you will be stronger for it. But surely, even if you don't die right away, going through the process must surely alter you somewhat.

♥ ♥ ♥ ♥ ♥

Alexis cherished both her Croatian and her Russian heritage, even with the failings arising from too much drink. Homegrown varieties of two-hundred-plus-proof spirits, aka 'Slivovitz' or 'Samohonka', if consumed in excess, would surely kill you. Still, she greatly respected the work ethic, values of camaraderie and ties that bound her to her culture through traditions and religion. Those were the building blocks that influenced who she had become as an adult, mother, sister and daughter. She was proud of her strength.

That culture is surely genetically based; it is evidenced by the deep pull of Shostakovich's melodies that would enter her ear lobe and spread, like Samohonka, into her soul. Her tendencies toward culturally based specialties like borsch and homegrown remedies gave Alexis strength from her roots. The daily family interactions, tending on the extreme, with her siblings who resided on the wrong side of the law also did not kill her – they simply 'made her stronger', she kept telling herself. She chose to link her connection, depth and meaning in life to those generations that passed long before, genetically transmitting that passion for living that ran the expanse of the widest steppes.

Mid-October was to present her with more opportunities for cultivating her strength. Increasing pressure was emitting from the masses at work, at home and in her personal life. Alexis was beginning to feel like it was pre-1917 Revolution with full-time kids, work and a new relationship on the boil.

MSN – 16 October

James Karlten 10:30:54 p.m.
Hello darling, how are you? Is everything okay?

Alexis Jordain 10:32:07 p.m.
Hello, just doing some work before bed. What time is it (are you still at home)?

James Karlten 10:35:19 p.m.
No, I left earlier than scheduled. I arrived in London this morning ... Are you okay? I get a vibe ... did I do something wrong?

Alexis Jordain 10:36:20 p.m.
Gosh, your instinct is good.

James Karlten 10:37:12 p.m.
Talk to me, baby. What have I done wrong?

Alexis Jordain 10:37:39 p.m.
You didn't do anything wrong. Work is just crazy and the juggling is getting to me a bit.

James Karlten 10:38:25 p.m.
I'm sorry, baby, I wish there was something I could do to make you feel better … I don't like it when you are sad …

Alexis Jordain 10:38:49 p.m.
I think I just need some sleep. How was your flight?

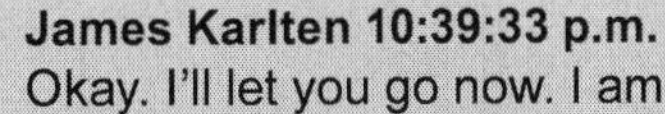

James Karlten 10:39:33 p.m.
Okay. I'll let you go now. I am a bit jet-lagged myself. I'll write you an email later. I miss you. Mike didn't want me to leave, he cried. But I've an early flight to Sri Lanka on Thursday, which I'm not looking forward to …

Alexis Jordain 10:40:23 p.m.
I miss you. Being pulled in different directions must be difficult for you also. How are you feeling?

James Karlten 10:41:27 p.m.
I just want to be with you right now, and kiss you and put my lips on every part of your body. Is that too much to ask?

Alexis Jordain 10:41:43 p.m.
I think it's very reasonable.

James Karlten 10:41:49 p.m.
I'd feel better in Hawaii ... u can do with me what you wish ...

Alexis Jordain 10:42:17 p.m.
I had better stock up on some sleep then, hadn't I – It's hard reconciling wanting to be in constant contact with not wanting to be needy, and trying to still 'live' normally when there is a budding relationship in the wings (distant wings, but ...)

James Karlten 10:44:05 p.m.
You should, but at the same time, I wish you didn't have to go. I love you, Alexis, I can't stop loving you ever ... please get better for me, know that I care about you. Baby, you can never come off as 'needy' with me. Come on. Text me, call me, email me, come pay me a surprise visit anytime you feel like it. You own me now. I'm your property. Love makes everything beautiful & perfect. Love heals everything & never dies.

Alexis Jordain 10:47:02 p.m.
I cannot own you, James. I do agree with your love sentiment, however.

James Karlten 10:47:14 p.m.
We've to come up with a story of how we met when we eventually get married … I'm looking forward to that as well.

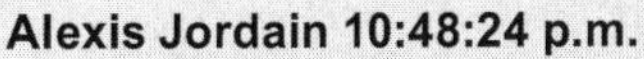

Alexis Jordain 10:48:24 p.m.
I called your cell this morning on the way into work to say good morning. I kind of felt you weren't there then.

James Karlten 10:48:57 p.m.
Did it ring? Cos I've no missed call from you, baby.

Alexis Jordain 10:48:58 p.m.
'The story', yes. You do like to plan, don't you? I rang the number I had from Jersey.

James Karlten 10:49:38 p.m.
Oh.

Alexis Jordain 10:49:50 p.m.
I left a message – gosh, I hope it was your phone (I'm sure it was).

James Karlten 10:50:12 p.m.
I am a planner, I'm sure you have noticed.

Alexis Jordain 10:50:19 p.m.
Oh yes, I have.

James Karlten 10:50:36 p.m.
I'll try to listen to it. You are too cute. There's nothing not to love …

Alexis Jordain 10:50:37 p.m.
You're making me smile with your craziness – give it time, I'm sure some quirky character flaw will surface. I'll remind you of what you said today – did I say I miss you?

James Karlten 10:52:58 p.m.
Yes, you did, but you can it say it again. Alexis, I don't say things until I absolutely mean them. I don't mince my words, baby … it's hard to believe that you love me like I love you sometimes, that you'd be there when I need you. The feeling is overwhelming.

Alexis Jordain 10:56:36 p.m.
I would like to be able to reach out when I need to. It is not something that comes easily. Any suggestions?

James Karlten 10:57:47 p.m.
Text me, baby. Or call me whenever, I'll pick up. I've a messed-up sleeping pattern, so I'm always up.

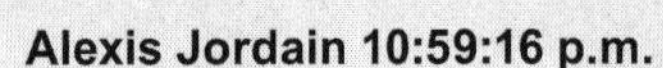

Alexis Jordain 10:59:16 p.m.
I'm not worried about you answering. It's the part before that, where I need to contact you, that I'm not great at. My past profile is tough and never show weakness – I want to learn to be vulnerable with you.

James Karlten 11:00:38 p.m.
Babe, that's why I am here, to turn your weaknesses into strength … and your vulnerability into care.

Alexis Jordain 11:01:51 p.m.
I believe that to be true. I really do. Just where to begin? It is a scary precipice.

James Karlten 11:05:17 p.m.
Anywhere, anyhow, I'm here to help you. I love you very much and that's what matters. So whenever u feel the urge to talk to me, call me. Whenever u remember something you haven't told me, text me. Whenever you have thoughts to share, email me … it's never too much …

Alexis Jordain 11:08:09 p.m.
Thank you. I know you care about me. Please be patient with me, James.

James Karlten 11:08:21 p.m.
We don't need any space between us. I am, I will. There's no rush. We have a whole lifetime together.

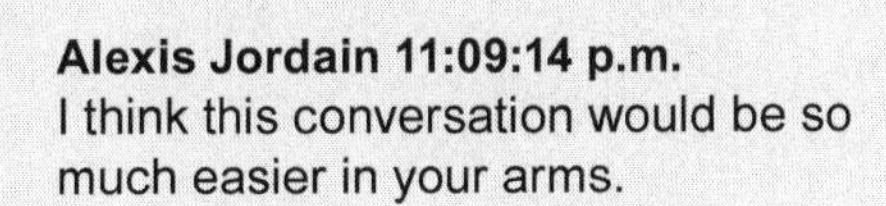

Alexis Jordain 11:09:14 p.m.
I think this conversation would be so much easier in your arms.

James Karlten 11:09:41 p.m.
I know, so I can kiss you with every word that I say …

Alexis Jordain 11:10:12 p.m.
Yes, please. I am glad you were here tonight. My heart aches a bit. It misses you. Does that seem possible?

James Karlten 11:11:04 p.m.
Me too. I'm always happy when I get to talk with you. It's all that matters these days … It's going to be worse after Hawaii …

Alexis Jordain 11:11:38 p.m.
Are you still trying to make me feel better? :) We'll sort it out.

James Karlten 11:12:40 p.m.
No, I mean it, baby. You make me really happy …

Alexis Jordain 11:12:58 p.m.
And just so you know, I have an elephant memory, and am counting all the times you are promising this multitude of kisses.

James Karlten 11:13:52 p.m.
LOL, if you ever lose count, just multiply whatever number you have by 3 … tell me what you have …

Alexis Jordain 11:14:07 p.m.

Just 3? Does that work for tenders too?

James Karlten 11:14:38 p.m.
LOL, tell me what you want baby …

Alexis Jordain 11:15:22 p.m.
You.

James Karlten 11:15:47 p.m.
You have me already …

Alexis Jordain 11:16:10 p.m.
Okay then. I guess I can go to bed then ;)
Are you going to get some sleep, or are you up for the day now?

James Karlten 11:18:43 p.m.
No, I have to sleep. I'm exhausted from that flight …

Alexis Jordain 11:19:00 p.m.
Okay, come to bed then.

James Karlten 11:19:06 p.m.
But I feel better talking to you – except you have to go.

Alexis Jordain 11:19:32 p.m.
I'm going to dream of the 'story' we will create in Hawaii of 'when we met'. You need to sleep … and yes, I need to go.

James Karlten 11:20:10 p.m.
LOL, okay. You do that and I'll just nod when people ask us. I love you. My number here is up & running, so u can reach me anytime, okay?

Alexis Jordain 11:20:48 p.m.
You realise it is probably the first time we will both be going to sleep at the same time – ever. Okay, I'll work on the script. I love you. (I don't want to go, but I will.)

James Karlten 11:22:16 p.m.
I know, baby. I love you very much. Goodnight ...

Alexis Jordain 11:22:21 p.m.
I still miss you, but you've made my night. Thank you, darling. Sleep well and sweet dreams, x

James Karlten 11:23:00 p.m.
You always make my night just by being you & loving me ... Sleep well, my love. Sweet dreams.

In October 1917, Russia's national debt had risen to fifty billion roubles. The country faced the threat of financial bankruptcy. Strikes by more than a million miners, metalworkers and oil, textile and railway workers were taking place everywhere. At the same time, peasant uprisings against landowners were becoming commonplace. Action against the demonstrations only served to enrage the peasants. By the tenth of October, the Bolsheviks' Central Committee resolved that 'an armed uprising is inevitable, and that the time for it is fully ripe'.

Texts – 17 October

Alexis Jordain 8:00:10 a.m.
Good morning, James. I hope you managed to get some rest. I fell asleep quickly, but was up early. I think I'm catching the children's cold. I don't get sick, so hopefully this feeling will pass. It will be good to see you soon. I wonder if you are a figment of my imagination at times. I need to apply for a visitor's visa for USA once I get hotel details.

Alexis Jordain 8:00:56 a.m.
Have a terrific day today. Sending you lots of love, A x

Alexis Jordain 10:25:23 a.m.
Hello. Are you there?

Alexis Jordain 7:27:18 p.m.
Hi sexy, I'm not sure if the UK cell number I have is working – it's doing the same thing it did when you were last in London – connects and then cuts out. I also tried MSN from work, but no joy. (See trail above.) I hope you are okay, and please let me know if you receive this. I love you, A x

Alexis Jordain 9:36:08 p.m.
Goodnight, James. I've got an early flight down south tomorrow. Sweet dreams, A x

On October twenty-fifth, 1917, the Bolsheviks led the uprising in Petrograd (modern-day St Petersburg). The provisional government was virtually helpless and unable to offer significant resistance. Lenin sent an early proclamation of the fait accompli, even before the final assault on the Winter Palace. While historians tend to depict the event in heroic terms, the Bolsheviks entered the palace without much resistance, with minimal gunfire and a rapid surrender. With all communication and contact with the outside world controlled by the revolutionaries, the royals didn't stand a chance. Some might say they didn't even see it coming.

MSN – 18 October

James Karlten 11:20:20 p.m.
Hello Alexis, how are you? I've sent you a number of msgs. I am wondering if you got them. I miss you so much and I am looking forward to this like never before. I love you, very much … you will get the hotel details today, no worries. I love you baby, very much …

Alexis woke to an email from Charles Col, James's infamous assistant:

> Hello Alexis, Below is your booking information as instructed by my boss. I hope you both have a nice vacation. Warm regards, Charles.
>
> The hotel was the Courtyard Waikiki Beach, 400 Royal Hawaiian Avenue, Honolulu, Hawaii. Confirmation 88136035. Check-in Friday, November ninth. Check-out Tuesday, November thirteenth.

Alexis was pleased Charles had requested a late arrival, as noted on the reservation. He had also booked her a deluxe room with a view of Waikiki. Excellent!

MSN – 19 October

> **Alexis Jordain 6:38:23 a.m.**
> Good morning, sweetheart. I received your lovely messages yesterday in Christchurch. I had a very busy day popping around to various locations, as I had three different projects/clients to spread my time around. It was a late flight back to Wellies. How are things for you in London?
>
> You must be getting ready for your trip to Sri Lanka – today? This weekend is Grandma's house move, so much to do on that front. Working in town today. I've been meaning to ask you more about your work and interests – I've so many questions. You still have been silent on the theatre, dancing and going out. All I know is you like movies and vampire books :). Tell me more!

There is one thing I have been thinking about and wanted to share. It is if you would consider not wearing your wedding band when we are together in Hawaii. Perhaps you have thought about this already. I feel it is important to have a clean start, and wanted to express my feelings so you have time to consider it. I will try to understand whatever you decide. We don't need a big dialogue about it.

I miss hearing your voice. Perhaps I should liaise with Charles and book some time in for us to talk (LOL). I thought about you a lot in Christchurch. I wished you were there. I wanted to take you to different places and share stories. I would love to show you around NZ. It is such a pretty country, and down south is my favourite part. One day I will.

You made me smile yesterday all day whenever I thought about you (which was often). I hope everything is going well with your negotiations with the Chinese, sorting the contract details in Madrid and prepping for Sri Lanka. Please send my regards to Mike. He sounds keen to connect (sweet lad). I had better go make school lunches and start breakfast.

The weather here is stormy. A perfect day to be tucked up in bed with you, with a couple of coffees, warm croissants and the newspaper. I would be fighting with you for various sections that I want to read (mostly just to tease you, selecting the ones you want most). Yum. You bring warm thoughts to a cold and blustery day. Have a wonderful evening and know I am thinking of you. I love you, darling. Safe travels, A x

The timing for brunch with the gang could not have been better. Meeting James face-to-face was becoming very real for Lexi. Too real. She was starting to mix arsenic into her excitement and could feel her judgment clouding. Edie and Oliver would need to sort her out.

On the way down the path, she was greeted by a delivery man holding a rather bland-looking bouquet of flowers. *Wrong address,* she silently hoped.

'Alexis Jordain?' he asked.

'Yes ...'

'For you.' Alexis received the flowers like a rugby hospital pass and opened the card. She suspected they were from James, but she had hoped he would have send something a little more perky and, well, alive. The note made up for it.

Slipping the card into her purse, she set off.

Alexis met Oliver in the queue partway up the stairs. It was always busy on a weekend, but well worth the wait for the coffee alone. She loved the chocolaty, smooth and strong blend of the Havana roast. Plus, she'd had a soft spot for Cuban anything since visiting years before.

Without a word, just a cheeky smile, she coquettishly placed the card from James into Oliver's hand and watched his reaction when he read it.

'Oh, Lex. This guy is good. I mean, fucking panty-remover good. Ahh.' He wrapped his arms around her and gave her a big bear hug. 'He's a keeper, babe, a real one-of-a-kind.'

Edie arrived just as Alexis and Oliver completed the emotional dissection of the bouquet, the card and the suitor.

Oliver concluded, 'Oh, and Lex, I'm going to use that line and not even footnote him!'

'Footnote who?' Edie inquired. Oliver passed her the love note, and the procession continued to their table.

'What the hell? Who writes this shite?' Edie read aloud, as if neighbouring tables might want to put an oar in:

If I had to choose whether to breathe or to love you,
I would use my last breath to tell you that ... I love you.
Always, James

'Good lord, this is way beyond sappy, it's sick. You're not buying this drivel, are you, Lex?' Edie pleaded.

'Yes, this is exactly what I needed, a well-balanced breakfast to start the day.' Alexis focused on the waitress. 'Long black, please, and an order of sour grapes for my friend.'

The brunch, as she suspected, would provide the perfect mix of cross-questioning of pros and cons between Oli and Edie. She could almost sit back while they investigated different angles about James and different actions she might take. They gave her the needed perspective on the fast-moving picture of her love life. In the end, she knew she was going to Hawaii and she was going to meet James face-to-face. With a little help from her friends, she felt she was going in eyes wide open. It was an adventure, and in a romantic setting like Hawaii, what could possibly go wrong?

Hearing from James put her in a good mood.

Being in love really does give you a spring in your step. Alexis smiled to herself. Life was really good. She felt happy, really happy. Happier than she'd felt in a very long time. James inspired her. She could only see sunny skies ahead. She was so grateful they had found each other.

From: Alexis Jordain
To: James Norman
Sent: Sunday, 22nd October, 1.41 p.m.
Subject: Hello

Hearing your voice this morning was music to my ears. I tried not to worry when I hadn't heard from you, but it is impossible, such are the feelings I have for you. So deep, so true.

I knew you were travelling, but as the destination is not mainstream, I tended to concern myself more than usual.

Finding out you are in a caravan (air-con exempted) and 7 hours from the main city in an abandoned rail line, well, darling, you have done little to ease my preoccupation with your safety and well-being.

You have survived 50 years without me and I know you are more than competent, but alas, it has taken so long to find you, I do not wish to go on a reconnaissance in Sri Lanka to collect you! Do travel safely. I imagine you there and I wish I was with you. So much.

The feelings you have unearthed in me are profound. They are so new, and in a way unfamiliar, while at the same time grounded in eternity, a knowing that resides so deeply in the soul and is such a part of my being that I connect with you at my inner core. Like we have been together forever, just reconnecting after a brief sojourn away.

You speak often of love and forever, and I know that is our playground. In some ways I know so little of you, and in others – where it matters – I feel I know everything. In the important matters of the heart, I hear what you say without words. It is part of my instinct to know your soul, to feel your heart, to reach out to you without reservation. Hmmm. I sigh.

When I got off the phone with you this morning, I physically was short of breath. The elation I felt sucked all of the air from my lungs, and my smile and mood stretched from Island Bay NZ to Sri Lanka and back. I can escape in our encounters, where it seems there are only you and I and distance dissipates into thin air. When I hear you chuckle, it makes me smile. Your happiness makes me happy.

I cannot wait to meet you. I am already counting down the days. And there are so many things to do before we go, but I will sail through these busy days on the wings of knowing I shall set my eyes upon yours in mere weeks.

I have searched your eyes in the photos for more – they are simply two-dimensional, and while stunning, the real thing I imagine will mesmerise me.

We must be careful not to exceed expectations with what Hawaii may bring in reality, but at present it is wonderful to imagine perfection. A blissful location, two people in love, meeting for the first time, looking into each other's eyes, at last, feeling the hands and arms wrapped around each other. It is all very intoxicating.

I better sleep. If I continue in this vein, I shall surely not sleep at all, and I must. My mind wanders too often, and I still have responsibilities that remain front and centre.

James, darling, soft-spoken, lyrical James. I cannot wait to see you and hear your voice whisper in my ear, to feel your lips upon mine and to gaze into your beautiful eyes.

How blessed we are. How grateful I am for us, and you. I miss you, darling.

Love Alexis x

Before she went to bed that night, Alexis sent James a photo of the neighbour's house listed for sale.

She felt it necessary to instruct him not to proceed with buying the house on a whim. He had intimated he might do so when they spoke earlier. If things didn't go well in Hawaii, it wouldn't be prudent to have ex James as 'the guy next door'. Better safe than sorry. She added a note:

Hi sweetheart, the neighbour's house as discussed.

Please don't do anything crazy before we talk ☺ xx

Alexis was happy with how things were progressing with James. She thought it sweet and cute that James would even suggest buying the neighbour's house. It was something she would consider. They were two peas in a pod. He was romantic and thoughtful and just a hint of crazy. It was nice that he had financial means as well. She hoped their chemistry in Hawaii would score highly to match all the other dimensions they shared. She was even better able to understand his accent on the phone.

She drifted off to sleep imagining all the wonderful places they would visit together and how amazing it would be growing deeper and deeper in love. She felt truly happy, in love, without any reservations. She was proud of herself for taking a risk with her heart.

In the morning, Alexis would wake to a different Risk – the game of strategy.

To play the board game Risk, you must understand the basic objective: conquer the world by controlling all the countries on the board. The rules state how you do this by 'occupying every territory and in so doing, eliminate all other players'. You win territory engaging other players in a game of rolling dice.

On MSN early the next morning, Alexis saw that James was indeed rolling his dice.

♥ ♥ ♥ ♥ ♥

If you don't believe your own lies, your lies will not survive, and you can make better choices based on truth.

—Don Miguel Ruiz[10]

Sounds like tons of fun (sarcasm), but a worthwhile reflection. It's great how the fluffy cat of the universe hops onto our laps at just the right moment, and, if we are aware, we can enjoy its presence rather than feel its claws perilously kneading nails to pierce deeply into our thighs.

A normal morning, like any other. Alexis logged onto MSN, looking for a love note from James. As usual, she was comforted to find it there, right next to a picture of her gorgeous honey. But as her gaze shifted downward to locate her cell phone, her thalamus relayed a sensory alert: something looks different, and off it went for processing.

As the frontal lobe engaged, the visual cortex played I Spy to report that today's message from lover boy had a larger-than-usual font.

'Hmm, that's different,' concluded Alexis. She also saw that right next to his sign-in name, 'James Karlten', it stated: 'I love you, Alexis. You mean everything to me.'

Processing.

A conclusion came quickly from her brain. 'That is pretty bold, putting a love note for Alexis on his homepage sign-on …'

Processing …

'Wow. There for all the world to see!'

Processing …

'He must love me a great deal for such a public declaration!'

More visual cortex action …

Just below, there in smaller font, was another message. She smiled and kept reading. Pour moi? This was cute fun. Or was it?

'Caryl? Caryl? Who the fuck is Caryl?' Alexis yelled so loud the seals several miles down the coast perked up.

Was this a joke? Some sort of sick game? Was James engaging with another player to gain territory? Alexis thought surely it must be a computer error. Some sort of glitch. A technology mix-up. Mr MSN just hadn't had his caffeine fix yet and had mixed up two profiles, surely.

Her frontal cortex forced a one-eighty course change, and her central nervous system initiated emotional lockdown, activating the poison-control centre. Her area postrema made her feel queasy, and her stomach began to churn. Her body would not physically allow her to ingest any more poison. She lurched to the bathroom.

Alexis stood over the toilet, poised like a five-hundred-metre swimmer on the starting block, waiting for the gun. She wanted to vomit. She wanted answers. She wanted to pull a Bobbitt. She wanted to know who the fuck Caryl was. Now. Right now. But only the dick-fuck James had answers.

'Step up, take your marks,' she told herself, but she was never a particularly good puker. Today was no exception. No false start, no start at all. 'Damn it.' She was disappointed to let the team down. 'I can't even barf properly!' she rebuked.

Alexis decided to take a gentler, 'make love not war' approach. She installed a new set of disposable contacts instead. As if biffing the old pair symbolically meant she would see things more clearly – like the old pair was to blame for the current mess.

She returned to the scene of the crime to immerse herself in the last of the Caryl Clerk/James Norman cup-of-cold-sick-overfloweth MSN venom.

Her reply to James's good morning message would be replete with highlights from the Caryl/James (aka slut-face/cock-breath) transcript. She felt like Chef Ramsay, simmering her rage while tenderising the control panel with a unique white-knuckle pounding of the keys. She typed …

6:42:34 a.m. (from cock-breath to slut-face)
'I love you Caryl Clerk and I will love no other woman ever.'

6:42:47 a.m. (from douchebag Caryl to fuck-knuckle James)
'Oh, I love you too.'

6:43:58 a.m. (from cock-breath James to slut-face Caryl)
'I will always love you, James Norman Karlten, no matter what. My heart belonged to you and only you, so there will be no other.'

6:46:11 a.m. Alexis to dick-fuck
Thanks, James, and thanks, technology. It seems someone is a busy boy indeed. A great day to receive this lovely message interplay with you and Caryl.

Part of me would love to hear an explanation. The other part is just smiling at my foolishness.
I guess the good part for you is that you can fall in love and out of love as easily as changing socks.

Silly Alexis.

Her mouth became dry. With each line she typed on MSN to James, the damning evidence of him and his beloved Caryl crawled upward, edging further and further from the screen into cyberspace. She feared that the wrongdoing would be absolved as swiftly as sin at Sunday confession. She needed evidence. Both to prove she wasn't imagining this and for a future conviction.

The solution escaped her.

It was like the time she took her first driver's test on her sixteenth birthday. In the practical, the instructor took her through a school zone located at the bottom of a hill. During the approach, Alexis noticed the car accelerating as they made their way down toward the playground. A glimpse back to junior high reminded her how much she hated physics. Removing her foot from the gas, she hoped the car would go slower, but faster they went. It didn't occur to her once to simply use the brake. Naturally, she failed.

What next? she thought. Had her frontal lobe shut down? Palm tapping to forehead, she attempted a reboot. Fortunately, her faculties engaged and threw her a lifeline. They must have felt bad about the driving test.

Of course. Alexis smiled, reaching for her iPhone to photograph her screen.

Cataclysm averted.

She exhaled, grateful for technology and relieved to be in sheltered waters.

♥ ♥ ♥ ♥ ♥

If you are an avid canoeist, or even one that loves being on the water but prefers the Sherpa does the heavy lifting of your water chariot, you know to heed white water and swirls.

The delicate crystal H_2O dance lures you with its beauty, but what of the dangers that lie beneath? What if these swirls are evident in the river of your mind? The confluence of a zillion thoughts: pressing timelines, pressures to make decisions, new information about the fidelity of a love interest? Such turbulence is as real as Homer's Charybdis in the *Odyssey* waters whirling between Italy and Sicily, or the Viking maelstrom circling off Norway.

Ancient civilizations explained away such phenomena as works of angry gods or sea monsters, but Mother Earth provides another explanation. In nature, the phenomenon results from rock formations below the surface, constant winds, narrowing waters or the meeting of currents.

So when faced with the mental maelstrom – do we provide an offering to the gods or follow nature's lead?

♥ ♥ ♥ ♥ ♥

Alexis sat there like a stunned mullet for what seemed like days.

She was undergoing an inner and physical turmoil resulting from hitting the wall like a crash test dummy in the TV ads where they test airbags. All her plans of their future together were smashed in an instant. She wallowed in the pain of it. Somehow the suffering made it more real, more awash with self-loathing, more shameful. She was deeply hurt and angry – almost more for the unplayed song than the past indiscretion. He had shat on her future and tarnished her hope.

During their premature relationship, Alexis had rammed her head so far up the ass of the future that her gaze was transfixed on tomorrow, not realising the cracks were there, plain as day, in the present. She knew she had to rally to get showered and dressed and engage herself with kids and work. She gently told herself, 'Everything happens for a reason, Lexi. Time to take a shower and have a strong cup of wake-the-fuck-up.'

When she left the house for a lunchtime meeting, she still hadn't heard from James. On the one hand, she was desperate to avoid the rancid exchanges typical of a post-infidelity exposé. On the other, the silence embedded the fate of 'the end'. At 11.33 a.m., she emailed James a copy of the screen photo, with the Re: line 'Hope the internet is up …' and a simple note: 'A special good morning message ☺'

To say that Alexis was distracted for the remainder of the day is like suggesting Channing Tatum's body is 'okay' to look at.

It was the physical side effects that were the worst – the repeated smacks to the back of the head with a crow bar. The dry mouth with the metallic taste of saliva that you notice every time you swallow hard – which seemed to occur at some frequency as she attempted one breath at a time.

How could breathing be such a challenge? she brooded. She also felt sick to her stomach. That and she wanted to vomit and shit at the same time.

The diarrhoea was not Weight Watchers' suggested approach to losing kilos. *Better out than in.* She tried to see the benefit. It was like the body's attempt to clear all the vileness of all the shite she'd swallowed, believing in a man who lied, cheated and stole as easily as tying a shoelace (actually, it was even easier for him – he said he wore slip-ons)! She was angry and upset and experiencing the whole grief cycle array of emotions.

Although crushed, she kept her news to herself. If she mentioned anything to Oli, he'd never get over it, and Edie would turn into RoboCop: shoot first, ask questions later. No, she needed some answers first. It could be technology after all. Maybe it was an old message? She wanted to run – she just hated running – perhaps just a brisk walk away instead?

She finally collected her range of emotions in a diary note that evening. The note, like Lexi's exercise, never made it out of the house.

She was just starting to get her life on an even keel – not jumping ahead to 'plan' anything for the future, but totally learning to get through the day, one hour at a time – a feat that had felt like climbing Everest most days. So she'd been pretty proud of herself of late. Now she found herself lying in bed crying (she was not a crier, remember, so the whole 'feel it to heal it' thing applied). She was totally without energy and felt endlessly tired. It is amazing how every molecule in the body seems negatively charged at the same time your bed is positively charged, and WHAMMO, the magnetic force prevents you from leaving the confines of this safe haven.

She recalled the only other time she felt so 'weighed down' emotionally and physically was trying to learn to scuba dive with that damn weight belt.

That belt and these emotional times had the ability to pull down tall buildings in a single bound. Well, except for her ass. No amount of weight could get that thing down ☺. She smiled remembering the pool scene when learning to dive, how her law school buddy Judy took great delight in her desperate thrashing around attempting to swim to the bottom with bodacious butt cheeks delicately skimming the surface of the water, just slightly less graceful than a hippopotamus. Even the instructor's attempts to 'take her down' were unsuccessful. She wished the instructor were there now to help her 'take down' James or Caryl or, ideally, both.

23 October, Alexis's diary entry

Hmm. Where to begin?

I was so busy caught up in the elation of being in love, I didn't appreciate the dizzying heights to which I had climbed. I knew the air was thin. I kept catching my breath, but I disregarded the simple mantra, just breathe.

All day I have been close to vomiting. My chest is so incredibly tight. I feel like a concrete block has been firmly placed upon it. I cannot breathe again, but for a very different reason.

I think part of me is in shock. I did not realise how deeply I had fallen in love. It would not feel one iota as bad if I had not jumped in with both feet. I trusted you. I reached out my hands to yours. You promised you would not hurt me. You asked me to trust you. I took your hand. I closed my eyes. I jumped. I flew. And now I have fallen. From a great height. Alone.

I am so extremely confused. The mix of emotions running through my head, my heart, let us not speak of the soul. Oh, God. I connected dots that weren't there – added others – and created some seventies Hasbro Lite-Brite picture of perfection. You were the leading man and I the love-swept damsel, being courted by a silver-tongued devil, speaking words that made me fall farther into an abyss that I am now trapped in.

Words that cut both ways. Good and bad. Happiness and woe upon the razor's edge reside.

I foolishly thought the words you spoke were mine – created and uttered to me alone. Like we were star-crossed lovers who, at long last, found each other. But the words were borrowed like a rented tuxedo with a limited shelf life. To be returned before the carriage turned back into a pumpkin.

The scene now features a large orange vegetable, a soiled frock and rats that used to be horsemen. Does that large one resemble your photo? Cinderella, meanwhile, has returned to the chores, while Prince Charming continues with whores.

I thought I was special. Ouch. Is that my bruised ego? My shattered heart? Or my traded soul? How could I have such low regard for such treasures? The essence of my being. To be flummoxed with not actions, not deeds but empty promises? Silent sounds. A mime without substance.

No scrap of evidence. Not one. I receive flowers as a peace offering from the dog box, not in celebration of love and happiness. Poor pathetic bouquet. Absent of any olfactory delight. Muted hues, like your communication. Now recognising the language barrier is actually more extreme than once teased in jest.

This language – the words have all become poisoned – tainted by God knows how many before and promises made to many to come – like some sort of blood sport for the rich and famous bored with yachts and Rolexes and manicures. Human sacrifice. Conrad's heart of the matter beckons. The hunt. The kill. For sport.

You win. I roll over and play dead. I have not the strength nor the desire to fight. I have been beaten. I gave everything I had. I entrusted a complete stranger. Bamboozled by love. For a short while I devoured three courses of love a day, nibbling on snacks of happiness and pure delight in between.

I allowed my imagination to take me away. I had no barriers, no emergency break. Anything was possible, plausible, true. I gave you God-like attributes and put you on a pedestal. You advised me you were not perfect. I disregarded the warning label. Silly Alexis.

All the red flags of loving too soon, faded by flying too close to the sun, became imperceptible, and all this without really knowing anything about you.

I mocked it all.

I thought a man surely wouldn't introduce his son into a fickle encounter. Wow. What happens here? I cannot bear to think what Mike has experienced of the revolving door spinning so rapidly round and around. I was of the impression (based on what you said – so more than impression) that you hadn't been with anyone since Angela. How does that work? Do you self-select which encounters matter and which to disregard?

How many women have you told 'I love you [insert name], and I will love no other woman ever'? Your letters bring new meaning to 'search and replace'.

You say to trust you and that you do not lie. In your MSN, you say you knew Caryl 3 weeks. On the phone you said you dated for months in London. Which is it? You love her so deeply after 3 weeks? You will love no other woman ever – again after 3 weeks? Really? You do move with speed and ease. I thought there was some sort of magic in our short rocket ride to love – but it's something of a common occurrence – normal for Norman.

I'm not even sure I know your real name. Caryl says it's James Norman Karlten; you told me it's James Karlten Norman – which is it? Do you change them around?

Did you want me on MSN to make it easier to manage your flock all on the same online paddock?

And why did you ask me to go offline on Be2 when you did not? How many others are there in the wings? I want to throw up. I feel so sick. Truly physically sick.

And you speak of sacrifices? Yet not once do you answer what these grave actions are. What kind of a sick joke is this? How dare you play with another human being's emotions like this?

I am a good, honest person with a good heart and tender soul. It is not a nice thing to do – playing with me. I have a wonderful family and great friends and I work hard and I support everyone. I am a simple and loving woman. It is not fair and you are not kind as regards what has happened.

I am grateful that I saw the MSN at least. Forewarned is forearmed. Now what to do???

I have no idea.

I have a non-refundable ticket to paradise, so I will start there. Maybe it will knock some sense into me to fly halfway across the Pacific on a whim. Investing 3k which I could have spent elsewhere, easily. Geez. The body slams just don't stop.

I need to have a good cry.

So much for never hurting me.

Words and actions. It's nice when they line up.

Alexis lamented, *Did I inadvertently stick my head into a bee nest last night?*

The good-morning glance in the bathroom mirror revealed excessive swelling around the eyes, possibly caused by violent and repeated stinging. Nothing could subdue the puffiness. After fifteen minutes of cold-water splashes and intensive index-finger press-ups around her red and veiny baby blues, she gave up and piled on two different types of concealer.

Even the epoxy-plus-activator mix could not cure that crazy inflammation that results from sleeping face down whilst intermittently sobbing uncontrollably and aggressively rubbing eyes, nose and mouth, as all facial orifices desperately try to purge the evil poison.

She had not slept well.

This was not the first 'gotcha' infidelity rodeo Alexis had been through. Unfortunately, it seemed each and every experience from her career of love and loss came and haunted her last night like Scrooge's Ghost of Christmas Past.

The first was long ago in high school, when her best friend was seeing her crush at the same time they were dating (she had accidentally picked up the wrong sweater present – same box, different yet familiar name on the gift tag). Skip ahead a few more cheaters to university, where the captain of the volleyball team she adored admitted he had a long-term girlfriend only AFTER Alexis recognized the familiar smell in his bed wasn't her own but the other woman's perfume. You'd think he'd at least have changed the sheets! Yuck. She walked out then and there, braving Ontario's snowdrift in sock feet. She nearly got hypothermia before the cheat's roommate came to her rescue in the park near the dorm. Fast-forward to present times, where her Aussie bloke was caught texting his 'tenant' during a Melbourne Cup after-party to 'come and play'. The list goes on. And last night, it went on and on.

Why was she so gullible? And always choosing the wrong guy?

She had argued to Edie and Oliver that her being a Pollyanna was a character strength, not a flaw. Didn't everyone deserve a second chance? But her willingness to trust and believe in the best in everyone translated to obvious naivety in love. Here, this 'feature' was not serving her well. A woman of high integrity and values, she expected others to act similarly, not visit her nightmares cloaked as 'learning experiences'.

She wanted to stop acting as prey for the next adulterer. But first, she needed coffee. Strong and black. Preferably served in a bucket. She reached for the largest mug in the kitchen.

'Was that three or four?' she asked herself out loud.

In her automatic, I'm-too-fucking-tired-for-all-this-shit good-morning mode, Alexis was unsure how many dark espresso pods she had already jammed into her flash, candy-apple red, metallic Italian coffee machine.

Francesco was more than persuasive that day in his shop, when he promised to service her every coffee need in the coming months. Very charming and a man of his word, he went on to expand into an Italian deli/restaurant and burgeoning import business. In Island Bay, you needed to have good Italian connections. She was glad that at least Francesco the male Italian was dependable – for coffee at least. He would always be there to kick-start her day with his foreign machine, creating a coffee heaven on earth.

She swallowed the first few sips.

While Dr Feelgood did his work, the caffeine satiated her sleepiness. Senses bamboozled in a good way, she finally conceded to 'good morning' as she read the inspirational message on the mug: 'Life is a journey, not a destination.'

She was not sure where the hell she was right now, and there was no 'you are here' destination sign visible nearby. Still, being a Pollyanna allowed her to at least see some sunshine to get her started on her day.

When James didn't hijack her thoughts, Alexis diligently tried to work from home. The two spoke only once through the day, and it did not go well.

James had monopolised the conversation, and Alexis ended the call abruptly. It was more than she could bear, hearing more pathetic explanations.

Alexis had wished the hang-up process was more satisfying. Something dramatic, like in the olden days, when you could slam the receiver on the base with a loud crash to rouse the neighbours, or pull the cord right out of the socket. Having to find then push a wee red end-call button on her cell just didn't cut it.

Caryl was a 'sex addict' in James's assessment, a woman of loose morals who liked to share intimate details of their liaisons in the bedroom with her friends. That and 'an adulteress'. Apparently after James took her to dinner one night with his colleague, Caryl contacted the guy and propositioned him, and the two started an 'affair' for a number of weeks. Guilt got the better of his mate, and he came clean to James. That's when Caryl explained her condition, and James compassionately decided she was nuts and that this was not part of his fantasy world. She had been stalking him since.

James hadn't mentioned Caryl to Alexis as he was ashamed of how ridiculously things turned out in his first online dating experience. Caryl was nobody to James now. It had ended months before he had met Alexis, and Caryl meant nothing to him now. Surely Alexis could appreciate his circumstance.

'Oy vey, my life!' she exclaimed of her latest nightmare. Ethnic phrases always add occasion to drama, she thought, and the Yiddish captured dismay well. Nice choice.

Later that night, the scoundrel James would once again try to turn down her boil to a simmer.

MSN – 24 October

James Karlten 8:26:14 p.m.
Alexis?

Alexis was there, but for all she knew, Caryl could have been on call waiting. She considered the real possibility that James – right now – could be jockeying between both mares, trying to keep track of names and stories to avoid a slip-up. Clearly, James applied the KISS principle, popular amongst males. He kept it simple, stupid, by explaining how each meant everything – that should do it.

She was angry and hurt, ignoring him for over an hour. It was the longest 'I'll show him' she could muster. Poor sap.

Alexis Jordain 9:52:38 p.m.
Hi James, In reply to your conversation this afternoon, I do not make assumptions about how you are feeling and would ask that you be responsible for your own emotions as I am for mine. I have been candid with how I have felt over the past 36 hours. Saying to me, 'I wish it was as easy for me as it is for you to concentrate on anything else, or leave this for later,' is not helpful.

I never said this was easy for me. It has been an immense challenge for me to conduct myself professionally in my work commitments, at a board meeting last night, with realtors and lawyers for the sale today, and in front of the children and my mother, who moved in last night. 'Easy' is not a fair word coming from someone who knows little of my circumstances.

I am a single mother who supports, leads and provides for her family. I do not have the luxury of a trust fund or independent wealth to fall back on. I work hard to enjoy a good lifestyle and have immense responsibilities that I take seriously. My needs come second, they always have. I thought for an instant that with you perhaps they might come first. So please do not make assumptions about how I am feeling. If you wish to know, simply ask me.

As I said on the phone, I have many questions. They have kept me awake at night. Now that the kids are in bed, I have my first opportunity to put pen to paper and ask you for some answers. I do not mean this to be an interrogation. I really just want to understand things better and gain perspective so I and we can move forward.

I have been completely honest since we met. Could I ask you to also be honest in responding to my questions whenever you have some time. No rush. I'm exhausted and will try to sleep tonight. I really hope I can, as I have a big paper to start and finish writing tomorrow.

Here goes, starting simply ... 1. You told me your name was James Karlten Norman. Caryl said it was James Norman Karlten. Which is it?

2. You said on the phone Caryl Clerk and you were together for several months (and that it ended in February), but on MSN (which says 60 days ago) you said you knew her only for a few weeks. Which was it, 3 weeks or many months? Either way, you appear to have loved her very deeply – was this after 3 weeks or several months?

3. You gave me the impression that you had not been in a relationship since your wife died. Clearly that wasn't the case. How many relationships have you had over the past few years? And have you fallen in love with them all?

4. What did you mean that you didn't want to tell me about Caryl so I would not be 'compared' to her? You seemed keen to tell me she has sex issues – was that part of the mystique? Are you still friends?

5. What do you mean about the sacrifices you have had to make to be with me? I am not aware of any.

6. Did Charles honestly load a profile for you on the net? If so, when was it? (You told me it was end of Sept, just around when I signed up.) How many women were you corresponding with? Is it possible you perhaps got me confused with others you were speaking to? (You commented on my lips and beauty and smile when I had never sent you a photograph … ?)

7. Why did you ask me to sign off Be2 (which I did) and yet you yourself are still on? Do you have other prospects now?

8. Do you have usual ways of communicating for all the women you meet/see (eg, I love you xx, and I will love no other woman. Ever.)?

9. Do you habitually introduce Mike to women that you are dating? How does he relate to other women you date?

10. Why me?

That's all I've got. Ten simple questions (aided by nectar of the gods to craft). I mean no offence in asking them, and apologise in advance if they seem crude or sharp in the asking. I do not want to offend, nor to hurt you. You may choose not to reply at all, and I would respect your right to do so. I simply need answers to move on.

I hope that other than this unforeseen drama, the work is progressing (I know this sounds trite, but I really do mean it). Distance and drama is a lethal cocktail. But you may know this already. You may feel that both (the distance and the drama) are not worth the effort (seeing you speak of sacrifice). This matter is something we both need to consider separately.

What an interesting hand we each have, James. I have revealed mine. It's your move.

Goodnight, sweet James, wherever and whoever you are.

A x

Alexis was confounded. She wanted to trust her instinct, but it was easier said then done. She felt her instinct had taken a sabbatical and she was left with a schizophrenic substitute. One telling her to take the blue pill after she had 'decided' on a course of action. Then out of nowhere, the bottom opened in the floor and she commenced descent like Alice through the looking glass, but with no soft bunny to direct her at the bottom.

All paths were leading away from the relationship. The situation was so straightforward based on the facts, yet she couldn't trust her head. Her overthinking and impetuous nature combined had her consistently run away from intimacy. She had to choose to do things differently or face similar outcomes of love and loss to those she had in the past. She felt herself pulled into the vortex to stay – led by an assault of both her head and heart. Why was she choosing to stay?

Alexis would eventually read the book *Daring to Trust*, which held the answer: 'If our deepest desire is to be sought and found by another, and so few people are willing to put energy into that project, we might come to doubt our own value, even our survival. This helps us understand why our most enduring anxiety is about separation, rejection, abandonment, excommunication. These fears can hold such terror for us that we will stay in relationships that no longer work, still clinging to the little that comes our way, still hoping, against evidence to the contrary, that our needs may one day be met. We stay because of the crumbs we occasionally receive, but we also stay because of our fear of the worst isolation that may follow. This is not healthy staying. This is stuckness.'[11]

Had Alexis read the book earlier, she may indeed have asked herself if she was stuck. She might have concluded that James needed the heave-ho (despite her feeling possible rejection and abandonment). She would have based her decision on the mounting evidence of the coming revolution – the whirlwind romance, the blind love (and faith), the 'if it's too good to be true' advice of friends and, now, the potential infidelity card, with 'who the fuck is Caryl?' Alas, she did not read the book, and, like the czar, did not effectively respond to the signs.

Alexis attempted to take the high ground, climbing into bed and assuming the position of the red star, perched over hammer and sickle. She was leaning toward the do-not-run-away option, to stay and 'put energy' into the James project. She would overcome this assault and lead the James/Alexis unification process. She would triumph as the larger-than-life Bolshevik in James's heart, with the bevy of 'mean nothing to me' peasants taking their rightful role into the backdrop of the steppes.

She didn't appreciate the hammer would defy gravity and force her to doubt once more. 'How many gals does this douchebag have hanging on the line? Bloody Rasputin.' She nodded off.

Oh, those Russians.

Chapter Six

He's 'The One' – Hook, Line and Sink-Her

Eat	Liver with some fava beans
Drink	A nice Chianti
Look	*Medea* (1889), by Evelyn De Morgan
Listen	I Will Survive, performed by Cake (original Gloria Gaynor)

♥ ♥ ♥ ♥ ♥

Women's lib has come a long way since Gloria Steinem, and since Irina Dunn's 1970 comment that 'a woman needs a man like a fish needs a bicycle'.[12]

The bunny-boiler Glenn Close gave that pendulum a good hard push in *Fatal Attraction*. And recently, her formidable role was substituted by a trio of beauties: sisters doin' it for themselves in *The Other Woman*. In this latest flick, the heroines glamorise infidelity through the unintended consequences of getting rich and creating lasting bonds of friendship. While incredibly humorous and entertaining, the story, if set in earlier days, would have played out much differently.

Take Medea's infidelity remedy in Greek mythology. She finds out her man, Jason, is leaving her for King Creon's daughter (asshole). In retribution for his betrayal, she kills their children. Now you're unlikely to get that scene on HBO anytime soon. So yes, Medea's approach is much more dramatic and extreme, yet, at the same time, more interesting and thought-provoking. What woman didn't exhibit mixed emotions about Bobbitt chopping off her partner's dumb stick after he popped his pecker into another Polly's panties. Hmmm.

These contrasting emotions exude from the most poignant version of Medea, by English painter Evelyn De Morgan. Portrayed with such sublime beauty and serenity, Medea also reveals darker aspects of her character, her pain, her crime, to contrast her lighter intensity and spiritual glow. One might expect to find De Morgan's rendition etched in glass on a country church somewhere in Yorkshire. Perhaps while enjoying nice Chianti on a picnic, De Morgan took inspiration from the great Renaissance artists during her study in Florence to create her own unique style. Medea screams softly, 'I will survive,' with a mostly beautiful result.

Others have created less intoxicating versions of Medea. One by Anthony Sandys was rejected for exhibition at the Royal Academy in London in 1868, causing a storm of protest. Some years on, in 1911, it would be sent to Italy as one of the 'best of Britain' pieces to celebrate the jubilee in Rome. Boy, how quickly times change.[13]

MSN – 26 October

James Karlten 3:35:24 a.m.
Hello Alexis, I was half away into answering all your questions and I didn't know how I felt.

I think that if you feel like this already, if you think that I might be talking to other women or I might have lied to you about a lot of things, then what's the point? I will always have to prove myself to you and we can't start like that.

I've never lied to you. All that I've told you since I met you has been nothing but the truth. I just didn't mention Caryl because I wanted to tell you about her face-to-face, and, to be honest, it was a part of me I was trying to forget. You have no idea how things like that have psychological effect and can mess with your self-esteem.
I can't live life that way.

I love you, Alexis, and I've never loved anyone this way. If these words don't mean anything to you anymore, I am not sure what I can do. I regret that this happened, but it was long ago. I should have told you. For this course, I apologise.

I wanted to take it slow with you. To get to know you more, get to meet you first. Kiss you, touch you. But I don't know how I started to love you. I just started to giggle in the bathroom because I'd remembered something you said on the phone or in your letter. I tried to get a grip, I tried to be cautious, but what's there not to love? I couldn't stop myself from loving you. I even told Mike about you. I never do that. I gave you all my addresses and numbers. I trusted you. I still do. There's no love without trust.

Thank you for giving me another chance. My promises to never hurt you and to love you forever are not empty. I do not throw words carelessly. Please, you need to trust me with all your heart for this to work. I love you with my whole heart, and I don't want to lose you.

The internet here still doesn't work. Please, I need you to help me do something when you wake up. Please call me when you wake up so I can give you details. It's urgent. I love you.

Alexis didn't want to the let the girls side down. How many women were prey to infidelity? She should stay true and strong. Sing 'I Will Survive' from the rooftops as she spit down upon the two-timing bastard. She had to tell him it was over. She was not that 'stupid little person' still in love with him. He messed with the wrong chick.

But she also wanted to believe what he said on the phone, and what he wrote. Could she ever fully commit to give him another chance?

Her mind remained steadfast in its overactive long and winding road to the place of second-guessing everything. Along the journey, Alexis successfully connected that James not being with anyone for eight years since his wife died had conveniently excluded the nympho liaisons: liar, liar, pants on fire.

She read his words over and over again. She wanted to give him, and their project, another chance despite the present turbulence. She so wanted the lofty red star status dreamt up in her head. Perhaps the remnant niggling question of James's intent would dissipate in time.

If only she had time.

James's business had taken him to Sri Lanka. Alexis worried about him working there. She had heard about the corruption. But was Sri

Lanka really any more fraudulent than other countries? Alexis asked Mr Google.

Yes, actually.

It ranks alongside Bosnia, Guatemala, Kiribati and Swaziland, tied at ninety-first place on the Corruption Perceptions Index (CPI).[14] The index is released by Berlin-based Transparency International, which ranks countries from zero to ten (zero being the most corrupt, ten being the least). Sri Lanka and its compatriots score just over three. New Zealand tops the charts with Denmark and Sweden at 9.3, and the United States is just over seven.

The most corrupt countries are also the poorest, often ruled by dictators or unstable governments. Corruption dilutes efforts to address intractable social problems like poverty and climate change. In the 2010 CPI, about three-quarters of the 178 countries scored under five, indicating a serious corruption problem.

So where are the anti-corruption measures from the international community?

The UN Convention against Corruption provides a framework but falls short on implementation. Alexis thought most people had heard of the global warming issues and naturally wanted world peace, but she hadn't really considered the full impact of the insidious corruption malevolence.

The Sri Lankan operating environment and 'way of doing business' would soundly explain any future communication gaps. Either party could legitimately indict 'the damn technology in that third-world country' as reason to miss a phone call or email.

Alexis was immersed in reticence to re-engage with James in their post-Caryl *détente.*

She attempted to balance her anger and hurt with self-awareness of her fear of intimacy. Perhaps he was actually telling the truth. Her delicate heart and overly sensitive nature, plus his current situation in Sri Lanka, in the backwoods on a random railway line, made her wonder. Should she end things now, before Hawaii? Or take a chance and believe in the possibility that Caryl was in fact a nutter? Which story was 'beyond reasonable doubt'? Was he guilty or innocent?

Deliberations were interrupted pre-judgment. Alexis physically lunged forward at her desk as the damn MSN lit up like the Leafs' goal scored against the Canucks. She knew it was impossible to avoid James forever, and that she'd have to face the music.

Damn it. She swallowed hard. Her time for reflection was up. *He knows I'm online.*

James Karlten 7:21:32 a.m.
Hello, baby.

Alexis Jordain 7:21:38 a.m.
Hi there, do you want to do this thing you need my help with now? Or do you need to get a few things together (in which case I'll dive through the shower)?

James Karlten 7:23:11 a.m.
No, it's okay, we can do it now. The site is: http://www.globalcbplc.com/gc-uk.

Alexis Jordain 7:24:54 a.m.
Have clicked the hyperlink. It says: 'This site isn't well known. Be careful – don't share your sign-in or personal information or download anything unless you're sure this site is trustworthy.' Continue?

James Karlten 7:25:06 a.m.
Yes please. Okay, on the top corner, you'll see internet banking. Click on it, please ... the top right corner.

Alexis Jordain 7:26:38 a.m.
Yep. User ID and password?

James Karlten 7:27:38 a.m.
Username: Jnorman Password: gcb4rfr48

Alexis Jordain 7:28:32 a.m.
Okay, into account summary.

James Karlten 7:29:04 a.m.
Please, what's the balance on the account as at today?

Alexis Jordain 7:30:19 a.m.
Three recent deposits, 08-10, 09-10, 09-10, giving balance of 6,567,003.

James Karlten 7:31:50 a.m.
Okay, thank you. Okay, proceed to the transfer on the bottom right corner.

Alexis Jordain 7:33:29 a.m.
Transfer activation code?

James Karlten 7:35:15 a.m.
GLCBK00902875764764789O

Alexis Jordain 7:36:21 a.m.
Okay, lots to fill out on next screen – destination bank name, address, branch, city, swift code.

James Karlten 7:36:59 a.m.
Okay, which is first? Let's take it step by step. I'll try to be faster.

Alexis transferred 32,750 GBP to Frontier Communications Network at the Hanseng Bank in Central Hong Kong. James asked the confirmation to be sent to her email to enable her to forward to Frontier. His internet connections were not reliable enough in his current location. She filled in the non-residential tax clearance code and financial action task force code, and was waiting on the retina scan.

James Karlten 7:58:38 a.m.
I love you. Thank you for being such a darling. You mean everything to me.

On one hand, Alexis was not impressed having to play secretary for James. He had Charles for this sort of thing, and why didn't he sort all this out before going to Sri Lanka? What if she hadn't been around that afternoon and could not have processed what was required?

On the other hand, she felt honoured with the level of trust James had in her. It was not insignificant. What was to say she wasn't a gold-digger who would jump at the opportunity to reuse his passcodes to deposit some of over six million pounds into her 'travel the world' account? Of course, she would never do that, and James obviously knew her integrity was beyond reproach or wouldn't have asked her in the first place.

Before she had too much time to consider if Caryl the slut had played admin assistant for James, Alexis received confirmation of the transfer. Mr Martin Wilson, Head, Transfer Department from Global Citibank copied her into an email to James. She immediately forwarded the payment confirmation to Frontier Communications like a dutiful secretary, alerting them the cash was on its way and, with it, the shipment to Sri Lanka at long last.

Chu Xing from Frontier Communications replied the next day.

Thank you Alexis/Charles. Consequent to the delay in payment for the last 3 weeks, the rest of the materials will only be released as soon as the funds arrive in the account. Thank you for understanding our position on this issue.

Regards, Chu Xing.

No doubt this would cause more delays. Alexis had to get a hold of James. He would not be happy, given he was already well behind schedule.

MSN – 27 October

James Karlten 8:57:13 a.m.
I miss you. I can't tell you enough. I can't sleep. You've no idea what you've saved me from. I was just speaking to the project manager and he said the government were considering withdrawing the contract if I didn't have this mess sorted out by next week.

I'm sure you are in some meeting or another. I love you. More than words could ever express.

Alexis Jordain 9:07:08 a.m.
James, given the reply, it may require a follow-up phone call at least, I think. Happy to also reply to try to prompt release of materials, but you'll need to assist on the wording if you want to proceed. Please let me know if you need anything today. I'm home and computer-bound all day, so happy to assist anytime. Love you. A x

'Bloody Sri Lanka,' Alexis said aloud as she read the note from James later that day:

James Karlten 11:57:13 a.m.
Hello baby, I was able to use the project manager's phone to get into my email this morning. It is very difficult to do anything from here, but I was able to forward the email from Chu Xing to you. I am not sure if you got it. I will try and call him again after I finish this. I am not sure why I can't do this from my phone as well. I thought I was very technologically inclined.
I will like to say more, but it is taking me almost an hour to do this. I just want to say that I love you and I will never stop. Please call me when you are awake. Love James.

A few more expletives were added by Alexis after receiving the reply from Citibank's Mr Johnston.

Email: info@globalcbplc.com
Date: 26 October
GLOBAL CITI BANK
Credit Control Department
No 110 Basinghall Avenue
London, United Kingdom EC2V 5DD
James Norman Karlten
36 Clayponds Gardens
West London
W5 4ER
United Kingdom
Dear James

RE: TRANSFER OF YOUR FUNDS

Notification: Your transfer of 32,750 GBP to HASENG BANK LTD 787-3633738-883 Hong Kong has been declined.

Reason: Transfer was done from an unfamiliar IP address. (cable.telstraclear.net)

All wire transfers from your account will only be authorized when effected from your registered IP address on our system. However, if you log into your account now, you will notice that the actual funds have been debited from your account. Please do not be alarmed as we have immediately placed a call back on the funds transferred.

Funds should be re-credited to your account within the next 48 hours.

We apologise for the inconveniences this action might cause but our security team has advised the immediate shut down of all transfers from your account.

Yours faithfully,
Mr. Martin Wilson
Head, Transfer Dept

Now what? thought Alexis. The words 'shit, piss, fuck' rotated off her tongue like animals on the merry-go-round, each with distinctive features and unique intonation. She felt silly for thinking she could log onto James's account and move money around the globe when she herself knew her bank had loaded various levels of security on accounts. Why didn't she – or, better yet, why didn't James the international consultant – consider Citibank would do the same?

Alexis remembered years ago, when living in North America, she held a Citibank Visa card, but she'd never come across Citibank Down Under. Of course a TelstraClear ISP account from the other side of the world would be unknown and suspect. Now Mr Bloody Wilson would not make the transfer until the ISP could be verified.

It was reasonably difficult to get a hold of James while he was out bush in Sri Lanka. Now there was this issue of the money not getting there for the materials. She forwarded the email to James, hoping his intermittent internet connection would connect him to this important message. The project, and indeed Hawaii, rested on his reply.

♥ ♥ ♥ ♥ ♥

Alexis received a brief call from James later that afternoon. The conversation lasted under five minutes before they were cut off. In it they discussed what options they had, and, after considering the possibility that James would not complete the work and not attend their rendezvous in Hawaii, they began considering that perhaps Alexis might help. Just as Alexis was talking about how she might use an advance on her line of credit, their cell call dropped.

In the mere minutes it took to reconnect with James on MSN, Alexis's thoughts travelled across the Milky Way and back.

She wanted to help and appreciated it was just for a few days until James could transfer the funds himself. He was in the back of beyond. Once he reached civilization, her money would be paid back and they would be enjoying the beach in Hawaii together. It would need to be only a few days, as Alexis did not have the funds lying around as savings. She would need to draw on her flexi facility. James would cover the additional interest charges, he said, and the whole thing would be done and dusted within a week max.

She had a niggle in her gut – why would a businessman of his purported calibre find himself in such a situation? It was overridden by her desire to feel needed. She viewed this as the start of future business dealings together. Perhaps after this, they might engage in joint ventures.

Alexis's intuition led her to LinkedIn. She didn't expect to find him but said to herself that if he was there, she should really give him a second chance. Sure enough, Norman Consulting Ltd, based in London, UK, had James as CEO for the past twenty-seven years, one month. His former roles included Senior/Principal Consultant at PWC, where he led, managed and delivered a wide range of professional advice and support in the field of rolling stock and depot strategy, specification, maintenance and operations for over six years. 'Norman's – integrity, professionalism, and excellence.'

She allowed the feeling of being needed by James to wash alkaline over the cynical gut acids. Arriving in her neutral state, Lexi joined James on MSN to get the details for the transfer. It wasn't as straightforward as she'd anticipated.

Alexis would need to transfer 32,750 pounds to Frontier Communications, but there was a number of Hangseng Banks, and of course limits on the amount of foreign exchange she could process in one transaction. The limit was five thousand pounds lower than the amount required for the materials.

WTF? she thought.

She only managed to transfer $55,608.94 NZD that night. The remaining $9975.25 NZD would need to wait until Monday.

Alexis concluded her personal assistant duties with notes to Chu Xing and James. Who would have thought she'd be spending her day on high finance across borders? It was a full day indeed.

To: Frontier Communications
Cc: James Norman, Charles Col
Sent: Saturday, 27th October, 12.51 a.m.
Subject: Re: 回覆: TRANSFER OF FUNDS Dear Chu Xing

Thank you for your email.

Further to the initial approved transfer via Global Citibank as communicated to you yesterday, a security protocol at Citibank has cancelled that initial transfer as the transaction was placed from an unfamiliar internet IP account. By now James Norman would have contacted you to explain the situation that resulted from a lack of internet access on site.

To remedy the situation, a subsequent funds transfer has been initiated (see attached slip). Due to foreign exchange limits in New Zealand, the amount transferred today is 27,750 GBP. The further and final transfer amount of 5,000 GBP will be processed tomorrow. I will forward you the confirmation slip once processed. Both transfers (27,750 + 5,000 GBP) will be in the system by Monday 29 October.

This matter is most frustrating for all parties. We thank you for your patience in this matter.

Kind regards
Alexis Jordain

Her note to James underplayed her financial apprehensions.

MSN – 27 October

Alexis Jordain 10:04:10 p.m.
Hi James, I hope your day got better than it started early this morning! I am glad I can help you given the circumstances.
I have developed a slight niggle this evening given I've drawn down on a flexi loan to cover the funds.

Would you kindly acknowledge the intent of the transfer by way of a return MSN, thank you. I think that would help ease my mind. I'm off to sleep as it's been a full day.

You have no idea how much of a stretch in trust and love this is for me. I love you, and I miss you.

In the morning, Alexis received a reply to her transfer payment update from Chu Xing.

From: Frontier Communications
To: Alexis Jordain
Cc: James Norman
Sent: Saturday, 27th October, 11.43 p.m.
Subject: 回覆: 回覆: TRANSFER OF FUNDS

Thank you Alexis/Charles

I've not been able to speak to James yet, I saw a couple of missed calls from him but I was asleep at the time. I've tried to call him back but can't get through as well.

However, as much as I understand the situation of things and I sympathize with you, I am bit concerned about the time limitations here seeing that these transaction has taken almost a month since when the first set of materials/equipment were delivered. I am hoping that there won't be another issue this time around.

Secondly, please indicate your interest in the RAIL TROLLEYS ($6,972.17) as you've excluded that from the payment. The shipment would go out today as soon as I hear back from you but will only be released when the funds arrive in our account.

I will remain patient,
Chu Xing

To lighten the mood and distract from serious matters of work, high finance and Sri Lanka, Alexis and James played MSN tag most of the next day.

MSN – 28 October

James Karlten 10:47:42 a.m.
Hello baby, are you there?

Alexis Jordain 12:03:12 p.m.
Hello James, I thought I would let you sleep in a while before contacting you. I hope you are getting some rest. Please let me know if you've reached HK and if you want me to proceed with the final 5k GBP payment today. I've been flat out here. Lots to do in a compressed time frame. One report down, another to go and I forgot also that GST is due for payment today, so spent a few hours on that.

They are having an open home today next door. I'm scaring off potential purchasers with snarly glances from my desk. I must get back to work matters, big facilitation session tomorrow. I love you and miss you terribly and am very much looking forward to some R&R with you in Hawaii. I can't wait. A x

James Karlten 4:18:29 p.m.
Hello baby, are you there?

I can imagine the pressure. I am sorry to double it with my own issues. I feel very horrible now. I miss you very much and I can't stop thinking about you. I was hoping to talk to you yesterday, but apparently your work had a better part of you. I love you, Alexis, and loving you is the priority for me right now. I hope you were able to finish everything you had to do. I love you.

Alexis Jordain 4:46:38 p.m.
Hi sweetheart, just back from a quick time out with the girls at the tennis court. It was my first time out in lord knows how many years. My racquet weighs a ton. I must get a new one. They are just learning (I am not a pro by any means) and we spent most of the hour chasing rogue balls!

I'm back at the desk now – well, soon – just need to pop some biscuits into the oven that Bella just assembled. So, if it's convenient, jump online for a minute :)
A x

Okay, cookies in. Back to work (well, almost … first James …). Please don't feel horrible about my helping out. Priorities are priorities. When two people are together, they share what needs to be done together. Honestly, would you have not done the same? I am sure you would also feel good about doing something to help the person you love when they need it.

Please confirm you want me to transfer the final 5k GBP to HK. Yesterday you told me to hold off until hearing from you. I also thought if there are any more issues, just send Charles to the nearest place with internet. Surely it cannot be that far. Okay, hope to hear from you soon. I love you. A x

PS – tell me what you are doing today …

Alexis Jordain 9:07:06 p.m.
Hi James, FYI I will need to complete the 5k transfer in the morning. My 'after hours' limit has been reached for the weekend, but should be fine to go again in the morning. We are ahead of you, so should all still go through in the morning so processing begins asap. I will attend to this and email HK, and message you once complete. Speak soon, A x

It was GST time and Alexis was CRAZY busy at work and didn't have a lot of time to think, just to get through things.

The next day, the to-do list just got bigger.

People in full-time positions can look with envy at the freedom and flexibility of self-employment. Around tax time, though, incarceration commences. Receipts descend like amnesia-injecting locusts, blocking any recall of what that significant expense was for, or who you were with for that client schmooze, and calculators and simple math formulae play hide-and-seek with any arithmetic skills you thought you acquired in high school.

'The admin side of invoicing and collecting payments also adds to the administrative burden of loving my job,' Alexis would offer Edie whenever she told her how easy she had it. Not having paid holidays or sick days was also problematic, especially with wee ones. But enough wallowing; she needed to get on with things.

MSN – 29 October

Alexis Jordain 6:26:32 p.m.
Hi James, I've just finished my day with a room full of property people. For one woman to manage that much testosterone – whew – I'm exhausted! Sorry I couldn't touch base earlier, but as the facilitator, I hadn't a moment spare. Will catch up now. I did get your messages and I would smile my head off amongst the endless background 'noise' :) thank you.

I had a meltdown today when the banking didn't initially go through – apparently it was a computer glitch to start with, but en route to town I managed to sort by phone. It was rather comical, on the motorway with cell in one hand and HK bank details in the other. The supplier will have 32,750 GBP TODAY (should be cleared in a day or two, the bank promises). I have emailed Chu Xing to find out what the balance is with the addition of the rail trolleys (less the payment to date). I should be able to pay the shortfall (it may be around 2k). I just have some commitments in mid-November to manage.

Hey – are you on the line?

James Karlten 6:34:54 p.m.
Hey gorgeous, Thank you so much for all the trouble. I don't know what I would have done without you.

Alexis Jordain 6:36:30 p.m.
Seriously, I nearly reached through the phone to throttle the unsuspecting bank attendant.

James Karlten 6:36:57 p.m.
I hate banks. I wonder how you manage.

I can't wait to start waking you up with a million kisses all over your body, instead of just a text.

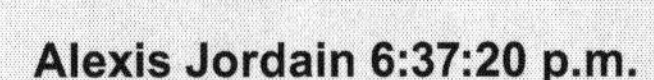

Alexis Jordain 6:37:20 p.m.
That will take some time – we will need to get up early … It's just as well I'm an early riser – 5 am work for you? I loved hearing from you today. My phone is dead right now too, FYI.

James Karlten 6:38:12 p.m.
Of course we would finish about 7 am.

Alexis Jordain 6:38:23 p.m.
Is that a short session? ☺

James Karlten 6:38:55 p.m.
LOL, Yes, it's the appetizer session.

Alexis Jordain 6:39:03 p.m.
Whew. I still haven't started writing my second report. I'm starting to freak out. What's happening with you … ???

James Karlten 6:40:01 p.m.
You have till Tuesday, right?

Alexis Jordain 6:40:11 p.m.
Which is tomorrow where I live …

James Karlten 6:40:25 p.m.
LOL, I keep forgetting.

James Karlten 6:40:31 p.m.
You want me to help?

Alexis Jordain 6:40:38 p.m.
I may need to do some serious smooth talking (I should send you …). You are perfect.

Alexis Jordain 6:40:49 p.m.
Yes please.

James Karlten 6:41:12 p.m.
LOL, don't call me a smooth talker, you hardly hear what I say. Now who's trying to be smooth?

Alexis Jordain 6:41:30 p.m.
How are we going on the really important issue of moustaches? I honestly have no issue with your moustache – whatever suits you …

James Karlten 6:42:05 p.m.
LOL, I've made the ultimate decision to cut it down.

Alexis Jordain 6:42:21 p.m.
What does that mean?

James Karlten 6:42:44 p.m.
I mean take it off so it doesn't cause any hindrances ...

Alexis Jordain 6:43:01 p.m.
Now who's trying to be smooth ...

James Karlten 6:44:13 p.m.
LOL, I love you baby.

Alexis Jordain 6:44:21 p.m.
I'm grinning like a hyena (again). What are you doing today?

James Karlten 6:45:29 p.m.
Well, trying to get more hands on deck. Getting ready for the materials to come in.

Alexis Jordain 6:46:51 p.m.
Are you sleeping okay?

James Karlten 6:47:20 p.m.
Not really, to be honest, but I am sure I will catch up.

Alexis Jordain 6:48:08 p.m.
I need to catch up also. I'm getting a sore throat. I need to be in tip-top shape, as I have an important meeting in Hawaii very soon.

James Karlten 6:48:08 p.m.
I wish we weren't so far apart. I miss you so much.

Alexis Jordain 6:48:15 p.m.
Tell me about it! I miss you also.

James Karlten 6:49:15 p.m.
LOL, Alexis Norman. You are so sweet.

Alexis Jordain 6:49:34 p.m.
You need to be on the computer with spell check :)

James Karlten 6:50:04 p.m.
LOL, you are so mean to me too.

Alexis Jordain 6:50:23 p.m.
Oh, if everyone was so mean, you would be the happiest man alive xx

James Karlten 6:51:04 p.m.
I know, your love knows no boundaries and I still can't get enough …

Alexis Jordain 6:51:33 p.m.
Let me know when you do, I'll shift into second gear.

James Karlten 6:51:41 p.m.
You are a perfect lover. I can't stop thinking about you and the whole package …

Alexis Jordain 6:51:50 p.m.
I don't want to overwhelm you.

James Karlten 6:52:06 p.m.
I am already overwhelmed. You are too late.

Alexis Jordain 6:52:16 p.m.
You are a very lucky man. You must have done something right in this lifetime. I wish I was there now. I hope I always overwhelm you. I hope you always need to catch your breath like you do to me – taking mine away.

James Karlten 6:53:44 p.m.
Aww, you say the sweetest things to me …

Alexis Jordain 6:53:48 p.m.
We are so incredibly lucky, Mr Norman.

James Karlten 6:54:06 p.m.
I need a picture of you, Alexis, a brand new picture, something really hot and sexy.

Alexis Jordain 6:54:50 p.m.
You in the middle of Sri Lanka, with a bunch of guys on the rails, that would just be mean.

James Karlten 6:55:32 p.m.
I still need it. I need to feed my imagination, before it dies …

Alexis Jordain 6:56:52 p.m.
I don't believe that. I figure your imagination is working absolutely fine.

James Karlten 6:57:40 p.m.
LOL, I take it that you are not going to send the picture …

Alexis Jordain 6:58:28 p.m.
I need to manage your expectations. I also need the element of surprise on my side. Is it really important to you?

James Karlten 7:00:00 p.m.
The picture? If it makes you feel better not to send it, don't … but I'd love to see one …

Alexis Jordain 7:01:13 p.m.
I'll see.

James Karlten 7:01:27 p.m.
OK love.

Alexis Jordain 7:01:32 p.m.
It may be hard to fit in a photo shoot.
Back to reality. I better start on dinner,
it's late.

James Karlten 7:02:27 p.m.
LOL, are you fishing for a compliment?
You gorgeously hot woman.

Alexis Jordain 7:03:04 p.m.
I never fish. I better run. Enjoy the rest of
your day. I love you also. Speak to you
tomorrow (I'll have my phone charged :))

James Karlten 7:04:07 p.m.
OK darling. I will leave you now. I love you
... very, very much ...

Ew, thought Alexis. James wanted her to send hot and sexy pictures. To a trailer in Sri Lanka. It had classy written all over it. Yuck. Not only was she worried who would be seeing the pictures, she was also feeling priggish about being respected as a person, not just some human female receptacle. She wasn't even sure they'd have chemistry or be attracted to one another!

Alexis knew she would need to manage expectations about Hawaii. Having sex was not a foregone conclusion in her mind. She would need to advise James of her five-dates rule. She didn't want to feel pressured to have sex with him and wanted to see how things might unfold naturally.

She could feel her breaths shorten, inhaling, exhaling. She was a combination of nervous and anxious. She'd never met him before, but he appeared to be a large man from his photos. What if he was more insistent about intimacy? She started to panic about the space between what James might expect in juxtaposition to what she was prepared to offer.

To ratchet up her anxiety, the logical reality check tossed in for good measure was the reality that it was only about a week prior that she found out about Caryl.

Was she truly satisfied with James's explanation of a February romance? Or was it more plausible that Caryl was a mere three weeks prior to Alexis, thus making her an August squeeze, like suggested on MSN? She was a sex nympho. Was he? Did the whole affair last only three weeks, or was it longer? He seemed to fall in love with her within nanoseconds or …

All the James thinking was creating a downward spiral. *My life is completely upside down,* she thought, considering the roller coaster in the Gold Coast, stopped midway, suspending her upside down, G-force making her eyes water and pressing her face backward. Not to mention the small matter of sending off over sixty-five thousand to Hong Kong. The feeling of barfing still followed her around like a rotten, smelly fart caught in her knickers. She recalled Edie's prior sage advice when asked if she should barf or shit – she said, 'Shit, because barfing is too hard on your system.' Great to have loving friends.

Alexis concluded she needed her head read, and knew just who could set her straight. She called to see if any of the bookies fancied splitting a bottle of truth serum.

Alexis was collected at hers by Oliver, and they went to Edie's for coffee and cake – which turned into pizza and beer from the local Four Square.

'I'm just a bit nervous about what he might expect – coming all the way to Hawaii from Sri Lanka and all,' Alexis explained.

'You're just having performance anxiety,' offered Oliver.

'Bullshit, Lex. You're not a man with performance anxiety. You're a woman whose radar is going off around the possibility that this dude is a bit of a headfuck! You've never met him, and you're scared he may be a serial killer or a Kinko the Clown weirdo. And fair enough,' Edie chortled. 'We don't know enough about him – or his sexual fantasies – to comfortably put you on a plane to the Hawaiian outback to reel in "the big one".'

'Edie, enough of the James-bashing session, love. We all know your opinion on matters of the heart and jumping into a new and possibly very real love situation.' Oliver gave her a childlike scolding. 'You'd do well to leave Ms Misery Guts to her own devices, Lex. She's just jealous 'cuz she's not been laid in ages!'

Oliver's smug look toward Edie signalled the discussion was moving on from Lexi's dilemma to the point of no return.

MSN – 30 October

Alexis Jordain 8:17:11 p.m.
It was great speaking to you at 3.30am this morning (sorry, sort of). I love hearing your voice. I hope all is going well on-site. Know I am thinking of you often and that you always bring a smile to my face. I am getting so excited about our rendezvous. I love you. Speak soon darling, A x

MSN – 31 October

5:51:26 a.m. Alexis Jordain
Good morning, sweetheart. I wonder if you can do me a favour and enter something in your 'write something new' space on MSN. Every time I log on to MSN I have to see your note: 'I love you Caryl Clerk and I will love no other woman. Ever.' I'm really over it. I don't know what other way to get rid of it, but if you can try that, I would appreciate it. Thank you.

It's another busy one today – need to write the presso that I negotiated instead of the report – yikes. I've got a structure for it though, so I'm feeling a lot better about it. Today is also Halloween here, so the kids and I will head to a friend's for a wee party (fish & chips dinner) and then go trick-or-treating. They are so excited. It's only over the past few years that people have started going out collecting candy.

I'm off for a quick walk now and then into work early. I loved getting your texts this morning. Thank you.

I was particularly intrigued by you 'not trading me in for anything else'. I am wondering if you are spending too much time in Sri Lanka and were considering trading me for a goat or cow. I assure you, you have the better deal with me ☺ – stick with me kid, we'll go far. I love you, darling. Hope you had a fantastic day. I will try to ring you on my way into work. A x

James Karlten 8:44:54 p.m.
I miss you. I can imagine how busy you are these days. I hope your work doesn't spill into our Hawaii time and then you would have to cancel. I am not sure what I might do.

I wish I can help with those reports, take some burden off you. I feel very terrible that I can't do anything …

I hope you're not getting tired of my random texting. Those words are just a small representation of how I truly feel inside. I love you, Alexis. I wish there were other ways to say it, different words so it still meant something to you after 30 years of marriage. I've experienced a different kind of love with you, baby, and I am overwhelmed. You are God's special gift to me, and I am very grateful to him …

I don't expect it to always be this smooth, there might be bumpy times as well, but I promise to always love you and be there when you need me. I promise with everything that I have …

James Karlten 8:48:50 p.m.
The materials arrived this morning, so we have swung into full action, all hands on deck to ensure that we finish this in 7 days max. Thank you very much, darling. You alone made this possible. I will try to ring you again now, just to tell you how much I love you. You mean everything to me.

Oh, I forgot to mention, I was so devastated when I heard about the Hurricane Sandy that has almost ravaged the whole of New Jersey and New York. I was scared that something might have happened to Mike, especially since I couldn't reach him for about 14 hrs. I was going crazy.

But he's fine. Alpine is still safe, but I am making arrangements to fly him to England ASAP, as I am not sure what might happen next. All schools have gone on break due to this, and it's getting worse by the day …

All New Jersey residents have been ordered to evacuate their houses as the hurricane approaches.

James Karlten 9:00:17 p.m.
I just tried to ring you again, but there is no response. I love you, Alexis. Please ring me when you get the chance to. I can't function properly when I don't hear your voice in such a long time.

Alexis Jordain 11:41:54 p.m.
Hello, darling, I truly hope in 30 years you are still trying to trade me for a goat :). I love you. I love your texts. I love that Mike is safe. I love that the materials are there. I love that I'm done my work for the night and can hit the hay. I wish I could stay up longer and chat, but I will speak with you in the morning. I never tire of hearing from you, James. I am missing you terribly and think of you always. Go well with work and know I am there with you in some small way.

I love you darling.
Good nite from New Zealand x
PS – I miss you.

She bounced back into her PA role. Hong Kong sent correspondence to Alexis regarding the additional equipment quote required to complete the work in Sri Lanka. They also requested the next payment in USD for ease of reconciliation across their accounting.

At one level it was fun for her to feel 'part of' her partner's business. She had always liked the notion of global business ventures with her 'partner' at work and at home. Working in Sydney and Singapore and across Canada brought Alexis much joy, discovering new places, people and ways of doing business. Even though it was indirect involvement, she still felt she was learning. She recalled a counterpart from HK discussing how business was done at the polo club in HK. Alexis was having a wee taste of this 'way of doing business'. It appealed to her sense of curiosity, exploration and a desire to acquire new skills – like patience. Some lessons are more challenging than others.

♥ ♥ ♥ ♥ ♥

Her impulsive nature beckoned Alexis to jump on the next plane and meet up with James in Sri Lanka. She was sure she would add value there. Certainly more than she felt she was contributing on the home front.

Work commitments were starting to weigh her down, as the pace of organisational change was not meeting with her anticipated progress goals. Her rational side kept her feet firmly on the ground. She wasn't even sure of the exact geographic location of Sri Lanka, let alone which forest grove James was perched in. Rather than google the required vaccinations for the deepest ends of the earth, she attended to business from the comforts of Island Bay.

MSN – 1 November

Alexis Jordain 9:03:29 p.m.
Hi James, quote from China follows – you need to confirm quantities required and quote price: Rail Skates: RB/BR/153 2@$13,200 Hydraulic lifting machine MOD. SI-300A 1@$17,880 Railband 950 RB/BR/153C 3 @ $7,250 Tamping systems MOD. TSR-300 1@ $6,960 TOTAL $45,290.

Once you confirm the above, Chu Xing will invoice and dispatch materials, but not release until funds have cleared. He wants payment in USD (what currency is the quote in?). When you come back to me I will send confirmation email to get the ball rolling. I'm afraid the amount will be too much for my flexi loan limit – what is Plan B? I will absolutely do what I can, but I think we need to have a contingency in place, OK?

Your MSN messages make me laugh. I cannot wait until Hawaii also. It just makes me think that is much more important than this one gig. It will be wonderful to meet you. I imagine your arms around me, feeling the small of my back and pulling me toward you to kiss me (sans moustache). Wow. Is it a gentle kiss? A passionate kiss? You have so many owing, you will need to mix them up.

Alexis Jordain 9:45:14 p.m.
I suggest lots of practice (with me, not goats). I am so hanging out for this. It will be perfect. I will enjoy hearing your laugh in person. You have a wonderful laugh, from what I have heard. I will enjoy making you laugh. I will tousle your hair, I may tickle you, the odd raspberry is not unheard of. I am so excited to get to know more about you. What is your ideal first date?

I better go. I know you are working very hard, and I hope all is going well. I am thinking about you and sending you lots of love and encouragement. I look forward to hearing from you, darling. Go well. I love you very much, A x

PS please try to get some rest, okay? X

As much as Alexis wanted to assist James, even if it was just in a clerical capacity, she also realised her financial exposure was significant. She felt like Scotty on the USS Enterprise. 'Captain, I'm givin' ya all she's got!'

She had always ensured she had a buffer for emergencies with a line of credit. She would need to dip into this at various points to pay tax, GST, body corp/strata fees for investment property and of course those whimsical trips to the jungles of Sri Lanka. The overdraft numbers were adding up, and she needed to get James's assurance that this 'short-term' financial fix was just that – i.e., she would soon be back in black – AND hopefully singing to Amy Winehouse at the 'performance bonus' her wealthy partner would surely bestow her way, especially with the interest accumulating on the flexi loan.

Alexis was usually very articulate in work settings. On the home front, and anything remotely emotional, actually, she became tongue-tied, defensive and confrontational. She wasn't the greatest at voicing her needs and concerns or, in this case, conveying her fears about being financially extended when she and James connected that afternoon on MSN. She enacted the next best alternative to speaking her mind – she spoke someone else's. She found herself taking artistic licence with the story of a 'friend' to encase her suspicions and reservations.

In retrospect, another approach may have been more successful. Hindsight is a wonderful thing, just not practical.

❤ ❤ ❤ ❤ ❤

MSN – 2 November

James Karlten 8:52:28 a.m.
Baby, are you there?

Alexis Jordain 2:52:17 p.m.
Hi James, I've confirmed the order to be sent from China and told him I'd send through the payment slip shortly. You must remember it is Friday here and so dates are askew on the other half of the world. I can only put this through if you can guarantee I'll have cleared funds back in my account on 7th November. I literally won't have ANY fallback if things are delayed beyond that.

I have a lump sum payment due on the 9th for 20k and mortgages due etc. Plus I'll have exhausted all cash reserves and my full flexi loan facility. This is quite a serious situation for me. I would have never been so exposed. I will proceed if you can assure me we can sort out banking on 7 November (you may need to send Charles back home to sort it otherwise).

I will await your call or return MSN – and OMG if this isn't sorted next week … I'm off to more meetings, must fly, A x

PS – I'm billing you for my time :)

Alexis Jordain 6:52:35 p.m.
Hi James, I've just had a quick wine after work with an old friend, ex-cop.

I told him of our situation and he's convinced I'm being scammed.

He said if he promises true love and it's too good to be true, it is. He asked about company websites and proof of identity and how this stuff happens all the time and that's probably what happened to Caryl etc. It all did happen pretty fast. He said I'll never see my 65k and to stop this nonsense immediately. He said I thought you were smarter than that, etc. He said a successful businessman would never be in a situation like this, and particularly where he couldn't ring the bank to sort out this stuff (and when I think of it, I called my bank to do the fx transfer – which they did by phone easily). I'm having an OMG meltdown. I should have never gone for wine – or maybe that was the best thing to do.

I'm so confused and feel like I've really foolishly put my family at risk. I'm not sure what to do now. He's a good friend, and wouldn't cause trouble for no reason. First the Caryl thing, now this, oh boy.

James Karlten 7:39:14 p.m.
I am very dismayed by your message, and I am in complete shock that you would even give in to such side talk. You are very much aware that it's not like I planned any of this and how uncomfortable I was with it at the start. Why would he say something like that? I feel very insulted.

James Karlten 7:39:14 p.m.
I am not sure why you are telling me this either? Am I supposed to prove to you that I am for real or reassure you that you will get your money back? You are not sure of this?

Alexis, please avoid side talks as much as possible. They ruin homes. I can't believe you got yourself involved in such petty talks.

Please, I need your account details ASAP. Euros 131,000 will be paid into your account by the 7th and the rest will be paid in on the 12th.

Alexis Jordain 7:43:02 p.m.
James, I cannot help what someone else said. I did not say anything to upset you. That was not my intention. Obviously in future, I will keep these interactions to myself. I am sorry I mentioned anything. I feel like I'm being scolded. Scolded like a child.

James Karlten 7:44:08 p.m.
No Alexis, what upset me is that you gave into this conversation.

Alexis Jordain 7:44:11 p.m.
Thank you for your understanding.

James Karlten 7:44:28 p.m.
I am sorry, that is not how I meant it. But you know how people ruin homes with just sitting there and assuming.

Alexis Jordain 7:48:36 p.m.
I'm under pressure here, and very tired. Perhaps it was a weak moment and I did give into a friend's assessment, in so much as I wrote to you about it.

Alexis Jordain 7:48:36 p.m.
Perhaps that was my mistake. I should have processed it by myself rather than discuss it with you. I have been taken to the cleaners before and nearly lost my house because of a guy. Forgive me for being cautious, but once bitten.

It doesn't matter. It's great that we can work through things calmly and respectfully.

James Karlten 7:50:12 p.m.
It's okay, Alexis. I completely understand. Please talk to me about anything you're not sure of. I will never put you in jeopardy.

I love you and I want the best for you. Your kids have become my kids now, and I know the same thing goes for you.

James Karlten 7:54:20 p.m.
Are you there?

James Karlten 7:59:41 p.m.
Please, I need your account details ASAP. 131,000 euros will be paid into your account by the 7th and the rest will be paid in on the 12th.

I don't know how you disappeared. Is everything okay? I waited for about half an hour and I need to get back to work. Please confirm to me when you make the payments and also details of your account. I love you to the moon and back.

Alexis Jordain 9:33:50 p.m.
Hi James, my phone battery died. Your materials have been ordered and paid for. I'm tapped out now so, sorry, cannot assist further. My account details are sent by email.

I've been invited to my friend's lake house for the weekend. There's no cell or internet coverage, so I will ring you when I'm back on Monday. I hope your work goes well. I will be doing the same.
Love, Alexis

PS – I have sent all the required docs to China, so you should be all set. Secretary Alexis over and out.

Well, that didn't go well, Alexis thought, signing off MSN.

She was pissed off at James's reaction, and at his inability to hear her concerns. She was annoyed with herself for doubting him in the first place. *I have a 'friend' who's an ex-cop.* Nice, alert the guy. *What was I thinking?* Would she continue to project her past hurts into the future, not trusting anyone because she was betrayed by some opportunistic assholes in the past?

She knew she would have been pissed off if James had questioned her integrity. But she also considered whether his reaction was out of proportion. A case of 'thou doth protest too much'? How would she ever know?!!

She half wished she could consult her fake ex-cop friend. He'd know whether she should make the second transfer to Hong Kong or not. Alexis was desperate to run away from the situation. But where to go? There wasn't even a real lake house. She wished she were an ostrich instead. She'd have her head down by now, and the only thing anyone would see would be a random bird butt on the horizon.

Time was of the essence. She needed to decide now whether she would make the $45,290 USD transfer.

It was the fundamental domino to get the remaining supplies, so James could finish the work, so he could leave Sri Lanka, so he could meet Alexis in Hawaii. In making the payment, she knew she was swimming at far greater depths than those at the grown-up end of the pool.

Treading water was already strenuous for her, and she was heading toward the continental shelf – the drop-off zone, to be exact. She wondered if she might reach that warm jet stream and travel to Hawaii with the turtles in *Finding Nemo*. She dreaded to think of the alternative: descending into the abyss of the dark, bottomless and penniless ocean floor.

She put on her 'be a big girl' swimmers and completed the transfer.

The USD converted to $55,651.99 NZD. She had never transferred that much money. Her overdraft amount made her dizzy. Steadying herself, Alexis sent the transfer slip once again to Frontier Communications.

Things will look clearer in the morning, she thought. *At least I gave James my banking details. Let's see what Mr Integrity does with that.*

♥ ♥ ♥ ♥ ♥

She needed to shift out of the headspace she was plummeting into before the pressure in her head exploded like a character in a *Looney Tunes* cartoon. She diverted her thoughts to relocate the GPS behind the wheel of her convertible. Hair blowing in the wind, her fake ex-cop friend sat next to her. They headed up the coast to the infamous make-believe lake house. Ah, daydream or nightmare – however this would turn out – Alexis was creating an excellent start for her weekend away – even if that meant getting lost in the meandering contours of Egyptian cotton on her Cali King.

♥ ♥ ♥ ♥ ♥

MSN – 3 November

James Karlten 9:24:15 p.m.
Hello baby, I miss you so much, I feel like I haven't spoken with you in over a year. Work here has been very hectic. I was on my feet yesterday for over 14 hrs. I think I might have gotten a bit of a tan.

I wish there was something I can do to take away this space between us right now. I wish there was a way I could look into your eyes right now and tell you I love you. To clear away every reasonable doubt. I wish there was a way I could give you all the kisses I promised you right now …

James Karlten 9:48:29 p.m.
I love you, Alexis, with all my heart. The last thing I want to do is hurt you. You have the most amazing heart, and I will never take your feelings for granted. I will love you forever, for as long as I still have breath in me.

I hope work is going on well. I can imagine how stressed you are right now, and I hope that one day it is me that you will be running home to, to take all the pain away.

I hope I can hear your voice before Monday. I am not sure what I would do if I didn't hear your voice for that long. I miss you so much already.

You mean the world to me, and I also want to be your best friend. Please talk to me about everything and anything. I don't need to say anything, I just love to listen.

The materials have already been dispatched. Thank you. I love you so much, and I have all the details you've sent to me. I will update you. My regards to your friend.

I will go back to work now. So much to be done, and I feel like I am losing my strength.

MSN – 4 November

Alexis Jordain 7:28:51 a.m.
Dear James, you may feel like you are losing your strength, but remember you also have mine now too. Perhaps you forgot temporarily – where your strength ends, mine begins – you have endless strength now. Just remember that ☺

I forgot about helping with first communion, so I'm off to the grocery store now to get bits and pieces and will run off to the church. I will write soon and ring you later. I can imagine you 'getting a tan' – it's kind of hot. Better go – duty calls. PS, my friend Sue says hi and is looking forward to meeting you. I love you, James, A x

Alexis Jordain 1:06:31 p.m.
Hi there, me again. Back at home and back to work. Sweetheart, please do not feel pressure to get things done to get to Hawaii on time. If you need to take an extra day or two, please do. I'd rather you take your time and get some rest in between tanning so hard :). If you are a bit later to Hawaii, that will give me time to work on my tan (see if I can get darker than you). No pressure, okay?

I'm glad the materials have been sent off. I followed up with China on Friday night asking to ensure things were in train (pardon the pun – I've got a million of 'em). I hope all goes well. I'm up to my eyeballs here. I cannot wait to get away. Give me a ring when convenient for you. It's Sunday here, so I'm mostly around (albeit it must be the wee hours of the morning for you, love). I miss you. A x

Alexis Jordain 9:10:27 p.m.
Hello love, apologies for again waking you during some much-needed sleep. I'm heading to bed to get some reading done and prep for tomorrow. Big day, and I really hope they are open-minded and listen to what I've heard during my 30 interviews with their senior leaders. Fingers crossed. Grandma is now sick (and very grumpy). Girls are back from Dad's, and I'm really ready for Hawaii.

I love you, James.
I'll leave it at that for now. I hope work is progressing smoothly and that your selection of men is as good as mine LOL. It's funny how the closer we get to seeing each other, the further away it seems. How is that possible? C'est la vie. Know I love you deeply and am thinking of you. You are an island of calm amongst some pretty rough seas. Soon we will both be on the same island. I cannot wait.

MSN – 5 November

James Karlten 12:31:33 a.m.
Baby, you don't realize how much I love to hear your voice. I miss you so much. I can't function properly without hearing from you in such a long time. I am glad that you've had a bit of a break from work. How was communion? Did you pray for me? I need all the prayers I can gather. My regards to Sue as well. I can't wait to meet everyone.

Unfortunately, work is not going as well as I thought it would. I had a disagreement with Chu Xing over the weekend as regards some of the equipment. It got heated up and we decided he would refund the money ($45,290) back to your account, including the GPB 5,000 for the unpaid rail trolleys. Charles is still in talks with him to find a common ground. I doubt that is going to happen, but I will keep you posted.

I am already in talks with some other suppliers as regards the equipment, and I will inform you of whatever happens by Monday.

James Karlten 12:31:34 a.m.
I miss you. I hope I don't have to push days for Hawaii. I really can't wait to see you. You are so sweet when you write me such lovely messages. I can't help but keep smiling. You mean everything to me and I love you very much … 'Where your strength ends, mine begins – you have endless strength now'. This is the best thing anyone has ever told me, and I say thank you. I love you.

Alexis Jordain 8:23:16 p.m.
Hello, darling. The presentation was a home run today. It went really well. I've passed one hurdle for a week in Hawaii today – the programme director was most impressed by the performance with the exec team, so I hit him while he was vulnerable about more time off next week :)

Just one more thing tomorrow and I'll be able to confirm my availability. No pressure at your end. I know you have a few things to fit in between now and Christmas. Keep me posted on what's up at your end. I hope you are making good progress today. Nothing happening in my accounts today, FYI. I will hope to speak to you before bed, but if not, sweet dreams and I love you. A x

PS – I cannot believe we will meet in less than a week – is this possible? Is this dream real? I have pinched myself many times, as it all seems so surreal. I do hope you are real, James. I am so excited about meeting you and spending time together getting to know you. I am in a mixed state of disbelief and believing in magic. If magic is to happen, then paradise shall be the perfect canvas. X

The implications that might result from James's disagreement with Chu Xing, and a subsequent delay in getting equipment to Sri Lanka, did not fully register for Alexis. Nor did the pending 'refund' to her account, of which she was cognizant. Her mind was squarely focused on getting her end prepared for Hawaii – work and kids and elderly sick parent, and her 'end' – should she get a spray tan? Book in a wax? And what about sexy knickers? There were far too many more important matters to attend to …

MSN – 6 November

James Karlten 6:37:12 a.m.
Hey baby, are you there?

Alexis Jordain 6:37:29 a.m.
Hey there, yes, just jumped on.

James Karlten 6:37:45 a.m.
Oh, there you are. I am so glad to see you here. How are you? Did you have a good night?

Alexis Jordain 6:38:03 a.m.
Good, thank you. How are you? Night was very good, thanks. Dreamt of you …

James Karlten 6:38:22 a.m.
I am hanging in there. I miss you. Really? Was it good? What was I doing in the dream? Did I have any clothes on?

Alexis Jordain 6:38:43 a.m.
I hope you are feeling stronger. No, you were completely naked.

James Karlten 6:39:07 a.m.
Oh wow, did you like what you saw?

Alexis Jordain 6:39:31 a.m.
It was lovely mood lighting, and yes.

James Karlten 6:40:04 a.m.
Hmm, I love you Alexis, don't ever forget that.

Alexis Jordain 6:40:45 a.m.
I won't. But you can keep reminding me just the same. How's progress?

James Karlten 6:41:14 a.m.
Of course I will, but sometimes I think you forget. You asked me if I was real last night. That hurt a bit.

Alexis Jordain 6:41:59 a.m.
Oh, stop it. All I meant is that it feels so good, it seems unbelievable sometimes.

Alexis Jordain 6:42:15 a.m.
You may be more sensitive than I am – which would be something.

I will try not to ever say things that hurt you, James. We both need to remember about each other's vulnerabilities. This thing with you is a big deal for me. I am really trying to trust and jump in without a safety harness. It is a challenge for me.

James Karlten 6:45:48 a.m.
No, it's fine. Sometimes I read things the other way around, but once you explain it to me, the way you meant it, then I am fine.

I miss you, baby. Very much …

Alexis Jordain 6:48:36 a.m.
I miss you too, very much. When you receive something from me, please try to first think that I love you so much and I would never do anything to hurt you.

Then, maybe be curious – Walt Whitman has a great quote – 'Be curious, not judgmental.' Try perhaps to understand why I might say something. I've done this a few times with notes from you that seemed abrupt. I think it's only when we are hurt or vulnerable that we say things that may not come across as eloquently to the other – they can be a bit raw.

James Karlten 6:50:01 a.m.
I totally agree and I apologise. You are so sweet.

Alexis Jordain 6:50:21 a.m.
I love you very much, James, and I cannot wait to see you. We are travelling halfway across the world for our first date. It's all very incredible, really.

How is your tan going?

James Karlten 6:50:53 a.m.
I know. It was your idea. I don't know how I managed to buy into it.

Alexis Jordain 6:51:15 a.m.
Maybe you've met your match in negotiations.

James Karlten 6:51:25 a.m.
LOL, I agree ...

Alexis Jordain 6:51:38 a.m.
I'm pretty excited. Are you?

James Karlten 6:51:40 a.m.
Do you have to rush off soon?

Alexis Jordain 6:51:44 a.m.
Yes.

James Karlten 6:52:03 a.m.
Yes, I am. I am looking forward to it with all vigour.

Alexis Jordain 6:52:07 a.m.
I need to do some work before an 8.30 am meeting, get kids breakfast, school lunches etc.

Good. I'm glad you too are excited.

James Karlten 6:52:29 a.m.
Okay, what time is it right now?

Alexis Jordain 6:52:34 a.m.
6.52.

James Karlten 6:52:52 a.m.
Okay, you're an early riser, good.

Alexis Jordain 6:52:53 a.m.
Will you sleep tonight? Very early. You?

James Karlten 6:53:32 a.m.
I hardly have any sleep these days, but when I am exhausted I don't wake up till about 9am.

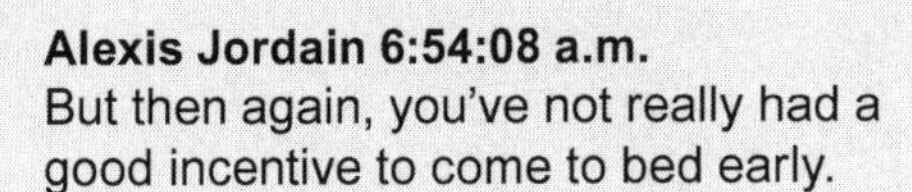

Alexis Jordain 6:54:08 a.m.
But then again, you've not really had a good incentive to come to bed early.

James Karlten 6:54:42 a.m.
You are right. Soon, baby, soon ...

Alexis Jordain 6:55:33 a.m.
Okay, love, on that fine note, I will bid you adieu. I must get moving here. Remember I love you and we'll speak soon.

James Karlten 6:55:56 a.m.
Okay, did you get the money in your account today?

Alexis Jordain 6:56:02 a.m.
I miss you, sweetheart. Nothing as yet.

James Karlten 6:56:33 a.m.
Okay, please let me know as soon as you receive it, so I can tell you what to do, okay? I love you.

Alexis Jordain 6:56:48 a.m.
Will do. I've got to fly. Speak soon, A x

James Karlten 6:57:00 a.m.
All right, I love you.

When you finally find what is beautiful, everything changes. You make me happy and give me a reason to smile, even when everything else seems difficult. I love you. I promise to be there in sun and rain; in pleasure and pain. I know how easy it is to make promises when you don't have any immediate situation, but I will never leave you, Alexis. I will never stop loving you, even if you stop.

Have a good day and don't stop thinking about me.

Alexis Jordain 7:04:23 p.m.
Hi love, just off to dinner with a client. Have checked accounts, and no action on this front. I'll try to ring you when I'm heading home from going out. Love you,
A x

When Alexis arrived home just after midnight, the living room downlights looked like they were playing checkers on the ceiling. She didn't realise she'd drunk enough for imaginary parlour games at her client dinner.

The financial stress was playing havoc with her subconscious. She welcomed the numbing of her central nervous system (CNS) at the start of the night, relaxing her body and mind. But then, overloaded with worry, the increasing depressant effect of the alcohol she kept consuming formed a lethal cocktail tailspin. Her slowed brain activity impaired her cognitive judgment, which failed to play liquor control board and press the stop-drinking switch.

Alexis was not the first person to drown her sorrows, and would not be the last. Her heritage of heavy drinkers was coming home to roost. She would also not be the first to pray to the porcelain god that she would never drink again if she would just make the room stop spinning and make her feel even a modicum better.

She finished in the bathroom, and the expelled intoxicant made room for sufficient sensibility to return. Alexis was reminded she should 'check in' with her overprotective (aka controlling) partner. She doubted she'd actually speak to James. He was often unavailable, what with working on the line, and in different time zones. At least she couldn't be criticised for not trying – she would leave a recorded message to capture her efforts.

'Voicemail full.'

Of course, thought Alexis. She felt her relationship with the telecoms 'voicemail full' attendant had more substance than the one with James. She hung up, speaking two short words to her companion, neither goodbye nor bon voyage. She groaned. His mail had been full most of his time in Sri Lanka. She would MSN him for posterity's sake and then go straight to bed.

Hi babe, tried ringing, your mailbox is full. Just in from dinner and drinks. A bit tipsy, but happy. Was a great night. Hope all is well your end. Speak soon, A x

The wing mirrors on cars carry the warning 'objects are closer than they appear'. This morning, in Alexis's head, the objects were sounds. They were everywhere – more trucks air-braking on the road doing the

tip run, waves crashing so ferociously they shamed the last big storm and those damn seagulls – squawking like they were locked in the line of sight down the hunter's barrel. One sound she would not hear today was James's voice.

Today, the happy couple would not directly communicate. They would try, of course, leaving notes and voicemails. Yet again, the tyranny of distance would dominate. Communication in this far away relationship was not just challenging; it was borderline ridiculous.

Alexis left James a note in the morning:

Good morning, I hope all is okay your end. Please ring and leave me a message when you can. I've changed my flights, returning Saturday night to NZ (17 Nov). Still nothing in the account and today is the 7th Nov here. Would you chase this up please. They've asked me to stay until Christmas at work. Speak soon. I love you, A x

James tried Alexis at night:

Hello gorgeous, I tried to call you again but still no response. I hope you are okay? I am a bit worried about you now. Please let me know. I love you.

And several times in between, both their attempts failed. 'Twas another day of telephone tag with no winner. Each missed contact only served to frustrate Alexis more and to further heighten the growing unease over money. She would have to wait to connect again tomorrow.

MSN – 8 November

Alexis Jordain 6:39:56 a.m.
Dear James, I couldn't sleep last night. I am sick with worry about my finances. I don't know what I'm going to do to pay my bills and mortgage. I thought you were arranging Madrid's payment to come into my account yesterday. What happened? I have now sent over 121k NZD and have no further loan facility, nor cash. I don't know what to do. Please do not leave me in this situation. This is the worst.

Her note was cut short by a phone call. Luckily, the brief chat with James talked Alexis off the ledge. At least temporarily.

Alexis Jordain 7:59:56 a.m.
Hi James, I must be head over heels in love. Despite everything going on right now, speaking to you makes me feel so much better. You are a wonderful island oasis amidst a choppy sea. We will get through this, James, and soon will be sipping on piña coladas and laughing about our 'interesting' early adventures. I love you, darling. Despite all the turmoil, that has not changed. I miss you. A x

Alexis Jordain 10:28:22 p.m.
Hi darling, heading off to bed now. I hope you had a good day. No action on the cash front. I'll let you know if anything comes through in the morning. I love you, A x

MSN – 9 November

James Karlten 8:16:13 a.m.
Baby, are you there?

I've just tried to call you. I miss you very much. I know how hard this situation is for you, and I know 'I'm sorry' doesn't solve the issue, but I'm indeed very sorry …

I assure you that by next week you will get everything back. I hope the money goes into your account by this morning so we would know the next step.

I hate for this to be an impediment to our relationship. I love you and I don't want to spend the rest of my life without you. This is just one hurdle we need to pass through together, and I promise that everything would be all right.

James Karlten 8:52:32 a.m.
I have great respect for the amount of trust you have in me, and I've taken none of that for granted. No woman has ever loved me like you have, and you've taught me a better way to love …

Even in your uncertainty and insecurity, you still trust me. I'm not about to take that for granted. I love you very much, Alexis.

How is work & all of that? I'm looking forward to Hawaii, baby. I'm trying not to stress out too much, so you will recognize me when I show up. I'm looking forward to kissing every part of ur body till you scream for me to stop.

I'm almost done now. My new suppliers have already dispatched the equipment I need. They're only just waiting for confirmation of payments …

I really hope this money gets into your account today. I love you. Call me when you get a chance to.

James Karlten 8:53:06 a.m.
I'm trying to get a quick nap now …

I want you to know that I love you. I don't want you to ever doubt how I feel about you, ever. I love love love you and I cannot wait to look into your eyes and tell you every day.

I cannot imagine a life without you in it, Alexis. You make me really happy. You are everything that I have ever wanted, and I hope I make you happy as well …

I want to wake up beside you for the rest of my life. I want to make you late to work.

Have a good day, baby.

♥ ♥ ♥ ♥ ♥

When she returned from work, she logged onto her bank account. Lo and behold, there was a deposit of $55,363.26, all there in black and white.

Alexis logged off and logged on again to be sure.

Yup, still there.

Once the bulk of Lexi's money was back in her account, she had an overwhelming urge to leave it there – to not re-transfer that money for the new materials in China. The feeling she had to endure after hitting the initial 'complete transfer send' button was causing her such angst she could think of little else. She now had an opportunity to relieve her suffering – just don't transfer the money again – leave it there.

But James needs it. He'll never get to Hawaii if he doesn't finish the job. This is your future, Alexis. It is an investment – short term at that – in your future life with James. She hated the Pollyanna dimension of her personality, which always saw the bright side of life, even when it was cold and dark and raining and her feet were soaked with a chill that climbed straight up her back and ended with a sharp ear flick …

Wake the fuck up, stupid, her rational ego cried. *Take your money and run! This guy is a loser if he's in the wop wops of Sri Lanka without his railway ties. He's going to run off with your money and choo choo away, never to be seen again.*

The Socratic approach continued in her brain.

James had more than enough money without her meager 'line of credit'. The flat in London, where he received her bouquet of sunshine, the house in Alpine with its pool and gardens and Consuela, who had probably already received the posted wee notes. And lest we forget his healthy Citibank account balance, which she had seen plainly in black and white with her own eyes.

She could contact him, let him know the cash had arrived in her account and at least see what he had in mind as the 'next step'. It would buy her some time to conclude the winner of the Harvard debate with her frontal cortex.

Alexis Jordain 7:50:58 p.m.
Hi James, I've just logged onto my account and received $55,363 NZD, FYI.

James Karlten 9:35:58 p.m.
Baby, are you there? Alexis?

Alexis Jordain 9:37:39 p.m.
Hi, yes.

James Karlten 9:37:52 p.m.
How are you?

Alexis Jordain 9:38:06 p.m.
Fine thanks, just packing now.

James Karlten 9:38:20 p.m.
Okay, you received the money?

Alexis Jordain 9:38:20 p.m.
How are you? Part of it.

James Karlten 9:38:51 p.m.
I mean the 45,290. It was returned, right?
I am in pretty bad shape.
I need that equipment by today.

Alexis Jordain 9:39:46 p.m.
Yes, the 45290.

James Karlten 9:39:47 p.m.
You said you were going to call me. You didn't. I couldn't sleep.

Alexis Jordain 9:40:03 p.m.
I sent you a note on MSN.

James Karlten 9:40:36 p.m.
I wasn't on. Sometimes the network is really bad, so I can't stay on. It logs me out.

Alexis Jordain 9:40:40 p.m.
What are you asking of me? I'm not sure of what you require.

James Karlten 9:42:02 p.m.
Okay, can you do a transfer to the new suppliers before you leave please? The money from Madrid will come in on Monday. At that time I should be in Hawaii as well.

And the 5,000 will also go into your account by Monday.

Alexis Jordain 9:43:39 p.m.
I have no details.
I also need to take part of the repayment for my overdue mortgage payment.

James Karlten 9:44:04 p.m.
I will give it to you now. Hold on one minute, let me get Charles.
Can it be delayed till Monday? I can assure you that you will get the payment from Madrid on Monday. Please Alexis, I don't want to stay any longer here.

Alexis Jordain 9:46:26 p.m.
Send through the details.

James Karlten 9:46:57 p.m.
Okay, I will send it now.

Alexis felt like a prostitute forced to perform tricks against her will. She knew what she was doing on one level, but resented that she was put in that position. She took down all the details. The new contact was Xiu Lee. She didn't like doing business in China, she decided.

Alexis Jordain 10:10:33 p.m.
Fine, I'll sort it.

James Karlten 10:11:53 p.m.
Are you okay? You didn't seem in a chatty mood at all. Almost like you are upset with me.

'Are you okay?' James had asked. But Alexis had what she needed. She was not 'okay'. Her slight niggle was growing into heartburn, and now she had urgent secretarial duties to perform before heading to bed. Not only was she NOT okay, she was ropeable.

She didn't know if she was more annoyed with James or herself. She didn't even give the $55,363.28 NZD deposit squatter's rights in her account before exiling most of it – $53,764.71 NZD back to some new Hong Kong supplier! What was she thinking?!?!

Her love-struck pea-brain decided to take the refunded monies – which were desperately needed to bring up her overdraft some – and send them, once again, sight unseen, to the never-never land of railway materials that may or may not make it to Sri Lanka before she arrived in Hawaii.

She was further annoyed with herself in the James's secretary role. She was an educated woman who, in the brief time it took to wait for James to confer with Charles, had pummelled herself back into angst about making her next mortgage payment. She needed her head read.

'Not in a chatty mood' – Really?!!, seethed Alexis as she typed to Xiu Lee. *Did James worry about his mortgage? Not likely,* she considered.

At least her efficiency in purchasing railway equipment from HK suppliers was improving. She clung to the hope that her faith in James was not misplaced. Hawaii was so close – palm trees in sight.

Alexis Jordain 10:44:20 p.m.
It's done – supplier notified and copy of details sent to yours and Charles's email. See you in Hawaii.

James Karlten 10:45:37 p.m.
Alexis?

Alexis knew she could never speak of the money-lending to her friends. She had enough trouble convincing herself that things would work out. She just needed to breathe until the whole thing was over. They would laugh about it once James had more than compensated her for the overt display of faith and trust in their new love.

In the morning, Alexis received confirmation from HK. It was her last official duty before going on holiday.

寄件人: Alexis Jordain
收件人: Tharapatong Limited
副本(CC): James Norman; Charles Col
11月9日 (週五) 10:42 AM
主題: Payment Slip for Materials – James Norman

Hello James/Alexis,

Thank you for the payment. Like I told you on the phone, since it is our first transaction/dealing with your company, we would not release the materials until the money has arrived in our account. We have had bad experiences in the past and I am not about to take chances. I understand the urgency of the issue but I don't directly run this company.

Subsequent transactions might be different once trust is established.

I will write you to inform shipment as soon as we hear news from our bank.

Plenty thanks my friend,
Xiu Lee

To: Tharapatong Limited
From: Alexis Jordain
CC: James Norman; Charles Col
Sent: 10 November
Re: Payment Slip for Materials – James Norman

Dear Xiu Lee,

We understand your position. I assume the materials have been dispatched. Could you please confirm estimated arrival date, thank you? The bank has assured me the funds should be cleared and with your bank within the next day. Please follow up with your bank, as I am confident all will proceed smoothly.

I look forward to hearing from you.

Kind regards,
Alexis

She never imagined she'd be playing ping-pong email with a man called Xiu Lee while she squeezed far too many strappy shoes into her suitcase.

The whole circumstance was surreal. Alexis boarded the flight to Hawaii not knowing what to expect, when, how or with whom.

At least there was an open bar on board and she was travelling premium. Alexis was thankful she coughed up the bucks for the upgrade. She would need an endless fountain of Tanqueray and tonic to cross the Pacific. Bar service in coach would be like travelling in an alcohol-free zone.

She knew she would be entertained on this intrepid journey when she heard the onboard music playing the Cake version of 'I Will Survive'. Smiling at the good omen, she walked down the aisle, containing her Medea-like contrasting emotions.

Buckled in her seat, the suspense-filled *Silence of the Lambs* seemed apt entertainment, even though it ruined fava beans forever. She looked forward to her favourite Hannibal line, 'I do wish we could chat longer, but I'm having an old friend for dinner …'

Could you imagine James turning into such a friend? She shuddered at the thought. No, James would be there and he would be wonderful. The alternative? Well, as Medea attests, hell hath no fury like a woman scorned.

Chapter Seven

Honolulu Rendezvous

Eat	🍴	Haupia (traditional Hawaiian coconut pudding)
Drink	🍷	Royal Chief (coconut wine)
Look	🖼	*Inside the wave* (2012), by Kenji Croman
Listen	♫	'Catch a Wave', The Beach Boys

♥ ♥ ♥ ♥ ♥

'Deadly Hawaii'. At first this sounds surely to be an oxymoron. But consider over one hundred dead tourists in a decade, and it does blow some grey cloud over the typical tropical paradise image in guidebooks.

Drowning is the leading cause of death for visitors to the Hawaiian Islands. Tragedies in Kauai top the list. Why?

According to an investigative report by NBC in 2013,[15] the guidebooks themselves cause part of the problem. Luring visitors to hard-to-reach locations featuring magnificent beauty with turquoise-coloured rock pools that conceal the dangers that lurk within the waves. A local legislator wants guidebook authors to take responsibility for leading tourists to dangerous spots. Is the wave the inherently dangerous object, or the participant in the activity of standing in harm's way?

In year one at law school, arguments about whether it is the person doing the shooting or the gun that is an inherently dangerous object tax the brain. We can safely leave that debate with the capable NRA advocates. Meanwhile, in Hawaii, does the danger of the rogue wave take away its beauty?

'I still remember my first decent photo. I was so stoked to finally get a clear photo from inside the barrel, looking out.' Kenji Croman is a commercial photographer born in the Hawaiian Islands. He is referring, of course, not to the barrel of a gun but rather to the barrel of a wave – much more breathtaking, so to speak, and a lot safer.

He has an impressive portfolio of wave shots from the North and South Shore beaches near Oahu – some might say they are simply mind-blowing. Hawaii can be like that. One just needs to avoid the dangerous places and avoid becoming another statistic.

Arriving in Honolulu again (she had been there several times on layovers), Alexis contemplated buying sunscreen at Duty Free.

To sunscreen or not, that is the question.

Blessed with her father's dark olive skin, Alexis was always a bronzed beauty in summer. Like most around her, she grew up slathering baby oil over her flawless complexion, in order to bake her skin slowly like a suckling pig. These were years prior to warnings of melanomas and skin cancer now commonplace in schools, on beaches and here, now, in Honolulu at the Duty Free counter.

Scanning the multitude of options, Alexis remembered that cool 'song' from the '90s: 'Ladies and gentlemen of the class of '99 … Wear sunscreen. If I could offer you only one tip for the future, sunscreen would be it. The long-term benefits of sunscreen have been proved by scientists …' It was from a column by Mary Schmich in the *Chicago Tribune* that went viral online. It gained notoriety when Baz

Luhrmann combined the words with pictures and glued it together with Zambian dance music performer Rozalla Miller.

Alexis ran through the many life truths of the song – to not read beauty magazines, as they'll make you feel ugly, that you're not as fat as you imagine, and to not worry about the future. Getting on the plane yesterday, she could tick the 'do one thing every day that scares you'. She was never reckless with other people's hearts, and hoped she was not the object of someone who might be reckless with hers. As she juggled a face screen, waterproof option and some good old-fashioned Coppertone Dark, she pulled out her MasterCard – at least she had control over wearing sunscreen. As for controlling her heart – that was out of her hands a while ago.

When she arrived at the hotel, she had a voicemail from James that he left that morning. It was short. 'I am sorry. The service here is pretty bad.' That was it. This was not the first sweet nothing she had hoped for on arrival. In her mind, she had considered where and when she would first meet James, desperately hoping she could 'freshen up' before he saw her for the first time with jet lag.

She imagined he would be at the bar and she would enter. He would stand and saunter over, take her hand, kiss it gently and reach for the bouquet of exotic flowers that needed two hands to carry. He would order her a piña colada, with a fancy umbrella. She would blush and be impressed by her new gentleman friend. They would laugh and get lost in each other's eyes until the bar staff would ask them if they would like to take the next one up to their room, as they wanted to call it a night. But alas, Alexis was solo. There was no James at the bar. She walked past to the front desk.

She asked if James Karlten had checked in. She knew he had not, but wanted any and all information she could get. She wondered if and when she would experience that first date she had dreamt so much about.

'We are not allowed to share information about other guests.' The exotic, strapping young Hawaiian man behind the counter held Alexis's gaze, momentarily distracting her from the purpose of her query.

Alexis tried to avoid staring at the dark biceps protruding from the red hyacinth-patterned shirt, politely explaining that she was meeting a colleague but that he was stuck overseas. She simply wanted to advise that he would not make check-in tonight. Fortunately, she was not overly gaga and was just present and careful enough to avoid saying 'boyfriend'. Imagine if that were truly the case. How would she have explained why on earth they weren't sharing a room? The well-trained Marriot clerk seemed satisfied with her explanation.

'That room booking was cancelled earlier today, miss.'

Alexis forced a gracious Medea smile on the outside. Inside, she was busy biting a huge chunk of cheek and pinning it to the mat in her mouth.

'Excellent news,' she lied. 'I was afraid he'd be paying for a room he'd not be using. Aloha.'

♥ ♥ ♥ ♥ ♥

In the elevator going to her room, she considered at least there WAS a hotel room booking to cancel. It could have been worse with no booking at all. James had planned to be there at some point – the Sri Lankan circumstances just got the better of him.

But really, how much worse could it be? she thought.

After literally weeks of foreplay, this was not the climax she anticipated on her first night in the Islands. It had been a long flight and she was tired and solo. So low, she unpacked her things in zombie mode. The dozen pair of shoes and matching outfits for each, the mood candles, dark chocolate, new lingerie, wine from New Zealand, jasmine and clary sage scented massage oil and one large package of condoms. It was the many years in Girl Guides that ensured she was always prepared.

Unpacking completed, she found it too depressing to stay in the room. It was a pathetic excuse of a room choice. A mistake she'd never have made. Charles needed his head read. The room he should have booked – the one Alexis would have selected had she been assigned the task – would have 180-degree views of the ocean and an expansive lanai to enjoy pre-dinner cocktails and, overall, would have been supersized – a helluva lot bigger than this shoebox!

A few welcome-drink double G and Ts later, at the hotel bar, which was clearly built for hobbits, like her room, she sent James a text:

Hi there, I've arrived in Honolulu safe and sound, just checked in and will unpack before doing some work. It's sort of weird being here and you are not. I see you've cancelled your room booking. I do hope you will be making a new one soon. The flight was fine. I'm a bit tired, so will try to sleep soon.

How's your day? A x

She couldn't have been more sarcastic. She actually didn't give a rat's ass how his day was. She'd have rather heard her Duddly DoRight was strapped to the tracks and the light up ahead was his beloved engine powering full bore ahead, unable to stop. One should be careful what they wish for.

She passed out shortly after taking the other half of an Ambien left over from the flight over.

She wouldn't wake up until lunch the next day.

MSN – 11 November

Alexis Jordain 12:46:23 p.m.
Hey hun, are u there?

James Karlten 12:46:54 p.m.
I am here, baby. I just got your text. How are you?

Alexis Jordain 12:47:11 p.m.
Whoopee! I can text via Skype, great!

James Karlten 12:47:19 p.m.
Yay … LOL. I didn't cancel my booking. They automatically cancel it when you don't show up and take $100 off your credit card. How are you?

Alexis Jordain 12:48:22 p.m.
I'm great after a good sleep. Wow. I was exhausted. I'm working for a bit on a report due tomorrow in NZ, then will venture out to the beach.

James Karlten 12:48:53 p.m.
I saw it, 12 hrs. Wow, did you snore? LOL. Oh, you wouldn't know.

Alexis Jordain 12:49:23 p.m.
Do you snore? What's happening your end?

James Karlten 12:50:18 p.m.
I am doing better now that I've heard from you. I was worried.

Alexis Jordain 12:50:40 p.m.
I sent you a text note last night, but, alas, you were not connected. I knew you would be worried. That's why I Skyped. We talked about you not worrying so much. Have you forgotten? (It was just yesterday …)

James Karlten 12:51:24 p.m.
LOL, I can't help it. I am sorry.

Alexis Jordain 12:52:03 p.m.
It's OK, I worry about you also, but I don't mention it to you. Don't want you worrying about my worrying.

James Karlten 12:52:34 p.m.
LOL, you're getting more hilarious every day. Have you ever considered stand-up comedy?

Alexis Jordain 12:53:00 p.m.
Wait until I'm caught up on my sleep, you won't be able to keep up. So, what are you and the lads up to today? AND how is Mike – what's happening on that front?

James Karlten 12:55:00 p.m.
Nothing really, one of the measurements was wrong apparently, so we have a fragile surface in one of the platforms. We had to work on that today from the top. More importantly, I am waiting on the materials from China.

Mike is good. I need to send him some money ASAP but I have told him to wait till I get out of here in a few days. He needs urgent attention.

Alexis Jordain 12:56:34 p.m.
How is he feeling? He must be out of sorts with all that's happening in the US.

James Karlten 12:57:01 p.m.
He is all right. He keeps asking about you.

Alexis Jordain 12:57:22 p.m.
I think about him often.

James Karlten 12:57:50 p.m.
I am sure you would love him.

Alexis Jordain 12:57:56 p.m.
He should come and explore Hawaii with me. I wonder if his dad will make it?!

James Karlten 12:58:34 p.m.
LOL, don't say that, Alexis. You know how much this means to me.

Alexis Jordain 12:58:57 p.m.
You know I'm kidding, James.

James Karlten 12:59:11 p.m.
How do you like it there? You like the hotel?

Alexis Jordain 12:59:14 p.m.
If you don't arrive in a few days, I'm coming to the jungle to collect you!

James Karlten 12:59:43 p.m.
LOL, I don't want to test you, baby.

Alexis Jordain 12:59:44 p.m.
I've not gone exploring yet. Hotel seems okay. I'm too tall for the beds – you'll be falling off.

James Karlten 12:59:53 p.m.
I miss you.

Alexis Jordain 12:59:59 p.m.
I'm used to a Cali King size.

James Karlten 1:00:05 p.m.
What time is it?

Alexis Jordain 1:00:36 p.m.
I miss you too. It's 2 pm I think (every clock in the room says something different).

James Karlten 1:01:11 p.m.
LOL, right? Yeah, it should be about that time. Have you spoken to the kids? They must miss you already.

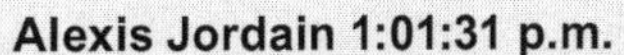

Alexis Jordain 1:01:31 p.m.
Oh, and you know the time??? Really, now that is funny. The girls have a dad's weekend, so they've texted me. I always think of them and vice versa. I am very blessed.

You should be here.

James Karlten 1:07:56 p.m.
I know. I am sorry. I really thought I would be.

Alexis Jordain 1:08:35 p.m.
You better be thinking up lots of ways to make up for all these sorrys, sir.

James Karlten 1:09:15 p.m.
You have no idea what I have planned. Brace yourself, baby.

Alexis Jordain 1:10:10 p.m.
We just need to get you, your plans and me in the same geographic space …

James Karlten 1:10:24 p.m.
That can be arranged. I haven't had a chance to look at the property close to you with all that has been happening, but I really want to buy it.

Alexis Jordain 1:11:33 p.m.
I just learned that the granny flat at the front of the house isn't first right of refusal to owner of the larger unit (house). Not sure that is a goer – I think that is why it hasn't sold yet.

How are you feeling? Other than missing me desperately.

James Karlten 1:13:53 p.m.
I feel very tired and I feel like I've put too much pressure on you over the past few days. I am so sorry.

Alexis Jordain 1:14:41 p.m.
We'll have a good talk when you are here, once you are rested. I seriously feel a million times better with a bit of proper sleep.

James Karlten 1:15:22 p.m.
I can relate. It's hard to sleep under these conditions, plus pressure from the government on the completion of this project.

Alexis Jordain 1:18:02 p.m.
Just breathe, darling. One step at a time, one task at a time. Strengthen the fragile platform and then strengthen your own. I look forward to helping you relax and chill out. It will get finished. You always deliver. Remember that. BTW, how are you going to get here – via England still or??

James Karlten 1:19:21 p.m.
Yes, I still would have to go through England.

Alexis Jordain 1:19:41 p.m.
That is good. You can see Mike.

James Karlten 1:19:42 p.m.
Thank you, baby, your words put a smile on my face. Well, I don't think I am stopping over for too long, considering that I am already late to meet you, but I'll see how it goes.

Alexis Jordain 1:20:53 p.m.
I need to be out of here on Saturday night – a week today. I hope we can spend some time together. It's important for us.

James Karlten 1:21:00 p.m.
I intend to just send him Western Union from Hawaii.

Alexis Jordain 1:21:34 p.m.
I won't be able to stay longer, James. This is already a real push, and I've much work to do while I'm here.

James Karlten 1:21:35 p.m.
Yes, love. I am looking forward to spending time with you, amongst other things.

Alexis Jordain 1:22:43 p.m.
I will focus on work over the next few days and get a lot out of the way.

James Karlten 1:23:30 p.m.
Okay, I completely understand that.

Alexis Jordain 1:23:40 p.m.
I'm going to head out now and get some sun and lunch. I hope all your work goes well today.

James Karlten 1:24:26 p.m.
All right, lovely, I will hit the bed. It was good to catch you here. I love you more than words could describe.

Alexis Jordain 1:24:57 p.m.
Try to sleep in the bed after you hit it.
Sorry, couldn't resist.
Dream of me, us, Hawaii … I love you.

James Karlten 1:25:28 p.m.
LOL, I love you more than you love me.

Alexis Jordain 1:25:47 p.m.
A kiss from sunny Hawaii (and … yeah, right …) :)

James Karlten 1:26:26 p.m.
Thank you babyyyyyyy.

Alexis didn't hear from James the next day, but she was working for most of it anyway. She couldn't believe that she had barely set foot outside.

Tonight she would at least try to make a Hawaiian sunset. Pathetic girl.

It was worth the effort of walking several blocks to finally feel the sand between her toes. So many people mesmerised by the setting sun. So simple. So incredibly beautiful – and it set so fast. Connecting to nature as she did on the beach touched her soul in a new way. The water rebirth provided focus. She wondered what the hell she was doing in this tropical paradise, by herself, catching a short glimpse of such beauty with no one next to her to ooh and ahh with. Holy Jesus.

Back at the hotel, Alexis sent James a text and decided she would no longer spend another day by herself in the godforsaken B-grade room.

Hi James, radio silence – hope all is going well at your end.

I'm nearly finished my mammoth report this end. I'm sending it off done or not done tonight. Last night I couldn't sleep – was up all night. Very frustrating needing to work in Hawaii. Got down to the beach today for sunset though. Lots of romance going on around me. Interesting scenario. Sipped a wine and came back to finish writing. A x

Up early, she went to the pool to enjoy her morning coffee and a croissant from the shop downstairs. Passing the spa on the way by, she thought, *What the heck? I'm on vacation. I will book in for a massage.*

As she sipped on Kona coffee and waited by the pool for her appointment, she considered the financial and emotional wave she was caught inside. She couldn't do much about the bashing her heart was getting. She could, however, try to get some balance, at least financially.

Alexis knew she would feel a bit better with some hard evidence confirming each and every last one of James's six million pounds was safe and sound in that Citibank account. She had all the passwords from their MSN discussion. She could just punch up the details and make sure everything was kosher. That would certainly buy her some surf time in the barrel.

Kicking off Operation London Calling, a small part of Alexis felt guilty for tapping into someone's account without approval. The bigger part of her told that smaller part to get stuffed and grow a pair. She looked up the passcodes, wrote them down, checked and carefully entered the information.

It was there. In black and white. The same transactions that she saw weeks prior. The withdrawal and subsequent deposit details of the botched transfer, voided because of the unknown ISP address and Citibank's security feature. The dates and times were recorded accurately from when Alexis had logged on that first time. Other than one weird date entry where the month and day were transposed and out of sequence, all appeared legitimate. And yes, the account balance remained at a healthy 6,567,003.00 GBP.

Whew. Well, that is something, thought Alexis. *At least he's not siphoned all his money from his account and skipped town without me.*

Speak of the devil. It was James calling on MSN.

MSN – 13 November

James Karlten 1:47:53 p.m.
I miss you so much. I do not know what to do. I spoke to Lee today. He says that they still haven't confirmed the funds in the account and there's nothing he can do. I feel like I am going crazy and I can't do anything about it.

Alexis Jordain 1:48:01 p.m.
Hello, are you there?

James Karlten 1:48:18 p.m.
How's Hawaii? What have you done? Did you make any friends? Yes, I am here. Oh, great, you are here as well.

Alexis Jordain 1:49:06 p.m.
I finished my work last night, so now officially in holiday mode. I cannot believe this predicament. This is such a romantic place.

James Karlten 1:52:23 p.m.
I know, I am so mad at this situation.

Alexis Jordain 1:53:01 p.m.
I'm heading to the beach early today for the sunset. It's spectacular. I caught the end of it yesterday, but today I will sit with a piña colada and watch every minute.

James Karlten 1:54:28 p.m.
I want to be there … I am missing out on so many things, and these stories are not helping either.

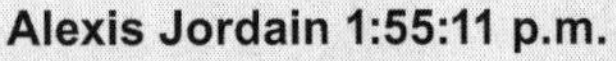

Alexis Jordain 1:55:11 p.m.
If it's any consolation, I hadn't planned on being here on my own.

James Karlten 1:56:42 p.m.
I love you, Alexis. I love you so much. I've never loved anyone the way that I love you. I think about you every second of the day, and I just keep smiling and wishing you were here. I am hoping I'd be there soon. I really want to see you, put my lips on your body, kiss you like I've never kissed anyone else.

I know I would have the most memorable experience. I can't wait to show Mike the pictures.

Alexis Jordain 1:57:50 p.m.
What is the plan at this point?

James Karlten 1:58:24 p.m.
Well, I am hoping the money arrives tomorrow and I'd leave here Wednesday morning.

Alexis Jordain 1:59:01 p.m.
You'd not be here until Thursday. Oh, and there are no funds in my account today either.

James Karlten 2:00:18 p.m.
I was just going to ask you if you checked.

Alexis Jordain 2:00:55 p.m.
This isn't turning out as we'd planned, is it?

James Karlten 2:01:09 p.m.
I will liaise with Madrid in the morning. I am not sure what to do, Alexis. Please be my strength at this point. I need you.

Alexis Jordain 2:02:30 p.m.
I was really hoping to get to know each other a little better.

James Karlten 2:03:45 p.m.
I had great plans as well, but all hope is not lost. I intend to come with you to NZ for a few more days after we leave Hawaii.

Alexis Jordain 2:04:21 p.m.
Sorry, that doesn't work for me. I'm flat out with work, mostly in Christchurch, working weekends to get submissions in to government.

James Karlten 2:05:26 p.m.
Even if I see you 30 mins every day, I wouldn't mind. I know how upset you are with all of this, but I didn't plan for it to happen this way. I am sorry. Are you there, baby?

Alexis Jordain 2:09:31 p.m.
Let's not get into this now. I'm trying to be understanding. I really am. I understand your situation in Sri Lanka. Things just seem pretty one-sided to me, really.

James Karlten 2:10:16 p.m.
I am sorry. I don't want it to seem like I am selfish. I just want to be with you. Please just give me some time to make things right. I don't want to lose you.

Alexis Jordain 2:11:01 p.m.
James, words and actions need to match up for me. So far there have been a lot of words and a lot of promises without a lot of action.

I need to get to know you more than words on a page. I cannot make promises and commitments to someone that I have never met. I have unanswered questions that I need answers to. We started as a fairy tale – I am such a hopeless romantic – I grew intoxicated by your words.

James Karlten 2:13:58 p.m.
This is hard for me as well. Please trust me a little longer. I know how hard it is for you. I am not sure what will happen if I were in your shoes, but I will never take your love for granted, baby.

Don't think about this too deeply. There are so many angles to this, but just trust me a little while longer. Please.

Alexis Jordain 2:16:07 p.m.
I am surprised at my own actions right now. I'm not sure what to think anymore. There are indeed many angles and I've misplaced my protractor.

James Karlten 2:16:45 p.m.
Sigh.

Alexis Jordain 2:17:08 p.m.
Sigh back. You need to finish up there. That is a certainty. I am here until Saturday dinner. Another certainty.

James Karlten 2:17:37 p.m.
I need you on my team. Please don't make this harder than it is already. I need you right now.

Alexis Jordain 2:17:55 p.m.
When in doubt, head to the bar for fancy drinks with little umbrellas.

James Karlten 2:18:11 p.m.
What?

Alexis Jordain 2:18:21 p.m.
Trying to be funny.

James Karlten 2:19:06 p.m.
I need to hear your voice. Can I call you?

Alexis Jordain 2:20:57 p.m.
Argh, you are so frustrating … I cannot believe you are putting it on me that I am making it harder than it is already – seriously???

James Karlten 2:21:54 p.m.
I am sorry. I am not putting it on you. I am not even sure what to say anymore. I don't want to say the wrong things.

Alexis Jordain 2:24:16 p.m.
James, you know I will back you – and I have – the proof is in the action. Remember that. Words are just words. Actions speak volumes. Please don't bust a gut. These circumstances are beyond belief. Nothing can be said to make them any better. Just breathe. And don't forget to smile. If things do work out with us, it's a helluva story. Smile for me, baby.

James Karlten 2:25:18 p.m.
I wish I could. I feel like I've disappointed you in so many ways …

Alexis Jordain 2:26:14 p.m.
It's easy. Lift your cheeks up and flash the pearly whites. I promise you'll feel better. Try it … and clear some messages on your phone! I can never leave a voicemail because others have beat me to it :)

James Karlten 2:27:46 p.m.
I LOVE YOU.

Alexis Jordain 2:28:45 p.m.
I love you too, you big goofball.

James Karlten 2:29:16 p.m.
Send me a picture, can you?

Alexis Jordain 2:29:56 p.m.
I'll try tonight.

Alexis Jordain 2:30:28 p.m.
I'm going to head out now. I've spent too much time in the hotel room as it is with that @#@(#*$ report. Draft is out now though, so yay!

James Karlten 2:30:36 p.m.
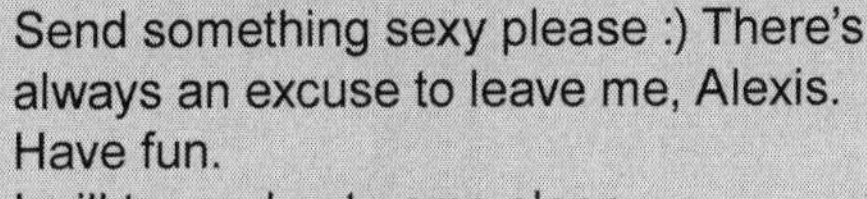
Send something sexy please :) There's always an excuse to leave me, Alexis.
Have fun.
I will try and get some sleep.

Alexis Jordain 2:31:35 p.m.
You are so far off sexy, sweetheart. Don't even get me started ... Sweet dreams.

James Karlten 2:34:01 p.m.
I love you very much.

Alexis finally grew to accept that even if James ever did come to Hawaii, she would have already left. The likelihood of seeing him, even just passing by him in the airport terminal, was slim to none.

Why on earth would he go there now?

James had overstayed his time in Sri Lanka, Mike was affected by Hurricane Sandy and the contract in Spain must surely be almost ready to commence. Slim to none was optimistic when it came to betting odds that Alexis would ever recover this colossal waste of time. She didn't come all this way to be disappointed and leave without a tan. She decided to make the most of her time in Hawaii.

For the final few days, Alexis hit the beach, walked a lot, read beauty magazines and tabloids she knew she shouldn't (they did make her feel insecure) and got a few more massages. As the days passed, the bad taste of the first-date disaster started to transform into a rather enjoyable mini vacation. At least she was catching up on much-needed sleep!

Her attitude toward interactions with James also shifted. When she'd get a text or email from China or Sri Lanka, she'd consider it in a different light. It was just 'stuff' that happened in her day – like having to fill out a customs form upon entry. Just housekeeping matters to deal with and move on from.

On November fourteenth, Lee emailed:

> As you know by now, the bank has confirmed the funds and the materials have been released. I hope to do business with you and your company soon again.

After that, Alexis found herself often turning the phone off or simply leaving it in the room. Sometimes if James rang, and she tired of his banging on, she would simply hang up. It was time that terrible internet connection worked both ways.

Alexis Jordain 8:55:07 a.m.
Hi James, are you there?

James Karlten 9:55:32 a.m.
I am here, baby. What happened to the phone call?

She continued to send James an odd text or MSN, all the while conscious of balancing her desire to give a knockout punch to the only one with keys to the cash kingdom. She had a great deal of cash – borrowed cash – in his business and needed to be careful her jabs did not jeopardise her investment.

On November sixteenth, she texted:

> Hi darling, I'm back in the room to shower and dress for dinner. I have decided to open the bottle of NZ wine I got for you in duty free, and I've already had 1/4 of the chocolate and started using the massage oil. I lit the candles last night then got paranoid the room fire alarm would go off. It was very romantic for about 10 minutes. Just one thing was missing ...

And just when she thought she was on the home stretch, seeing the shoreline from inside the barrel, things with James grew even more thought-provoking.

Alexis was foggy recalling the details of the call as she sipped on another piña colada at the beach bar. It was far tastier than that pathetic bitter Hawaiian coconut wine – bleurgh. She was emotionally exhausted. She felt the injection enter her veins and the warm drug fully take over her hyper nervous system. Like pins and needles of a foot gone AWOL after a long cramp, the dull, stoned headfuck had stormed and overtaken her body.

This should be the national drink of the Islands. They are so yummy, she thought she said to herself, but it could also have been out loud, as, soon after, she found herself conversing with the fella sitting adjacent.

Lucas was a pilot for Air West on a layover from Japan, just trying to watch basketball. Alexis needed an unbiased observer to hear James's latest story and give an honest opinion. Poor unsuspecting bloke.

'So after all the delays in getting the equipment to his site, James thought he would try to make up time by hiring more labourers. Problem was that there was quite a process that Charles, his assistant, had to go through to hire the initial set of local workers. When James tried to speed things up, the latest hires didn't get vetted through the appropriate government process.

'None of the last hires had the correct paperwork when the inspectors came by today. The officials charged a fine for each employment breach, stopped work on the project and were taking the culprits into custody until the matter could be sorted. As the man in charge, James was also held as responsible. Both he and Charles were sitting "in jail" along with a group of labourers when he rang me with his story.

'According to James, he figured that since the project was nearly complete, the local authorities were trying to squeeze the last bit of money out of the "rich foreigners" before they left the country. He needed to pay the fines in order to be released, get the project signed off by officials and at last be paid by the Sri Lankan government.'

'Whew, that's quite a predicament, Alexis,' Lucas remarked, ordering another round before starting into his own 'business in Sri Lanka' story. Lucas knew a guy who knew a guy who did business in Sri Lanka.

'This guy always spoke about how corrupt dealings were and how you'd need to grease the wheels of government to get things done,' the stranger started. 'While your story sounds pretty far-fetched, I dunno.' He shook his head and grimaced. 'It could also be true.'

This was not the answer Alexis wanted to hear.

She, Queen of all the Pollyannas, had exhausted all 'could be true' scenarios and concluded James was full of shit. Diarrhoea. The kind that would take ages to clean off the cream-coloured rug of her life. If Lucas wasn't prepared to say with one hundred per cent certainty the story was total fabricated bullshit, why was she still sitting there? *Geez, I thought we were meant to trust a man in uniform.*

'Could I get the bill, please?' Alexis asked the barman.

'Look, don't worry. I'll cover you. You sound like you could use a bit of good luck. And so does James. Either way, I'd hate to be in your, or his, shoes.' Lucas managed a kind, well-meaning smile. 'Things always work out in the end. Take care, Alexis. It was lovely meeting you, even in such circumstances. Remember everything happens for a reason.'

Who was this guy, Deepak Chopra?

Alexis was grateful that Lucas picked up her tab. In part because it was a really nice thing to do, and she needed some really nice right about now. The other thing was she wasn't sure if the MasterCard that she had slid into her bra was still located in an easy-to-reach place. It might have gone walkabout to her knickers area, had she remembered to put some on. She was desperate to avoid any further humiliation. Feeling herself up in a public place just to find a credit card that may or may not be 'accepted' to pay for her few drinks seemed extreme.

Those drinks helped her get to sleep that night. Another thing she could thank Lucas for: a good night's sleep.

Lucas inspired her so much the night before that Alexis immediately called downstairs to book in for a facial when her wee eyes welcomed the morning light. Today she would do at least one nice thing for herself.

They could only take her right away. Fine. Breakfast could wait. She seized the moment, enjoying ninety minutes of bliss. This was her first facial in what seemed like forever. She loved every minute. It was not quite the couples' treatment she had dreamt of when she and James had discussed it weeks ago. Still, she was grateful for the tremendous talents of today's therapist.

Not feeling much like venturing to Waikiki, she decided to hang at the hotel. She could give it a chance – it wasn't the hotel's fault that El Stupido Charles booked such distant accommodation. Alexis would play hermit by the pool, reading and dozing like a normal tourist. What fun!

Sited on her single lounger, Alexis felt her confidence begin to evaporate.

It seemed she was the recipient of sets of cold stares. First from happy couples giggling above their drinks with fancy umbrellas. Next, several young, catty women, who combined could fit into her one pair of swimming togs. They appeared to be saying with their eyes: 'How pathetic and lonely Alexis is …' Were they wondering how she could be so dumb as to think that James – or any other man of substance – would be interested in her? Alexis was certain that was it. They probably also thought she was mutton dressed as a lamb in that silly bikini, which revealed those horrendous stretch marks and a more-than-ample muffin-top belly. 'Look away … No yummy mummy here,' she wanted to scream!!!

By mid-afternoon, she had created innovative condescending comments from everyone poolside. By late afternoon, she had associated additional criticisms from anyone walking by and/or within those areas inside the hotel that were visible from her deckchair.

She really wasn't feeling very good about herself when she hit the tuck shop on the way back to the hotel room.

Alexis decided not to go out to watch the sunset that night. She had her social interaction yesterday. Tick. Today she turned in early with a six-pack of beer, a bag of candy-coated peanuts, a canister of Pringles, an ice cream sandwich bar and an assortment of three-for-one chocolate bars.

♥ ♥ ♥ ♥ ♥

Alexis felt different when she woke the next day.

Geez, do you think that dinner was a very good idea? She interviewed herself on behalf of her digestive system. But it wasn't just her lack of balance in the five food groups and what she ate. She reviewed the bigger picture in her head. She certainly had enough sleep. Six beers and several ZzzQuil later, she had most certainly covered the sleep angle. But her head felt different, and it was more than the hangover.

Maybe it was the poolside self-flagellation session, she mused. *Or maybe it is the reality of having only another day or so left in glorious, warm and sunny Hawaii.* Her head finally caught up to what her body knew instinctively.

She had to face facts. It was physically impossible for James to fly to Honolulu from Sri Lanka before Alexis got on a plane to leave Hawaii for New Zealand. The conclusion was clear. James wasn't coming. Soon she would return to cold, windy and harsh weather. She would arrive home with nothing, less than nothing. Just a huge hole. Two, actually – one in her heart, the other in her wallet.

What a loser, she chastised herself. *I'll come back dejected, rejected and pasty white.*

Alexis maintained her deficit thinking to conclude there was zero appeal in lying around the beach like a Shake 'n Bake chicken. Thankfully, vanity prevailed in the fallacious notion that brown fat is more attractive than white. She also told herself a walkabout on Waikiki held the appeal of an adventure, concluding the end would justify the means. She would return dejected and rejected, yes, but her lard-ass … it would be golden and brown.

She donned her Sunday-best camo: the beige mesh dress pretending to be a cover-up, her flowery fashionable flip-flops accessorised with functional bear-bell-like GUESS tag, and the most perilous of all the togs she brought – her elegant yet functional LBB (little black bikini). Later she would remember how it got its name – the danger, of course, being in breasts tipping out of said swimming garment. She wished she had brought her military cap and scarf to complete the ensemble.

'Today,' she declared in Che Guevara style, in front of her fans in the Narnia wardrobe behind the full-length mirror, 'I will not heed the advice given to the ladies and gentlemen of the class of '99.'

Alexis gave herself a final front and back stare. She would live to regret not wearing sunscreen on the return flight home. But that's tomorrow's story, not today's. Today, she would defy the odds. Smiling, she strode across the room with fake-it-till-you-make-it confidence and opened the handle to exit the room, only temporarily detained when her arm jammed from that pesky security latch that was still poking out. Austin Powers, anyone? Behave.

Safely out the door, she walked – no, marched – the blocks down to the beach. She was owning dem bitches, step by step, breaking stride only to wait for the little green man at crosswalks (no point in dying en route to the adventure).

Today Alexis (code name Bear Grylls) would explore the most dangerous and less beaten paths of Waikiki Beach. She would lunge and dash to catch iron gates as they closed, managing to enter just before the hidden hideaways disappeared and were lost forever. Her daring quest would take her into and out of 'private beach' areas and 'hotel guests only' zones.

With each step, Alexis felt her soul start to reconnect to her consciousness. *It will be okay,* she told herself. She would find a way through this. She didn't know how, but with the sun shining on her back and water lapping at her heels, she was glad to come to the realisation the James fiasco was real, not a dream. She was well and truly duped. Admitting it was the first step in her healing process. That was something. The something else was the silver lining that came with the admission. The unexpected gift with purchase wrapped in the uniform of an Air West captain – well, that was just plain unexpected.

'Alexis? Alexis?'

Did she just pass a seemingly familiar face, or was her subconscious thought trying to wake her out of her daydream? Her brain chided, *You know no one in Waikiki.* She dismissed the voice and kept on.

It repeated, but more deliberately.

'Alexis! Alexis!'

She thought, *Oh dear, now I am hearing voices!* She turned and looked back. Filtering visible cues, her brain connected the dots.

'Lucas? Oh my God.' She had forgotten she did know one person in Waikiki. 'What are the chances, right?' Alexis was thrilled to see his smile and welcoming glance. 'Aren't you a friendly face amongst this sea of unknown tourists? How are you?'

'We just got in from Japan last night.' Lucas's compassionate face warmed Alexis more than the sun. 'I'm a bit tired, but hate to waste the day, so I went for a walk to clear the head. How have you been?'

Alexis was determined not to bore her new acquaintance with the messy and embarrassing details of no-show James. She was also thankful that Lucas was too much of a gentleman to ask. They exchanged pleasantries about Hawaii's perfect weather and skited about the piña coladas and amazing fish tacos. Alexis mentioned she was due to return to New Zealand the day after tomorrow.

'A few of the pilots I flew over with are meeting up at five o'clock tonight for drinks. We are going to that same bar we met at. They're really nice guys. I think you should come. I told them about you on the way over, and you'll have a nice time if you join us.'

Alexis never expected an invitation. *Does he feel sorry for me from the other night?* She reasoned with herself. *But it would be lovely to watch the sunset and sip on piña coladas in company other than my usual Nelly-no-mates manner. Last night was surely nothing to write home about. But what would I possibly have to say to three pilots?* On the other hand, she remembered, I did say I wanted an adventure today.

'Thanks so much for the invitation, Lucas. Let me see how I go this afternoon. I still have a few work things to finish,' she lied. 'I might see you tonight, but if not, have a safe journey home.'

Alexis wanted to hedge her bets just in case she lost her nerve once her head had a chance to do the maths of three pilots + one chick = ??? She leaned in for a departure hug and Lucas complied with a genuine back pat. They parted, and, after a few paces, Lucas called back to her.

'I really think you should come tonight.'

Alexis turned, smiled and kept walking.

On the walk back to HQ, she swung her Naval Special Warfare Command-issue flip-flops slowly as her mind ticked over the serendipitous events of the day. *What a sweet guy,* she thought. What were the chances of meeting up with Lucas again? Waikiki Beach wasn't exactly small. She knew Lucas was happily married. She also felt like his daughter, in that he was telling his co-pilots about this lovely woman he met. Surely he wouldn't introduce her to a bunch of piranha guys, not his daughter, and not given he knew her Sri Lanka story. She put the possible meet cute to one side and continued on her walk. Today was turning into an adventure for sure.

Alexis slowly scanned The Edge of Waikiki bar, trying not to make an entrance by jamming her floral stilettos in the uneven pavement. Her matching brown-and-fuchsia seventies-style halter dress contrasted with the patrons' attire. She could have got away with a t-shirt and sandals, not the four full outfit changes, three shoe-pairing options, two hairstyles and a partridge in a pear tree make-up session. She knew she would nearly miss the sunset when she left the miles-away Marriot (cheap suit shite James). Now she feared, at well past five o'clock, that her trio of flyboys had flown the coop without her.

She would not walk around the bar twice, she told herself. In the final arc of loop one, she considered she would still stay, with or sans pilots. Piña coladas would be her friends. Changing focus to find a single stool at the bar, or considering a total possible bail, she caught sight of Lucas and an older fella perched near the pool's side tables.

'Lucas, there you are.' Alexis casually sauntered over, conducting her own pre-flight check: undercover tongue licking stray lipstick from teeth – check, boobs safely in dress – check, panties safely in … she smiled, remembering tonight Grylls was going commando. Chuckling aloud at the thought, she playfully said, 'What took you so long?'

'Alexis, we were afraid you weren't going to show. We were nearly out the door for dinner.' The trio got acquainted, sharing stories of their various holiday homes, recreational vehicles and flight attendants. She would later learn pilots always had something to say on this latter topic.

'What have you done with your other co-pilot, Lucas?' Alexis asked, remembering he mentioned two would be joining him for drinks.

With perfect army precision, right on cue, Jack appeared. He was absent when she first approached the group and, upon joining, immediately stole the show. He was funny and charming and markedly less arrogant than Bill, who couldn't stop referring to all his acquisitions: chattels and, from the way he referred to them, women. With Jack, though, there was a playful attraction. His dark brown eyes hinted at a sincerity and sexuality at the same time – not in a weird and creepy way; he seemed genuine and friendly and deep. It would be months later before Jack would confess how, even before speaking to her that night, her regal and self-confident poise attracted him as she sat, this beautiful stranger, alongside his newfound friend and co-pilot.

Alexis had turned down the group's kind offer to join them for dinner. Even Bear would not hike in high heels down the Waikiki strip for steak and chips at a sports bar. That, plus she didn't fancy playing the only female role in the current blockbuster: *Conductor of the Charming Testosterone Trio*. Jack seemed truly disappointed, but perhaps not nearly as much as Lucas.

'At least give Alexis your phone number, Jack,' he prodded.

'Who is this guy?' thought Alexis. 'My love guardian angel as well as dad?' Jack had already made a passing reference about coming back to the bar if Alexis would still be there. He suggested they might meet up for a drink after dinner.

As he dictated his cell number to Alexis, the heat of Jack's breath landed on her shoulder. Perched to ensure Alexis entered it correctly, she suspected he was actually conducting his own cleavage check. It would be the first of several that night.

♥ ♥ ♥ ♥ ♥

Alexis knew Jack was a pilot. He was on a layover (operative part being 'lay'). She was not a one-night-stand kind of girl. She quickly set aside any reservations and negative connotations in favour of 'living in the now' (Eckhart Tolle would have been proud).

From the moment the handsome stranger returned from dinner and found her waiting at the bar until they parted a dozen hours later, the pair was inseparable and intricately connected.

They talked non-stop and effortlessly, like old friends. They laughed – both with a similar quick wit and sarcastic nature. They shared an incredible intimacy and bond that was palpable. When seeking refuge from an unexpected light shower, the pair ended up under a fairy-lit gazebo at some random private party.

Continuing the adventure, now amongst the strangers, Alexis and Jack fit in like an old married couple. The onlookers assessed their 'couple status' at well over a decade, as Alexis and Jack bullshitted facts to support some cockamamie 'how I met your mother' story. They veiled their mere hours' history with two Oscar-winning performances.

Of course, there was alcohol involved: several piña coladas, assorted beers and the carefully selected New Zealand Pinot gris in Alexis's hotel room. The pair would make jokes about who invited whom to taste that last unopened bottle. The only thing left that was still waiting for James.

Later that evening (or rather early morning), the ceremonious consumption of the said bottle was the final challenge for pilot Indiana Jones before he enjoyed the lost temple between Alexis's legs. She felt it fitting that this perfect gentleman, who carried her shoes on their walk on the beach, opened the door for her and walked her home, aptly positioned on the street side (lest a horse-drawn wagon spray muck on her beautiful gown), would now end the torment and suffering of her James-induced coma.

The way Jack engaged Alexis made her feel wanted, not only physically (God knew it had been ages) but also with the intensity of his kisses, his touch, the way he made her feel alive. As a woman, she felt vindicated.

She told herself she *was* desirable, someone *did* find her attractive, she *was* lovable and had something to offer. She was not just the loser and the victim that James had led her to become. Jack found a crack in Alexis's armour, sufficient to summon within her the strength to let go of James. To stop waiting. To eat the chocolates and light the candles and wear the sexy lingerie she was saving. To reclaim Alexis Jordain.

His caress was firm but delicate, full of emotion, as he pulled back the bedclothes to climb inside more than her B-grade bedsheets. Alexis had made so many mistakes in the lead-up to this encounter. She would not diminish this new lease on life as a one-night stand.

She enjoyed the company of this stranger over and over that night. It was a magical dream, and the perfect end to one amazing, mind-blowing adventure of a day. This final encounter was the turning point in what had been absolutely the very worst possible trip to Hawaii one could ever imagine. Well, aside from shark attack or drowning.

Jack was gone the next day when Alexis managed to climb out of bed. She was happy performing her morning ritual, recalling the events of the past twenty-four hours. She was also excited as she and Jack had made plans to meet for an early dinner. Jack would fly out later that evening.

The next morning, she woke up big time. With no Jack to distract her, Alexis knew she needed to get organised. Today was home time. It was time to put away her toys and wash her hands and tell her children that Mummy was coming home.

She called Wellington to confirm her return arrangements and to check in with the girls. In the middle of the conversation, James appeared online.

Was he stalking? Just waiting for her to light up on MSN? Her anxiety grew as her patience diminished.

MSN – 17 November

James Karlten 1:27:28 a.m.
Hey baby, this situation has become a roller coaster. Please call me when you get a chance. I can't get through to you. I've no one else to talk to. I love you.

James Karlten 10:06:57 a.m.
Hello, baby. Are you there?

Alexis Jordain 10:07:14 a.m.
Yes, just talking to my girls right now.

James Karlten 10:07:28 a.m.
Are you okay?

Alexis Jordain 10:07:49 a.m.
Yes. How are things with you?

James Karlten 10:08:40 a.m.
Not too great. I was hoping you would call me.

Alexis Jordain 10:09:11 a.m.
I was going to ring after speaking to the girls.

James Karlten 10:09:21 a.m.
Okay.

Alexis Jordain 10:09:39 a.m.
What's happening now?

James Karlten 10:09:59 a.m.
I miss you. I don't know what to say to you.

Alexis Jordain 10:10:35 a.m.
Well, I figured out you aren't coming to Hawaii. I have to leave.

James Karlten 10:11:50 a.m.
I have a tough predicament here. I am not sure you will ever forgive me.

Alexis Jordain 10:12:13 a.m.
What's happening now?

James Karlten 10:13:49 a.m.
Well, I am kind of in a dead end.

Alexis Jordain 10:14:00 a.m.
Why?

James Karlten 10:14:38 a.m.
I have not been getting any more cash. And I can't leave here either, they won't let me.

Alexis Jordain 10:15:18 a.m.
You need to ask Charles's partner.

James Karlten 10:16:08 a.m.
It's more complicated than you think. She's deaf.

Alexis Jordain 10:16:20 a.m.
Why? What r u not saying?

James Karlten 10:18:21 a.m.
I am saying everything.

Alexis Jordain 10:21:38 a.m.
Okay, off the phone now.

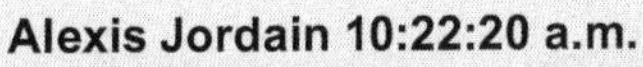

Alexis Jordain 10:22:20 a.m.
So Charles's partner is deaf. I'm sure she has technology that can work with phones. I do work for the Foundation.

There is still no cash in my account, so I cannot do anything either.

James Karlten 10:24:27 a.m.
Well, I don't know how Charles communicates with her, but it's pretty hard on him. Did you get the 5K from China?

Alexis Jordain 10:25:22 a.m.
Yes.

James Karlten 10:25:51 a.m.
Okay, can you help with that?

Alexis Jordain 10:26:24 a.m.
That's already been swallowed up. I had a 20k bill plus mortgage to pay, remember?

James Karlten 10:26:33 a.m.
Okay.

Alexis Jordain 10:27:07 a.m.
I have a flexi loan that I've overdrawn on – the bank is not happy.

James Karlten 10:28:25 a.m.
Yeah, you said that. I am working on how to get that to you by next week.

Alexis Jordain 10:29:27 a.m.
James, I know you are in a pickle right now. How will you manage to come through on the other 110k +? At least if that money came through I could move things around, get some cash to Mike etc.

Is it still just the 5k per person you are looking for? If so, Madrid may be your only option.

James Karlten 10:32:31 a.m.
I am confused. I don't know what to do. I have never been in such a horrible position before.

I basically need $25,000 to get out of this mess. This is absolute rubbish. I can't believe my ends are so loose. I could never imagine being in this position in my life, ever.

I just need some time alone. I need to figure out what to do.

Alexis Jordain 10:34:14 a.m.
Keep it simple. Get the $ from Madrid to me. I will transfer $ to Sri Lanka to pay for the guys & Charles, and send $ to Mike. Unless you have another source of $ not in UK – anything in USA? You said you have a friend in Canada. Can he help?

James Karlten 10:35:50 a.m.
I don't know when Madrid is going to come through. I can't afford to mount any pressure on them because I've not done any job. It was supposed to be mobilization money.

I spoke to them and they say they having a bit of a mobilization problem and they will let me know as soon as it is sorted out.

Alexis Jordain 10:37:04 a.m.
Well, if it's not tomorrow, I'm on a plane, so there will be a delay.

James Karlten 10:37:25 a.m.
My friend in Canada, Richardson, he's the one in England at the moment and he helped with the 15k.

James Karlten 10:37:54 a.m.
Is there anything you can do at all?

Alexis Jordain 10:38:03 a.m.
Absolutely skinned. I've even got cash advances on my credit card, which is now near the limit. I've never been in this position – it is the worst thing ever for me. I am so worried about my responsibilities for my kids and home. And I'm sitting in Hawaii wasting more money I don't have. It's all pretty unbelievable.

James Karlten 10:40:05 a.m.
Don't worry too much. I got you covered as soon as I leave here.

Alexis Jordain 10:41:02 a.m.
No offence, darling, but how can I be certain of that, all things considered?

James Karlten 10:41:14 a.m.
Oh wow … Well, that's okay, Alexis. I will go now and talk to you later.

Alexis Jordain 10:42:01 a.m.
All right.

James Karlten 10:43:02 a.m.
I don't want this to come between us. You mean everything to me.

Alexis Jordain 10:44:49 a.m.
I've given you everything I have, James, my heart, my time, my love, my finances. I've put you first ahead of everything else to give this a real try. I set aside my fears and insecurities and jumped in with both feet. It's all so surreal now.

I hope you figure out what to do, James. You are a clever man and I know you will. It sounds like you need to go now, so good luck with everything. I will hear from you when you are ready to speak again. Go well, darling, A x

James Karlten 10:47:00 a.m.
I am sorry. I need you here with me. I don't want to lose you. It seems like I've taken all the wrong decisions and I don't even know the right ones anymore.

Mike is there in dire need and I can't even get him help. I am just helpless at the moment and I am losing my grip.

Somewhere between Charles's deaf wife, the delayed mobilisation payment from Madrid, 101 ways to recycle five thousand pounds, London Calling Mike, who was running from Sandy, and James needing a $25,000 USD get-of-jail-free card, Alexis developed a screaming headache. Not the perfect state for plane travel halfway across the world.

Drugs were her only saviour. Lots of drugs. She examined the daily limits for Tylenol, Advil and paracetamol, created an equation that factored in travelling forward in time to New Zealand and tried to focus. She had a plane to catch and hadn't started packing.

In the taxi heading to the airport, she chuckled, sending James one last middle finger salute from Honolulu:

> I've just been to the front desk and found out the hotel wasn't paid for in advance. This situation just keeps getting better. I really hope my card works on check-out. BTW I'd never use this hotel again. It's at best two star. Aloha.

Alexis had travelled a lot in her life, but boarding today was probably the most welcome. She felt her encounter with Jack was not her last, and made a mental note to send lovely Lucas a thank-you card for his gentle prompting.

Her adventure complete, she buckled in for the long journey home. She had not only faced the barrel but also managed to turn herself around to ride it. Catching the wave, she really was sitting on top of the world.

'Take me home—' She stopped short. That bastard nearly stole that too. Alexis continued, 'Take me home … James.'

What a crack-up, she thought. He would not take one more thing from her.

Ever again.

'G and T, thanks.'

Chapter Eight

Like Father, Like Son, Like Really?

♥ ♥ ♥ ♥ ♥

The globe is littered with places as testament to the human desire to explore uncharted territory, whether in search of treasure and wealth or new lands or to satisfy the simple curiosity to explore something more 'out there'.

L'Anse aux Meadows, at the tip of Newfoundland, is home to the earliest European settlement in the New World. The UNESCO World Heritage Site contains evidence of timber-framed turf buildings in the excavated remains of an eleventh-century Viking settlement – the earliest and only known site established by Vikings in North America.

Not much of this early Scandinavian connection is mentioned in history class growing up in Canada. Instead, contradictory cultural clichés of savage Vikings or noble warriors limit one's greater appreciation of the Viking legacy.

Norway, one of the Viking homelands, for example, is famous for inventing the ostehøvel, or cheese slicer, in the 1920s. The brunost, or brown caramelised whey cheese (quite similar to fudge), is popular with locals but an acquired taste for foreigners. A little more popular is akvavit, or 'water of life', a staple feature since the fifteenth century. Important at festive celebrations, like Christmas, Easter and weddings, it's reputed to ease digestion of rich foods – helping that pickled herring or smoked fish to 'swim down to the stomach'.

Akvavit is distilled like vodka but flavoured with herbs, spices or fruit oil, such as caraway. Often a yellowish hue, it can take on a darker brown colour if aged longer in new barrels, or be clear if aged in old casks. Olav Engelbrektsson, the last Roman Catholic Archbishop of Norway, received a gift of akvavit in 1531 from the Danish Lord of Bergenhus castle, who sang its medicinal praises: 'a help for all sorts of illness which a man can have both internally and externally'. Yes, you can imagine the poster featuring the strapping Viking male: akvavit vodka for health.

Being in remote northern climes most certainly influences the food and beverage palate, but what of its influence on the Norwegian art palette?

Edvard Munch, Norwegian painter, described the landscape and nature inspiration for one of his most famous works on January twenty-second, 1892: 'One evening I was walking along a path, the city was on one side and the fjord below. I felt tired and ill. I stopped and looked out over the fjord – the sun was setting, and the clouds turning blood red. I sensed a scream passing through nature; it seemed to me that I heard the scream. I painted this picture, painted the clouds as actual blood. The colour shrieked. This became *The Scream*.'

It may be slight ignorance to not know of Munch's Norwegian heritage, but to be unaware of several other significant aspects of his famous print is more than a little embarrassing.

First, take for example the fact that the original isn't the black-and-white print sold in contemporary Art for Art's Sake shops but rather colourful, luminous combinations of various media, including oil paints, pastels and crayon. Second, there are four versions, produced between 1893 and 1910. The first painting is a favourite, featuring a

CSI-like murder scene with nature seriously kicking human butt in the nature–human saga. Third, who knew Munch named his works *Der Schrei der Natur* (*The Scream of Nature*)? The scene is more about the surroundings and the psychological impact of nature – perhaps reflective of his manic-depressive sister, Laura Catherine, a patient at the asylum nearby.

The main works remain in Oslo, but the fourth pastel version (1895) was sold at Sotheby's for $119,922,600 in 2012. Not bad for some Viking descendant from the Norse (north). Go Munch!

♥ ♥ ♥ ♥ ♥

The approach to windy Wellington was typical. As they commenced descent, swaying back and forth, up and down, Alexis remembered the regular commute she'd make to Sydney's sunny shores, most often on the red-eye.

Some trips were for work; most were to visit the investment funds manager she fell in love with. The long-distance relationship lasted several years, and the pair clocked up many air miles both sides of the ditch. He was a typical ballsy, obstinate, opinionated but very loving Aussie. It remained a mystery which of them coined his nickname, 'Hurricane'. She did remember, however, Hiatt's lyrics to 'Loving a Hurricane', which, at this particular point in her journey, hit home, so to speak:

The whole foundation just went flying round past her…
She might have known you'd get her sooner or later
Livin' in that trailer park down by the sandy beach
Where tides roll in like the dream generators
Forces of nature, blow everything out of reach …

Hiatt had been a favourite of Alexis's from the first time she heard him sing 'Feels Like Rain' in a movie soundtrack. Today, she did not appreciate her resemblance to the object in his hurricane's reckless path.

♥ ♥ ♥ ♥ ♥

'Was he everything you'd dreamt he would be, Mum?' asked Bella.

At home, Alexis would keep up a brave face. She smiled and said,

'Darling, everyone's dreams come true in Hawaii – it's paradise there. I can't wait to tell you all about it, but now let's get ready for school.'

She had work commitments to attend to that next morning. She would also have to report back to Oliver and Edie, both of whom she'd avoided pretty much the whole time she was in Hawaii. They had agreed to meet for a coffee debrief early that morning.

Alexis really did not have time for the MSN update from James with the never-ending Sri Lankan saga, though part of her was curious about the new angles he was able to connect in his imagination.

She put in a holding-pattern response and drove off to meet the gang at Maranui.

She needed to soak in the energy from the bays to collect her thoughts and get the story straight – she wasn't sure how much she would, could or should share.

She felt she had been most irrational now, back in the cold light of day.

MSN – 20 November

James Karlten 1:50:37 a.m.
The last couple days have been very onerous. We've a bit of a situation here. I've been able to raise $30,000. Charles's partner was able to raise $15,000, and they are still not bending. They want the complete thing. I am doing my best to get out of this situation, especially because of you. I know how desperately you need cash.

I've tried to call you a number of times as well. You haven't answered the phone. Most of the time, I am exhausted, especially with Charles still locked up for several days now. I am almost handicapped. I am on the verge of breakdown.

I love you, Alexis. A lot more than you can even imagine. I will never take your feelings for granted or make you look like an idiot. You gave me everything, no reservation, no second thoughts. Even though people tried to discourage you, you still trusted me. That's the kind of love any man would die to have, so don't think for one second that I will let you go.

I love you.

Please Alexis, if there's anything you can do, anything at all, just let me know. I will really appreciate it. P.S. DON'T LET ANYONE YOU KNOW EVER COME TO SRI LANKA.

Alexis Jordain 7:24:51 a.m.
Good morning, James. Thank you for your notes. It's so difficult, I know, but I'm glad things are getting closer at least with Charles's partner. I haven't been not answering your calls, they just don't seem to make it through. Whenever I ring you it goes to voicemail. I will say some prayers for more money and let's try to speak on the phone today. Love you, Alexis x

James Karlten 7:50:12 a.m.
Hello baby, I've just tried to call you again, but still no response. I miss you. I can't believe I haven't heard your voice in more than 3 days. I miss you so damn much, like a part of me is missing. I love you, Alexis, I really do, from the bottom of my heart. I've loved no one else like this.

I hope we get to talk today.
I will try to stay awake till you can phone me.

♥ ♥ ♥ ♥ ♥

Lucas's comments about Sri Lanka unsettled Alexis enough for her to yet again seek enlightenment from Mr Google.

Beyond the underlying corruption, there was a bit about tourist scams and internet fraud, but nothing terribly new, exciting or relevant.

Like many poor countries, it had credit card scams. The old ATM fraud where pairs of scammers hit tourists – one watching the PIN keys while the other tapped your shoulder saying 'you've dropped something' as the first stole your card. And then there was a version of the 'Teacher or Student Scam', which Alexis experienced first-hand travelling to the Forbidden City in Beijing.

In China, two young and attractive 'students' wanted to walk with Alexis and her companion, not wanting any money but rather to simply practise speaking English. Nearing their destination, the girls mentioned how they were art students and that right nearby they and their friends had an exhibit where today there was a special promotion to sell their paintings. They emphasised how much the school and students needed funds and said they would ensure the tourists got a good price. They stopped into the 'gallery' on the main street.

The shop featured dozens of beautiful wall hangings, some large, some small. All very well made. However, once inside, the girls locked the door, saying this way they would not be interrupted by other tourists and could have first choice of anything for sale.

On cue, as the door lock clicked shut, several men came out from the curtains and the hard sell started. Sensing trouble, Alexis's companion took the lead, communicated they had no money with them and skillfully negotiated an exit without altercation. Disaster averted. Barely. Driving to meet her friends for brunch, Alexis thought, *Where is my clever companion now?!*

♥ ♥ ♥ ♥ ♥

Maranui made the best coffee in Wellington. For Alexis, it was her office.

She spent several hours there each day when writing her thesis, and often arranged to meet clients there for lunch. They enjoyed the stunning 180-degree view over raucous Lyall Bay. The staff were the best ever, always funny and interested, and gave great service. The food was brilliant and healthy with good-sized portions. All in all, two thumbs up.

She was the first to arrive and got a table. Gazing at the crashing waves, Alexis felt she had her head under water, having been caught off guard when the funnel collapsed upon her. Would she become the next drowning victim? How would she ever get her money back?

Oliver and Edie arrived about the same time and scanned the café, anxiously looking for Lexi as if she were four years old and lost in some clothing rack at the department store.

Smiling and waving frantically, Alexis caught their eyes, stood up and simultaneously lost any resolve acquired in the drive over. The movement immediately activated a downpour of tears that made Niagara Falls recoil in shame at its mere trickle.

Wrapped up in the safety of her three-way whanau support, the next few minutes (which seemed the duration of a one-act play to their circling waitress, desperate for an appropriate 'in') consisted of four Kleenex tissues filled with nose-blow snot, two cloth hankies (compliments of Oliver and which would now be binned due to the bad juju of Alexis's bitter JC tears) and a riff of dozens of 'bastard' and 'fuckwit' sets from Edie (whose profanities, in retrospect, probably qualified her positively in a Tourette's assessment).

'Coffee?' the patient Maranui angel sheepishly edged in.

'YES, please,' the trio pealed in unison. It was too early for drowning sorrows. First order of the day, get the goss.

Alexis tentatively began her story in the safety of Oliver and Edie's loving ears. She would recap how it started and why she was so affected after such a short time, almost seeking answers herself as to how she got into the present situation through the retelling.

'For a start, I told myself that he loved me just the way I was. He had never set eyes on me, so he wasn't mesmerised by my beauty

– ha ha. He didn't know if I was successful in business or had a lot of wealth. It was also so important to me that this man could see me for more than the 'tits and ass' that Mommy Dearest taught us was the sum total of a woman's worth. He didn't know I lived in a big house on the beach in New Zealand's paradise. These were massive issues for me. He loved me without ever having slept with me! He hadn't even really alluded to sex! He was mine, hook line and sinker, even before I had a chance to bedazzle him face-to-face with my charms.'

Oliver gently held Alexis's hand. 'He scratched that itch of total belonging for you, sweetie. He gave you affection, acceptance and that unconditional love we all crave.'

In a most un-ladylike manner, Alexis slurped up the accumulated snot in her running nose and redirected the runaway streams down her face into the sopping wet serviette. Edie handed her a new one. 'Take this and blow your fucking nose. It's gross and you look awful.'

Lexi took Edie's loving message in the spirit it was given, but Oliver defended her.

'No one is attractive when they're crying. C'mon, girlfriend, let it out. Keep talking.' Oliver threw a dagger at Teflon Edie, who didn't register she might be remotely insensitive. Alexis continued.

'I really thought I knew him! We had spoken on the phone and corresponded by text, email and MSN messenger. I felt I had a reasonable overview of his business, followed him across the globe in his international travel, provided advice on the various trials and tribulations he encountered running his company. We had so many common interests. I love transport and trains and international commerce. He was romantic and attentive and never demanded anything of me.'

'His story was tragic but tender: a widower of six years,' Oliver added.

'Eight. And yes, with the bonus of no ex to contend with,' Edie chimed in.

'He was raising his only son, a dashing if somewhat awkward-looking boy, tucked under the shoulder of his doting dad. His deep belief in God and higher purpose in life was comforting, and that he was getting set to retire meant just on the horizon was plenty of time for us to build a relationship, relax and enjoy the spoils of decades of hard work. He wanted to share this life with someone … me. This loving, kind, intelligent man chose me! And all this BEFORE having slept with me. I felt like the luckiest person on the planet – my first online dating encounter was the only one I'd ever need. Fate dealt a match made in heaven in the first hand – how amazing! Incredible!'

'Well, incredible is exactly what it was, Lex,' began Edie. 'Let's break it down. "Incredible" is from the Latin, *in-* meaning "not" and *credibilis* meaning "believable". Put together, ah, yes, that makes sense: not believable! The story is so implausible that it is unbelievable! Now here you sit, like hell in a handbasket! The whole romantic tale was just that – on course for disaster from the very beginning. And it got there fast – the deterioration was so rapid it only took mere weeks!'

Alexis corrected Edie. 'Don't you mean "hell in a handbag?"' The group chuckled. Sweet Alexis was always mixing her metaphors. Thankfully, good friend Edie, crossword queen, was able to set her straight. She could lecture on an entire topic without taking a breath. They needed a diversion from the Alexis kamikaze dive-bomb.

'Actually,' Edie began, '"Hell in a handbasket" is a phrase most often used in America, where movies popularised handbaskets as the catcher's mitt for guillotined heads of criminals whose souls were "headed" straight to hell – pardon the pun. This is not to be confused with Monty Python's "bring out your dead" wagon, where these souls could go either north or south. The earliest print reference related to an imaginary decapitated head is in Samuel Sewall's diary, 1714. Sewall was born in England but emigrated to America at age nine. Naturally, the Americans claim it as their own, but most likely the phrase originated in England, where the thought of wheeling sinners to hell was common from the seventeenth century. There is a mediaeval stained-glass window at Fairford Church in Gloucestershire showing a woman being carried off to purgatory in a wheelbarrow pushed by a blue devil.'[16]

'Well, no matter how you get there, the destination sure feels the same – clearly I've arrived in hell!' Alexis gave one last sniff and blow and tossed the last dead-soldier tissue into the empty tulip cup.

Leaving Maranui, Alexis realised that the time change and jet lag didn't seem to affect her as much as the crashing comprehension of the amount of money she had loaned James. It was difficult to focus on work being tired, having had a grilling from Oliver and Edie and now getting home to find a new angle on matters – a note from Michael. The son.

Now, this is unexpected, thought Alexis. *The boy is in on the action – WTF?*

From: Michael Karlten
To: Alexis Jordain
Sent: Tuesday, 20th November, 10.12 a.m.
Subject: Hello Alexis

Good morning, Mom (I don't know if it is okay if I call you Mom yet, but I feel very comfortable calling you this already).

I hope you are doing very well. Dad gave me both your number and your email address, but I thought it was better to email you, as I know you are very busy. I was hoping to get a chance to talk to you when Dad was back home in Jersey, but each time we tried to call, there wasn't any answer.

How was your trip to Hawaii? Dad told me what happened. I hope you can find it in your heart to forgive him. He speaks very fondly of you. Like he has never done with anyone else. He is a passionate man, and, to be honest, I've never seen him this happy. He says you made it so easy to love you, and I won't have a problem loving you too. He doesn't stop talking about you.

I'm happy for both of you. He truly deserves a good woman, because he is a good man. I am sure you know that already. Sometimes I think he's too nice and people take advantage of him. I miss him as I talk about him now. I just can't wait until I see you two.

Dad says you might be able to help me with some money to cover my ticket and some other bills I've incurred during my stay here, but I don't want to bother you, especially with all that happened in Hawaii, and the process of transferring the money all the way from Australia. It might take too long to get here, so I will just wait till Dad gets here.

Whatever you both do, never stop loving each other. It's important.

Have a good day. Greetings from London.
Mike

It was the first direct contact she'd had with Mike. Alexis once tried to speak to him on the phone when James was in Jersey, but it was a weird connection and his voice was incomprehensible. He sounded like Daffy Duck – like he was speaking through some voice-altering device. Alexis had seen these gadgets used in movies, like when a kidnapper calls to set the ransom drop or when secret agents disguise themselves to hide their identity.

So Michael, the lovely prodigal son, is now in on the action.

It was possible that Michael did send the note. He assumed Australia and New Zealand were the same place, a plausible teenage faux pas AND very American – but his dad knew the difference and had commented prior. This was good. But what teenager calls their dad 'passionate' or gives relationship advice when he's surely still a virgin and – judging by the picture – quite possibly never even been kissed!?!

Alexis set out to catch the James 'mini-me' thief.

From: Alexis Jordain
To: Michael Karlten
Sent: Tuesday, 20th November, 8.12 p.m.
Subject: Re: Hello Alexis

Good morning, Mike, what a lovely surprise to get your email first thing this morning!

Things must have been pretty crazy in Jersey before you left. What a devastating situation for all concerned. I hope things are starting to resume normality (all things considered). When Christchurch had the series of big quakes last year here in New Zealand (and they continue) the mood of everyone was affected – so low and despondent. I hope NY bounces back more easily, given the greater resource base.

I asked your dad to give you my contact details because I know it's important you get back to school, particularly given Christmas is just around the corner, and you mustn't have many weeks of school left. We don't know how long the Sri Lanka mess is going to take to sort, so I propose that we at least get you a plane ticket back home as a start. Would you be able to organise the flight through an agent and then get them to invoice me to my email so I can charge the fare to my credit card – at least we won't need to cause delay with money transfers, and we can get you some certainty of getting back to NJ. Hopefully we can sort the rest over the next few days.

It's been a most challenging time, as you can imagine. Hawaii was meant to be a paradise rendezvous, not the storyline for a melodrama. Still, first things first, let's get you back to school and then sort your dad.

I hope you've been okay in London on your own. You dad said Richard (??) was there from Canada for a while. I hope you two were able to catch up. I must see my girls off to school now and then get to work myself, so I'd better jump in the shower quick smart.

I look forward to hearing from you, Mike. Thanks for making contact, and we shall speak soon.

Warm regards
Alexis ☺

From: Michael Karlten
To: Alexis Jordain
Sent: Tuesday, 20th November, 2.13 p.m.
Subject: Re: Hello Alexis

Thank you, Mom. To be honest, I wasn't expecting a reply so soon, so nice of you. I know how busy you are. I feel like I know everything about you already. Dad doesn't complete a full sentence without 'Alexis', LOL. Sometimes it's annoying. You can't imagine what went on in Jersey. For a minute, I thought I wasn't going to make it. From what I see in the news, things are gradually returning to normal, but to be honest, if not for my finals coming up soon, I would not be looking forward to going back.

I am so sorry about Hawaii. I am so sad that it had to happen that way. Dad has plenty of making up to do. I am looking forward to meeting my new family. What are the names of the girls again?? We should all spend Christmas together and take plenty of pictures so I can show the boys at school next term.

Richardson was here, but he was very busy. I think he has work problems as well, so we hardly spoke, but he says he would visit Jersey soon. Have you met him?

I am not very certain about agents. That might be a bit tedious. I spoke to my friend about it and he says my best bet might be to get the money through Western Union and get it directly from the ticket office. Haven't heard about it before. Do you know how it works? I owe him some money as well. Dad couldn't send any money for me to get to London during the crisis, so he lent it to me. Everything I need might come to around £2,300.

I don't know how this will work out. I have tried to reach Daddy the whole day. He hasn't responded. Have you spoken to him?

Well, thank you so much for your help, Mom. It feels good to have both parents again. I can't explain the feeling. I am gonna go to bed now.

Have a good day at work. Mike.

'What a little shit,' Alexis scoffed. Mike had learned well from dear old Dad.

Western Union may be easier – sure. Cash is king – oh, and is not traceable. Playing the 'daddy' card – for a mum, of course that would totally pull at the heartstrings. Nice touch. Focusing on the happy-families Christmas special with the new sisters – love it. Bravo! It was 'good to have both parents again' – how incredibly Charles Dickens. Insert 'highly offensive term for the anus' here . . .

Even Western Union advised against young lads like Michael: 'Don't fall victim to fraud – Criminals wear many masks.'

The brochure caption leapt to Alexis's attention in the queue at the grocery store's WU kiosk. The warning featured a bald fella with 'intense' eyes and paper mask with lots of phrases on the mask, some familiar to Alexis, including 'can you please help me?' and 'I need you to send me money' and 'you can trust me', among others.

Not now, she thought. Feeling green around the gills, she put it into her purse. She was sure she might drop to the ground from the wave of building nausea. Alexis would read it fully at home from the safety of a piece of furniture located close to the ground to prevent injury when she would, once again, fall from a great height.

The warnings were all over the tiny A6-sized alert: 'Don't be fooled.' 'Stay alert.' 'Do not proceed with your transaction if it's: for an emergency situation you have not personally confirmed … to someone you personally don't know or have met online … remember … you cannot obtain a refund from Western Union, even if the transfer was the result of fraud.'

Alexis figured it was about time for tough love from Mommy Dearest.

♥ ♥ ♥ ♥ ♥

From: Alexis Jordain
To: Michael Karlten
Sent: Wednesday, 21st November, 9.31 a.m.
Subject: Re: Hello Alexis

Hello Michael/Mike – what is your preference?

I'm off travelling from tomorrow morning. That's why I thought the credit card would be fastest. We can sort it when I'm back in a few days. Please look into Western Union offices nearby, as we would need the address and location details for a transfer.

I'm sorry I don't have more time to reply. Things are a bit busy here. I spoke to your dad briefly during the day. Nothing new to report. He was having trouble connecting with Richardson. He gets on MSN from time to time, though, so perhaps try that route first (and keep fingers crossed this all sorts itself soon).

I will answer your questions on the weekend. The girls' names are Paige and Bella (aged 12 – 13 in a few weeks – and 10, respectively). Thinking of you and wishing you well,

Warm regards
Alexis

Alexis felt like Caesar, given the current state of play with Michael. 'Et tu, Brute?' came to her lips, like Caesar. Having been betrayed by those around him, he is aghast at the final blow, the knife in his back from the most unlikely source – Brutus, his best mate. Alexis never anticipated this young scoundrel-in-the-making would go to such lengths to strike the final blow.

From: Michael Karlten
To: Alexis Jordain
Sent: Wednesday, 21st November, 1.59 a.m.
Subject: Re: Hello Alexis

Good morning, Mom,

I feel like I am making this worse and putting too much pressure on. I am sorry. I don't know what to do anymore.

Anyway, I called the Western Union here as you asked me to do, and they say what I need to give to you is my full name and address, and what I need to pick up the money is a 10-digit number from you.

Name: Michael Karlten
Address: 36 Clayponds Gardens
West London
W5 4er
United Kingdom

Say hi to the guys for me. I can't wait to meet you all.
Thank you so much for helping out. Mike.

It didn't take long for Mike to come back with the details for Western Union, thought Alexis.

It would take considerably longer – some might say until hell froze over – for her to organise another transfer to the Jersey boys.

MSN – 21 November

James Karlten 7:04:23 a.m.
Hello Alexis, I miss you. I am sure you are asleep at the moment. I can't stop thinking about you. Sometimes I don't think I deserve the kind of love you have for me. I can't contain it. I can't wait to show you how much you really mean to me.

I've not heard from Richardson. He hasn't answered the phone all through the day. I am so worried. This situation keeps getting worse. I don't know what to do …

I hope to speak to you when you wake up. I LOVE YOU VERY MUCH.

Are you there?
I've been trying to get a hold of you.
Are you okay? No, I am getting worried.

Alexis Jordain 4:09:32 p.m.
Hi James, I'm finished in town and with the kids' sport. I'm back at my home office now and need to prepare for tomorrow's travel. Before I start, I will drop you a line to say hello. The weather here today is magnificent. I got burnt watching sport, hotter and sunnier than in Hawaii even – that hole in the ozone layer over NZ doesn't help. I will reply to Mike's reply today.

However, I doubt we'll be able to sort his travel this side of the weekend, as I am away in Christchurch for work until Friday. I hope Richardson comes through for you, James. There is much going on for me here. Mum staying with me is not going to work for any long duration. I will need to find her a place to stay or we will kill each other. My patience is so tight right now and I have such pressure financially that the skip in my step is long gone. I am most unsettled with how I find my situation at present. I have not been in such a position in many years and I dislike it beyond words. I wonder if it is something I will ever bounce back from. The responsibilities of kids and home and extended family and business etc are back full steam, despite my short reprieve in Hawaii last week.

I hope you have better news today and that you are able to speak to Richardson. Good luck, James. I'd better keep working, much to do before bed tonight. Sending you love and well wishes, Alexis

Alexis flicked a quick holding message to Mike and then James. She was really 'over it' with all the time she'd wasted liaising with father and son. *Who's next, the Holy Ghost?*

With her money well and truly 'lost' somewhere over the internet, she wondered how and when any of this would/could possibly be resolved.

She buried herself in work. She would need to earn an awful lot to get herself out of this growing muddle.

From: Alexis Jordain
To: Michael Karlten
Date: Thursday, 22nd November, 9.22 p.m.
Subject: Re: Hello Alexis

Hi Mike, I tried to get an advance on my credit card today but unfortunately I have exceeded my limit after all the Hawaii expenses and money loaned to Sri Lanka. They suggested I apply to have the limit extended, and I will do this when back in town. It would take a few days to process if it's successful, no guarantees. Sorry, thought it would be easy.

Speak soon, regards, Alexis

MSN – 22 November:

Alexis Jordain 7:32:17 p.m.
Hi James, thanks for your note. I am travelling now and been up since 5 am so very tired. I hope to speak to you soon. Kind regards, Alexis x

♥ ♥ ♥ ♥ ♥

James went into radio silence for the next week. As much as she welcomed the silence, it was also foreboding – no contact cemented no possibility of ever recovering her investment.

She poked the bear on November twenty-seventh, via MSN. She needed to stay connected to the asshole, even though the thought of it was revolting:

James, it's been days.
Please contact me.

Enter the Holy Ghost.

A few days later, a new character entered stage left – the infamous Richardson from Canada, eh.

One of the early photos from James included a visit to Richardson's place in the Great White North. Richardson was an older fella, complete with well-stocked grey hair, a rotund physique (characteristic of frequent visits to Tim Hortons) and a warm, simple smile. Richardson rang Alexis on the way to work.

She was dumbfounded.

First, that he had her phone number, and second, that this band of merry men was still attempting to extract blood from a stone. How many ways could Alexis say 'I have no money'? Several, actually. Maybe she needed to globalise her protestations:

- Je n'ai pas d'argent (after all, Canada was bilingual. Maybe French was a better language choice for Richardson); or

- No tengo dinero (Spanish was rapidly growing in the USA, so much so that by 2050 it would have the world's largest Hispanic community); or she could try
- У меня нет денег (Alexis's grandparents would be proud her uni education wasn't wasted); or
- E kore ahau e moni (to do her part in the Māori language revival for cuzzies back in NZ); or, maybe better still for the Chinese recipients of the unwitting Alexis Jordain philanthropic fund
- 你有沒有錢 – Nǐ yǒu méiyǒu qián? (she wished she had known this one earlier).

Richardson would not have heard any of the above. He was on a mission to explain how James's plight rested in 'their' hands.

The Holy Ghost emphasised that no one else could help James, and appealed to Alexis's Christian nature and good heart.

Alexis countered with 'the Lord helps those who help themselves', and, again, what part of 'no money' don't you get? She was terminally wounded financially and had not another penny to access from anywhere! Not that she would!

Persistent as Richardson was, he followed up his call with an email the next day. The cynic in Alexis figured he wanted to convey the financial details in black and white.

God loves a trier.

From: Richardson Hess
To: Alexis Jordain
Date: Thursday, 29th November, 9.08 a.m.
Re: Ms Alexis Jordain

Dear Alexis Jordain,

I am writing as I stated to you on the phone. I must say that it was a pleasure speaking with you on the phone yesterday. All your concerns have been duly noted, and I would like to state that they are not in any way unreasonable. It is to be expected that you will feel the way you feel right now. However, we need to put our heads together now to see how we can help James.

I sincerely hope that the contents of my e-mail do not seem to you as a deliberate avenue of putting more pressure on you. Should that be the case, please accept my apology, as that is not the intention.

As I stated on the phone, all that is required now for all issues to be resolved is $40,000.00USD. My hope is that we can both come to an arrangement on how to put down a permanent root on this matter which will resolve everything once and for all.

We must sympathise with his situation and try to help him. I do understand that you have always done your best for him, but the only way all you have spent will be paid back is when he is out of this problem.

One thing I can assure you is that once he is released, I will personally ensure he is out of that country and all funds you have spent are returned to you within 24–48 hrs at the most.

I have enclosed with this e-mail the required account details where the funds should be sent. Should you be able to find a way of raising the $40k, please wire into this account and inform me and I will move into action immediately and get everything resolved.

I will wait to hear from you.

Richardson Hess
CEO, Esber Group
Tel: +852 8193 0652

Alexis politely replied to Richardson that he should go and fuck himself, hoping that he too appreciated and understood messages in black and white.

Apparently not.

From: Richardson Hess
To: Alexis Jordain
Date: Saturday, 1st December, 2.47 p.m.
Re: Ms Alexis Jordain

Dear Alexis Jordain,
Thanks for your email, which I have read and understood. I delay a little bit in responding because I needed to see if I can raise the required amount.

Unfortunate I can't but I might be able to raise $20,000.00USD. If you can get the balance all can be completed.

Thanks and I wait to hear from you.
Richardson Hess
CEO Esber Group
Tel: +852 8193 0652

From: Richardson Hess
To: Alexis Jordain
Date: Wednesday, 5th December, 9.37 a.m.
Re: Ms Alexis Jordain

Dear Alexis Jordain,

I still have not heard anything from you. Please let me know your next line of action.

With the Holy Ghost being the only one still in the confessional box, Alexis played the game of 'try and find the money'.

It was a bit of an insurance policy. While she remained in contact with at least one of the unholy alliance, there was hope to connect to the others (if in fact they were more than one person).

From: Alexis Jordain
To: Richardson Hess
Date: Wednesday, 5th December, 6.09 p.m.
Re: Ms Alexis Jordain

Hi Richardson, I heard back from the bank this afternoon. They will not lend on current figures, as I suspected. My income last year doesn't support my borrowing level. I need this year's accounts (due March) before they'll look again at my lending. I am completely wiped out now and paying interest on the 140k loan that I do not have. I have been so foolish. I do not know what next to do. Do you have any other avenues to explore?

There was only one thing Alexis dreaded more than being part of the ongoing drama with James and Mike and Richardson. That was silence.

The silence fed the subconscious, which begat the nightmares, which begat Alexis becoming a murderer.

A few days later, she awoke in the middle of the night, writhing around and wet with sweat.

She had gone to Clayponds to find James. The bank had repossessed her home, and she and her children were now out on the street. She had lost her work contracts because clients felt that anyone who could fall for such a scam certainly would not be worthy of providing quality advice. Even her best mates walked away from her because she did not confide in them when she made the grave error in judgment of sending the money in the first place. They insisted they'd certainly have stopped her from making such a colossal mistake.

She berated herself from every possible angle. She woke in England, in a full-on attack of James. She was punching and screaming at him, wishing she had completed the course on how to become a lethal weapon at the school of martial arts. That was December eighth.

She was cold from the sweat. She changed her bedclothes, grabbed her phone and, despite seething with hatred, sent the bastard a text.

Staying connected to him was keeping Alexis stuck.

She knew saying goodbye to James was effectively saying goodbye to any hope of seeing any money at all. She knew without the money, her nightmare had a chance of coming true. She also knew she could not endure the continued torture of pretending there would be a different ending.

She swallowed hard and hit send.

Dear James, I should be out buying presents and getting excited about Christmas, but that is not to be. As I sit in a pool of tears, I have reached my limit on everything. I have had this heaviness in my heart now for far too long. My melancholy, like a brick on my chest, must be removed. I cannot contact you further until you are back on solid ground and things are sorted between us. I know you will understand this. I wish you a safe and speedy return. I will continue to pray for things to get back to normal for us both.

With love and light, Alexis

With still nothing from Mike or Richardson, Alexis set her pride aside and tried resurrecting the Holy Ghost.

To: Richardson Hess
From: Alexis Jordain
Date: Thursday, 13th December, 2.39 p.m.
Re: Possible assistance?
Hi Richardson

I hate to drag you into this mess further, but not sure what else to do. James has dropped offline. Christmas is so close and I have absolutely no cash and credit left. Is there any chance you might be able to assist with just a few thousand dollars to get us through until my client pays a pending invoice? I truly wouldn't ask if I had any other options. I am too proud to go to friends here, as I would need to tell them the whole story, and I'm quite embarrassed that I've put myself, and my family, at such risk. If you cannot assist, I understand.

Thank you.

The only thing worse than silence, for a 'now' person, was chronic silence. Alexis didn't hear anything from anyone the next week. She was going to Skype James on December twentieth, but the technology fairy came in and kicked her offline.

The drama addict in her had started writing ...

> Merry Christmas, James.
>
> My letter was returned from NJ this week – ANK scrawled on the front. I had to look that up – it's Addressee Not Known.
>
> It sums it up, don't you think?
>
> I suspect you have packed up your yurt and moved on. Confirmation of this would have been appreciated, but not surprising, I guess, given the past week's reported events.
>
> It is not the season I thought in my heart it would be. I expected a large extended family with you and Mike here with us, or the girls and I with you. Mike never replied after I ran my resources dry, nor did you.
>
> What does that say, at Christmastime? Not so much as a word from you, in protest or otherwise, at my request to stop ...

And THAT's when the technology fairy came in.

Whenever Alexis had prepared a text, email or MSN note of dubious content (i.e., conveying feelings that were NOT for human consumption and certainly better NOT shared), the technology fairy would step in. S/he was like Alexis's online communication guardian angel. Saving her from herself. Alexis learned not to argue with the fairy.

Things in time would eventually correct themselves, and she was always grateful the fairy had her back.

From: Richardson Hess
To: Alexis Jordain
Date: Thursday, 20th December, 6.28 p.m.
Re: Possible assistance?

Hi Alexis,

James is still under police custody. I have tried everything I could to raise funds, but nothing at the moment. With regards to what you asked me, will it be okay if I send you $200?

I hope that is not too small. Let me know what you think.

Regards
Richardson

From: Alexis Jordain
To: Richardson Hess
Date: Thursday, 20th December, 9.53 p.m.
Re: Possible assistance?

Hi Richardson,

Thank you so much for your kind thought, and while I appreciate the gesture very much, it would not create sufficient impact to warrant the effort, particularly given my circumstances. I am sorry to hear things have not changed in respect of James's situation. Please do keep me abreast of how things progress. I hope you and your family have a safe and peaceful Christmas.

Warmest regards, Alexis

The Christmas holiday season came and went.

Alexis was weighed down by the financial circumstances she had created for herself. She would beat herself up thinking of how all that money was wasted on some charlatan, particularly at Christmas, when one's thoughts go to charity.

Imagine all that money going to sick children or needy families or, geez, MY friends and MY family!

It was money she did not have – it was borrowed money, and now she was on borrowed time. It would only be a matter of time before the payments on the flexi loan would outstrip her already weighty monthly expenditures.

Why oh why did I go to the spa in Honolulu and drink so many goddamn piña coladas?

On New Year's Eve, after a bit too much Pinot noir or Tanqueray or both, Alexis was feeling lonely and nostalgic.

She tried her own version of the *Sleepless in Seattle* approach with James:

James, I've tried to reach you several times. I wanted to let you know that meeting you and our virtual world brought me extreme joy and happiness. I fell in love with you without reservation, trusted when you asked me to take your hand and said you would never let anything happen to me. My haste to give myself to you meant no due diligence, and I quickly found myself in a quagmire of creations unbelievable, even to my most romantic heart.

In Hawaii, I told myself each day you would come. I wonder in retrospect how entertaining my emotions must have been for you. I know this seems absurd, but despite everything, I am still in love with you. I cannot move forward while my heart is connected to yours. If there is a chance you feel the same, please contact me before the year ends at midnight tomorrow. If I do not hear from you, I will start my 'new beginning' when the New Year arrives.

On New Year's Day, Alexis closed the loop to start the year afresh:

Dear James, I've tried ringing you again and am still unable to reach you. I promised myself a new beginning. I will now accept a few dates. Perhaps you might ask me out one day. Then, at last, we will have our first date. At least we need not invent a good story – the real one is remarkable on its own. The experience has changed me forever. I would very much look forward to going on a date with you. I do hope you will ask me :)

Until then, I will think of you fondly, and with love, truly, Alexis x

Nothing from James, but Richardson (whoever the hell he was) sent a 'happy new year to you' email to Alexis on January fifth.

Alexis needed to take some sort of action. She wanted something to happen, well, now! She made a last-gasp effort to get some form of document to set out the money transfer she loaned James. She realised it was too little, too late, but didn't see the harm in trying.

She drafted a promissory note.

Naturally, she had one after lending other boyfriends money that they didn't pay back without prodding. Why are some people destined to keep repeating mistakes? Oh, that's right, until we learn from them! Enough said.

The note outlined the money Alexis had loaned to James, broken down with the payment dates and amounts, converting different currencies for transactions in GBP or US dollars. All up, after the conversions, she was in for $140,634.03, including the interest on her flexi account. His London and Alpine properties were listed as collateral. All she needed was his actual birthdate (which she thought she had somewhere), a driver's licence or passport number and then to get him to sign up with a witness.

Sure.

She may as well have assisted the Yanks to find Bin Laden.

C'mon, Alexis thought, *at this point it would probably be easier to perform a self-root canal.*

Nonetheless, it felt good doing it, doing something. It almost made things more real (and scarier at the same time). But it almost felt like there could be some legal remedy if, by chance, she could get some documentation in place.

Alexis sent a note by email to James and Richardson and blind copied in James's son on the off chance his son (if he existed) would prod Papa to send the nice lady (aka Mom) her money back. Was that another pig flying by? Alexis had hoped that sprinkling some emotional blackmail into the request from Richardson might tweak at some compassion – if, indeed, Richardson was a different individual from James and/or Mike.

She was desperate and would try anything.

From: Alexis Jordain
To: Richardson Hess
Date: Thursday, 10th January, 8.32 p.m.
Re: PCL Promissory Note James Karlten

Good day, Richardson,

I hope this note finds you well. I'm writing directly to you as I've tried to reach James numerous times, to no avail. I've texted a few times also and heard from him once last week, but he really isn't communicating.

I have attached a draft promissory note outlining the 121k loan to James. It is missing a bit of information (birthdate and driver's licence and/or passport info). I need to record the lending via my business (it is simply too insane to consider otherwise). If you (or Mike) might assist to complete the document, then I can finalise the details and perhaps you or Mike could arrange signing by James. That would be brilliant and much appreciated. Once finalised, the document will help me hopefully secure an emergency loan that I have been trying to negotiate with the bank. Unfortunately, it's looking like I may need to wait until financial year end in March, but with the promissory note in place it should help a lot. At least the girls and I aren't on the street yet, thank God. It's been such a trying time (thank goodness for new credit cards – yikes).

I look forward to hearing from you and to your assistance in this matter. Many thanks in advance.

Kind regards
Alexis

PS – I've attached a recent pic of the girls and me with their grandparents (dad's side) just for fun ☺

That done, Alexis went on with her life. Having friends around for dinner was just the ticket to get her mind off James and money and onto living!

♥ ♥ ♥ ♥ ♥

Just when she thought it was safe to go back in the water – remember the dun, dun (long dramatic pause) dun, dun (pause, but shorter), then, repeatedly, and growing to crescendo, dun dun, dun dun, dun da dun da dun da – da da – theme from *Jaws*? Well, don't break out the Coppertone yet, honey. At some time in the wee hours, while everyone was nestled in their beds, Jaws (aka James) came ashore with a voicemail for Alexis.

Captain Brody Vodafone put the time at 3.49 a.m. The voice was garbled – perhaps he had just ingested a small dingy – but it sounded something like: 'Hi Alexis, it's James, um. I'm sorry I've missed your calls and your messages. I've been in the hospital, in Semindecker Hospital in England. I'll have a doctor send you an email so you can know what is actually wrong with me. I need a heart transplant. I haven't forgotten about your money or whatever. I still love you very much. I'll fix this, all right? If you just give me some time. If you could come here in England I'd be very glad, um, so you could see me in the hospital. Things have gone from bad to worse, but I'm trying my best to fix them, all right? Hopefully I can talk to you soon. I love you, and I'd like to pick up if you call me, but if I don't I'll call you back later. I love you so much, my heart to you and the kids. I'll talk to you soon. Bye.'

In the song that spoofs the movie, James's message was saying: 'Why can't we be friends, why can't we be friends?' Alexis thought, *I know sharks are stupid, but you must think me completely certifiable.* But this wasn't the spoof song, and it wasn't the poor original mechanical shark (shameful compared to modern technology, although still spooky as hell if you watch it now).

No, this was real life, and really happening.

Imagine the surprise, after days of nothing, to hear, of course, dramatic pause – James needed a heart transplant.

Now, first off, who didn't know time differences when ringing overseas? Professional engineer? No. Asshole.

Who was awake (or coherent) at 3.49 a.m.? With all his 'ums' and pauses, Alexis wasn't, um, sure that, um, he was coherent either! So, he was back in England, then. Interesting.

Up until this morning, Alexis thought he was still rotting away in Sri Lanka, with staff locked up in the brig. Clearly things had moved on, even without her 40k to bail him out. She couldn't wait to hear his story of how the Sri Lanka scene ended. And what of Charles and his deaf wife? Had they been happily reunited? She had likely acquired an additional disability in the interim.

What about the work in Spain? Surely the big businessman couldn't perform a miracle with a 'broken heart'.

Did the Holy Ghost get a call to action?

Alexis could only imagine what James's physician, Doctor Feelgood, might write. She also thought it nice that the money 'or whatever' hadn't been forgotten. He had previously said that as soon as he got back to London, he would sort everything. Wouldn't that be amazing?

Maybe the cheque's in the mail, Alexis joked. LOL ☺. Steady on, girlfriend – don't get too excited. But she did remember Lucas's story that crazy things happen in Sri Lanka. Anything was possible in this Shark Tale.

Alexis failed miserably in her trawling around the internet to try to find any hospital that remotely resembled what she thought marble-mouth said about 'Semindecker' Hospital. She took James's nibbling as her chance to catch her own fish. She replied and reopened the lines of communication on January thirteenth.

Hi James, I received your voicemail yesterday, thank you. I'm glad you are back in London and out of godforsaken Sri Lanka. I had no idea where you had got to. What happened in Sri Lanka in the end? Please write me the details of the hospital and I look forward to receiving the notice from your physician. At least you are back in civilisation, you must be happy about that. I would be happy to come to London, but obviously cannot without cash. I'm looking forward to hearing from you. Please check the time difference so we might connect easier. Thanks. Love you, Alexis

Saying 'love you' was the best Alexis could do for the communication façade. Saying 'I love you' would require her to eat glass as she sat straddling the two countries of Contempt and Pity, paying due regard to Lucas's friend-of-a-friend's wise words that the Sri Lanka story was totally plausible. Time would tell either way.

I'm still so impressed by my ability to engage with Fuck Knuckle, Alexis thought. Still, a few 'love yous' for 140k didn't feel like too much of a values compromise. When in Rome and all that …

But the nibbling fish took the worm and the line and the 140k and jumped into the Pacific to some exotic paradise without Alexis. She would not hear from the cardiac patient again.

♥ ♥ ♥ ♥ ♥

Richardson tried a few times over the coming months to interest Alexis in investing in a new business venture, sending an odd email, making the odd phone call.

One 'opportunity' was in Spain, where Richardson had colleagues that had $8.6m USD and felt that she, with her 'skills', would know where and how to invest the cash to earn his colleagues a sizeable return. Richardson was offering this to Alexis to try to make up for the difficulty she'd suffered with James. Another time, he sent through an official-looking document from the Bank of Dalian in Hong Kong, showing an account balance of 92,477,654.98 euros, with the following email:

From: Richardson Hess
To: Alexis Jordain
Date: Wednesday, 27th March, 8.46 a.m.

Dear Alexis,
Many apologies for not attending to our last phone discussion so promptly. I noticed that you were not so interested in such a proposal.

I would not want to get you involved in anything you are not interested in. I have known these investors for over ten years so I am very sure of what I am introducing to you.

I have attached with this e-mail proof of funds. These funds are available but the only reason why I want to get you involved in this is strictly on the grounds that you can be creative and come up with a great investment plan you think we can invest these funds in and get very good turnover. Please let me know what you think and we will proceed from there.

Thanks
Richardson.

♥ ♥ ♥ ♥ ♥

Alexis would let the interaction with Richardson die from lack of water and attention rather than stoop to repeating her earlier strategic advice.

She couldn't call the local Viking to rough anyone up, and so, like after any natural disaster, she had a lot of repair work to complete: emotional, spiritual, physical and the all-important plus time-sensitive financial. Unfortunately for Alexis, several areas suffered irreparable damage. Her attempts at financial recovery would be in vain.

There was not a lot left to do but take a few shots of akvavit, hold her hands against her face and scream.

Chapter Nine

Is it Me, or Does My MasterCard Look Big in This?

Eat — McDonald's – your choice from the $2 value menu

Drink  1.5L bottle of Baby Duck

Look  *Migrant Mother* (1936) by Dorothea Lange

Listen — 'Money, Money, Money', ABBA

♥ ♥ ♥ ♥ ♥

'Help me. I'm poor.'

Kristen Wiig's comment in the first-class cabin en route to Vegas in the laugh-out-loud-funny *Bridesmaids* movie is the perfect opener. We all know she is not poor, just like we know she is not Mrs Julio Iglesias. The spin-off sales inspired by those four words on coffee mugs, prints and t-shirts would surely feather even the least frugal of nests. It would certainly leave Ms Wiig with plenty of dosh to drink the good stuff.

Remember when the good stuff was sold in a 1.5 litre bottle for just over eleven dollars? Yes, you guessed it – Baby Duck, the classic. On the bottle, it recommends serving it 'chilled, with animal crackers'. The sweet, pink, tickle-your-nose-with-bubbles drink was an easy transition from soda for those in high school way back in the 1970s and 1980s. What the kids refer to as 'the olden days'. Serve that swill up now to the ritz brigade at your peril – but back in 'the day', Andrés Baby Duck became the most popular wine in Canada, selling eight million bottles a year in the early 1970s. It was simple to drink, simple to say and the price was right.

Getting value for money is important not only to 'starving students' but also to those on a tight budget, say, like people who have suddenly found themselves 140k out of pocket.

Luckily, the McDonald's marketing gurus also target the cost-conscious in their menu options. A variety of 'value' meals are on offer for just a one- or two-dollar price point. Great for those poor single-mum families, right? Ah, but what if I told you the typical McDonald's customers weren't actually the poor but rather those lower–middle-income families who earn up to sixty thousand dollars per year?

So if we were wrong about the poor – is it possible we may be overstepping around the single-parent families also?

Believe it or not, all children growing up with solo parents are not destined for a life of prostitution and drug-smuggling. Barack Obama, Bill Clinton, Tom Cruise, Julia Roberts, Angelina Jolie and many other famous and highly successful people all come from single-parent families. Even if not famous, thousands grow up to live happy, healthy and successful lives. Each helps dispel the negative stereotypes, even when sometimes the parents of such children continue to disparage themselves with guilt.

There's a black-and-white photograph from the Great Depression featuring Florence Owens Thompson and her children taken in 1936 in Nipomo, California. Titled *Migrant Mother*, it is one of the most reproduced images in history. The photographer was Dorothea Lange, who grew up – yes, you guessed it – with a single parent.

Lange was forty when she took that photograph. She had recently transformed herself from a portrait photographer of well-to-do clients to one capturing images of 'people in trouble'. The first day she crossed over on San Francisco's skid row in 1933, she made the celebrated *White Angel Breadline, San Francisco.* Her print of that image would sell in 2005 for $822,400 at Sotheby's in New York. Not bad for the mother of two small sons, who was also principal breadwinner and, oh yes, living apart from her husband.

Lange's experience, raised by her solo mother after her father abandoned them during the Depression of 1907, echoes stereotype-busting through her success, but then matters of family and money are never easy, whether or not one can legitimately or otherwise say, 'Help me. I'm poor.'

♥ ♥ ♥ ♥ ♥

Not having sufficient funds to stay at a hotel meant Alexis needed to fall at the mercy of colleagues or a social acquaintance or family friend when called out of town for work.

Once in the wop wops, she struggled for a clean bed, a decent meal and somewhere to wash her stinky used garments, including knickers and undershirts – the one she had on was already recycled for several consecutive days, first as an undershirt, then a nightshirt, then an undershirt, then …

Tonight she needed to shower, despite feeling like she needed a tetanus shot before entering the stale old room with cracked basin, missing floorboards and constantly leaking showerhead. Surely things had not got so bad, she thought as she glanced from the lofty perch of the toilet throne, assessing Gulliver's landscape: the dead bugs in the corner resting on the bed of hair carefully accumulated from geographically diverse regions of the human body; the nineteen-sixty-something floral wallpaper peeling under the open window that stubbornly refused to close, likely from around the same period when the paper-layer came to visit.

The bowed wooden sill wasn't the only bathroom accoutrement needing assiduous amputation. The skull and crossbones on the bright-orange lid lying adjacent to the high-potency wart remover next caught her eye. Subconsciously, her visual senses triangulated the distance between the orange lid, the shower floor and her bare feet below. By the second navigation, her conscious brain caught up. The assessment connected her precipitously prickly feet, with a likely fungus (with a really long, hard-to-pronounce name) growing invisibly in the nearby stall. The bacteria now engulfing her canoe-sized feet, like Jim Carrey's face in *The Mask*, sent a shudder down her spine, shifting her attention to another sunny reality. She was not only in a pathetic kingdom, left wanting for OCD, but was also physically chilled to the bone.

She wished there were more blankets on the bed when she tucked herself in and saw her breath against the moonlit room. The one where the absence of curtains meant the little body heat generated by her slow and steady, heavy panting escaped through the single paned straw, sucking up what, if any, warmth from the wee bedroom.

She was grateful for a room, but knew that the icy temperature would inevitably leave her sick. That, between the cost of the doctor's visit, resulting antibiotics, probable wart-removal treatment and numerous hostess gifts of wine and dinners out, she would have been financially better off down the road in a motel. In that faraway land, guest rooms came complete with thermometer, heating blanket and the indispensable sunblock curtains.

Next time, she thought. If, indeed, there would be a next time.

She calculated the odds. Chances were pretty good that hypothermia would set in and kill her as she slept – or passed out, whichever came first. Would it be so bad if she did die? Before her subjects conceived of any other brilliant coup d'état, Alexis realised it was time to remove her royal bottom from its humble throne.

Would anyone REALLY care? she thought again in bed. As she pulled the sheets well up over her head to incarcerate additional warmth, the moonlight drew her to focus on a collection of yet more furry deposits, too curly to be from her blonde mane.

Dear God, I'm lying amidst someone's pubic hair.

Dressed in her five-dollar pants, bought on holiday in the South Island, Alexis escaped reality by going for a drive. Stopped at the red light, she recalled the happier times in the history of those pants.

Visiting Mr Porsche's family in Kaikoura, she needed something warm when the summer heat evaporated nearer the coast. The Warehouse had a bargain bin with these black cotton casual cargo pants. A deal at five dollars, they became her staple pants for hanging at home, embarrassing the kids at school drop-offs and walking the dog. One small problem: they were two sizes too big and now fit perfectly. Hmm.

With this new girth and weight, she could almost hear Louise Hay roll down the window in the car next door to comment, 'Your stomach is telling you to stop eating your anger and worry. Time to start digesting your life, Alexis.'

♥ ♥ ♥ ♥ ♥

Alexis had driven past the Catholic church in their new neighborhood at least twice daily on school pick-ups and drop-offs. Since they left New Zealand, her dignity long since evaporated, the mustang with a wounded leg decided to go inside. Today it felt like the barrel was loaded and cocked. She knew no safer place and had avoided it, and the truth, far too long. The holy water penetrated her weary soul as she made the cross on her forehead and pulled up a pew with handsome Jesus bleeding on the cross above her. She would contemplate those final transactions in New Zealand before the fat lady sung. The Big Guy had certainly seen and heard a lot worse in his time. She was in excellent company and had a captive audience to hear her reminiscing. Pinned to the wall, Jesus wasn't going anywhere in a hurry.

For weeks after her last interactions with Richardson, and the newly bedridden, heartbroken (pardon the pun) James, the financial reality of losing $140,000 that she did not have came home to roost. Part of her senselessly believed James would come through in the end, but that part was losing out to the rational brain. *Idiot,* she told herself. *How hard does one need to work to earn and save that amount of cash?!*

The aftershock of the detonation created such devastating wreckage – fragments of self-esteem, crumbs of remains in what once was her retirement nest egg. It brought new meaning to the saying 'don't put all your eggs in one basket'. The reality of losing her home for the first time began to set in – like power walking into a plate-glass door.

The facts were one thing, but the physical effect on Alexis's body just seemed unfair. The blow to her guts sent the bowel into overdrive. The amount she shat, you'd think she'd be giving Twiggy a run for her money, but nope, her binge eating ensured she was actually gaining weight! At times, her mouth was so dry she couldn't swallow. Other times, excess saliva required her to spit.

Meanwhile, the financial throat choke going on was up there with Jack the Ripper enthusiasm. The lack of oxygen circulating in her body was as if her autonomic nervous system had sent out an all-points alarm to every corner of the body, pulling to the side of the road, she could hear the ambulance siren grow nearer. And then, just when she thought cardiac arrest had arrived (along with the screaming hospital bus), the Chinese wall kicked in and sent a numb and floaty 'scene from *Gravity*' (without all the spinning – that was just way overdone in the movie). So, physical stress and panic attack relocated behind the Chinese wall, Alexis could compose herself enough to commence interrogation.

She asked herself unanswerable questions: *What can I possibly tell my kids?* She couldn't possibly subject them to this crazifuckingness (technical scientific term). *How will I sell my home whilst investing tens of thousands in reconstructing the backyard?* Her heaven-on-earth haven – gone, gone, gone, because of some whimsical, silly act. For love. When they said it was better to have loved and lost, surely they couldn't have meant lost your family home – whoever 'they' are, anyway.

If the primary relationship blowing up is considered 'ground zero', what is the impact radius for secondary relationships? Those friends and family that absolutely are affected by the aftershock of the detonation? Is carnage or wreckage the better descriptor?

While 'carnage' colourfully captures the meat-and-flesh people dimension of a 'massive slaughter', wreckage, in all its auditory grandeur, powerfully calls to mind the act of wrecking – leaving 'debris' or 'remains or fragments of something' that aptly link the ruin or destruction impacting secondary relationships.

Alexis decided to dress the remains from the wreckage up as a 'time of life' move. People would not suspect it was too extraordinary. They'd say, 'Is it her third or, perhaps, fourth "mid-life crisis"?' Everyone knew how she could be impulsive. After her first relationship, with the girls' dad, ended, she bought a shiny, red, hot sports motorcycle. The adventure lasted about three months before she realised she was likely to kill herself and leave motherless children (plus let's not even go there on the helmet hair).

Right, so this will all be about a life change. Yes. That seemed one hundred per cent feasible. She'd mentioned giving the kids a 'year abroad' experience. Her sister lived abroad – they could go there. Her sister was flaky and in need of support – they could 'save' each other, perhaps. *Yes,* Alexis concluded, *that story will work. And it will be a good experience for everyone.* Time for the Academy Award-winning performance in a lead role …

They left for Canada three months later.

Alexis would steady herself on and off, consoling her quandary in her journal. She was a single mum, of course. Such stories were commonplace, were they not?

10 October, Alexis's diary entry

It seems I can only write in the dark. So no one will see me indulge in this forbidden ritual. Forbidden at least in my own eyes, for more months than I care to mention. Amidst the normal background traffic noise creeping in through the slightly open window, the same one where the pot smell wafts in to remind me that we now live in Beautiful British Columbia. I get a jolt from the occasional motorcycle burst as it accelerates along the seemingly wet roadway below our apartment.

It isn't the most grandiose of writing spaces, not the least bit inspiring. The low din of the computer screen illuminating the large dark shadows that surround me. The pillow pouf patterns cast shapes onto my half of the bed. It's not that anyone else is even inhabiting the other side.

So why the secrecy? The hidden screen, the creative juices that only flow at the wee hours when I'm supposed to be asleep. Instead, it appears that part of my brain is only just waking up. The part that has something to say. Why can't it wait until morning?

The debate goes on between content and timing. I take the first half an Ambien to sleep, get drowsy and dopey and might nod off, but never before a paragraph or two that seem so insightful, so important to write down. So I fight the hazy smack at the back of my head calling me to sleep, the sharp taste at the back of my throat from the pills that lingers long into the day. That almost metallic flavor on your tongue, like licking a metal bar on the schoolyard when you were little – like a Popsicle – and don't deny you've ever done it. There's no one here to judge you. Remember it is dark. I certainly cannot see you. Nothing to be embarrassed about here. Well, maybe just one thing.

The small matter of a relationship that went wrong and totally changed the course of my life forever – in a good way? Hmmm. The jury is still MIA on this one.

From: Alexis Jordain
To: James Karlten
Cc: Richardson Hess
Sent: Thursday, 12th September, 2.07 a.m.
Subject: Perhaps you might buy my house back for me ... ?

James, I've not contacted you for a long while now – it is around a year since I met you and my world came crashing down around me shortly thereafter. I mentioned to you that I needed to take out an additional mortgage on my home to loan you the money I did. I said that I desperately needed the money back as the bank would foreclose on my family home. Well, that is exactly what has happened. I am now homeless with my two young girls. Perhaps you might buy my house back for me? I am truly in a bind without any cards left to play ☹ totally tapped out.

I still do not understand – why me?

Alexis recalled the process for selecting a real estate agent. She met several, ranging from totally pragmatic (and unemotional) – a him-and-him team – to immensely intuitive (so touchy-feely that she couldn't possibly respond to how she'd market the home until she had a chance to let the aura of the place settle into her psyche). For real. Upon reflection, Alexis should have gone with the middle-of-the-road, pragmatic marketing expert, but let's just say she could chalk up another 'life lesson' in this incredible, ever-growing 'learning' journey.

The financial comedy of errors continued when Be2, the dating website, automatically charged her credit card an additional $270. It wasn't until she saw her MasterCard statement that she remembered James had mentioned something like this in their early correspondence. Wow, it was twelve months later and so much had happened. She was still in disbelief and shock. The extra financial cost just added insult to injury, given her financial loss.

She wrote customer service to request a refund:

> I have just been charged $270 NZD to renew my membership and I do not wish to renew. I met a guy on your site, was scammed out of $140,000 NZD (that I did not have – I got a loan!) and will NOT be paying to stay connected. What a farce! I did not authorise this purchase. Please re-credit my account $270. The details of my initial payment follow, and the subsequent one a few days ago just appeared on my MasterCard e-statement.
>
> User name on your site: Funny Girl
> I await your reply ASAP. Thank you.

It was two weeks before Alexis heard from Be2.

You'd have thought they had an alert for words like 'scam' or 'fraud'. Apparently not, as what she received was a standard reply: sorry to hear you wish to cancel, blah blah, we can delete your profile, you can transfer your premium days to a friend, re-register whenever, and then step-by-step instructions to cancel. Oh, and of course, 'Thank you for using Be2.'

No mention of the scam, the loss, the catastrophe.

She was incensed and replied:

Please cancel my membership and refund my credit card of $270. I have lost over $140,000 NZD via a scam by Jcarl (James Norman Karlten). What a nightmare! I have reported him on your site. I had tried to put the whole experience behind me, until I received your receipt for $270 charged to my credit card! Enough already. I will be pursuing with government scam channels next. I expect you will promptly refund my membership fee.

In anticipation, sincerely, Alexis Jordain
(Attached: Termination of membership sheet!!)

She finally received some acknowledgement of the disaster from Be2, but barely any! They apologised for the inconvenience, noting how 'some people on the internet try to trick others into giving them money' and how it was their goal to 'take strong action and prevent this kind of activity'. The Be2 note told Alexis they reviewed their system on a daily basis and were 'very grateful for any information that clients can provide us concerning dubious users of the system'. Would James be considered 'dubious'? She chuckled considering which adjectives Edie might choose.

'He's a fucking asshole, Alexis. You know that. He is well beyond the "doubtful" or "uncertain" Latin *dubiosus*, and has far greater mental illness than "of two minds" from its Latin root *duo*. The guy is a lying, cheating bastard – no two minds about it!'

Yes, well that is exactly what Ms Edie did say when Alexis shared her Be2 refund news at the New Zealand leaving party.

So much had happened in that wonderful country in the antipodes.

New Zealand was home to her two gorgeous Kiwi kids. She had spent nearly two decades working and living in the land of the long white cloud. How could it end this way? So unexpectedly, so unbelievably, so dubiously.

♥ ♥ ♥ ♥ ♥

How did it all go so wrong so quickly? Alexis pondered.

No answer in sight, she got up to light a few candles. Her butt was sore and she welcomed a brief diversion before returning to her headspace amongst all things holy.

She sighed, glancing at the flickering candles she lit: one for Tata, one for each grandma – Baba and O'Mama – and the one for herself. Life was so fragile and so short. She wasn't much younger now than her dad was when he got sick and started with blood transfusions.

She considered parents and parenting and wondered if Mary, looking down on her gracefully, all motherly like, had the same issues with baby Jesus that other mums had – and what about those troubled teen years without Nigel Latta to be politically incorrect with advice for raising them? Child-rearing, wow, now there was a lesson in life. They taught us so much. Alexis considered how quickly the beach-sick Kiwi kids were growing up.

She recalled her return from Hawaii, Bella's innocent words ringing in her head: *Was he everything you'd dreamt he would be?*

That was the problem. Alexis had dreamt the perfect scenario, then shoehorned the most unlikely candidate into the glass slipper – sight unseen.

Too bad Alexis had not heard 'Hollywood', the Angus and Julia Stone song, earlier. They debunked fairy tales, including *The Sound of Music*, where, in reality, 'they all would have been killed'. The Little Mermaid 'wouldn't have made it to shore', and her prince would have 'married a whore from a wealthy family; after all, he was royalty'. She would have realised 'it's a cruel world' and not have been lured in as 'a young girl' to believe in happily ever after.

For Alexis, and modern fairy tales, the reality of lying and cheating bastards would take a few more years to surface. In modern times, Cinderella's original Disney debut in 1950 was supplanted in 2015 by *Into the Woods*. Hot and sexy Chris Pine, aka Prince Charming, cheats on Cinderella – yes, no one could believe it – go Rob Reiner. When caught out two-timing Cindy, his defence? 'I was raised to be charming, not sincere.' Priceless.

Too bad for Alexis, reality did not 'bite' sooner. Why wasn't she part of Cinderella/Anna Kendrick's three million Twitter followers? She would have got her sage advice for Prince Charming: 'Okay, let's get one thing straight, I can do whatever the fuck I want.' Maybe then the score at half-time would not have been lying, cheating scoundrel = one. Epitome of integrity = zero.

Back at home, she wrote in her journal:

7 June, Alexis's diary entry

It would be impossible for anyone to say anything that would make me feel worse than I do right now. I have asked myself 'how could I?' in a zillion different ways. I've tormented my brain with the whys and wherefores. I have relived the sick – vomit please, I've drunk too much gin – feeling over and over again. Unfortunately, there are no logical answers that appease my mind. Time does not fade my scarred heart. Underneath the smiley façade, my soul remains unsettled. Little stops me from berating myself with words like stupid, blind, ridiculous, naive, damaged. How did I let this happen? What could I have done differently? Why me?

You can run, but you cannot hide from your past. We are destined to repeat mistakes if we do not learn from them. What I am meant to learn from this catastrophe? I had to stop trying to sweep the whole sordid affair/ordeal under the proverbial carpet and share the story. According to Brené Brown, the only way to rid yourself of shame is to talk about it. Well … here I go, talking. I can only hope that in addition to consolidating my own learning, I might shed some of my shame, guilt and self-deprecation for being so gullible. I want to stop bullying myself.

At forty-something (a term which I'm told can last up to two decades or more – whew), I find I can carry around quite a lot of emotional baggage if I allow myself to indulge in life's little 'oops … I didn't do that'. Umm, except in this instance, I'm afraid, yep, I DID do that. I have the financial scar perfectly situated next to the emotional one – the design simple – a few more circles – or, looking closer, maybe they are zeros. Nonetheless. This actually isn't a boohoo entry about my baggage. It is meant to be a 'learn from the mistakes of others'. Hopefully my 'duh' experience will be a lesson for others. That's another part of why it's important to write it down – to share the lesson.

The other part is about my learning 'self-love' journey. It requires me to face my past 'choices' and to be totally comfortable with them. To not beat myself up about things like falling in love with the 'wrong guys', to not feel like my Pollyanna tendencies create a blind spot with the male sex and maybe even to drop the self-fulfilling prophecy that 'I'm just not relationship material'.

James had me dancing on the head of a pin for months. Boy, I have got work to do …

♥ ♥ ♥ ♥ ♥

Isn't it remarkable how even after your head says, 'Yup, the signs were all there – you were duped,' your heart still wants to go in for another round and get a bashing? Of course, it isn't intentional. Alexis remembered the song about not letting anyone be reckless with your heart. *I wonder if she meant to include herself?*

What causes our self-love, our self-esteem, to be so downtrodden that we are able to take more and more punishment, abuse, neglect, pain and suffering and still turn up for yet MORE?! Jesus, it was so obvious when you saw another going through it – but not so much for yourself. Alexis needed a window washer for the heart – her approach was not working.

She was finally ready to tell her story. Though her scars would remain forever, the immediacy of the bleed-out had passed. Her wounds were sufficiently healed to share the story, to stop the shame and secrecy. When she left, she didn't even tell her bookies the truth. No one needed to know, she thought. Until now.

As she packed up her boxes of books – her most prized possessions – she stopped and opened the one she had purchased in Honolulu on that fateful trip. It was marked with her boarding pass at this exact place: 'She was the one she was waiting for.'

Smiling a bittersweet smile, Alexis called to her girls: 'Bella, Paige, come here. Family conference time. I've got something to talk to you about …' She had a new reality tale to share with her girls … one that would no doubt serve them better than Cinderella.

Fin.

Chapter Ten

Online Pathology – Social Media Post-Mortem

♥ ♥ ♥ ♥ ♥

And now for the author's amuse-bouche – a bite-sized hors d'oeuvre offered according to the chef's selection alone. You won't find it on any menu. You don't ask for it. It just simply arrives. There is no evidence of it on your bill; it is provided free of charge.

Today's amuse-bouche is a bite-sized serving of humble pie, complete with a dollop of unsolicited relationship advice on the side. *Bon appétit.*

In the days of Robin Hood and his Merry Men (the real ones, not the made-for-TV version), a huntsman would provide his well-to-do clients with lovely Bambi meat and leave the less-to-do with the numbles – a French word that sounds much more palatable than 'deer innards'. One way of cooking numbles is to chop the heart, liver, lungs and kidneys and bake them into a – yes, you guessed it – a pie.

So how did 'numble pie' make it to 'humble pie', you ask?

Consider the connection to who is eating numble pie – those that are 'humble' – modest, or of low rank or status. So it isn't too far a stretch now, is it? *The Merriam-Webster New Book of Word Histories* records 'humble pie' from before 1642, though 'umble pie' was also in use, possibly with the British penchant for deleting h's.

Webster attributes the resurrection of 'humble pie' to Americans, which is where we now pick up its common usage and relevance to our story: to eat humble pie is to be humiliated and forced to admit error or wrongdoing. It is similar to having to eat crow and may also refer to a general drop in social status.

And to wash down the humble pie? 'But of course, the beverage selection features freshly squeezed lemonade,' spoken in perfect French by the same waiter in *Monty Python's The Meaning of Life* restaurant scene. You may recall he suggests to the *très grand* diner, after he completes enough food for a dozen Friar Tucks, that he might enjoy 'a wafer-thin mint'. He partakes just prior to violently expelling the contents of his stomach, acting as a catalyst for other diners to follow suit and ending by exposing his own numbles. Yes, the beverage selection is the perfect accompaniment and puts to good use life's particularly abundant supply of lemons this season.

Psychiatrist and Holocaust survivor Viktor Frankl once wrote: 'Life is never made unbearable by circumstances, but only by lack of meaning and purpose.'[17] Definitely a more profound account of 'when life hands you lemons, make lemonade', though both point in the same general direction.

The meaning and purpose of Alexis's catastrophe (everything is relative, right) was to share her story with others – to prevent similar nuclear fallout from others genuinely looking for love.

'Maybe this is the universe's way of putting me in the right emotional state to write a book on internet-dating scams. Yes – I bet that's it.' She tried to make sense of things, discussing her experience.

Alexis had started her path of spiritual growth years prior, but even with the preparatory work in the lead-up to the James series of events, she was still feeling like she was climbing Everest, hitting a hell of a lot of slippery bits, falling over and appreciating falls from Everest are not fun.

For Alexis, life certainly was having sincere meaning and purpose at this moment. Watching her emotions and the physical manifestation of them, she let the feelings wash over her like a warm summer rain, fading in and out of her mind when they grew overwhelming. She didn't realise how much she'd learned on her quest – there was an awful lot of Mr Miyagi 'wax on, wax off' – but now was the big fight. Alexis appreciated her soul coming to her emotional rescue, acting like a compass to wade through the experience.

'While we're at this tell-all clusterfuck, we may as well throw in some learning on "radical forgiveness".' (It's actually a thing.) Alexis was really starting to tell two different stories, one about online dating, the other about learning self-love. To share her online dating experience, Alexis would need to get over 'looking like a fucking freak' and her self-assessment of being a 'total dumbass'. The meaning and purpose of that personal self-discovery journey is a different lesson, another story. Every author has a story...

♥ ♥ ♥ ♥ ♥

The featured portrait of Virginia Woolf in London in 1939 evokes melancholy, considering her mentally troubled life, yet her handsome beauty emits a stronger character below the slender fingers casually partaking in a cigarette. Deep in thought – about her next book, perhaps? Perhaps not. What does occur behind the scenes of a photo, a painting, a portrait?

In her diary, Woolf admits sitting for portraits was 'detestable and upsetting'. She was not holding the cigarette for effect; she chain-smoked through the whole sitting. The poor second-hand smoke recipient, German-born Gisèle Freund, who captured the writing diva in this rare colour photograph, was an early adopter of this medium, claiming it was 'closer to life'.

Some years later, Woolf would feature in a 'closer to death' manner, weaving together intergenerational stories of a wealthy, pregnant 1950s housewife (who wouldn't be caught dead eating numble pie) and a 2001 New York now lesbian, both reading *Mrs Dalloway* while Woolf, a character in her own right, is writing it back in the 1920s.

The film, *The Hours* (2002), begins and ends with Woolf (played by Nicole Kidman) putting stones inside her pockets before drowning herself. (Sorry to spoil the end, but we all know Woolf committed suicide in real life – and if you didn't, you really need to read more.) There are lots of death and near-death scenes, one where husband Leonard asks Virginia, of *Mrs Dalloway*, why somebody must always die in her novels. She tells him, 'So that we all appreciate life.'

Later, just before the 'end', Woolf writes to him: 'Dear Leonard. To look life in the face, – always, – to look life in the face – and to know it for what it is. At last to know it, – to love it for what it is, – and then, – to put it away. Leonard, always the years between us, always the years. Always the love. Always the hours.'[18]

Does her 1939 photograph capture her 'knowing life for what it is', or is it the 'putting it away' part? Hiding her breath so well no one would ever remember where she placed it. Never to be found again. What would the topic of conversation be between Viktor Frankl and Leonard after the fact? Certainly Woolf's life had meaning and purpose, yet she still found it unbearable.

No matter how destructive the James experience had been, Alexis did not want to wittingly add more stones to her coat and wade into the river. At times, aspects felt unbearable, but she was not ready to know love and life and put it away. She had her girls to think of. They still needed their mother. Alexis just needed a life preserver, a raft – or maybe just David Hasselhoff to find her and give her mouth-to-mouth … ah, 'the Hoff' – things seemed so much easier in the 1990s.

♥ ♥ ♥ ♥ ♥

There is a saying I've heard so many times it has to be true: 'When the student is ready, the teacher will appear.' Too often, things happen to give this validity. Whether a not-so-random teacher appears on a flight between Seattle and San Diego or you meet a new lifelong friend just moments before they set off to their new home overseas. For Alexis, it was that book that landed in her lap at the perfect moment – when the student was ready.

Brené Brown's research into self-esteem and her book Gifts of Imperfection were pummelled at her from the most unlikely cheerleader – a boyfriend's ex-wife …

Right?

Alexis had first come across the concept of having to face the shadow side of her personality through *A Course in Miracles*, which states: 'The hidden can terrify, not for what it is, but for its hiddenness.'[19] Brown suggests turning our efforts to keep our shame hidden on their head. She guides how shame loses its hold on you, or the power it has, when you talk about it, when you expose it to the light.

There are so many teachings with a similar message – bring into the light that which is keeping you stuck – that which is holding you back. Don't be afraid of looking silly, being judged – you just made some not-great 'choices' – how liberating! Everyone – each and every one of us – has made a poor choice now and again. The difference, the freeing part, is when we can stop, reflect and talk about it WITHOUT associating some judgment that makes us feel we are unworthy to go on.

Alexis needed to tell her story to extricate herself from the self-deprecation, contempt, scorn and condemnation of the 'I love you, send money' experience. To bring her story to light would take courage. Alan Cohen sums it up perfectly: 'It takes a lot of courage to release the familiar and seemingly secure, to embrace the new. But there is no real security in what is no longer meaningful. There is more security in the adventurous and exciting, for in movement there is life, and in change there is power.'

Alexis tentatively but bravely told her story – to share her experience with others. In so doing, she was able to surrender the yoke of thinking of herself as a bad person. She appreciated that she had made some bad choices – and thank you to Brené Brown, who has no doubt helped thousands to be free and start to understand what it means to love ourselves, glorious imperfections and all.

It was Alexis's wish to share her true story with others, to heighten awareness of online-dating traps and to consider the need to love ourselves first before we desperately seek love from another.

So, as this story comes to an end, we've come full circle, back to the beginning and where the seed was planted. You've received the full picture, 'the whole truth and nothing but the truth, so help me God', so to speak.

And for the online diagnosis good doctor, the social media post mortem follows.

♥ ♥ ♥ ♥ ♥

The word 'pathology' is from the Ancient Greek *pathos*, meaning 'experience' or 'suffering', and *-logia*, meaning 'study'. The investigation into the 'why' of a disease, if you will – the diagnosis, or progression, as with different forms of cancer (pathologies) or with psychological conditions, like psychopathy.

I am not a pathologist, though, on occasion, particularly when bedding down an attractive male, I have used my 'doctor' status in a professional capacity to encourage the removal of superfluous articles of clothing. I do like applying the notion when dissecting Alexis's story as part of the wider social phenomenon of online dating. In this post-mortem, two essentials need to be covered: the people part and the technology part.

(i) The people part.

Let's remember that Alexis, a novice on dating sites, actually found the whole 'getting to know you' part pretty 'user-friendly'. Where else could you 'bare all' in the comfort of your own home and really get to know someone – because, of course, you assume they too are baring all? Technology afforded her the ability to be vulnerable – she had always struggled with getting to know people on a deep level, exposing herself to another, but with technology, she felt she could 'dig deep' and SAFELY expose her soft underbelly to another without ANY repercussions. She could go as slow or as fast as she wanted. She could expose as much or as little of herself as she was comfortable with, and she had the luxury of time between interactions to reflect and consider her responses. As a solo mum with a busy career, she could get on with her life WHILE finding/falling/being in love! She could be working and taking care of the kids, house and businesses WITHOUT being in a relationship that weighed her down. It had all the conveniences and no downside. In a word: perfect!

The stats support a move to more online relationships, as compared to organically meeting partners through friends, at work or at a bar. The UK *Daily Mail* (7 March 2016) reported more than fifty per cent of new UK couples were expected to meet online by 2031, with that number increasing to seventy per cent by 2040. At the same time, these couples actually seem happier!

A University of Chicago-led study (2013) notes over a third of marriages between 2005 and 2012 began online, and those online couples actually had happier, longer marriages.[20] The reasons are inconclusive, but could include 'the strong motivations of online daters, the availability of advance screening and the sheer volume of opportunities online'.

And opportunities are aplenty (of fish.com)! In just .35 seconds, search online dating sites and you'll get over forty-seven million hits. The website Top 10 New Zealand Dating Sites discusses how online dating 'has totally revolutionized the manner in which people search for friendship and love in the modern world'. The site helps you sift through the myriad of options, services and platforms, taking away the 'confusion, frustration and time wasted' so you can find the 'right site and ultimately, a new partner, friend or one night stand'. Fabulous – who could ask for more?!!

The social attitudes toward online dating are also changing. Pew Research Centre (2015) reports that from 2005 to 2015, more people see online as 'a good way to meet people' (increasing from forty-four per cent to fifty-nine per cent) and that people are less apt to think those that date online are 'desperate' (down from twenty-nine per cent to twenty-three per cent). They note that sites such as Match.com,

OkCupid and eHarmony are playing a significant role in American romance, with twenty per cent of online daters enlisting the help of friends to create and review their online profiles. Those age cohorts growing most rapidly are under-twenty-fives and the fifties and sixties set, which has doubled and continues to grow.

Forbes reported on the wider social impact from four in ten adults that are 'single and looking for a partner' online.[21] Citing the 'social' and 'public' dimensions of online dating, the article notes the behaviour shifts of technology providers to accommodate more users on mobile devices with the creation of Tinder and other apps that draw on Facebook information to enable a 'match' more quickly and easily. 'It's common for groups of friends to sit around "playing Tinder" together, showing each other pictures and messages. Online dating is not a private, semi-embarrassing activity anymore. It's now part of how we spend time with friends and entertain ourselves at parties.'

So, to conclude the people part, we can safely say society is coming to grips with – embracing, if you will – the whole dating-online scene AND partaking in a wider social activity associated with human relationships facilitated through technology. It is a good thing – no, great – people meeting people, getting into happier relationships (or more plentiful bonks). So what went wrong with Alexis?

What makes some relationships online work and others not so much? Does 'being online' expose us to greater risks – the 'sight unseen'? Is the new 'role of technology' in human interactions cause for alarm with the potential for fraud, as with, at least, Alexis's case?

(ii) The technology part.

Technology is just technology. It doesn't change human nature. That, at least, is what I understood danah boyd[22] to be saying during her interview with Krista Tippett on the phone app On Being. I found some interesting insights about the role of technology in relationships from the author.

'Steeped in the cutting edge of research around the social lives of networked teens, danah boyd demystifies technology while being wise about the changes it's making to life and relationships. She has intriguing advice on the technologically fuelled generation gaps of our age – that our children's immersion in social media may offer a kind of respite from their over-structured, overscheduled analog lives. And that cyber-bullying is an online reflection of the offline world, and blaming technology is missing the point.'[23]

danah focuses upon the impact of technology and children/youth, and I feel almost more at ease listening to her – that it's not such a bad thing – technology, that is. But her research also makes me think about the gap in understanding between technology and adult relationships, particularly for those of us that grew up in the 'olden days' without computers, let alone cell phones and all the latest social media. It is many of these relative newcomers to technology that are using it – technology – to find romance and love and adult relationships – while facing the generation gap that pummels us into 'how does that thing work?' and 'is this on?' and a general lack of understanding about how the whole interweb thingy works. Combine the naivety of the tools with the already social gap of 'looking for love' (approaching relationships from a deficit position?) and this seems to equal a recipe for disaster.

But is the disaster the fault of the user or the inherently dangerous object (aka technology)?

(iii) The people part + the technology part = the social phenomenon of online dating.

If all the romance stories had a happy ending, and Cinderella didn't get shafted by Heir Fucks-a-lot, we wouldn't have much of a story today, now, would we? So, what does happen when 'dating site connections go wrong'? Is it just Alexis? Was she just some dumb bunny who picked the wrong profile?

Sadly, Alexis's story is not unique.

There are similar stories with the sad reality featuring the dark side of online dating. These stories feature other characters as prey, 'catfished', and losing more than just dignity and self-esteem. Yes, this is about cold hard cash – around $1.5b USD a year, if my calculations are correct!

Let's take a closer look.

In the UK, statistics issued by the National Fraud Intelligence Bureau (NFIB) show the UK public lost thirty-four million pounds to 'romance' fraudsters in 2014, a thirty-three per cent increase in fraud cases compared to 2013.[24] Meanwhile, *Newsweek* magazine reported that cybercrime cost Americans eight hundred million US dollars in 2014, with romance scams making up around eighty-seven million dollars of the losses.[25] Victims included women and men (4088 and 1795 cases reported, respectively). In the same year, seven Kiwis lost over one hundred thousand dollars each, as online romance and dating scams cost victims over $1.3m NZD, according to New Zealand's consumer affairs network, Scamwatch. In Canada, CBC News reported online-dating fraud cost Canadians seventeen million Canadian dollars in 2014, jumping the queue to become the number one source of fraud on the internet in Canada. In Australia, the Competition and Consumer Commission (ACCC) says online dating scams costs Australians twenty-eight million dollars in 2014 (reported July tenth, 2015). 'About 30 per cent of victims met the scammer through social networking sites,' according to ACCC data. 'This allowed scammers to stalk victims on social media, getting a sense of someone's likes, dislikes and social values, so it felt as though there was an instant connection when they did make contact online.'

OK, so based on this 2014 data for the UK, USA, NZ, Canada and Australia, love scams cost about $171.5m US dollars. Now remember this figure is based on fraud actually reported.

A study out of the University of Leicester confirmed law-enforcement suspicions that online-dating fraud is a grossly under-reported crime.[26] Between 2010 and 2011, the study estimated over two hundred thousand victims of romance scams, compared with the 592 notified to ActionFraud, the UK's national reporting centre – less than one per cent! The study also asserts over a million in the UK personally know a romance scam victim. 'This is a concern not solely because people are losing large sums of money to these criminals, but also because of the psychological impact experienced by victims of this crime.'

In the USA, the Federal Bureau of Investigation's Internet Crime Complaint Center (IC3) reports 'only an estimated 15 percent of the nation's fraud victims report their crimes to law enforcement'. The IC3 estimates they receive less than ten per cent of victims filing directly through them.

Alexis falls into the eighty-five to ninety per cent who did not report.

Consider this: if the annual reported loss from our five sample countries is only ten to fifteen per cent of the actual romance-related internet victims, then their real loss for 2014 was more like $1.5 billion US dollars!

Extending figures globally beyond these five countries means there's a lot of cold hard cash involved with this 'I love you … send money' syndrome.[27] As a social issue, the problem is likely to intensify as romance fraud stats continue to rise and online relationships are projected to flourish into the future.

This burgeoning economy provides a new income source for organised crime, where the internet allows scalability with relative ease. Any who have had 'more than one fish on' while trolling the rivers of potential possibilities knows how simple it would be to deplete more than one prey at a time. This is especially true across geographies, where different time zones and a plethora of prospects can keep you busy twenty-four seven, all year round! The charlatan need never meet his/her mark, and time is not of the essence – why rush a good thing? A victim might be strung along for weeks or months or longer if the lure of a big payout is pending. Meanwhile, the pipeline of cash from others they've cheated trickles or pours in, as the case may be. Why would you get up and dressed to go to work when the money can come to you?

♥ ♥ ♥ ♥ ♥

Alexis has a snowball's chance in hell of ever seeing her 140k again.

Even when fraud is exposed, international jurisdiction often makes prosecution difficult, if not impossible. Compounding this legal nightmare is that so many of the crimes are unreported, as with Alexis, where victims can stay stuck, often suffering in silence, because they are just too embarrassed about what happened. Those who do find the courage to speak up are recognising that staying silent just allows the culprits to retain power over them. While talking about it or reporting it may not bring your money back, telling the story DOES shine a light on the experience and can dissipate the shame. Telling her story allowed Alexis to start to heal, finally feeling some closure on her up-until-now dark cloud from the past.

So why did Alexis hang in there?

Why did she stay, when it was clear that she should have taken Tom Hank's lead in *Forrest Gump*: run, Alexis, run!!!

It's simple – the die was cast when she accepted that he loved her 'just the way I am'. This most intoxicating feeling kept her 'stuck', like the *Daring to Trust* book suggested. Alexis had abandonment issues and feared rejection and separation. She knew it was 'not healthy staying' but endured. She didn't trust her instinct; she got carried away with the romance – the allure of being loved 'just the way she was'.

♥ ♥ ♥ ♥ ♥

The online dating stories are endless. Alexis's experience is but one of thousands, hundreds of thousands. This doesn't mean you should not go online dating! There are thousands of happy couples who started out online. What it does mean is go online with eyes wide open. Know what to watch for and stay alert.

So how can you protect yourself? Here's a checklist of what to avoid:

The Top Ten Traps of Online Dating Scammers

1. Has a MacGyver-type profession. While he might not be devoted to ensuring world peace, he may profess to have a *Mission: Impossible*-type career – often in engineering or a highly skilled trade profession – one that is often involved in offshore business operations (meaning they are 'away' out of town, travel a lot or are frequently in a different time zone). Do they really live in the USA but are travelling abroad? Remember James's letter came back 'addressee unknown'? While Mac may not carry a gun, he can be deadly with paper clips, duct tape and a few misguided emails.

2. Often shares some tragic family situation or past event. James was widowed for eight years and, other than the nympho Caryl (yeah, right), was without a partner 'for a long time' (poor baby). They may say they are a parent, often with a child living apart from them (MacGyver cannot be held back by a small child). That said, they remain 'close' and share a special connection to their progeny. It all makes them ever so sweet, vulnerable and in need of your tender loving care, well-meaning advice, oh, and cash.

3. Asks you to relocate from the dating site to a personal email. Staying online in a dating site is too close for comfort for potential scammers. They want to 'go offline' as soon as possible to isolate their prey. Have you ever seen large game animals hunt? These predators may cite reasons like their membership is ending soon or they won't be on the site for long. Remember James asked Alexis to go off Be2 in his second email to her, yet in checking later on, James was still listed on Be2 months later. Dating sites often mention this point in the 'fine print'.

4. No hablas Engleesh. This tell is not an attempt to be politically incorrect or disenfranchise any non-English-as-a-first-language speaker. In fact, if I were fluent in Spanish, French or German, I'm sure I'd find the same thing happens in those country's dating sites. This dating tell is more apparent than simple grammatical or spelling errors. We all know a plethora of men are missing that spelling gene. No, this is more stick-out-like-dog's-balls, OMG! If your Shakespeare confuses the name of a rose and doesn't know it smells, assume something is fishy and hang up, delete or simply adios that amigo ASAP.

5. Has arrived at his future 'someday' now. Is your potential suitor ready, or nearly ready, to retire? Do they talk about how they're soon to be enjoying the fruit of their hard-earned labour? If only they could find their one true love to share it with? If you think about it, MacGyver's been working hard since the mid-1980s, so it is possible that he does have a healthy nest egg. Trouble is, your online love might be strongly suggesting his work has been lucrative without actually proving it – well, until his subtle 'click into my online accounts filled with millions of pounds' comes into play. Pick me ... pick me not ... pick me? ... C'mon, ladies, he's not really MacGyver.

6. Epitomises retch (as in vomit) romance extremist. Does he talk about how destiny or fate brought you both together? Does he intoxicate you by saying 'all the right things'? How money means nothing without that special someone to love? It is also hard to resist that ego boost of someone claiming to love you 'just the way you are'. But if that were truly the case, such affection should not cost you a single solitary penny – it, like you, is priceless.

7. He really needs your help. Have you all of a sudden become his 'next of kin' on his personal forms? The 'one call' he makes when landed in the slammer, er, huh? Scammer suitors will inevitably fall upon a difficult time and need your help. It may start simply with cashing a cheque, or perhaps they do not have access to technology 'on the offshore oil rig', or James's 'remote' mystery locations. The players always seem legitimate – often self-employed, have a good job – so when they need your help, it seems like the most natural thing to do. Plus, everyone likes to feel needed, right?!

8. Makes inappropriately early personal encroachments. Does Mr Wonderful ask for your address to send flowers or gifts? The only reason Mr Not-So-Wonderful James sent Alexis flowers was to volley back to her (she had originally sent him some). It also had little to do with romance and everything to do with stalking his prey. Does it seem 'too soon' when he starts to speak of money issues, or your net worth in the first few interactions? YES, a resounding yes. Your personal information is personal – keep it that way.

9. Sends lots of photos. People become more real when you put a picture to a name and email correspondence chain. Seeing them in lots of different scenarios, with family, friends, casual and business-like, gives them an off-the-page personality. But how do you know the photos match the person? You can try dropping them into tineye.com, or use a Google images search in the first instance, but meeting them in person, face-to-face, is the only way to be certain they exist. Seek to meet your Mr Wonderful as soon as possible. If he refuses? Well, that brings us to red flag number ten.

10. Avoids meeting face-to-face. There are copious excuses for why James couldn't make it to Hawaii, ranging from being stuck at work and held in a Sri Lankan prison to recovering from a heart attack in London. All very interesting, but if Mr Right cannot also be Mr Right NOW and come to say hello in person, consider it a potential red flag. Every justification should give you pause to think. If he's really looking for love, he'll want to meet you and will find a way. If he's not really that into meeting you, run, Forrest, run.

And so ended Alexis's twenty-six-week soirée with online dating.

She started her online-dating adventure on September nineteenth, and, in exactly six months, while waiting for the man of her dreams, she had:

- fallen in love, twice: once online and once while waiting to meet the man she fell in love with online;
- spent an unplanned and most unexpected week in Hawaii: having previously been to Honolulu for layovers, she strongly recommends it is much more fun to go there to get laid; and
- loaned (and lost) the princely sum of $140,000 NZD, disregarding every one of the top ten traps of online dating scammers.

♥ ♥ ♥ ♥ ♥

In closing, you really should read the fine print. Important not only for assembling tricky furniture and making technology 'work' but also to be au fait with how dating sites actually work.

Alexis wished she had. But, then again, if she had, and had avoided her encounter with James, well, then there would not have been a story to tell and a lesson to share.

Alexis the Pollyanna is often heard saying, 'I truly believe everything happens for a reason. We just don't always know exactly why at the time.' Her silver-lining outlook is refreshing.

In retrospect, we will not ever know all the whys and probably don't need to. What we do know is that through sharing her story, Alexis gained meaning and purpose from an otherwise unbearable circumstance. She made some really special lemonade and took it, along with her humble pie, down a different path. One filled with discovery of self-esteem and self-love.

But that's another story.

Endnotes

1. The original quote, 'the rules of fair play do not apply in love and war', is found in poet John Lyly's novel *Euphues: The Anatomy of Wit*, published in 1579. The first use of 'all's fair in love and war' was by English author Francis Edward Smedley, in his 1850 novel *Frank Fairleigh*.
2. Schama, Simon. *The Power of Art*. New York: Ecco, 2006.
3. Kelly, Ian. *Casanova: Actor Lover Priest Spy*. London: Hodder & Stoughton Publishers, 2008.
4. http://quotepixel.com/picture/love/paul_acquasanta/a_blind_person_in_reality_is_the_only_person_who_can_truly. Last accessed 24 March 2016.
5. Richo, David. *Daring to Trust: Opening Ourselves to Real Love & Intimacy*. London: Shambala Publications Ltd, 2010, p 25.
6. http://www.nzherald.co.nz/nz/news/article.cfm?c_id=1&objectid=143028. Last accessed 14 July 2016.
7. http://mentalfloss.com/article/64727/15-things-you-should-know-about-klimts-kiss Last accessed 08 August 2016.
8. Lambert, Angela, *The Independent* UK, 3 March 1994. (http://www.independent.co.uk/life-style/talking-pictures-with-annie-leibovitz-from-jagger-to-trump-she-summed-up-the-seventies-and-eighties-1426695.html) Last accessed 08 August 2016.
9. "Barbra Streisand, the way she is," by Michael Shnayerson, in *Vanity Fair* (November 1994) http://barbra-archives.com/bjs_library/90s/vanityfair_94_streisand.html last accessed 20 August 2016.
10. http://www.miguelruiz.com. See also *The Voice of Knowledge: A Practical Guide to Inner Peace*. Amber-Allen Publishing, 2004.
11. Richo, David. Op cit., pp 59–60.
12. Gloria Steinem wrote to *TIME* magazine in Autumn 2000 to credit 'Irina Dunn, a distinguished Australian educator, journalist and politician … [who] paraphrased the philosopher who said, "Man needs God like fish needs a bicycle." Irina Dunn later confirmed: http://www.phrases.org.uk/meanings/414150.html Last accessed 24 March 2016.
13. 'British Art for the Rome Exhibition', *The Times*, 20 March 1911, p 7.
14. http://www.transparency.org/cpi2010/results. Last accessed 14 May 2015.
15. Kirchner, Elyce and Paredes, David. NBC investigative report, 13 May 2013. First aired May 13 at 11 p.m. (Published Thursday, May 16, 2013). Last accessed 17 February 2016.
16. http://www.phrases.org.uk/meanings/hell-in-a-handbasket.html. Last accessed 2 May 2015.

17. Frankl, Viktor E. *Man's Search for Meaning.* Boston: Beacon Publishers, 2006.
18. Hours Quotes, Quotes.net. STAND4 LLC, 2016 (http://www.quotes.net/mquote/44477) Last accessed 08 August 2016.
19. *A Course In Miracles: Combined Volume.* Glen Elen, CA. Foundation for Inner Peace, 1992.
20. http://news.uchicago.edu/article/2013/06/03/meeting-online-leads-happier-more-enduring-marriages#sthash.UUtsMW98.dpuf. Last accessed 24 March 2016.
21. http://www.forbes.com/sites/katherynthayer/2014/01/14/mobile-technology-makes-online-dating-the-new-normal/#309bfdbd122d. Last accessed 24 March 2016.
22. This reference adheres to how dana boyd styles her name in lower case.
23. (http://www.onbeing.org/program/transcript/7463) Last accessed 08 August 2016.
24. According to the Internet Crime Complaint Center, scams cost victims an average of $8900 USD each. See also http://www.actionfraud.police.uk/news/new-figures-show-online-dating-fraud-is-up-by-33per-cent-last-year-feb15. Last accessed 24 March 2016.
25. http://www.newsweek.com/2014-year-Internet-crimes-334067. Last accessed 08 August 2016.
26. Respondents were questioned about dating site fraud by internet pollsters YouGov. http://www.huffingtonpost.com/2011/09/27/200000-suffer-dating-s_n_984192.html. Last accessed 24 March 2016.
27. There are 195 countries in the world, 196 if you include Taiwan. A conservative 'guess' would increase the number tenfold to $15b – but who knows how high the losses actually reach? Nearer $60b if we extrapolate the five-country data for 2014 to the rest of the globe. Yikes.

Objects d'Art

Chapter One: *The Armada Portrait* (circa 1588), attributed to George Gower (http://www.woburnabbey.co.uk/abbey/art-and-the-collection/the-armada-portrait/)

Chapter Two: *Allée au Parc de Saint-Cloud* (The Avenue in the Park Saint-Cloud) (circa 1908) by Henri Rousseau (http://www.lesarbres.fr/peinture-600-496-huile----261-1133.html)

Chapter Three: *The Kiss* (1907) by Gustav Klimt (https://upload.wikimedia.org/wikipedia/commons/4/40/The_Kiss_-_Gustav_Klimt_-_Google_Cultural_Institute.jpg)

Chapter Four: Photograph of Barbra Streisand directing movie, by Annie Leibovitz in *Vanity Fair* (November 1994) (http://barbra-archives.com/bjs_library/90s/vanityfair_94_streisand.html)

Chapter Five: T*he Bolshevik* (1920), depicting the 1917 Russian Revolution, by Boris Kustodiev (http://www.gettyimages.co.nz/detail/news-photo/the-bolshevik-painting-by-b-m-kustodiev-representation-of-news-photo/170982958)

Chapter Six: Look: *Medea* (1889), by Evelyn De Morgan (https://en.wikipedia.org/wiki/Medea#/media/File:De_Morgan_Medea.jpg).

Chapter Seven: *Inside the wave* (2012), by Kenji Croman (http://www.gokenji.com/gallery/ – see Ocean Photography Gallery photo #28 (4 of 16))

Chapter Eight: *Der Schrei der Natur* (The Scream of Nature, aka The Scream or The Cry) (1893) by Edvard Munch (https://en.wikipedia.org/wiki/The_Scream#/media/File:The_Scream.jpg)

Chapter Nine: *Migrant Mother* (1936) by Dorothea Lange (http://www.npr.org/templates/story/story.php?storyId=92656801)

Chapter Ten: *Virginia Woolf in London in 1939*, by Gisèle Freund (http://www.nytimes.com/2011/10/20/arts/the-elegance-of-gisele-freund.html)

About Jordan

Jordan Marijana Alexander was born in the blue-collar town of Oshawa, Ontario. The *Automotive Capital of Canada* attracted many European immigrants like her Croatian and Ukrainian parents. She became educated at Queen's University in Kingston before completing a Master's at the University of Windsor, and a PhD at the University of Auckland. Jordan has travelled widely. She left a policy role in British Columbia to work for the New Zealand government in 1994. The past twenty years, Jordan has enjoyed working in operational and strategic positions across government, private and community sectors in North America and Australasia. Currently Managing Director at Pangaea Consulting, Jordan engages in strategic and change projects, facilitates groups and enjoys coaching individuals. She currently lives in Wellington with her two daughters. This is her first novel.

Tell me about it...

Please contact me with your comments and stories about love and anything else that tickles your fancy at jma@jordanalexander.me or visit my website at www.jordanalexander.me

Want more love?

I love you, send money is available in different formats, including an audio version. To see more love-ly options, visit iloveyousendmoney.com

I love you, send money is the first book of a trilogy about life, lessons and love. The sequel will be released for Christmas 2017 and gives the next instalment of the Alexis drama, with more lessons and more love. Visit the author's website for more details jordanalexander.me